Praise for What This River Keeps

"With vivid, lyrical prose, Greg Schwipps has taken an age-old theme — man's relationship to the land — and made it new. You don't have to know anything about fish or rivers or even country living to be swept up in this story about how a vanishing landscape can tear apart a fragile human ecosystem. His characters are a delightful crew of misfits who sneak into your affections and set up camp. They fish and cook and fight and lie and love and take off down the highway in search of answers. We worry for them and celebrate their wit and perseverance."

—Lili Wright, author of the travel memoir *Learning to Float.*

"Often very funny, always lyrically beautiful, *What This River Keeps* is a powerful reminder of the cost of the American romance with profit and progress, and of the abiding strength of the people of America's Heartland. Even more, it's about that eminent domain, the heartland, and the complicated ways love — for a friend, a spouse, a child, a parent, a dog, a river — endures, even when the waters are rising and all hope seems lost."

—Beth Lordan, author of *And Both Shall Row* and *But Come Ye Back: A Novel in Stories*

WHAT THIS RIVER KEEPS

What This River Keeps.
Library of Congress Cataloging-in-Publication Data.

Ghost Road Press
ISBN (Trade pbk.)
13 Digit 978-0-9816525-5-9
10 Digit 0-9816525-5-7
Library of Congress Control Number: 2008937328

Ghost Road Press
Denver, Colorado
www.ghostroadpress.com

WHAT THIS RIVER KEEPS

A Novel

GREG SCHWIPPS

Ghost Road Press

ACKNOWLEDGMENTS

I grew up on a working farm outside of Milan, Indiana, and while almost nothing of this novel is autobiographical, that land is where this story begins. I thank my parents, Richard and Mary Lou, for showing me the value of places and for their never-ending support. When I was a boy, they were the kinds of parents who thought crows made good pets, and I owe them a great deal for that.

My writing professors at DePauw University changed my life with their inspiration and knowledge. Tom Chiarella, Barbara Bean and David Field were, and still are, some of the best teachers a young writer could have.

In the MFA program at Southern Illinois University at Carbondale, I was blessed to write among a wonderful group of peers and with gracious professors like Lisa Knopp, Ricardo Cruz, KK Collins, Beth Lordan and Kent Haruf.

While researching eminent domain, I spoke with many people who shared their stories and helped me understand the process. Many thanks to Jo MacPhail, the world's best reference librarian, along with Reese and Susan Nicholls, Wayne and Karen Snyder, and the U.S. Army Corps of Engineers.

For their medical expertise, I offer thanks to my buddies Dr. Matt Pisano and Dr. Jeff Bohmer. And for his legal advice, Tom Nolasco.

Thanks to fellow Hoosier Richard Fields for capturing the essence of the story with his amazing photography.

I thank most earnestly first readers Lili Wright, Chris Biggs, Tom Chiarella, Beth Lordan and Kent Haruf for their insight and patience.

For her stories and unique grandmotherly support, I am indebted to Luella Schwipps.

For their encouragement, Sue Harris, the Coffeys, the Caytons and the Longs have my heartfelt thanks, as well.

I've taught at DePauw for over ten years, and during that time I've had the honor of working with many wonderful students. There are far too many to list, so I thank them collectively but sincerely for their support and friendship.

I would also like to acknowledge my colleagues in the English Department at DePauw, and the University itself, which has been incredibly supportive of my professional development. Thanks in particular to the Amy Braddock Fund and the John and Janice Fisher Fund.

I am grateful beyond words to Matt Davis and Sonya Unrein at Ghost Road Press for bringing this novel to life.

This book owes much to the East and West Forks of the White River of central and southern Indiana, and to every catfish I've caught from those waters.

It's not easy to fish all night, through storms, snakes, mosquitoes and slime. With a muddy hand I salute my brothers, who are almost as obsessed with catfish as I am: Ron, Tim and Ben. And the four-legged: Indy, P-Dog and Grizzly. As Shipley would say: Hold Em Hook.

And finally, where would I be without the support of my Kentucky Sweet Wife, Alissa? She is all these things – editor, fishing partner, friend, wife – and more. Her love and encouragement made this book possible.

To all, again: many thanks. Love and respect.

For Alissa,

And in memory of Helen Millican and Clyde Schwipps

"No person shall . . . be deprived of life, liberty, or property, without due process of law; nor shall private property be taken for public use, without just compensation."

—the Fifth Amendment to the Constitution

"Loss of sentimental value, of historic interest, and emotional trauma associated with having to sell property through condemnation are not compensable under the law and may not be considered."

—Your Rights to Private Property: What to Do When the Government Wants to Acquire Your Land.

CHAPTER ONE

The two old men slept on the bank of the dirty flooded river, and from above they would've appeared as dead men—corpses washed ashore and left to rot in the coming sun. The river, swollen and thick in the predawn light, looked capable of carrying bodies along with its load of sticks, spinning logs and bottles. Here and there floated a child's ball, a doll's head. The men were not yet dead, but the morning's heat hadn't arrived to revive them from their jagged sleep. In a small depression in the sand between their prone forms smoke crept from a chunk of wood. Both men lay partially covered by sleeping bags, and they reposed with pieces of clothing knotted under their heads. They slept as men who had spent many nights on riverbanks. They slept on the sand that the river had carried for miles and for centuries and they slept on the earth as if they belonged to it.

Even in his sleep Frank was aware of his spine. He opened his eyes and his back woke up with him, and its pain yawned and grew. Above him was the soft gray light of early morning. His backbone felt as cold and dead as a lead pipe, like rigor mortis had set in and fused the vertebrae together. The pain hadn't been a dream. Waking up to it was like feeling the first cold splashes of rain from a storm that had been thundering just over the ridge for hours—a confirmation.

Clouds of mist hung over the current, a ghost river flowing. Above the woods around them the fog wasn't there, only the pale light of sunrise, but wherever the water ran the mist rose. He lay on his back and studied the sky. It was always strange to be given sight again, after staring into darkness all night long. But now different birds called. He'd been paying so much attention to this particular place it was as if he'd never known another life. Maybe he'd been here, on this riverbank, forever. Maybe he didn't have a wife, a son, a farm? Of course he did. It was time to get up again.

He looked over at Chub. Across the fire—it was still smoldering in the heavy dew—Chub lay stretched out like a side of beef. His mouth hung open and a cloud of gnats suspended over his face. Some were walking across his cheek, and Frank wondered how anyone could sleep through such a distraction. He took a hand out from his sleeping bag, picked up a smooth pebble, and threw it in Chub's direction. It hit his bag with a soft pop. Chub slept on. Frank threw another pebble and this one hit him in his thick neck. Chub's eyes opened slowly and deliberately and a giant hand came up and wiped at the gnats around his eyes and hairy brows.

"You got a pack of pecker gnats swarmin you," Frank said.

Chub said nothing but rolled over and reached for the zipper on his sleeping bag. It had worked down as he slept and was wadded around his midsection.

His naked upper body lay on the bare ground, and as he moved sand stuck to his skin. He was a big man. His skin was tanned but wrinkled and hairy. Under his arms the skin was white. He coughed and lifted himself up on his elbow. He coughed again and sucked furiously with his nose and throat, working it up. He spat into the sand next to his bag. Frank saw something pendulous drop.

"What time is it?" Chub asked.

Frank looked at his watch. "Just after five."

"Thought so."

"You look like an angel this morning."

"Shut the hell up."

Chub sat, pulling himself out of the bag. He still wore his brown pants and gray socks. His rubber boots were there and he tugged them on. He took the thin cotton shirt from the ground where he'd slept with his head on it and shook it rapidly. Sand sprung from the fabric. He pulled the shirt on and buttoned it.

Frank watched this with bemused interest. He waited for the pain in his back to subside even though he knew it wouldn't. The sun lit the trees across the river. Christ, the water was high. Thick and brown with runoff. He pulled his legs free of the bag and jerked on his rubber boots. His cane lay there in the sand and small pebbles where he'd left it at two in the morning when he'd gotten into his bag to get some sleep. He picked it up and it was cold and wet from the dew and he brushed the sand from it.

Standing up from this position was the worst. He pushed the bag down out of the way and turned onto his stomach. He could smell himself—the river water and dried sweat. By doing a pushup of sorts he rose to his knees and took his cane upright in front of him. When he got to his feet he stood there, leaning over the cane, and waited for the dizziness to pass. He felt as if he hadn't slept for days. Had there been a time when getting up meant nothing, took nothing? He did not believe it.

Both men took long steaming pisses in the tall ragweed around camp.

When they turned and walked toward it, the river looked different—somehow it had completely changed since they'd lain down. They'd grown to know it in the moonlight. They knew where the snags were because of the sound the water made as it sucked around them. They knew where the hole started and where it stretched into a run. They knew how hard to cast to reach the edge of the submerged tree that had toppled from the far bank sometime this spring. They knew where to expect the catfish.

Now the river ran naked before their eyes, shrouded only in a rising layer of mist already dissipating in the sun. They could see the ripples and the chunks of trees breaking the surface. It wasn't a big river, but one too wide to cast across. The pool in front of them was almost twenty feet deep.

Frank's jon boat swayed in the current, nosed onto the sand where they'd beached it. Their rods stood upright in the rod carriers he'd made from sections of PVC pipe fastened to the back of one of the boat's metal benches. They began to rig their lines for chunks of cutbait. Three-ounce sinkers sliding on the line above 3/0 hooks. Channel catfish would be out this time of morning, feeding in the shallows and in that riffle there.

A dead bluegill floated in the livewell, and Chub pulled it out, placed it on the plywood board, and started cutting with a knife. The fish barely bled. The bluegill had a hole in its back, under the pectoral fin, where one of them had hooked it the night before. Its bones crunched and the scales crackled as the knife reduced the hand-sized fish to pieces of its former self. He bent, swished the knife in the river, wiped the blade on the leg of his pants, once for each side, and dropped it back into the boat. There were still bluegills swimming in the livewell, ones that hadn't been hooked and cast the night before.

He handed two pieces to Frank—not the head, Frank noticed—and they put them on hooks without talking. They made sure the scales of the fish were not covering the points of their hooks. Their rod holders were still sticking up in the sand of the bank and they cast and set their rods back in the holders. Engaged the reel clickers. Their lawn chairs had sunk into the mud of the riverbank and they sat back down in them. They were on one of the few beaches still left dry when the river ran this high. Most of their usual overnight spots were underwater.

The river now met sand about three inches below the stick Frank had stuck upright to mark the water level before he went up the bank to sleep. He examined that—how the river had dropped so much in the last hours. If it rained tomorrow it would rise again. The river rose and fell, rose and fell. It was harder to catch fish as the river dropped and he didn't expect to catch many this morning.

"What time somebody expecting you?" Chub asked.

"I told Ethel I'd be there for lunch. She thinks Ollie'll probably be there."

Frank knew she was wrong even as he said the words. His son would not be there. Chub said nothing. He knew it was false, too. Ollie was a lark and didn't come to eat with his parents on Saturday or any other day anymore. Chub knew all about Ollie, but he didn't bring him up or talk about him to anybody else. He'd been friends with Frank for most of his life and he knew that a man could create a son and then lose control of what the son became. Chub had a son, too.

Chub lived alone now and no one expected him at any time. He'd stay until Frank said it was time to reload the boat and head out. He could stay out two nights in a row and no one would miss him or notice he'd done so. He'd been out many nights in a row and, in fact, no one had noticed.

The channel cats swam out of hiding now that the flatheads were going back to sleep. The smaller catfish felt safe, and even with the falling water, they'd eat for an hour or so. Almost immediately Frank's rod started to bounce and the clicker on the reel made its song as the line spun off the spool. He could stand without his cane for short spells, and he stood and grabbed the pole.

He set the hook by bringing the rod back over his head and fought to turn the fish. It headed downstream and levered its body against the current. Holding the rod tip high, he waited for the fish to tire. He could see where the dancing line entered the river, but the brown water hid the cat.

"Good one?" Chub asked.

"Feels good."

"I thought I'd get one on this head first."

"I know you thought that. I seen you keep it."

The fish ran a few times and circled back upstream. Frank gained line and brought the catfish to the beach in front of them. It splashed in the shallow water and made short bursts. Now he could see flashes of a black tail, a gray side. Four pounds or so.

"Want to keep some for lunch?" Chub asked. He kept most of what he caught. The Indiana DNR told you not to eat fish from this river more than once a month. Chub ate fish several times a week. It hadn't altered his health or appearance. He'd always looked like shit.

Frank got the catfish in hand and it was a good size to clean. Silver and slick-muscled. He popped the hook out and dropped the fish into the livewell. The bluegills, intended for the cave-mouthed flathead catfish they'd been fishing for last night, were too big for the channel to eat. The catfish swam, hit the end of the livewell with a splash, and then returned and thumped into the other side. The bluegills fled to a corner.

Before Frank could cut another piece of bait, Chub had a run and hooked the fish. The midsummer sun came over the trees and bathed them in a glorious burst of heat and light.

The men kept silent on the one thing they were both thinking about—the occurrence that would affect them almost equally, like the sun fizzling out or the sea lifting and washing over the continent. They'd talked about the matter some late at night when it seemed possible to say anything in the moonlight, and they weren't ready to talk about it yet this morning.

They caught three more channel cats and kept all of them. Then the sun grew too hot and they loaded the boat with their sleeping bags and the clothes they'd shed. They poured water over the fire pit, and its still-smoldering stub of wood, sending forth angry clouds of steam. The burnt firewood hissed like a snake uncovered under a flipped log.

Frank reached into the livewell, where the four channel cats swam and bumped against the walls, and began netting out the remaining bluegills. One by one he dropped them into the river. The bluegills hit the water and righted themselves in the current, but they didn't leave. Instead they finned there in the muddy water, near the boat, and tried to get accustomed to their new surroundings. They were lost and many of them would be eaten before the sun set again. They'd been raised in a farm pond, and they weren't prepared for this current or the predators that waited.

When he'd taken everything out of the livewell save the four catfish, Frank closed the lid. Chub pulled the boat parallel to the shore and Frank waded into the river. The water was so cold now, even though he'd gotten used to it yesterday, and his movements were slowed by the current and weight of the water. He sat back over the gunnel and swung his dripping legs aboard. Chub pushed the boat off and climbed in without grace or dignity. The bow dipped under his heft. Frank started the outboard with one pull and turned the bow back upstream. The prop ate sand and gravel for a bit—the sound of metal striking stones—before it slid into deeper water. There the boat settled into the current and the motor dug deep and pushed them upstream toward the waiting truck. A pair of mallards was frightened to see them coming and took off, flying farther upriver. The boat would approach them several times more, causing them to move again and again until they went past the gravel bar where the boat would stop.

Frank knew even before they rounded the first bend that he could probably count the number of times he would camp again on this river. After so many years, it had come down to this: a few times left, some countable number, something finite. He did not speak of it.

CHAPTER TWO

Ollie drove to the hardware store in Logjam on Saturday morning because all but one lightbulb in the trailer had burned out. What were the odds of such a thing? Only the light in the hallway still worked. He could see into the bathroom with its glow, but the bedroom and kitchen were secured in darkness. He had to use the TV to illuminate the living room. Coming in late last night, still drunk and tired, he'd pretty much fallen over in every room as he made his way back to bed. He could no longer see what in the hell he was doing.

The bell hanging from the door jangled when he walked in and the air conditioning was already on. He walked across a concrete floor painted red and the entire store smelled pleasantly of metal tools and rubber tires. He felt pretty good this morning. His mouth stunk and he was thirsty, but really he felt pretty good. It was early enough that he could still do something with the day once he got this one errand run. Then he remembered that Coondog wanted him to come over in the afternoon to make final adjustments to the demo car before that night.

A woman stood at the cash register, in the process of ringing up a sale for a customer—an old man with hair standing straight like he'd slept hanging upside down. He was talking about something. The rest of the store was quiet. Ollie nodded hello to the woman and looked at her ass as he walked by. He scanned the aisles to see if any other women were around, so he could change his trajectory through the store and walk by them, maybe smell their perfume. There were none. He had acted in this fashion for so long it'd become ingrained into his habits, like a hungry dog might trot through a roadside park with its nose down, looking for bites of hot dog bun or chunks of cookies. He watched for women in other cars as he drove and swiveled his neck to study them as they worked in their yards. He stared at girls in the grocery store.

He selected a box of generic sixty-watts and carried them to the counter without shopping around for anything else. He didn't have a lot of money on him, and with this one purchase, it was going to be close. This was a four-pack of bulbs and he knew he couldn't buy fewer. He imagined himself going up to her register and asking for one bulb. What the hell. Besides, he didn't intend to make this trip again. He'd get four bulbs and light the bitch up for another year. About three dollars rode in his wallet.

Amazingly, the other guy was still paying, so Ollie got in line behind him. The old dude smelled like he'd been mowing wet grass. The woman at the counter looked familiar but she didn't seem to recognize or even acknowledge Ollie. He thought she owned the store with her husband. Ollie waited while the old man counted out exact change for two bolts and three washers. He kept spilling more coins out of a felt sack that advertised a kind of liquor. Ollie knew the name but had not tasted the whiskey. There stood a rack of keys there—different colors and sizes that could be cut to fit—and the countertop lay covered with glass. Under the glass, business cards were spread out. House builders. Excavation work. He scanned the cards, looking to see if his friend's was there. The old man finally got his receipt and left without saying anything further. The bell on the door jangled when he left.

"Is that all for you," the woman said, reaching for the lightbulbs. She seemed like she wanted to get it over with. She was older than he was, but she still looked pretty good. Her breasts pushed against the red employee vest she wore.

He handed the box to her. "I was looking to see if you had 'CD's Tree Service' here."

The woman looked confused and he pointed at the business cards. She glanced down and then back to the register. She hit the final button.

"Two-oh-eight," she said.

He handed her the three singles. "He's got a tree-trimming business. Cuts down your problem trees and around power lines."

"You got problem trees," she said in a tired voice.

"Nope. Just looking."

She popped the drawer open and he noticed at least one twenty in the slot for the biggest bills. The woman seemed to sense him looking at the money. She handed him change and looked down the counter as if someone stood there waiting. No one else was in the store. Her husband must've been back in the storage room, checking inventory. It was a Saturday morning. She probably wouldn't make another sale until the lunch hour. Everyone was over at the fair, anyway, since it was the final day. He took the change—she dropped it into his palm without touching him—and stood there.

"Thank you, come again," she said.

"You know what the 'CD' stands for?" he asked.

She looked at him for the first time and raised her eyebrows.

"Coondog," he said, loudly. "Coondog Calhoon. Nobody's ever called him different."

"That's nice." There was something akin to fear or alarm sneaking into her voice. She kept glancing around the empty store.

"Yep, he started up a tree trimming business. Got his own bucket truck and everything. Your full-service tree man."

"Well, that sounds good. Maybe I'll call him up if me and my husband need a tree cut."

"He's real careful. He won't hurt your other trees or nothing."

"Good to know," she said. "Well, I think I better get back to my stocking. Come back and see us." She took a step away from the register.

"If you want to see him in action, you oughtta head to the fairgrounds tonight. He'll be runnin a demo car in the derby."

She looked at him like he'd delivered his last line in Spanish, or some other tongue undecipherable to her.

He stared at her, then took the bulbs and walked out. He wondered why no one could make time to talk. The problem seemed to be getting worse. He didn't care about the men but he sure as hell wanted to talk to more women. The bell clanked against the glass of the door as he swung it open and stepped back into the sun and heat.

He drove to the four-way stop in town and turned left at the gas station. Logjam had never seen a green light. It kept one electric stop signal, and it blinked red all the time. Water stood in the ditches in front of the houses, and the air hung humid.

It took ten minutes to get to the trailer. He parked his truck and carried the bulbs inside. He looked into the fridge, but there was little to eat there. A bottle of ketchup and half a loaf of bread. A container of pickles. A plate with spaghetti on it, covered in mold. Milk in a gallon jug. He thought about putting the bulbs up, now that he had sunlight to see what he was doing, but instead he lay down on the couch to wait for lunchtime to grow closer. It was too early to call Coondog—he'd be asleep because he'd been up late working on the car—so he had the morning open. But it was going to be damned hot. And he would need his rest for tonight. He clicked the TV on and a talk show materialized, and before long he was asleep, mouth open in the growing heat of the trailer.

Outside, instead of a sidewalk or a path of footstones, the way to the trailer was a worn track in the yard. If it could be called a yard—it was more like pasture land. The grass was mid-calf high and the edges of the lawn fell into fescue tall enough to be seeded out. Because it'd rained every week for the last month and a half or so, the grass grew faster than he cared to mow it. For the first couple of years, he'd kept the place mowed pretty well—even cutting a swath down either side of the driveway. All this with a push mower. Then, gradually, he started to mow less and less, and the weeds reclaimed the yard. Soon he was only mowing the square in front of the trailer, and now he barely did that.

There wasn't much out here—just the trailer and the propane tank. A rutted gravel driveway led up the hill, and that's where his truck sat parked. When his dad first set all this up, Ollie had talked about building a little shed to put the mower and stuff in, maybe even a pole barn for his truck, but it was easier to just shove the mower under the trailer until the handlebar hit the siding. And as long as he remembered to roll up his windows, he could leave his pickup outside.

The trailer itself lay baking in the sun like a wounded animal. It didn't sit level, and even an untrained eye could notice. There were three windows and a door on the front side, and only four shutters. The siding was dark brown, meant to appear like stained cedar boards. No one would be fooled now, if they ever had been. It had torn away in strips and the missing shutters were marked with bright, unfaded rectangles. There was a white skirt around the base of the trailer, but in most places it'd fallen away. In some of those spots, old bales of straw sat hunched, gradually collapsing back into the soil.

He'd lived here, always alone, for about five years. But he was still on his parents' farm—this was just the other end of it. His old man had come across the trailer and gotten a good deal, so they'd put it back here in a cornfield. Hauled in the gas tank and dug a septic. A few small trees stood by the drive, but mostly he was surrounded by his dad's fields. Some corn, some soybeans, the edge of the woods visible beyond them. The fields were hilly and in the evening it was a nice view. His parents' house was within walking distance, but from here he couldn't see another man-made structure in any direction. It was nice having his own pad, but this place was a shithole and he knew it. Still, things had gotten rough with his dad and he'd been forced out of there. Now he had about two miles of separation by the roads, and that was far enough, because he and his dad hardly saw each other.

When Coondog pulled up, he didn't look at any of it—not the listing trailer, the missing shutters, the overgrown yard with the crops beyond. He'd seen it all many times before. Now when he came out here, everything felt familiar and constant. He approached as he always did: he roared up the driveway in his truck, jammed the brakes, and slid to a stop. When it was dry the dust from the gravel would roll away across the hills like a cannon's smoke. Today the gravel was mired in mud and it limited what should have been an impressive entrance. He parked by Ollie's truck and noticed the windows were down, so he reached over and picked up a rock from the driveway and put it on the seat behind the wheel. He didn't think Ollie would miss it and sit on the rock, but it'd be funny as hell if he did.

Coondog knocked on the flimsy screen door and the whole apparatus shook. Maybe the whole trailer shook. He heard his friend yell inside. Then there was silence. He hammered the door again.

"Who the hell is it?" Ollie asked.

"Sheriff!"

Something creaked—the sound of someone getting off the couch. Then

Ollie appeared at the door. He was disheveled. His hair looked greasy, which in fact it was, and it lay flat on one side of his head where the pillow had pressed it up and across the top of his skull. He looked out and laughed, a smirk on his face.

"I knew it was you, asshole," he said.

"Ha! No you never, either! You come out like, 'Oh shit! I'm fixin to get arrested!'"

"Sure I was." He swung open the light screen door and it squealed as he pressed it wide with his leg. "Make yourself at home."

Coondog bounced up into the trailer. Ollie hardly ever saw him at anything less than full speed. They were both in their thirties now, but Coondog had been the same since they were kids.

"This whole place smells a little like hot garbage," Coondog said.

"Does it? Shit. I've been meaning to take the trash out, but I went up to Fix-It this morning and got sidetracked." He yawned and stretched his arms over his head. His T-shirt lifted over his stomach, which was not fat yet but no longer flat.

Coondog went to the fridge and opened it. Ollie watched his face as he looked around. "No beers at all?" Coondog asked.

"I'm gonna get some on the way there tonight."

Coondog nodded and shut the fridge. He pulled out a stool from the little bar there and sat down.

"You get the other piece welded in there?" Ollie asked.

"Pretty much. I had to cut a notch out of it where the bracket for the bumper comes in, but I think it'll help."

"Cool." He went over and sat down on the couch.

"Well, here's what I'm thinking now," Coondog began. "We need to make some calls fore we head over there tonight. We need to get some women to go over there with us, hang out while we're working on the car."

"Which ones?"

"That's what I been thinking about. Which ones to call. I come out here on account of I need to get some gas in my truck so I can trailer the car, and I wanted to see if you could call someone. Shirley, maybe."

Ollie laughed. "Oh shit. I ain't callin her."

"Why the hell not?"

"You oughtta know why the hell not. I can't stand her, and she don't like me too much, neither."

"I never seen that stop you."

"Leaving the bar with her is one thing. Callin her up and takin her to the fair is another. No. I ain't doin it."

"Fine. Well, who else then?"

Ollie sat and thought. The TV was still on—some news program or something. He couldn't recall what he'd been watching before he dozed off. Probably nothing.

"Maybe you need to call that one," he said. "You know, her. The one you was talking to the other night over there."

They'd gone to the fair most nights this past week for different grandstand events. Coondog had sat down next to a woman two nights ago at the three-wheeler drags and talked with her almost the whole time. She hadn't looked that good to Ollie, nor had she looked very young. They were talking about cats and even gardens at one point, Coondog bullshitting heavily. Ollie hadn't gotten into the conversation at all.

"I'd like to, but I never got her number," Coondog acknowledged.

They both stared at the TV.

"Damn, I'd drink a beer if I had one," Coondog said.

"Maybe we should just look around once we get there. Then we can ask em if they want to hang out with us in the pits."

"Well, that'll work." Coondog stood up. "With your looks and my charm we can't miss. I just thought I'd swing by here first and see if you had a better plan, but I see now you don't."

"I don't know who it would be."

"All right then. You coming by a little later, help me load her up?"

"Yeah, I'll be around about two or so."

"Cool. See ya out there." He pushed open the door. Ollie saw a fly come in at that moment. "Clean your garbage out, too, you lazy sack," Coondog said.

Ollie stood up and went to the door and caught it before it slammed. Coondog headed out across the yard in his long-legged gait. He looked like some kind of bow-legged cowboy. He wasn't, though. He was a long-legged tree trimmer wearing a hat with the Chevy symbol on it.

"Hey," Ollie called. Coondog turned around. "What the hell you know about driving in demos anyways?"

"How the hell hard can it be?"

"Bout like us getting some damn women to go with us to it."

"Nah. Ain't nothin that hard."

CHAPTER THREE

The act of leaving—motoring upstream against the current and will of the river, trailering the boat, and throwing gear into the truck bed— broke the night's spell and made Frank worry about getting home to his wife. He left her alone many nights, even now, but always to fish. Still, Ethel was not as strong as she once was. Years ago they'd owned a dog they kept tied to the barn, but it'd died a long time ago and these days there was nothing around to protect her. He hadn't worried all those hours they'd been fishing, but now they weren't, and he just wanted to get home and make sure she was all right.

Frank took Chub to his house but couldn't leave until he'd looked at his old garden tiller. Frank knew the routine—Chub would find anything he could to postpone being left alone. Even though Frank was tired and knew she'd be waiting lunch on him, he had to take a look, at least. Chub had been talking about his tiller the entire drive home.

"It ran fine last week but now the old girl is actin like she got fed bad gas," Chub was saying. "Yesterday I couldn't start it."

They walked through the side door into the garage that sat slightly behind and to the right of his house. It was a two-car garage with dented and faded metal doors. Chub lifted the big doors overhead, grunting with each one. Here came the midday sun into the place. The garage smelled of oil and gas. On one side he kept his boat—a jon boat like Frank's. A sixteen footer with a big dent in the side. They hadn't fished in it yet this summer because he'd let the registration expire. The Conservation officers rarely checked the river around here, but you never knew. On the other side of the garage he'd built a workbench. You couldn't see a flat spot on it. It sat heaped with old belts and parts from different machines. There was, among other things, the front of an oscillating fan and the motor from a push mower, leaning off kilter on its shaft. The wood of the bench was black from grease. It would never look like wood again. In front of the workbench stood his tiller and two riding lawnmowers, neither of which ran well. He left his Dodge truck outside in the elements. Only a tornado could do further damage to it.

The men paused over the tiller and Frank bent to inspect the engine. The tiller was probably fifty years old and some ancestor of Chub's had built it. The frame had been welded together solidly enough that it'd withstood the gardens of fifty seasons, but now maybe the motor was worn out. Frank took off the spark plug wire and scraped the circular end with his pocketknife blade. He opened the fuel tank and sniffed the gas. It smelled normal. He removed the air filter cover and knocked the foam on the side of the frame. Dust flew.

"You got a screwdriver?" he asked.

Chub got one and he twisted the cap off the oil reservoir. It was filthy black but high enough.

"Hell if I know," Frank said. "Why don't you try to start it?"

Chub propped one foot on the frame and the tiller leaned under his weight. He pulled the starter rope. The motor turned over but didn't catch. After one pull Frank could hear that the motor was fine and would probably start. Two pulls later, it did. It popped loudly in the small garage. Chub pulled the throttle lever back and the motor revved. White smoke from the burning oil piled around them.

"I'll be damned," Chub yelled over the noise.

"Why don't you go get them fish and I'll sit here and watch it."

Chub nodded and got down a five gallon bucket that hung from a nail on a rafter. Frank watched as he walked out toward the boat and opened the livewell. He pressed his gut against the gunnel and reached in and lipped the catfish one at a time and dropped them headfirst into the dry bucket. He got three out and Frank laughed as he struggled to catch the last one. It had more room in the livewell now and was able to swim away from this strange bear-like creature hunting it. Chub stood on his toes, grabbing. He was too old and big to do anything that required more than the most basic of movements. He even looked odd walking across level ground.

Chub finally caught the last cat and closed the top of the livewell. Frank could see two tails sticking out of the bucket as he walked with it into the backyard. The fish were flopping and the bucket swayed in his hand. Under the big oak tree he kept an old cattle tank full of water and the catfish would swim in there until he made time to skin them. It was a two-hundred-gallon tank and sometimes they'd filled it to the top with fish they'd caught.

The motor continued to run as well as it had for two decades and Frank wondered if his friend had even tried to start it yesterday. He looked around the garage. There was nothing that'd been bought new in the last ten years. Things were stacked up and buried. The garden that the tiller was for looked like hell anyway—Chub might get a few tomatoes if he was lucky.

Chub walked in carrying the empty bucket and put it against the wall. There was slime and some blood on the inside.

"That thing's runnin good!" Chub said. He grabbed the throttle and goosed it up. The motor went there. Satisfied that he couldn't kill it, he throttled it back down and the motor died when it slowed past the point of running. Clouds of white exhaust hung against the open joists. It grew quiet again. Chub didn't even have a dog to bark.

Once he'd asked Frank if he had any old coins lying around. Suddenly, wheat pennies fascinated him. Frank gave him an old Jim Beam bottle filled with pennies and other things like little screws and bolts. The bottle was one Ollie'd left in the barn. Frank hated to see somebody spend a day sifting through a bunch of old coins, although he'd done similar things, sure. But he didn't think he'd sunk that low.

"I reckon I better head on over to the house," he said, moving toward the open mouths of the garage.

"That sonofabitch wouldn't fire yesterday for shit."

"Might've been moisture in the tank."

"Guess I oughtta go to Stickel's and get some of that water remover?"

"Wouldn't hurt it none. Tell Jack my mower's runnin. He helped me get a belt for it last time I was in there."

They walked toward the truck. Each time Frank pushed down on his cane foot he felt his back tense up. He hated that he'd walked that extra way to look at a damned tiller that ran.

When they got to the pickup Frank hooked his cane over the side of the bed and climbed in. Chub stood there and put his hands through the open window and rested his meaty arms on the windowsill.

"You reckon this time they'll really get it built?"

For years they'd discussed damming Big Logjam River to create a reservoir. The lake level could then be controlled, cutting down on the floods that took the bottoms back almost every spring. Like the flooding they were experiencing this summer. The new reservoir, some said, would flood out half the town and all of the land that Frank had lived on for forty-five years.

He started his truck. "I reckon I'll be dead and gone fore they ever get around to doing something."

"Probably so," Chub said. He looked at the cornfield across the road. The truck idled roughly for a few beats. "I might get a bite to eat before I clean them cats. Might get some shut-eye too."

"All right."

"Well, I guess I'll talk at you later. You and Ethel want to come over and eat them filets tonight you'd be welcome."

"Sounds good." He backed the boat into the yard like he always did and nodded before he drove out the driveway. At the road he turned left and went toward his house. If he didn't make it home for lunch she'd be upset. He knew because he'd done that before.

The Chevy truck pulling the olive-green jon boat drove so slowly Norman Fisk thought the old bastard driving it had probably died behind the wheel. He pushed the grill of his big dually right up against the little outboard motor hanging off the rear of the boat. Let him get the hint that way, he thought.

The road was too narrow to pass along here. All you could do was tailgate somebody until they pulled over, or turned off onto some other county road. Fisk had places he needed to be, too. The appraiser was waiting on him, for one thing, out at the Simcox property. Then he had to run by the old home place to see if they'd finished running his wheat yet. All this before three, when he had to meet Deckard at the bank to go over the loan.

And yet here he was, wasting time behind some old fart out going fishing, probably with a blind white-faced dog and a can of worms.

Fisk thought he probably should know the guy, but he didn't recognize the truck. He knew a lot of the landowners out this way. He tried to keep tabs on who owned what. You had to be aware of what was coming up for sale. Sometimes these old suckers died in their sleep and their land was auctioned off. If you talked with the surviving family first, you might be able to buy before anyone else had a chance. If not, you could always outbid the crowd. But it paid to know who was putting what parcels up for sale, and who owned the land bordering it.

Damn, he didn't want to resort to honking at this old guy, but if he went any slower the whole day would be gone. He let off the throttle and fell back, then floored it and made the big diesel engine roar back up on the boat. Right then he blared the horn.

Sure enough, the old man noticed. Fisk saw the hand go up in front of the rearview mirror and make a fist.

He chuckled. The old fucker still had his salt, anyway. Fisk flipped him off and stayed right on him, his bumper inches from the prop. He was thinking of what he could do next when the old man slowed even more and then turned on his signal. The trailer lights were practically under his bumper, but Fisk could see the flashing light on the truck. About damn time. He was turning off on 500 West.

The old man slowed almost to a stop before he made his turn, but he finally did and got his shit out of the way. Fisk put the hammer down and the diesel roared. He looked over as he passed the intersection, and the guy had his arm extended out the window and was shaking his fist again. An old farmer wearing a cap.

Fisk shook his head. "Screw you too, buddy," he said.

He was coming up on one of his properties now. Just a stretch of flat cropland bordering a county road. He saw the familiar yellow signs in the ditches. FISK REAL ESTATE, they read, with his phone number under that. He checked them as he drove by, going a little slower now himself. They looked fine. You could read the number, which was all that mattered. Keep the damn phones ringing.

The property looked all right too, but it wouldn't hurt to get somebody out here to mow. If you looked at it now, you'd see open fields of fescue. Last year, there'd been a dilapidated farm house and a couple of outbuildings standing there. He'd bought it at an auction and then hired his dozer guy to come in and clean it up. There was nothing you could do with the house. Beyond repair—the barns, too. Better to knock them all down and start over.

This particular place had been about ninety acres, but now it was marked off in ten-acre increments, to sell them off as horse mini-ranches. He had a horse himself, for his daughter, and he knew they were the biggest money-suck you could own. But people wanted them, and they needed land for horses. He could sell five ten-acre lots and get back his investment. The other four parcels would be gravy. Driving by the lots now, he remembered that two couples had called about them already. They were supposedly talking with the bank. Sometimes the buyers never called back, but enough of them did. Even if it took all year for every lot to sell, they'd go sooner or later. He didn't need the money right now, and land prices would only go up.

There really wasn't anything to it. Buy a farm, break it up, sell it off. Put money back into the next one. To tell the truth, there was usually only one other guy bidding against him at these auctions, another local land developer named Dwayne Lovell. But really, he and Dwayne were the only ones looking. They were too far from any cities to make any big-time developers interested. Mostly, the competition came from farmers who wanted to expand or young couples wanting to buy their first farm. If you took the price over a thousand an acre you left them in the dust. He didn't really like Dwayne, but he couldn't blame him for playing the same game.

Still, these little farms and this backwoods wheeling and dealing would only get him so far. Take this little hobby farm out here—he only bought it because he knew he could make money off it with little investment. But he had something bigger planned that was going to set him up for good.

Because he'd already figured out where the lake was going.

And the key was not to buy those places they intended to flood. Hell, the government wouldn't give you jack shit for those properties. But if a guy could buy land on the edge of what the government would claim, then all of a sudden he had lakefront acreage. Somebody would want to build a marina, a general store. Sell off half-acre lots with cabins on them. Hell, you couldn't miss. The government would keep a lot of land, maybe make a park, but somebody had to own the land right next to that. Even if that plot stood a mile from the water, it would still be the closest residence to the lake. And people loved to live by water. He'd started digging two acre ponds on the properties he owned. Instantly the lots sold faster and houses would pop up like a ring of ducks around a puddle.

So as he rolled along in his big black diesel, going about sixty now, he thought about all the money he stood to make. And he had a leg up on Dwayne and everyone else, because he knew more. He knew where the lake would be, and he understood for certain that the lake was coming, although some of these hilljacks around here would fight it. It didn't matter. The water was coming anyway.

He owned about 10,000 acres at any one time, making him the county's biggest single landowner. And his sister had married the Governor's nephew, back about five years ago. Fisk had even met Governor Collins a handful of times. Which was about three times more than anyone else in Shipley County.

The Governor, now at least sixty and on his second term, stood behind the reservoir project. Indianapolis was where his bread was buttered, but he figured if he could throw the hicks a lake he'd be forgiven for never visiting and maybe even get a body of water named after him. There were a lot of floods down this way, and no reliable source of drinking water. Fisk and a few of the others had made calls and even written letters. There'd been a lot of talk for a long time, but now things were happening.

So Fisk had been approaching landowners, those with houses where he'd calculated the line would be between government and private, and asking them about selling their property. He hadn't gotten too far in that yet— most of them hadn't even considered selling until he came to their doors— but he told them that the government would be paying a lot less later on. He explained to them that they could get a better deal from him now, but they needed to act fast. Most of them had heard about the lake project and were already scared.

Some were not listening yet, but others were. All you had to do was throw dollar amounts into the air. Almost all were farmers anyway, tired of dealing with flooded fields and yellowed corn. Put dollar signs in front of their eyes and they'd start listening. Most of them knew him, he'd discovered. Or knew of him. A few did little to hide their disgust. But still, talk about those big amounts of money, and almost every one of them let him into their homes to sit down at their kitchen tables to talk further. They would have their wives pour him a cup of coffee.

Frank pulled down the long driveway that led past the old white farmhouse to the barn. After backing his boat into the lean-to, he shut off the truck. He was still mad about the jackass who'd followed him, honking and swerving like he intended to pass. He'd been driving these roads since he was fourteen or so, and to have someone try to run him off like that made him so mad he was ready to call the sheriff. But nobody from the sheriff's office would do anything now, and he knew that. He slammed the truck door and grabbed his cane.

He crossed the open area between the barn and the house. The yard needed to be mowed again, and he wondered if he'd have time to get it done today. Hard to say. He climbed the three concrete steps at his back door.

A pot with a lid on it sat on the stove. The smell of vegetables cooking floated in the air. He walked into the living room and sat in his recliner.

"Hey," he called out.

There was no answer. The house stood so quiet he heard the grandfather clock ticking in the hallway. A stack of folded laundry sat on the ottoman across the room, in front of the other easy chair. So she'd brought it in from the line.

He knew she was probably in the garden, and been hidden behind the barn when he pulled in. Maybe she was getting something for lunch. A lot of times she'd cut up a few tomatoes or bring in leaf lettuce. The lettuce was usually all but fried up by early July, but the rain had kept it on longer.

"You in here?" he asked.

When there was no answer he reached for his cane to lift himself out of the chair. He did this with the usual number of pains. Standing at the kitchen window, he had a good view of all he was used to seeing: the barn, with its chipping red paint, the white chicken coop, the grain bin and the pole barn that had housed the tractors. There was also a pumphouse, where he and Ethel brought up the well water they drank.

"Hey wife," he called. He'd lived long enough to know there was some reason to worry. Still, he was drowsy and it was not hard to stay calm. Probably she was in the garden yet, weeding or even tilling. He couldn't hear the tiller, though.

He hoped nothing had happened to the chickens. He didn't want to deal with that today. The coop would already be over one hundred degrees inside, and he wouldn't be strong enough to stand in there in the midst of the swarming chickens and their dust.

Walking back across the yard, he thought about what they might have for lunch. She'd made so many meals for him he no longer thought about where they came from. It was as fixed as anything in his life—his wife would have food ready for him when he wanted it. But now he wanted it, and he was still waiting.

He checked the coop first, but he could see right away that the chickens were calm and behaving normally, milling around in the lot.

When he reached the barn he hollered out again.

"I'm back here," she said.

He made the corner of the barn and he could see the garden then—the half acre her father had plowed for the first time over seventy years ago. She stood near the tomato plants, doing something with the metal cages that enclosed them.

"Didn't you hear me come in?" he asked.

"The tomatoes are so heavy they're bending over their traps," she said.

"I been in the house. I got back a while ago."

"I heard you come in, and I said 'I'm back here,' but you must not've heard, cause then I heard you go in the house."

"Well, I'm back. Lunch bout ready?"

"In a minute. I just want to get these plants upright. Some of them are falling over, their tomatoes are getting so heavy."

Their garden was constantly ravaged by raccoons. Beyond the garden lay only pasture ground and then the woods. Big Logjam River, the same one he'd fished last night and this morning, flowed through his woods for almost a mile, past sycamores and maples. He looked over his pasture now, grown up with seeded-out fescue, and the woods, dark green and shimmering, and it all looked like he expected it to. It was the perfect habitat for coons. They came into the garden at night and knocked the corn down.

Back when he was more concerned about such things, he'd sometimes waited in the hayloft as the sun set, and shot the raccoons as they appeared against the lighter soil of the garden. They wouldn't be there and then they would be, making their hunched-over way through the garden, pausing to dig here and there and biting off plants. He shot them with his .410 shotgun and hefted their bodies just over the pasture fence, where others coming toward the garden would have to step past their fallen brothers and sisters. He thought this would stop them, but sometimes it seemed more coons came every night, regardless of how many carcasses he piled.

Eventually, the smell got to be too much, and she got sick of looking at the rotting corpses. He started hauling them back to the woods with the trailer behind his three-wheeler, loading their heat-swollen bodies onto the cart with a pitchfork. The smell was about enough to kill a man. He'd heard that if you hung a dead animal over the river, you could catch catfish under it, because maggots would fall off the carcass into the river and provide steady food for the fish. He had thought about doing that with these coons, but decided against it. He didn't know how to get the body out over the water and it was just too nasty to mess with. Later, he stopped shooting them altogether. To hell with it, he thought. Let them have part of the garden.

She finished what she was doing and walked over. She carried some lettuce in a colander and a hoe she used for weeding.

"Seen any coon sign out here?" he asked.

"Let them coons be. I told you not to hurt them. They ain't hurting nothing, and you know that."

They walked into the barn, where she leaned her hoe in the corner.

"Did you catch any fish last night?" she asked.

"We caught two flatheads apiece, but they was small ones. Nothing too big. This morning we caught some channels and took em to Chub's. He said we could come over and eat them later, if we want."

"I don't really want to eat at his house."

Ethel and Chub had had their moments. He lacked the refinery she preferred in a man. That is to say, she wanted a man to wear socks to the table. She wanted a man to not wear a shirt day after day if it had something crusted on it.

"Anybody stop by after I left yesterday evenin?" he asked.

"Not that I know of."

"What did you do the whole time?"

"I worked on my crossword puzzle and then listened to the ball game. The Reds won in extra innings. I was up until almost eleven."

"So the sucker chubs won." He did not care about the Reds in the way she didn't care about fishing. But they asked each other about it. She wore a white blouse with a faded gingham pattern, and it moved here and there against her body in the light breeze. She had to walk slower so she didn't get too far in front of him. They made their slow careful way across the yard.

Inside, she scooped the stewed tomatoes out of the pot and placed some in a bowl. She put them in front of him, skinless and tender. She poured some milk into a glass and put that near him, too. She got crackers down from the shelf and put them in the middle of the table. She'd made tuna fish salad earlier and it waited in the refrigerator. She got it and a loaf of bread and put that on the table. She made sure he could reach the salt and pepper shakers.

Then she toasted two pieces of bread because that's how she liked it with tuna fish and sat down across from him. He'd already begun to eat. He looked decrepit and dirty, as he always did when he returned from the river. His hair stuck out on the sides from under his filthy hat.

"Take your hat off," she said. "You ain't eating in a barn. You know better than that."

"Sorry," he said, lifting his hand to remove it and place it in the chair between them. "I'm so wore out I forgot I was still wearin it."

"You're getting too old to be out on the river all night long anymore."

He pushed his fork into a pile of spilled tuna fish and put it in his mouth. He chewed several times and then took a bite from a piece of bread he held in his other hand, folded over double. Their eyes didn't meet, and after a while he took another bite of tuna fish.

CHAPTER FOUR

Saturday afternoon came around, and the Shipley County Fair had been held in the outskirts of Green City, the county seat, since Sunday, so the week was about to reach its pinnacle. The 4-H'ers had held their "Breakfast of Champions" that morning, the animals were sold at the auction shortly thereafter, and tears were cried as the prize and prized animals were loaded into strange stock trailers bound for slaughterhouses. Kids from every town in the county were starting to wander down the muddy driveways and through puddled parking lots. Heavy bass beats emanated from their rusty but polished cars. Country music played from loudspeakers mounted on utility posts, and the smell of popcorn and fried batter wafted across the grounds. A few animals remained in the barns, those headed back home instead of the meat locker, and some people went in and gazed on them and reached over the fences to pat their noses. Most of the younger people passed on the barns and walked the pathways of wood chips, eyeballing kids from towns ten miles away.

Ollie had gone almost every night so far, just to walk around, bird-dog the girls and maybe pay to get into the grandstand. He'd paid good money to see the three-wheeler drags and the mudsling, but he'd skipped the grandstand event Tuesday night, the antique tractor pull. He'd watched one a couple of years ago, and it about bored him to tears to sit there and watch old tractors pull weights a healthy lawn mower could move.

But in this county, this particular Saturday night meant the annual demolition derby. It meant Coondog Calhoon would finally run the car he'd spent most of the summer fixing up, with Ollie's intermittent help.

Coondog promised to pay him two cases of beer if he'd help fix the car between heats and, in essence, be the Crew Manager. And Ollie wanted part of the action. He wanted to be somewhere in front of the grandstand, where everybody was looking, instead of sitting inside where no one could even tell he was there.

The car ran, but not well. He knew he could keep the car running—he'd always had a knack with cars, especially those built in the seventies. Coondog'd found the car in the yard of an old woman living out near Stumpy's corner. A dented '74 Chevrolet Impala, white with a green top. There was enough steel and iron wrapped around the engine and transmission to make it difficult to rupture or twist something out of place. She didn't want to part with it, but Coondog offered her five hundred in cash and she grabbed the money like he always grabbed the first beer on Friday and produced the title from an ice bucket on top the fridge.

Back when they were in high school in the early seventies, with everyone scared sick they were about to get draft notices for graduation presents, Coondog raced cars for money. Two light posts stood in the high school parking lot, each one with a shrub and a curb of concrete around it, exactly a quarter mile apart. They all came up on Friday and Saturday nights and raced from post to post. Island to island, they called it. He won ten or fifteen bucks a weekend.

At that time, he drove a blue Ford F-150, but it'd been traded long ago for a three-wheeler and two motorcycles. He kept it fresh with his vehicles. There had probably been about thirty of them since graduation, now almost thirteen years ago. Every last one of them a piece of junk, but he loved them like brand new Corvettes. He would never, in all his life, sit in a brand new Corvette.

But he needed somebody to fix his demolition car between heats. Or needed his friend there to watch him do it. After five heats, there'd be a consolation round, and then they'd drop the flag on the grand finale. If your car ran long enough to drive back out there for the consolation heat, you could keep racing and have another shot at getting into the finale.

It was so hot Coondog wore no shirt, only jeans and black boots. And his Chevy hat. Most of the drivers had trailered their demo cars in, and now an assortment of junkers were being driven or pulled off trailers. Ollie met him there, back in the pits, the open expanse of grass out beyond the track. Ollie had gotten some beer, as promised, but only a twelve-pack of Pabst. He hadn't called Shirley nor anyone else.

They stopped tinkering with the Impala to go to the obligatory drivers' meeting, held on the track itself right in front of the grandstand. Old Jerry Sallus stood on a concrete platform in the center and read from the list of rules. He was the operator of the ag co-op and somehow connected to all the grandstand events. He spoke through a bullhorn, even though there weren't many drivers. Mostly guys about their age, arms smeared with grease and hair curled around their ears and necks.

Jerry finished with the rules, handed out sheets of paper with the lineups listed, and the drivers and pit crew workers walked back to their cars. The ring had been assembled: the volunteer firemen had placed telephone poles in a giant square, and pushed dirt around outside the poles to reinforce them. Inside the ring, they were wetting the dirt with the hose on the tanker truck. The tanker was new—the town had raised the money by hosting fried chicken dinners prepared by the firemen themselves.

At the Impala, Ollie pointed in the backseat. "Gonna wear that, are ya?"

Coondog nodded. "You heard him. 'Gotta wear a helmet at all times.'"

"You gotta wear hers, though?" Ollie laughed.

"Shut it, asshole. It's the only one I could find today."

Her name had been Margie, and no one had seen her in five years—not after Coondog caused her to leave the area. But while she was still around, for several months they'd been Hapgood's hottest couple. They'd ridden three-wheelers together. The Dog had picked up a helmet for her, and in an effort to personalize it, he'd taken a black marker and written MARGIE over the visor. Later it'd been x'ed out with the same marker.

But he couldn't be distracted with memories of lost loves now. Ollie watched him as he stared at the ring of mud, the field of battle. Tobacco juice leaked out of his bottom lip. The event was still hours away but the man was in the zone.

"I can hear music in my head," Coondog said. "Can you hear it?"

They'd already finished the twelve-pack he'd brought, along with a little whiskey hidden in the glovebox. Ollie was on his way to getting drunk. He knew for a fact his driver was too. "What kind of music is it?"

"I think it's Iron Maiden. It might be my theme song." Coondog lowered his head and closed his eyes and listened. He hummed a bit of the riff. "It is. It's 'Run to the Hills.'"

The Impala had been painted black the week before with three and a half cans of Rust-oleum spray paint. The green vinyl top had been painted over, too. Coondog had sprayed "Kiss my Ass" in yellow paint on the side. On the trunk's lid, it said, "Coondog Rocks" and "Watch Out!" He tried to come up with something the kids in the audience might get a kick out of. Not so much that he saw himself as a role model, but he understood he was there to entertain. On the hood, in a gesture that was more honest than he would've admitted, he'd sprayed "Looking for Love." Under that it said "Bend Over." The other side paid tribute to the sponsors: "Stickel's Service Center" and "The HollyWood Tavern." Each had given him fifteen bucks. The HollyWood Tavern, a bar built over someone's basement, gave him free beer one night instead of cash. When enough people got out on the dance floor at that place, you could feel the floor shake and sag. Several times Ollie'd been out there, swiveling his hips into some girl's ass, beer held high, and thought the floor was going to go any second. It was the kind of bar where you thought you might die.

"Sallus said we only got three hours before the first heat," Ollie said.

"Are we in it?"

He checked the sheet he'd been carrying. "Nope. Second."

Coondog jumped up on the hood of the car. "You all ready for this?" he yelled, arms out like a champion boxer. He'd welded the doors shut, so he put his feet into the driver's window and slid in. He fired the motor up. There was no muffler or tailpipe, and the engine roared. Black smoke all but obscured the car. He powerbraked it and dirt flew from the rear tires.

People turned to look. Then the car lurched forward and died. He slammed the shifter into neutral.

"Bitch took and died on me," he yelled out the window. The engine fired again and he jerked it in gear.

"Where the hell are you going?"

"Take a little cruise. Check out the competition."

He drove off between the parked cars, black smoke rolling from beneath. People were walking around, working under hoods or crawling underneath the junkers. Ollie noticed the circle of light from a welder down the way, brighter even than the sun overhead.

Ollie walked to the grandstand to gain access to the fairground. He wanted a hot dog if he didn't have to stand in line too long. The fairway was crowded— the demolition derby crowd was out here now, waiting for the race to start and watching the people try the games. He walked along the fairway and the carnies yelled at him. He looked at the prizes—gaudy stuffed animals and mirrors with old rock bands emblazoned on them. He didn't need any of it, and he was proud of himself for knowing it.

He noticed two young girls walking ahead of him and he sped up. They wore bluejean jackets and jeans. One of them had boots on, like maybe she showed horses. They might've been sixteen or so.

He walked right behind them. He could smell their fruity scent and the hay on their clothes. So close now he could reach out and cup their asses with his grease-stained hands. He fought the urge.

"Hey girls," he said.

Both of them turned, and Boots spoke. "Hey guy," she said. They kept walking.

"You ladies here for the demo?" he asked.

"Maybe," the same one said.

"I got a buddy that's runnin."

"That so," the girl said. They hadn't stopped walking. The girl answered him over her shoulder. The carnies kept interrupting him.

"Win them girls a bear!" one yelled.

"My buddy got me a pit pass, cause I'm working on the car. You ladies want to go watch from the pits?"

The girls finally stopped walking and studied each other. The talker read the other's eyes and said, "No, we got things we gotta do."

They stood in front of a dart game. You had to throw darts at balloons pinned on stars. The carnie sat on a bench that formed the front of his stand.

"How aboutcha? Break three, take your pick," he yelled.

The girls turned and kept walking. Ollie watched them saunter off. The carnie was so heavy it looked like he might break through his bench, but obviously it had held him maybe a hundred nights already this year. It would not break tonight, of all nights. He looked at Ollie.

"Them girls gonna be with you tonight?" he asked.

"Don't look like it, do it?"

"Huh? Do a little three-way action? Huh?"

Ollie stared at him, smiling halfway.

"Wanna throw some darts?" the fat man asked.

Ollie studied the board the red balloons were tacked to. The red stars made it look like you couldn't miss. It was red everywhere you looked, but it was those stars, not always a balloon. Hitting a star got you nothing. You had to pop three balloons. He turned around and walked back the way he'd come. He'd missed the turnoff to the Jr. Leaders stand, and they had the best hot dogs.

"Always a next time," the carnie yelled after him.

"Sure there is."

He bought five hot dogs and went back into the pit area. The tag around his neck let the deputy at the gate know he had access. When he got back to their designated spot the Impala sat there.

Coondog lay under the car. He slid out on the trampled grass. "Where you been man? We got this sewed up. These other bitches brought nothing but junk in here. Is one of them dogs for me?"

Even before the sun set the event started. They watched the first heat to get ideas, since Coondog had never driven in a demo.

"Don't look too bad, do it?" he asked.

"Keep your ass end first. Hit em from the back."

While they watched an old Lincoln Towncar backed across the pit, building speed, and rammed a station wagon between the headlights. The grill shattered inward with a tremendous crunch and steam burst up from the busted radiator. The station wagon sat there, crippled.

"Got him," Coondog said.

"Don't let them hit your front end."

"Shit yes."

They watched the heat end. A guy they didn't know won. Jerry Sallus, who also announced the event on the PA, said to all that the driver was from Hawesville, a guy named Ferris Post.

"Never heard of the fucker," Coondog said. Then it was time to climb into the car to get ready for the second heat. The firemen used two tractors to pull the broken cars out of the pit.

He still held his whiskey bottle as he sat in the driver's seat. "Maybe I won't even wear that helmet," he said. Ollie stood outside the Impala, looking in the windowless door.

"Do it. Sallus will throw the blackflag on you."

"I guess you're right. I gotta race if I'm gonna win the money." He pulled on the helmet, which was orange with a guard covering his mouth and chin. Over the face opening you could still make out MARGIE, marked over with x's and squiggles. He looked like an idiot. He leaned out the window and tried to spit. The tobacco juice hit the mouth guard and hung in a drip.

"Wish me the hell luck," he said.

"Go get em, you son of a bitch."

Ollie knew Coondog had little chance of winning any money. Ollie thought he'd be lucky to survive this heat. The car was running like it'd been rebuilt with parts from other models and makes, some altogether incompatible. Coondog was too drunk and he wasn't a good driver sober. Ollie thought there would be nothing to repair after the first heat. He was thinking about going to the horse barn to find those girls. He carried high hopes at least one of them would be interested in him. He hadn't kissed a girl since three Friday nights ago when he pressed Debbie Brandise against her car in the parking lot of the Depot. She'd been separated from her husband for two weeks before that, but she was back with him now. Ollie was overdue some action and those girls were cute. They were young but nobody was talking about marriage here tonight.

Coondog drove the car into the ring of telephone poles with great flourish, goosing the motor and spinning the tires. Jerry Sallus introduced him by the name on his license: Chester Calhoon. You could hear the crowd over the engines, laughing and clapping. Seven more junkers went into the ring.

The fire department boys soaked the ring again, since the previous heat had slung the mud around enough to sufficiently dry it out. The crowd hated to see the ring wetted, because it slowed the cars and lightened the impacts.

Ollie walked as close as he could to the ring. There was a rope strung up to keep people in the pit area away from the collisions. Four cars lined up on each side—rear bumpers facing the four across the ring. The drivers gunned their motors. The flag dropped and the first of the cars shot backward.

The crowd loved this moment. They cheered wildly as the first two vehicles crunched together. Coondog held back, his engine revved and waiting. A strategist.

The rules stated that every car had to move every three seconds, or it was disqualified.

"Move you dumbass!" Ollie yelled.

Whether he heard him or not, at that moment Coondog jerked the car backward and coasted into the center of the ring like he was backing out of a spot at the Dollar General. He was knocked sideways almost immediately, and turned in such a way that a station wagon had a good angle at the driver's door. The wagon gunned it and slammed into the Impala, and Ollie could see the metal buckle inward.

But Coondog's helmet was still visible, swiveling around frantically.

He pulled forward and bumped a car on its side, hardly denting it. Coondog was too drunk, and the Impala was experiencing the demolition derby version of whiskey dick.

"Move! Move!" Ollie yelled. "Backward!"

On the other side of the ring, a car was struck in the front bumper hard enough to cave it in and bust the radiator. Steam shot into the air. The crowd roared its approval.

The wagon backed into the Impala again and Coondog's ride seemed to settle lower on its shocks. Suddenly another car shoved into the back of the Impala, hitting it cleanly enough to push its front axle over the telephone pole marking the edge of the ring. Coondog spun his wheels, but he was stuck. It was finished. It was the most pathetic display of demo driving Ollie had ever seen.

He held up his arms, forming a question that couldn't be answered. Who knew what had happened, what had gone wrong? He wanted to laugh about it, but the work put into that Impala hadn't amounted to much. Here it wasn't even full dark yet, and the highlight of the day, maybe of the whole summer, was already over. He was in front of the grandstand for once, even now full of people, but he almost wished nobody could see him, see his part in all this.

CHAPTER FIVE

As the afternoon wore on, the sun slipped below the peak of the barn roof, momentarily setting it ablaze, and then the house fell into shade and immediately cooled. Frank knew exactly what time the sun would drop behind the barn in July. It changed about a minute, later or earlier depending on the season, every day. In winter the sun fell to the side of the barn, but he still timed it. He'd watch it set and then consult the clocks. As soon as it was completely hidden by the roof and the barn swallows were out swooping around the yard, he said to Ethel, "You better go feed your chickens."

He no longer had cows to feed and worry over. His father had kept a herd of about twenty Herefords, even before Frank was born, and so some of his earliest memories were of his father holding him over the cows' heads as they ate from the manger in the barn. And Ethel's father Tarif had also run cows. Over the last forty years, Frank had cared for as many as fifty head at one time. He'd been there to check on pregnant heifers in the blue cold hours of the night, gone into the barn to feed them on sunny days and on days when tornados threatened. He'd buried some calves and bottle-fed others to health. There'd always been cattle in his life, but there were none now. He knew something of the life of an amputee.

He'd sold the last of his cows about five years ago. He could no longer watch over them the way he wanted to, and things kept happening. An old girl got hung up in the fence back by the woods and died after she finally strangled herself. Another lost a calf after it fell into an old well. Another time several of them got out back by the river and Pearson found them first and told Frank his cows were out. He'd been busy planting corn that day, but he still should've known. It wouldn't do to have somebody else telling you your cows were wandering around off your land.

So that fall he loaded them all up and hauled them to the auction barn over in Green City. He sold the calves that had just been weaned off, their mothers, and the old bull, Hoosier. He drove home that night thinking about the barn standing empty. No animals to feed early in the morning. Nor any out in the pasture to look over and count from the back of the three-wheeler. The place grew a lot quieter overnight. Sometimes he thought about how those particular cows—Grandma Moses, Dolly, Princess, Lil Baby, White Face among them—would forever be in his memory as his last. It was a hell of a thing to let your mind stay on for long.

Ethel worked on a puzzle in the other room. She heard him call for her, but she'd already fed and watered the chickens. She'd done this while he was asleep in his chair and he'd not woken up for it. She fed her chickens without fail every day before evening, but he always said something, like it wouldn't get done if he failed to remind her.

He started talking again, and she could only hear bits and pieces of sentences. She heard the word chicken.

"I already took care of them," she said.

"Did you check their water?"

"Yes yes yes!" she hollered. "Are we going somewhere for supper or not?"

"Come in here," he yelled.

She got up and went into the living room and sat down across from him on her chair.

"Are we going out for supper, or do you want me to fix something for you to eat here? It's late already."

"Let's go over to Chub's."

"You know he won't have nothin to eat but them catfish."

"What?"

"He won't have nothin to eat—"

He grimaced like he still couldn't hear or understand.

"Turn that tv off!" she yelled.

He reached for the remote on the arm of the chair, and after pushing several buttons with varying intensity, the tv went black.

"I said," she began again, "that he won't have nothing to eat but water and those fish."

"Maybe we could take some slaw over there. Maybe a loaf of bread."

"I'll have to make the slaw."

"Okay." He struggled out of his chair and went to the kitchen to call his friend.

They pulled into the driveway at Chub's house and parked behind the garage. Ethel climbed out with a Tupperware container of slaw and a bag of bread. Frank reached around the bed of the truck for his cane and got out. They walked toward the house. It was mostly dark, and the light on the utility pole in the backyard illuminated the picnic table and the big man sitting there. Moths and bugs flew around the light.

It was apparent that Chub had showered. He wore dark blue overalls and a newer hat with a DeKalb seeds patch. Frank had given him the hat. Chub took up most of one side of the picnic table, a stainless steel bowl and a small sack of breading resting in front of him. Near the table sat a propane tank hooked to a burner on a raised stand, holding a sputtering pot of oil. On the back fence, Chub had nailed a board between two posts, and four catfish heads were nailed to the board in a row. Below the heads hung spines and guts to the tails. The heads and tails were still dark gray, but in the failing light of evening the rest of the carcasses were white and pink.

"Hello there, Clarence," Ethel said.

"Woman, you know my name." Chub made no effort to take the slaw from her hands or even to tell her where she might put it. The kitchen light was on inside the house and a pale square of illumination hit the grass.

Frank peered into the pan of bubbling oil. The smell of grease hung around the table. The oil spat out of the pot with a hiss every so often.

"I'll take these things inside," she said. "Is there a place where I can find some glasses and a pitcher? I can make us some lemonade. I brought the mix."

"Damn, you're a good woman," Chub said. "Glasses are on the left above the stove, and the pitcher should be under the sink."

She left and Frank sat down at the table across from Chub. There was a light bulb burning over the back door and she went through the light and they heard the door open and fall shut. Then they could see her head in the kitchen window.

"I don't know that your wife likes me," Chub said, and they both laughed.

"I wasn't joking, though. You got a good woman there. You know that."

"Yeah, I know."

Ethel had been close with LuAnne, Chub's wife. But LuAnne had died from breast cancer almost eight years ago. Chub had been on his own since then, mostly putting on weight, and Ethel hadn't been able to replace her friend. Chub and Ethel had lost something similar when LuAnne had gone on. They'd spoken for hours in the hospital during the last months, but now they seemed to have lost the ability to speak civilly to each other. It was as if the hospital provided a different universe where they could be friends. But LuAnne was gone, and no one needed to go to the hospital now.

"How'd them fish look?" Frank asked.

"Good," Chub said. "But they was a little pinker than normal."

"Eggs?"

"No, no eggs. I think the spawn is about over for all of them."

"It's a wonder, what with the wet spring we had."

"I know it."

Ethel came out of the house with three plates and three forks. She put the plates down in front of the men and put a fork by each plate. She went inside and the men sat there in silence. Chub turned every so often to check the temperature of the oil in the pot. It was still heating up. He took the chunks of raw fish from the stainless bowl and put them into a bread sack with cornmeal breading and shook them.

When she returned, she carried three glasses of lemonade pushed together in her fingers. She put them down on the center of the table and the glasses rocked on the uneven planks. There were bugs on the table under the light but Chub didn't like to eat inside. Frank had told her to put on some repellent before they got in the truck.

"I reckon I'll just drink a beer," Chub said. "There's some in the fridge."

"Maybe you should drink both," she said. She didn't leave to go back into the kitchen and instead sat on the bench next to Frank.

"Why don't you get him a beer?" Frank asked.

"I will when I go back in for the slaw," she said.

The oil finally reached 375 degrees and Chub pushed the pieces of breaded fish into the bubbling oil. They fell in with a great spatter.

The fish turned and surfaced and dove in the oil. They browned quickly. She looked around the shadows of the yard. It was grown up and unkempt.

"You get any of that tilling done?" Frank asked.

"No, I never got to it. I cleaned these fish and then took a nap. A little bit later the boy called from Massachusetts." He said the state's name like he was taking a sip of an unfamiliar liquor.

"How is Charles?" she asked.

"Oh, he seems to be doing all right. Tells me Sarah might be looking at getting a new job. Said his job is all right. Don't reckon they'll ever move back this way, now."

"They still paying him like a king?" Frank asked.

"I guess so. He never tells me that stuff."

Charles had gone to Purdue on a scholarship and chosen the unlikely area of study of chemical engineering. After college he'd gone on to graduate school for a time and now worked on the east coast. Chub hadn't visited him there, because he didn't like the idea of flying and so had never flown anywhere, and Charles hadn't been home since Christmas. He would come again at Thanksgiving.

"I think it's a shame them two never had any kids," she said.

Chub made a sound with his throat. He looked to the back of the yard, where the fish carcasses hung. "I reckon I woulda liked having some grandkids round here," he said as he stirred the fish chunks in the oil. "But I guess maybe she was sterile or something."

"Maybe they just decided not to have kids," she said. "You hear of that more and more."

Ethel looked sad then, and Frank knew she was thinking of Ollie, and maybe of their other problems they'd toted in the past. She'd suffered several miscarriages, as her mother had, both before and after the birth of their son. When Ollie was born, and they finally had a baby to raise, she was thirty-five and Frank was forty-three. At one time or another, they'd both thought that Ollie's problems in life were their fault, for being older when he was born. She still felt that way, but Frank had put it out of his mind long ago. He didn't want his wife to bring it up in Chub's backyard.

"That fish about done?" Frank asked.

Chub looked at her. "Will you run get me a plate with some paper towels on it? And maybe that beer too?"

She brought the plate and the beer. Then she walked back in to get the slaw and another beer, because Frank asked for one.

They waited for the fish to cool. Chub shut off the valve on the gas tank. When the fish was ready they put it on slices of bread and put the slaw on the fish inside the sandwich. The food was good. It grew dark. Last night at this time two of them had been on the river and they missed that now but they were full and happy and this felt good too. When the mosquitoes got too bad finally they all walked back out to the truck. She'd left the remaining slaw with Chub to eat the next day.

"Send the bowl with Frank sometime," she said.

"I will. You all come back anytime."

Frank put his cane in the bed of the truck and pulled himself up into the cab. He started the truck and they drove the county roads back to their farm. It was a pleasant night to be out driving. He drove slowly and watched for deer. He looked again at the fields alongside the road, as he had earlier today and again on the way to Chub's. Now they were lit up with moonlight.

"That poor old man," Ethel said as they stopped at the intersection where 500 West met 300 North.

"What about him?"

"He just needs some company out there. The inside of his house looks like pigs has been in it."

"It's good enough for him. It suits him fine."

"I just wish Charles would come home once in a while."

"He never does, though."

"Well, he should. Chub shouldn't have to live without seeing his son like that."

He drove without saying anything.

"Still," she said. "Seeing the way he lives out there makes me think you'd be the same way, if something ever happened to me."

He looked over at her. Her glasses reflected the lights in the dash. "I might be," he said. "If I even had it that good."

CHAPTER SIX

Now what do ya think of that folks?" Jerry Sallus yelled through the PA system, addressing the grandstand crowd. "He calls the car 'Every Mudder's Nightmare' and comes from Logjam! Name of Trent Smalls. And folks? The boy is only seventeen!"

Ollie watched as the tractor pulled the wrecked cars out of the ring. The station wagon that'd done so much damage to the Impala had won the heat, and now to find out the driver was some punk kid from their town? Some kid half their age, almost like a version of themselves before they grew up? Coondog would be hot. The lights overhead burned, illuminating the busted cars in the ring. The open mouth of the grandstand looked dark, but Ollie knew it was chock-full.

The volunteer fireman driving the tractor left Coondog for last. When they finally looped the chain around the Impala's bumper and pulled it back into the ring, Coondog came squeezing out of the window of the welded-shut door, orange helmet leading the way. Even from where he stood, Ollie could see it was the wrong thing to do. The firemen yelled at him and told him to stay the hell in his damn car.

The tractor pulled the Impala back to their pit area, the chain jerking tight, sagging, and jerking tight again. The car's tires were still up, but the vehicle sat hunched down on its rear like the springs had collapsed. Out the window came Coondog, the ridiculous helmet still atop his neck like a melon on a broomstick. He clawed and jerked at its strap.

"This damn thing!" he screamed, his voice muffled by the mouth guard. He ripped the helmet off his head and threw it into the backseat, where it bounced and careened off the other door.

"The car?" Ollie asked.

"Hell yes, the car! What'd you think I meant? I shoulda had enough power to get back over that shittin pole!" He stared at the Impala, his face streaked with sweat and grime in the outline of the helmet's opening. He looked like he had plugged a small pipe with his face until an explosion rifled out it, singeing his eyebrows and sooting his cheeks. Suddenly he slid back into the driver's seat. He cranked the ignition furiously.

"You gonna want to go back in there for the consolation heat?" Ollie asked. He'd assumed, after such a limp display, that they might call it a night and maybe go drink in the Depot, or go look for those girls.

Coondog continued to twist the key. The motor ground and ground as his foot hammered the gas pedal.

Then he stopped, and merely stared at the steering wheel as if he'd never been let down by anyone or anything so severely.

Coondog lived alone in a little house outside of Hapgood. His parents had only borne one child, perhaps thinking that they'd done so well the first time they could never hope to surpass or even match it. He'd lived with his parents, in the same house, until two years ago, when his pop hit the lottery. His father had only won about $25,000 after taxes, the result of buying a ticket every day on his way home from work over the last fourteen years, but they'd taken that money and moved to Florida. They imagined, and so did Coondog and Ollie, a mansion overlooking the beach, a pier with a boat tied to it—maybe a servant to bring drinks and run errands. It went without saying they never intended to work again, although Coondog's dad, a heavyset bald man, talked briefly about how he might want to open a small engine repair shop just for fun. They had, in fact, won the lottery, and those people didn't work.

Instead, once down there, they put money toward a house they could barely afford in a suburb ten miles from water, and found themselves working six days a week in a dirty seafood restaurant just to make payments. Coondog's dad was a cook for the first time, and his mother waited tables and carried trash out back to a dumpster filled with seafood that rotted in the constant sun. Somehow living in Florida made it all right. They were still lottery winners, with no intentions of coming back to Indiana.

They left Coondog the house and the understanding that he'd pay them for it. The mortgage had been paid off, so all he had to do was send his parents some money every now and then in a haphazard way of officially buying the house he'd grown up in. His tree trimming business provided enough for him to send three-hundred bucks, give or take, every two months. He spent the rest of his money on beer and almost junked-out cars and three-wheelers.

He climbed out of the Impala, his greasy face shining in the overhead lights. Another heat started, and the audience clapped over the jarring noise of crunching metal.

"Help me start this son of a bitch again," he said.

"What you gonna do with it?"

"Let's you and me take this thing out and trash it the rest of the way."

Coondog jerked the hood open—it had to be pried after the dents it'd suffered—and took off the air filter. He asked for some wd-40 and Ollie walked to the toolbox and got the can and handed it to him. He sprayed a healthy amount into the carburetor. He then reached back into the car and turned the engine over. The juice caught and the motor started, shaking and sputtering. Black smoke rolled out from underneath the car.

"Get in this shitbox," Coondog said.

Ollie went around and climbed in through the window. He knew from experience a night like this sometimes ended in an arrest or a serious conversation with a person of some sort of local authority or renown. But he couldn't be expected to see everything coming as it happened.

"Where's the seatbelt on this deathtrap?" Ollie asked.

"I took em out. Everything to make it lighter."

"How much can a seatbelt weigh?"

Coondog pumped the accelerator. The motor went up and down. Sitting in the car was like sitting near a gas fire, and the smell hung around them like curtains. Jerry Sallus said something over the PA, but Ollie couldn't hear it. The heat had just ended, and a winner was being announced.

The Impala bolted forward as Coondog dropped it into gear. He swung the wheel and the car began to turn in a slow arc, like the turning of a big, ocean-going ship. They drove down the rows of cars, some now completely junked and others still being repaired. Coondog waved to some of the competitors. Others he drove by with hard stares. The car rolled with a gentle up and down motion, one of the wheels out of round. Ollie could feel the vibrations of the motor through his seat.

They cruised toward the exit of the track.

"Where we going?" Ollie asked.

"Where do you want to go?"

"I don't know. The bars'll be empty. Most everybody is gonna be at the fair tonight."

"I'm still not ready to give up on some split-tail tonight," Coondog said. "Despite the fact that the demo did not turn out exactly as I planned it."

He nodded to the fair employee who sat on a stool near the exit, and took a right on the road leading past the track and then another right at the first street in town. No license plate and one taillight. He turned into the main entrance of the fairground.

The man in the booth next to the drive said they'd need to pay to park in the fairgrounds. He studied the car as he spoke. The engine sputtered like it might die.

"Entries to the demo should've come in off Orchard Road, back by the track," the man said. He wore glasses and his eyes went two different directions. You couldn't tell which one you were supposed to look at.

"We done entered that," Coondog said, too loudly.

"Then why are you over here?" the man asked. A car pulled up behind the Impala, its headlights filling the cab.

"We done won it."

"Look, if you want to go the fairgrounds, yous shoulda walked over. No need to drive your car in here. Parking's tight enough as it is."

"We want to show it off. We want to show the people a winner."

Another car pulled up in line and the man grew visibly exasperated, one eye focused intently on them. "All right. I'll let yous in. But no funny stuff in there." He motioned them on, and when Coondog let off the brake the car jumped and the engine almost died before it caught and the Impala lunged forward, into the fairgrounds proper.

"I never even had to pay him," he said, and they laughed.

The parking lots were nothing but fields of gravel behind the different barns. They drove by the lot behind the sheep barn, and then by the lot next to the hog barn. People stopped walking and stared at the car. Coondog honked like they were in a parade.

"Park this bitch," Ollie said. He was laughing his ass off, but enough was enough.

Coondog steered the car down the main drag, past the cattle barn and toward the horse barn. Crowds of people clogged the road, causing him to slow down and making the engine sputter and choke. When they reached the end of the cattle building, he turned the car down a little path that was not meant for cars. A tractor hooked to a spreader stood there, parked so the 4-H kids could throw the crap from their show animals into the trailer. Someone on the Fair Board distributed the manure on a nearby field every day or so.

"I reckon we can park back here," he said.

Ollie looked around. People were staring. A man dropped a length of rope and started walking toward them.

It was dark, but bright lights mounted outside the barn revealed an open expanse dotted with trees standing over stock trailers. The 4-Hers often slept in their trailers during the week.

Coondog cut the wheel to the right to steer around the spreader. The tractor, Ollie noticed, was a John Deere 4030, just like one his dad had owned. The headlights bounced across the open field, glinting here and there off the reflectors of the trailers. It looked muddy.

"Let's take this bastard car back here," Coondog said.

"This ain't no parking lot."

"Better put that helmet on, then."

With that, he goosed the engine and it sped up, almost died, and then coughed and roared again. The back tires started to spin and the Impala bounced out into the grass.

"Don't you dumbass!" Ollie yelled, grabbing the door.

The car bucked twice as it sped across the uneven ground, slinging mud in graceful arcs. Suddenly it bogged down, lurched to a halt, and screwed itself noticeably lower into the earth. The back tires spun furiously, brown soup splattering against the wheel wells and quarter panels.

"Shit! It sure is wet back here," Coondog said.

Against the sensation of the car slowly shifting back and forth and the sound of mud slapping metal came two things: the angry shouts of men and a powerful smell.

Coondog floored the gas pedal and the tires spun and sang falsetto against the mud. There was a sense of urgency to his actions now. He jerked the shifter back to reverse and floored it again. The car rocked back maybe a foot. When he shifted back into drive, the motor died. For a second or so it was very quiet.

Then men could be heard yelling, all of their voices blurred together. Words like "get" and "there" and "dumbass." Coondog stuck his head out the window. Against the light of the cattle barn, at least ten people stood silhouetted, madly gesturing.

"Hey!" he yelled. "You all, I thought this was a parking lot!" He laughed so hard he squealed.

Ollie sat there, looking back at the crowd. He wanted to laugh, but he couldn't. The smell was getting to him. Something rotten was seeping up through the floorboards.

Coondog pulled back into the car and looked at him. "I guess these pigsuckers don't want you to park back here."

They lifted out of their seats and climbed through the windows. When they dropped to the ground they instantly sank up to the tops of their boots. The sour smell swelled and hit Ollie in the face and he felt his stomach start heaving.

Together they staggered toward the men, jerking their feet free from the mud with each step. Ollie bit down on his tongue and fought the retches. Waiting were the parents of the 4-Hers, who didn't like cars cutting donuts where their kids and expensive animals spent so much time.

"We better get ready to throw down, looks like," Coondog whispered. "This time don't leave me all the big fuckers."

The group near the John Deere started hollering at once. A man with a mustache and a chest as wide as a door got in Coondog's face.

"What the hell you boys doing back there?"

"Wrong turn!" Coondog yelled. "We just won the demo, and we come over here to celebrate! We got lost."

"Well, that car can just stay there," the man said. Another said something about it being stuck for life.

Ollie looked at the men. He knew some of them. No one seemed to be a cop or a fireman. Just fathers. One was the local veterinarian, whose two boys showed beef cattle. Another man ran the bank. If they started swinging now, it would look like the town's two biggest roustabouts versus the city council. They'd end up in jail for sure.

"Maybe we could pick up around here tomorrow," Ollie said suddenly. The men all looked at him. "We'll pick up trash for you all."

Coondog looked over at him, eyes wide. He would've rather fought than suggest self-imposed community service.

"You boys better get on out of here, fore the sheriff shows up to ask questions," the man with the mustache said. Little kids were starting to gather, pointing at the car stuck out in the mud and the two men wet with brown slime up to their knees.

One little boy pulled the arm of his dad. "That's the mudhole where we dumped all that bad milk from the Breakfast of Champions," he said. Ollie looked at him and then down at his legs. He could feel the wetness soaking through to his skin. His boots were full of it, too. Milk cooking in the sun all day long.

His stomach had never been that strong and rotten food had always been his weakness. He bent deeply at the waist as he felt it rise up in his throat. He bit down and stopped it. He heaved again and the puke burst forth from his mouth. It splattered on his boots, which reminded him of the milk and he heaved again. The smell was everywhere now. He couldn't escape it. He puked again and again. He kept trying to walk away but he couldn't walk and puke at the same time.

"What the hell?" he heard Coondog say, now several steps removed. "What the hell is wrong with you?"

He turned, still leaning over, and looked at the Impala. They'd fish-tailed around when they hit the puddle, and now the car faced them, one good headlight still glowing weakly. It sat in the mud up to the bottom of its doors. The bottom half of the wheels were completely hidden in gunk. "Bend Over," the hood read.

He did just that and another rope of vomit churned and fell from his mouth.

When he finally finished puking, he stood up. Coondog had walked over by the barn and was leaning against a fence, talking with some man, explaining how the mistake had been made. He gestured wildly with his hands. The man didn't seem impressed.

Ollie looked the other way, toward the open area of the fairgrounds and the rides and carnival booths. People were walking by. The Ferris wheel, lit up with Christmas lights, went around and around. Groups of teenagers scampered by in packs.

While he watched a woman came into view. She was walking alone on the woodchip path, heading toward the horse barn. She didn't look his way; she didn't notice the car sunk in the mud. But from her profile he could tell she was hot. Even with puke dribbling from his chin he could tell she was the woman of his dreams.

"Oh there she is," he whispered.

Then, like a witness scrambling to note details of the getaway car, he memorized what he could: jeans, white shirt, blonde hair just below her shoulders. A walk that said she knew where she was going, tonight and in life at large. A butt that stuck out just right. The kind of woman he'd never had but always wanted.

But she strolled on, completely oblivious to the demolition derby drama reaching its denouement behind the tractor and manure spreader, and he lost sight of her behind a small cluster of people waiting on the Tilt-a-Whirl.

He'd have to go find her.

"Where the hell you think you're goin?" Coondog stood alone near the tractor, his face still ringed from the helmet, his left arm muddy from having it hang out the car door as mud splattered. He was wearing his shirt that bore a picture of a rottweiler. He didn't own dogs but he'd put it on before the demo because he liked the symbolic message it carried.

"Man, I need to talk to her," Ollie said.

A look of excitement darted across Coondog's face and he started in his direction. Ollie put up both hands in a kind of panic.

"Let me talk to her," he said. "You wait here by the car."

"Where the hell is that piece of shit goin?"

"Just hold on, now! We don't want to spook her. I'll be right back."

Ollie turned and jogged into the cattle barn. Coondog stood there and smiled, as if he had somehow managed to make all of this occur. Which, of course, he had.

Rows of show steers and heifers kept their asses to Ollie as he walked down the aisle of the barn. Little kids with shovels and teenagers standing in groups slowed his passage through the bovines. A little girl pushed a wheelbarrow as big as she was and he almost fell over her. At the end of the aisle stood the show ring and bleachers. He quickly scanned them— the bleachers now mostly empty except for a few fair moms sitting in pairs talking—and exited the rear of the barn.

The wash rack. A concrete pad bordered with a stout fence with tie rings, plumbed for multiple hoses. Here's where the show animals were washed and shampooed. He grabbed a hose, cranked the valve, and squeezed the nozzle. Cold water sprayed on his other hand. He turned the hose on his legs, blasting the nasty milk mud from his jeans and boots. The water was so cold it stunted his groin. He sprayed off what he could before dropping the hose and running back through the barn.

The pathway outside was littered with cups and wadded up hot dog wrappers. Here and there a popped balloon skin lay discarded.

"Jimmy you asshole!" a teenage girl called, right next to him. Ollie turned, startled. She was looking ahead, not at him. The girl next to her laughed and said, "Let's cut him off by the grandstand."

What the hell is Jimmy running for, he thought, watching their butts as they ran off in the other direction.

Darkness had fallen and the horse barn loomed lit from within, like some kind of skeleton with a glowing heart. He entered the building through the open side and tried to look around, but the high borders of the horse stalls prevented him from seeing much. It smelled different in this barn—now the distinct smell of horseflesh and sawdust overpowered even the smell of the fried tenderloin booth across the way. He turned and went down the first row of stalls. His legs and feet felt numb from the water. His socks squished in his boots. Horses peered out at him with their giant marble eyes, past their ribbons and boards proclaiming their names and maybe something else about them. One board read in wood-burned letters: "Ginger Snaps. Pierceville, IN. Do not touch me! I Bite!" After this last bit there was a wood-burned frowny face.

Amid this nonsense he searched for her, who had already grown in his mind into the most glamorous girl he'd ever seen, including those on television. He knew it was possible she'd been walking toward a parking lot, and was even now driving away. Maybe she'd be back at the fair next year. Or maybe he'd never see her again! If only he hadn't been forced into that impromptu shower. He turned the corner at the end of the barn and went down the center row of stalls. A woman was sitting in a lawnchair in front of a stall, and she called to her husband as Ollie got closer. He reached the middle aisle, looked left and right for her, and crossed into the stalls on the other side.

He'd only gone about three stalls deep when he heard female voices coming over the boards of one decorated with a blue ribbon and a poster of a pedigree. He had to lift onto his toes to look over the door. A girl of about ten was brushing a horse, a giant sand colored gelding that swished its tail in his face. The girl started to say something and then saw him looking in. She stopped brushing and stared at him.

A woman moved out of the corner of the stall to see who was there.

And there she was, in a horse stall, of all places. Not ten feet from him. She'd pulled her blonde hair back in a loose ponytail, but he recognized the white shirt. She was even better up close. He couldn't imagine how good she'd look if he didn't have to peer through bars.

"That's a nice horse," he said to the woman. The girl said thanks and he was surprised to hear that voice.

"His name is Mr. Pickles," the girl said, resuming her brushing.

The woman looked at the girl and smiled. It occurred to him that he had all three of them penned in the stall, and he could stand there and gawk all night if he wanted to.

The woman finally spoke. "Tell the man what you won with Pickles today."

"Me and Pickles got first place in our division," the girl said. "Last year Nina Mendelson beat us, but this year we won, and then we went on to the champion drive, and at first . . . ."

He stopped listening to her and watched the woman. She was staring at the girl, listening intently. He could see the way her fine, soft hair curled around her ears. The small earring that might have been a diamond. He studied the curvature of her ear and felt the desire to lick it. She continued to smile at the girl, who, amazingly, still had things to say about her wondrous horse, Mr. Pickles.

He looked around for a man but there was no one on either side. Just him, standing on his toes, peering into the horse box. He kept trying to smell her, but all he could smell clearly was Mr. Pickles.

"I'd like to buy Porkles a milkshake," he blurted out.

He heard the word come out wrong and grimaced. His tongue couldn't be counted on in times of need—he knew that—but now?

"His name is not 'Porkles!'" the girl exclaimed. She'd been not only interrupted but insulted.

"Yeah, I know. My bad. It's Mr. Pickles," he said. "Maybe we could walk over there and get the big champion one."

"I want one, too!" the little girl said, jumping around the horse. Christ, this one is a handful, he thought.

But the woman said all right and the girl put her brush in her back pocket and hugged the horse's neck. Ollie stepped back to let them out.

He then remembered he had thrown up on himself just minutes ago. He grabbed his pocket and felt for the thin pack of Big Red. He tore it out and popped two pieces in his mouth. He should've swung by the restroom to look at himself in a mirror, but there'd been no time and the mirrors had been shattered by punches long ago anyway. He'd have to go with what he had.

The woman followed the little girl out of the stall. She was shorter than he was. When she turned to throw the bolt lock on the door, the little girl stepped in front of him, produced the brush from her back pocket, and tore a handful of horse hair off it.

"Do you want some of Pickles' hair?" she asked, shoving a handful of the stuff up to his face.

He grabbed her hand and brought it down. The woman turned in time to see this, so with his free hand he took the hair from her grasp and made a big show of shoving some down into his pocket.

"The lucky fur!" he said. "That'll come in handy."

They both smiled and he knew he had done the right thing in taking it.

"Hair!" the girl screamed. "Horses have hair!"

"I got ya." It was almost eleven at night—Jesus! Did the kid sleep? She was high on cotton candy and horse showmanship.

"I'm Ollie, by the way," he said to the woman as they turned to leave the barn. He held out his hand and she shook it.

"Mine's Summer."

They continued walking.

"And I am Cheryl!" the little girl yelled. People outside the barn turned to look.

"She's my friend's daughter," Summer said. "I babysit Cheryl sometimes and every year I come to watch her show Mr. Pickles."

Cheryl hadn't seemed like her daughter. They were too polite with each other, too considerate. And Summer was clearly only twenty-five or so. Still, he knew other twenty-five year olds who had ten-year old kids. Several, in fact. He knew one girl who'd gotten pregnant at thirteen back when he was in high school. The father was a senior, about half retarded. They lived together in a trailer out by the dump at Stumpy's corner. They had about five kids by now, last he heard.

Summer walked next to him, and he kept trying to look at her. She wore cowboy boots, the tips just barely coming out from under her jeans. Little feet, then. Her shirt wasn't tight but it looked like she had a nice rack for a small-frame girl. Now, out in the open, he could smell her. She'd put on a perfume of some kind that reminded him of open plains and cowgirls out on the range. Damn, it felt good to be back in the hunt.

Summer led like she knew where they were going, so he followed her. But the path they walked went by the cattle barn, and the buried Impala. As they got closer, walking slowly among the groups of people, he could see the stupid car out in the mud. He prayed to God his clothes did not stink as bad as he thought they did. There was so much damn mud over here this year, he hoped his boots just looked muddy from walking around. His jeans were still cold and damp.

He suddenly noticed Coondog, talking with two kids. He was retelling the tale—his hands were up, pretending like he was driving. Ollie looked down, but not before Coondog spotted him.

Don't you do it, you bastard, Ollie thought.

But no yell came, and when he looked back up, Coondog just stood there, watching. It was as if he'd never seen such a sight—the three of them walking along, pretending to be some kind of family. Here was his friend Ollie with two blondes. The taller one good-looking like some kind of damn TV actress. The little one an annoyance but he wouldn't be able to see that. Coondog stood as if he were in a church as the three of them passed.

Summer started to say something, and she glanced up at Ollie and saw him looking over there.

"Who in the world put that car in the mud?" she asked.

"I heard something about it," he said, and they walked past the cattle barn on their way to the Junior Leaders building. "Some drunk asshole, probably."

There was no line because it was so late the 4-Hers were ready to close. A kid with red hair finally took their order for three chocolate milkshakes begrudgingly and trudged off to make them. They sat down to wait under fluorescent lights. Ollie hid his legs under the table. Cheryl spotted a fellow horse shower at the next table and went to talk with her. Thank God for small favors, Ollie thought.

"So. What's your story?" Summer asked.

"Not sure I got one, I guess."

"Oh you have one. We all do." From where they sat, the back of the grandstand was visible. People were streaming out—the demolition derby was over for another year.

She looked at him but he didn't know what to say.

"Cause you look like you got a story, is all," she said.

"Trust me. It's not a cliffhanger or nothing."

"The people with the best stories a lot of times can't tell them. Or they won't."

"It's probably both for me."

"What's your name from, then?" she asked.

"Uh, great. Thanks for asking that." He tried to laugh, but it sounded like a snort. "Well, my full name's Oliver, if that's what you mean."

"What's wrong with that?"

"It's a kind of tractor."

"So? So's John, as in John Deere. Doesn't mean that's why your parents named you that."

"No, this time it is. My dad named me after his first tractor. It was an old piece of shit Oliver."

She laughed. Her teeth were so white they looked like they were glowing. "Okay, here's another one. Why are your pants wet?"

He felt his face get red and he tried to laugh it off. He was thinking he'd tell her he fell into a giant puddle when the red-headed kid brought their milkshakes to the window and interrupted. Ollie jumped up and went to grab them, conscious of his wet jeans the whole time. He was relieved to find he had enough cash.

Back at the horse stall, this time with all three of them crowded inside ("Because this is the way Mr. Pickles would like it," Cheryl had said), they finished their milkshakes and sucked noise through the straws. Ollie was thankful for the horse, and he tried to keep part of Mr. Pickles between him and Summer so his jeans would stay hidden. The horse was huge and warm to the touch. Ollie hadn't been near one in years. He kept trying to talk to Summer, except Cheryl would not shut the hell up.

But it was almost midnight now and the girl was finally showing signs of slowing.

"It's about time for me to take you home," Summer said to her.

"I really think I can stay," she said.

"Norman'll kill me if you stay."

"No he won't. Rebecca said I can sleep in her trailer."

"I'm going to take you home, instead. Mr. Pickles will be here in the morning, and then you get to take him home. Thank this nice man for buying you a milkshake."

"Thank you," she said.

"I'll walk you all out," he said. Anything to prolong the night.

Cheryl gathered some of her things into a backpack and then put a padlock on the stall door. She really did seem competent when she kept her mouth shut, he thought. Not that he watched her too much. The girl then said a lengthy goodbye to Mr. Pickles. She told him tomorrow he'd be going back to their barn, and that she couldn't wait for that day to come.

The walk would be short because her car was behind the horse barn, Summer said, but he walked with them anyway. Back into the comfortable dark, where maybe he could keep his stains out of the conversation a little while longer.

When the girl ran ahead, he quickly asked Summer if he could call her.

"I don't see why not," she said.

"Cool."

"Do you want it now?"

"Yeah, I'll remember it."

She recited her phone number to him and he said it back. The first three numbers were the same as his.

"So you live in Logjam?" he asked.

"Yeah, out by Peterson's Market."

"How come I've never seen you?"

"I don't really get out that much."

"I don't really get out all that much either," he said. "Although I wouldn't mind it." He kept trying to think ahead, think of what he was going to say next. As a result, he barely knew what he was saying as he said it.

They were at the car then, a dented Dodge Omni. It looked like a demo car itself—hubcap missing, rust showing around the wheel wells.

"Well, bye," she said.

"Bye!" Cheryl said.

"You really can call me."

"I will."

"Ooohhhh," Cheryl said.

Summer opened the driver's door, and then reached back to unlock the back door. He stole a glance at her ass. Perfection. Cheryl clambered into the backseat, her backpack on her lap. She had to sit next to a baby seat, he noticed. Summer said goodbye once more, got in behind the wheel, and gave a little wave. She cranked the window down.

"Seriously, though," she said. "Nothing wrong with being named after a tractor." She laughed and he thought he would remember later how some light from the barn behind him reflected off her teeth.

The car started with a rattle and she drove forward, dipping and lifting in the ruts left by the horse trailers. She turned on the main path and disappeared around the corner of the barn, taillights glowing.

He stood there. His pants were still soaked and cold but he no longer noticed the awful smell. Instead, he felt like a red glow emanated from his body, and maybe it did. Was Coondog still around? He'd need to hear this damn story. He wouldn't believe it, Ollie thought. But he saw it! He would have to believe it!

Ollie couldn't wait to call her. He wanted to call her right now.

He wondered why she needed a car with a baby seat. Cheryl surely didn't require it, and what was she, a full-time babysitter?

That was something he could ask about when he called her. He turned and started back to where he thought Coondog might be—still at the stuck car, still talking about how it got there.

Ollie didn't know how he'd ended up here, but he thought, I'm sure as hell not going to look a gift Mr. Pickles in the mouth.

CHAPTER SEVEN

Frank woke up and noticed the breeze lightly blowing the faded curtain that hung over the window by their bed. Ethel had sown the curtains herself, and now the white fabric with its flowered border rose into the room and billowed up before being sucked back against the screen. He watched it do this for some time. It followed the same path but it didn't. Not an exact pattern he could predict, anyway, lying on his back this Sunday morning in their bed where he'd slept regular nightly hours for the last forty-five years. The window frame had been painted white, but it was chipped in places where he'd hit it with his cane coming around the bed. Dead flies and other insects collected in the corner of the windowsill. The wind blew the curtain in, where it hung in the air for just a moment, before the undercurrent pulled it back to the window frame. Then the breeze would lift the curtain again with almost, but not quite, the same motions. He watched it and thought about how the river breathed the same rhythms.

It was not yet fully light out. But the rooster had crowed several times, as it did every summer between five and a quarter after. During autumn, the rooster crowed later with the fall sun. In the winter, when the chickens were penned up in the coop, it barely crowed at all. But now, in the middle of summer, the rooster could be counted on.

He had gotten up without the use of an alarm for most of his life. At least for the last thirty years, now that he was what? Seventy-four. Didn't seem right, but what the hell was that feeling worth. Today, he found himself wondering about Ollie, in the absent, loose way he always thought about his son. He had no way of knowing that the boy had spent last night puking over the smell of soured milk and then falling in love, and was even now asleep and trying to dream about his new love interest, and would, in fact, wake up in several hours and start thinking about her. Frank didn't know any of that and didn't wonder about it. He knew his son was lazy and a late sleeper, though.

The morning's haze was burning off, and the dew that covered everything like a layer of the softest gauze began to steam and evaporate. The dew on the roofs and leaves collected and dripped like raindrops. She was still in the bed behind him. He could feel the warmth coming off her body. He knew she was awake, too.

She would be worrying about Ollie—he understood that, as well. She worried about him more than he did, and with more desperation. She wanted him to be all right; she wanted to suddenly cure him. Ollie hadn't been all right since before he graduated from high school, and his class had already held their tenth year reunion. He'd skipped the reunion, which was up at the VFW Hall, and he hadn't been all right during any of those ten years. Nor had he been all right in the several years since the reunion. He wasn't all right and showed no signs of ever being all right.

Frank tried to let it go—the memories of the fights and arguments. The problems with drinking that weren't problems until they were, and how those problems had refused to go away and instead only grown. The women he carried on with whom Frank couldn't stand the sight of, because he could look at them once and see everything they had been or would ever be.

Most of the men around here close to Ollie's age had fought in Vietnam. Several of the boys from the county had died over there. Ollie was too young by a year or two, so he missed the peak years of the draft, and as a result, went nowhere. Frank had never served in the military, but he held the idea that if Ollie had gone he would've become a stronger man. Not that he wanted something to happen to his son. Jesus, no. Just let him learn something about life from it.

The breeze continued to lift and drop the curtain, but now the sun lit the white fabric and it glowed.

"You ready to get up?" he asked.

"I guess so," she said. "You already woke me up, with your tossin and turnin."

"You were up."

She rolled over and he felt her looking at his back. "I guess I was. Do you want bacon or sausage?"

"Bacon."

She got out of bed and took off her nightgown and hung it on the hook behind the door. The floor creaked as she walked to the dresser, as it had every morning for at least the last ten thousand days. He heard her pull out a drawer, sift through clothes, and then sigh as she sat on the bed to get dressed.

He turned over and looked at his wife. Her white hair looked like she might want to get it permed again. He could scarcely tell the difference, but he knew when it started to look soft around the edges she would have Hattie make it permanent again. Her back looked white and small. It sloped in every direction—from neck to bottom and side to side. Her body was rounding out. She pulled a light blouse on, stood to pull up her polyester slacks, and looked down at him.

"Still can't keep your eyes off your beautiful wife, can you?"

"No," he said. "I guess not." And she was still beautiful to him.

She stepped into her shoes, which were waiting by the dresser, and walked across the hall to the bathroom. She was in there for a moment, then the toilet flushed, the faucet ran, and she left to go start breakfast. The stairs moaned as she made her way down them. It had become inconvenient to sleep on the second floor, but they always had and it seemed too strange to try to make a bedroom downstairs at this point in their lives.

He lifted himself to a sitting position. His back hurt. With his feet carefully spaced on the floor, he reached for his cane and rose. He went slowly around the bed to the closet. He took down a short sleeve shirt with buttons dotting the front and put it on. His overalls hung on a sixteen-penny nail and he put those on by leaning against the wall. He then went across the hall to piss and use Listerine from the glass bottle. He had almost grown used to the ridiculous amount of time all of this took.

The county paper came twice during the week, and one of those times was Sunday. He read the paper (she had gone out and gathered it from the driveway) while he ate his bacon and eggs and drank two cups of coffee. The pills she'd counted out for him waited by his plate. Young Dr. Mulferd had him taking several pills a day for various things. He lost track of what all they did. She kept tabs on them. Every couple of weeks they went to Green City to get the prescriptions refilled and celebrated by eating lunch out at a diner. He took the pills all at once with the glass of water she provided and then he stood and went to the door. She continued to work on her crossword puzzle. He put on his hat.

"I think I'll go check the fences," he said.

She nodded and said nothing. She knew he'd do it anyway. With the cows all sold the fences had nothing to keep in. Still, he wanted to maintain them—make sure trees didn't fall and mash them flat, their wires pulled taut as piano strings or popped like a fishing line that had tethered up a flathead the size of a calf. Once in a while a deer got tangled up in one somewhere.

"What about the eggs?" he asked.

She looked at the clock on the wall. It showed just before six. She fixed a look on him.

"You know I get the eggs at six-fifteen. Same as every day for the last umpteen years."

"Well. You might want to check your garden here in a little bit, after you get them eggs," he said.

She wrote something in the little boxes and said nothing.

"Make sure the coons didn't get in there last night. That, and the weeds."

"All right."

"I don't think it rained last night. But it might later on today."

He walked out and she turned and stared at the door he had since closed again.

Frank sat on his three-wheeler, his cane across the rack behind him. He pushed the little button to fire the engine. This one had cost a bit more but it had reverse. He backed out of the barn and the dew from the grass slicked the tires black and they squeaked against the ground. When he got past the barn he could see the garden, and it looked good from this angle: the corn was up, the tomatoes grew in their circular wire cages, the cucumbers were spreading. Still, it could stand to be weeded, he knew that. The barnyard gate had been tied open now that the cows were gone, and so he drove on through and out into the pasture. It was already warm and the air felt good against his arms.

Ethel's father, Tarif, had owned this land before they had. He'd bought the place back in 1910. Some of the farms out here were marked with a blue and white metal sign that read "Hoosier Homestead—Owned by the Same Family for over 100 Years." They had another twenty-five years or so to go, and Frank knew if they ever got a white Hoosier Homestead sign, he wouldn't be the one to mount it on the mailbox post.

Ethel's mother had died in her thirties, when Ethel was only nine, but Tarif had stayed on the farm until it took him back. For three painful years, the first three years of their marriage, Frank and Ethel had lived on the farm with him—with Frank doing all the work and listening to Tarif tell him how it ought to be done.

But he was young then, and he could take being bossed around a little bit. Now the place bore Frank's fingerprints—he'd paid the Rolls brothers to build the tool shed and later the grain bin and he built a lean-to onto the side of the barn himself. Only the chicken coop and the house looked largely the same as they always had.

Although he had to admit they didn't look the same anymore. Nothing did. He hated, especially, to see his barn lapse into disrepair. The red paint was mostly gone, and the barn looked gray where the bare, weathered wood showed through. He'd always kept his barn painted—red with white trim around the doors and windows. He'd done it himself, lugging around the long wooden ladder and occasionally having someone, usually Ollie, lift him up with the loader on the tractor to paint the high spots. It had been hard work, but he'd done it for forty years. The barn needed paint every fifth year or so. He'd kept the place up.

But now it looked rundown. If he drove by his own place today, as he'd driven by countless farms—going slowly and really checking the operation out—he would have to say that the place looked shoddy. He'd distrust the owner. And yet now, despite his best efforts and intentions, he'd become one—a paintless barn owner.

But it was too damned hard to paint it. For one thing, he couldn't get up in the loader like he could before. Nor could he use the ladder, with his back failing him like it was. And it would look worse to paint just the lower parts. It was too hot for Ethel to do it, and Ollie wouldn't help. The only other option was to hire it out, and you couldn't trust those traveling painters. They used colored water and moved on, is what they did. So the barn grew grayer every day.

The white chicken coop was also losing paint. Weeds had grown up around the buildings and under the gas tank. The fence on either side of the barn needed replacing. The posts looked like they could be pushed over with a human hand. The tool shed and the grain bin looked solid, but that was because they'd been built only twenty years ago. He hated like hell to see things fade away around them.

He drove the three-wheeler down the trail he'd worn to dirt. It followed the fence for a while, then cut down into the pasture and across the ditch. The pasture was hilly, and the three-wheeler bounced over the ruts and tracks. The cows had been gone for five years, but you could still see some of their trails, where their hooves had worn the earth into itself.

About fifty acres were in pasture, and the woodlot held another seventy. The trail ran through the woods, and already it felt cooler in here, in the shade thrown by the tall maples, oaks, and beeches. He could smell the leaves rotting. A squirrel ran up a shagbark hickory and he wished for his rifle. He hated cleaning squirrels anymore, so he hadn't shot one for years. He still liked the taste of fried squirrel, though. This new three-wheeler was so quiet he could hardly hear it running, even under him. Sometimes he drove right up on deer, and they'd bolt off, kicking through the saplings, white tails waving like flags.

He looked at things and it was all familiar to him. This was his land.

Deeper in the woods, Big Logjam River flowed across his property. This was the section he visited daily, the length of artery he rested his fingertips on. He fished from the bank because the river ran mostly shallower here, where it carved over limestone layers. There weren't many deep holes, but once he'd caught a twenty pound flathead from an outside bend.

It did flood often. On the other side of the woods, he owned a big field that'd been drowned more times than he cared to count. He'd seen corn standing in water many times, the tassels waving just over the surface. Or carp tailing among alfalfa in the spring. But some years the river didn't rise. And he carried some flood insurance for his crops, anyway. These woods, they got flooded, too. It didn't hurt the trees. Hell, everything back here was halfway soaked now, they'd gotten so much rain. Mud splattering up under the fenders as he drove.

He parked the three-wheeler where the trail cut along the river and killed the engine. Now birds could be heard. A kingfisher yelled at him from across the river. He sat there in the morning sun and watched the water. Still plenty high and stained, the river ran from bank to bank. Leaves and small sticks floated by. He watched them pass. Eventually, all the flotsam went around the slight bend downriver, and he couldn't see where it went.

He didn't think they would dam it.

On mornings like this he didn't think they could. He tried not to look at the barn back home because seeing it paintless made him mad, and on mornings like this he didn't allow himself to think about them damming his river. But as he watched so much water roll by, he knew that fifty gallons of red barn paint were nothing next to what they wanted to do.

CHAPTER EIGHT

Sunday morning came down hard on him, sleeping in the hot, airless bedroom of his trailer. The window stood open, the screen behind it torn and pulled away from the frame, but no breeze came through. The dew had long since burned off and a green fly that had spent the night outside on the windowsill felt the sun warm its wings and walked through an open corner of the screen and buzzed over Ollie's sleeping mouth on its way to the smells of the kitchen. It was gravid with eggs and seeking a rotting mass suitable for the raising of maggots. Somewhere in his unconsciousness he sensed the reverberations of the fly's wings and woke up. He was sweaty and waking up hot pissed him off, but then he thought of her and he felt himself smile. Summer.

The room smelled of sweat and beer and the sheets clung to him in a dank mess. On his wall, the antique Pabst Blue Ribbon sign with the built-in thermometer read over eighty degrees. He closed his eyes again.

He had found Coondog, and they'd walked the emptying fairgrounds together until they ran into Troy Beasley, someone Coondog used to work with. Troy gave them a ride back to Coondog's place in an old '69 Firebird that had been painted red with black flames on the hood and front quarters. Once there, all three of them got drunk while throwing horseshoes under the security light in the backyard. At close to four in the morning, Troy gave Ollie a ride back to the fairgrounds, where his truck was still parked in the pits. Troy was leaving then anyway to go wake up his ex-girlfriend to try to have sex with her. A long night, but today Ollie would not go to work, and that pleased the hell out of him.

He lay there in his dirty bed, which felt like it might be steaming, remembering everything that had happened with Summer. He recalled the little things: the way she first turned to look at him from the horse stall, the way her cheeks pulled in when she sucked on the milkshake's straw. It made sense to start at the beginning, right when he saw her while puking up bites of hot dog so familiar he almost remembered taking them. He wanted to start there and slowly revisit the whole night with her.

But he couldn't do it. He'd be reliving their first conversation when suddenly he'd think of her ass as she bent into the Omni. Then he'd go back, work his way up to the milkshakes, and think of something stupid Cheryl had said. Finally, he'd thought so much about the night he could hardly remember if any of it had happened at all.

But he knew her phone number! He also carried a vague idea of where she lived, and he seriously thought about getting up and driving until he saw her car. What if she saw him, though? Would he seem weird? He didn't want to seem too creepy right away. He wondered how early he could call her. It was—what time was it?—he opened his eyes and looked at the clock. The sun coming through the window cast a glare on the clock face and he couldn't see.

Jerking the damp sheet aside, he walked down the hallway to the bathroom, where he urinated in the moldy, piss-splattered toilet. He could smell the filthy toilet standing over it. Cleaning it had been on his list for a while now. But if there was one thing he hated to do, it was scrub a toilet with that flimsy little brush. Another thing he hated to do was clean anything in general.

Once back in the bedroom, he noticed it was almost ten in the morning. When he picked up the jeans from the floor to remove his keys he found the tuft of horse hair. He threw the jeans out behind the trailer because they still smelled but he put the hair in the drawer of the coffee table. He would get something to eat and call her. Maybe she could do something even today. Not that he usually went on dates on Sunday—he tried to recall if he ever had—but he didn't think he could wait until Friday to see her again.

A car show came on while he ate a bowl of off-brand marshmallow cereal, so he sat there and watched it in its entirety. Nothing looked that special, but he suddenly felt too nervous to call. At eleven oh seven he thought here goes nothin and went to the phone. He dialed up the numbers he had memorized.

After two rings a woman's voice said hello. He couldn't be certain it belonged to her.

"Um, yeah, hi. Is Summer there?"

"This is her."

"Hey, this is Ollie! I met you last night at the horse barn."

"Hey! I know who you are. Tractor Guy! How're you doing?"

"Fine. Just got up, though."

"You mean you just got up?"

"Yeah, well, a little while ago. I ended up goin back to a buddy's house, and me and him and another guy ended up playing horseshoes all night."

"Sounds like a good time," she said. He thought it sounded like she didn't believe it was indeed a good time.

There had been muffled sounds during the whole conversation: a TV on somewhere, a plate being hit by silverware, a voice or two. But now someone was talking to her directly. Couldn't they see she was on the phone? Christ, this was hard enough already. The receiver shook in his hand.

He heard her move the phone away from her mouth, saying something.

"Sorry about that," she said when she returned.

"That's cool. Who was you talking to?"

"My daughter wants to know when we're going to eat. I told her she was going to have to wait a little bit, cause I was on the phone."

He felt his stomach drop. He wanted to say something, but couldn't think of a single thing.

It wasn't unusual to find a single mother in Logjam. Coondog had a saying: throw a pacifier, hit a single mom. The follow-up was, then you run like hell the other way. Now that Ollie was over thirty, many of the women he met in the Depot had kids. You just accepted it, if you wanted to get any action. Many nights he had ended up in cramped little houses and apartments over offices downtown, kicking over toys and stepping on things that squeaked as he tried to drunkenly grope some lonely mother. But those were short-term deals. He always left long before the paper hit the doorstep. Or the baby woke up.

Damn. He didn't want her to have a kid. Give the rest of them twins, but just let this one come without any of that.

Although suddenly the damn baby seat made much more sense! He hated himself for his ignorance. She just hadn't looked like a mother. She looked younger than that, for one thing—much younger than most of the ones he picked up in the bar, anyway. But mostly he was mad because a kid meant another man, and he didn't know how far gone this one was.

"Uh, how old is she?" he finally managed to ask.

"About two and a half. She'll be three in April."

"I got ya."

And then no one said anything, and in the silence he knew he was making himself out to be an asshole. But he couldn't think quickly enough, and he was trying to sort out if he even cared anymore.

"I bet now you're wishin you didn't call, huh?" she asked.

"No, it . . . no! It ain't that at all."

"Well, let me just say, my daughter is the most important thing to me. She's got me through some tough times already."

"I bet she has! I bet so. You, uh, still married?"

"I never was. Spring's daddy and me split up before she came along."

"Oh, yeah? So just you two live together?"

"Yeah, me and her live in our own little house, used to be my grandma's. She goes to daycare at the Methodist church there in town. Crayons and Cradles, it's called."

"I got ya."

The conversation was so far beyond what he had planned he didn't know what to do. He started to ask how old her daughter was, but then he remembered he already had.

"Well, I better let yous go eat then," he said.

"Oh, you don't gotta run off. We're just gonna have a pizza here in a little bit."

"Nah. Well, I mean I better go. Maybe I'll call you sometime this week, after I get off work."

"All right. Where do you work?"

"Over there at Sellers Sawmill."

"I know where that's at."

"Well, I better run."

"Thanks again for calling. And thanks for getting me and Cheryl milkshakes."

"Any time. I liked doing it."

"She loves that horse, doesn't she?'

"I'd say she does."

"Yeah, I always go with her on the last day at the fair. That's been a tradition since I used to babysit her. Not like I don't have enough going on of my own. But you can't say no to good money, can you? Her daddy's rich."

"No, you can't."

It was quiet again and his ear felt hot against the plastic. He had never, in his entire life, been good at this.

"Hey Ollie," she said.

"Yeah?"

"I don't want you to see me as a desperate woman. Spring and I do all right on our own. We make a good team, the two of us. But if you want to do something sometime, I'd be open to it."

"Oh, sure. That's what I want. I mean, I don't think that. At all. Maybe just go out to eat or something."

"Yeah, I'd like that. Just let me know so I can take her to her grandma's house. I need a little time in advance so I can call Mom and make sure she ain't too busy or something."

"Okay. But I bet you're already seeing somebody, probably."

"No way! I . . . uh, nope, no dates for months now."

"Well, that sounds good. I mean about you being able to, not that you haven't went in months."

She laughed. "I can go out. But remember what I said about me not being desperate, okay?"

"I don't think that." And then, as if to prove to her that he wasn't so shallow as to not be interested in her just because she had a kid, he heard himself say, "I could even do something today, if you wanted."

"You could? Today? Well, let's see. Like what?"

"We could run up to the Dairy Queen or something. Nothing big."

"That sounds fine. But she'd have to come if we went today. Is that all right?"

"Yeah, that's fine."

"Maybe at like, two?"

He said that worked and she gave him directions. They said goodbyes and hung up and he sat on the couch in front of the muted tv. This morning he would've given away his truck to get her to see him again and now he felt like he'd been lured into a trap.

He drove to her house for the first time ever that afternoon in his pickup, and it bothered him like hell that he hadn't washed it beforehand. There was still dust from the fairgrounds all over it, and the truck looked all right really shined up, but it showed every one of its eight years when left dirty. But there was no water spigot out at the trailer, so he had to wash his truck at Coondog's. And there hadn't been time to do that. It took him longer than normal just to get himself cleaned up.

Peterson's Market was a little rathole of a place, but it was the only store near Logjam itself where you could buy food. It squatted at the corner of 450 East and 100 North, barely ten feet above the pavement at its highest point. Like the converted garage it was, the store had one entrance and low ceilings. Peterson had installed a pump out in front to make a little more money by selling gas. Any more, a lot of people drove over to Green City to do their shopping at the shiny new Jay C store. Ollie's parents still shopped at Peterson's. Most of the old folks did.

When he reached the store, he turned left and headed down 450. He was nervous now. His hands were wet, and he could feel sweat running down the back of his neck. Damn it was hot. He wore jeans and a clean T-shirt—he would not be seen in shorts. His lower arms were so dark when he wore shorts it looked like his legs had been sawn off a pale stranger and reattached to his torso. Dr. Frankenstein building a skinny-legged honky with spare parts. He chuckled at that. He had both windows down but the air that blew through off the road was too humid to do anybody good.

He followed the directions she had given him and turned into the second driveway on the left. The mailbox, a little black box with only numbers on it, looked like it would fall any day now, maybe even later today. The driveway was gravel, but weeds poked up through it with regularity. It looked like you could mow it. Big trees stood over the driveway, obscuring his view of the house. Then it was time to park, and he pulled in slowly next to her dented Omni. It had been parked crookedly, the windows left down in the heat.

He shut off the truck and opened the door. Now that he had safely parked (he just knew he was going to hit her cat or something) he got a look at the house, which was made entirely of bushes. He could see white siding, the old-fashioned kind made of wide strips of aluminum, and a door over a little concrete stoop. The rest of the house lay buried in green, overgrown shrubs. It looked like an old person's house.

A picnic table stood in the backyard, and some plastic toys lay about. He saw a shovel and a blue wheel off something. The grass had been mowed, but not trimmed. You could see where the taller grass had been left to stand around the house and shrubs. Big trees shaded the whole thing. Parts of it reminded him of his trailer.

He pocketed the keys and went toward the front stoop. Both the screen door and the wood door had been shut. He heard a window air conditioner rattling somewhere around the corner. He knocked on the screen door. It didn't seem loud enough, so he opened the screen and knocked on the wood one. His heart thumped.

Then suddenly the door swung open. There she stood—blonde hair and bright eyes and sweet smells. As soon as she opened it she turned again, bending around to do something with the little object behind her, which he took in only as a blurred shape.

"Come on in," she said, her back to him.

"This is a nice house," he said, although he had barely looked around even the room he stood in. His head swam. He looked at the ceiling, at the corners.

"Thanks. It used to be my grandma's, but she died so I moved in here." She was still bent over.

"I'm sorry to hear that. About your grandma."

"Yeah. Well, she was old and had Alzheimer's. She thought she was Katherine Hepburn there at the end."

"I'll be damned." He did not know who Katherine Hepburn was, but it was obviously not her grandmother. It was clear to him that the woman had been delusional, and that was the point.

Summer stood and faced him now, and with great fanfare she swung her arms and said, "This is Spring!"

He looked down in the direction of her arms and was surprised to see another human standing there.

In his entire lifetime, he had never held a baby. Never spent more than eight hours in the presence of someone under ten once he himself had gotten past that age. Never talked to a kid without the presence of an adult nearby. Never really talked to one with an adult nearby. When he walked into a room with children present, he often ignored them completely. It shocked him to realize he hadn't even looked at this one yet, and he'd been standing right next to her.

The child stood on her own power, but she was no taller than Summer's thighs. Her hair stood out from her head in little wisps and spouts and she kept her hand in her mouth. She wore a little white dress with something like orange pop splashed across the front of it. The girl looked over her hand at him. She had pretty blue eyes—her mother's eyes.

"Hi," he said.

She looked away disinterestedly and tugged on Summer's shirt.

"Ju-ju," she said.

He glanced at Summer, who was looking down at her daughter. She then knelt to be eye level with her. "Do you want your juice?"

The little girl nodded and Summer picked her up. Suddenly, the girl was right in front of him!

"She's a cute one," he said. He stood with his hands on his hips, rocking.

"Thank you," Summer said. "She's a good little girl, aren't you? Yes." She turned and scanned the room, the toddler on her hip. "I need to go in the kitchen for a minute. Can you make yourself at home out here?"

He said he could and watched her butt as she left, still carrying the child. Summer wore shorts, and her legs were tan and matched her arms. When he lifted his eyes he was shocked to see the little one watching him check out her mother's ass. Jesus God, eyes on the back of her head. He studied his hands until they were out of the room.

Summer really looked good. Better than any girl he'd dated, for sure. He didn't know what to make of this situation, though. For example, he didn't think the baby could tell her mother what she had just seen, but he couldn't be certain.

A TV stood, on, in the corner. Some cartoon muted. There was a couch that looked like it had been trampled by cows along the wall, under a window. The window was shaded by the shrubs outside it. On the couch lay two dolls and a small blanket. Against the other wall stood a play kitchen-type thing, and one of those cars a kid could sit in and scoot around. The child drove the toy with her feet, like the Flintstones. He was still dizzy from being in a new place and his ears felt swollen. The whole room was awash in reds, blues, and yellows. The colors of little kids.

Summer returned with Spring, and the little one carried a plastic cup with a lid on it tipped up against her mouth. The child now wore a little hat, and he was reminded she was going with them to the Dairy Queen. This woman and her daughter.

"Are you ready to go get some ice cream with this nice man, Mr. Ollie?" Summer asked.

He knew he was not being spoken to, and he stood there with what felt like a dumb grin on his face. His insides felt hot, like a bout of diarrhea was coming on.

"We're ready," she said to him and smiled.

He went out first and Summer pulled the door shut with a slam. He started down the walk.

"I think we'll need to go in my car," she said. She still carried the girl on her hip and lifted her a bit for emphasis. "Spring needs to go in a baby seat."

"Oh sure," he said, and he reached for the car's back door to open it for her. Summer placed her daughter in the seat and fastened all the different straps securely. The little girl's head rolled on her neck and she didn't seem to care if they went anywhere or not. Like she had been put into the car seat a thousand times.

He was secretly glad Summer was driving, because suddenly he couldn't remember how to get to the Dairy Queen. But it felt a little weird to climb into the passenger seat. She started the car—her seat seemed so far forward!—and put it in reverse.

"Is that your truck?" she asked as she backed up.

"Yeah, but it ain't too clean now."

"It ain't? It sure looks clean! I need to wash this car. I haven't been able to wash it for months."

He had noticed the inside was dirty. The seats they sat on looked stained. They were red cloth, but had faded to pink where the sun hit most often. Behind him the girl made cooing sounds, and Summer kept glancing back at her as she turned onto the road.

He put his hand on the roof of the car, his elbow on the windowsill. He was not a big man but he felt like a giant in this ride. Since he didn't like having girls back to his trailer, he often made out with them in their cars. He wondered if she'd ever done it in this tiny car. Maybe with the father of that little girl.

"So. Did you still want to go get some ice cream?" Summer asked.

"Oh. Yeah! If that's okay with you."

"First you get me and Cheryl some ice cream, and now me and my daughter. I see a pattern here."

"Well, I do like ice cream. And that's no joke."

"I like it too." They were driving between fields on the narrow road and the hills rose around them. She looked over at him. "So what did you do today?"

"I talked to you and watched some TV. That's about it."

"Where is it you work at again?"

"Over at Sellers Sawmill. It's in Hawesville."

"Oh yeah, that's right. You like it?"

He shrugged. "It's all right. I ain't goin to do it forever, I don't think."

"Me neither. I work at Logjam Electric & Power. I get almost six bucks an hour, though, so that part isn't so bad."

"What do you do there? Read meters?"

"Oh no. I don't get out in this heat. Hank does that—he's always got to walk around. I work as a secretary. I work there in that little brick building next to the post office."

He had seen that building a million times but had never really looked at it. He never would've guessed someone hot worked in there. What else had he been missing? Were there hot girls in every building downtown? There were only about five, counting this one and the post office, but he'd have to start looking.

"How long you worked there?" he asked.

"About three years. It's not bad. Fore that I worked as a janitor over at the elementary school, and this beats that."

The child said something and Summer turned to address her. She told her daughter to wait a little bit, the child garbled something else, and Summer ignored her and turned back to the road. He reckoned she knew when it was important and when it wasn't. He was already surprised how calm she seemed to be around babies. He felt like he'd never be able to relax.

As they got closer to town, he looked at his watch. Almost two-thirty. He hoped it wouldn't be too crowded up there at the Dairy Queen. It always was on the weekends. It was the only fast food joint anywhere near Logjam.

He wasn't sure he wanted to make a big scene of this. Being seen with a kid and all. He wondered if she'd take offense to the drive-thru.

"I'm glad you called today," she said.

"Me too. Did you all want to eat up here, or get it to go?"

"Oh. Well, I thought we would eat up here. It's real hard to get Spring to wait for it until we get back home. Plus it gets messy."

"Oh that's right."

She stopped for a sign and had to wait for a car to pass. "Not too comfortable, are you, Tractor Guy?"

"What?"

"I said you act like you're nervous. You're sitting over there like we're going to bite you."

"Nah," he said. "I'm fine. She don't bother me at all."

"Because we can go again, you know. We can go somewhere without her sometime. I done asked my mom, and she said she'd watch her. I realize this is a lot to throw on you."

"All right." He tried to smile. The thought of going somewhere with Summer alone—and the knowledge that she wanted to—excited him. On the other hand, you had to realize that something like that was temporary, while what was in the backseat was permanent.

At the Dairy Queen, only three cars sat parked, with several more in the drive-thru lane. They pulled in and he waited while she got the child out of the backseat. This DQ didn't have indoor seating—you ordered at the windows and then sat around tables out in front. But other people in line stood right by the tables. There was no damn privacy.

He told the high school kid behind the screen he wanted a blueberry milkshake and was so nervous he didn't hear what she ordered. He paid when it was time—actually he tried to shove the cash across a little early, before she'd finished ordering—and they sat down to wait. Summer sat across from him, one arm down around her daughter, who wiggled on the bench and played with a napkin. He wondered if the high school girl who took their order was talking with her friends about him while she made the shakes. He wondered what she'd say. He knew he was being too quiet as he watched Spring tear up the napkin.

"Them little napkins sure are shitty, ain't they?" he asked Summer.

She glanced up at him quickly, surprised. He knew then he'd messed up cussing around the baby and he said, "I mean, they aren't very good."

"That's better." She smiled.

The girl at the window called to them and Summer started to stand up. He stopped her, saying, "No no, let me get it."

He handed the pink milkshake to Summer and started to lower the cone with plain ice cream to Spring's waiting hands, but Summer took it from him and held it in front of her daughter.

"She needs a little help yet," she said.

"I gotcha. I bet she likes ice cream, though, huh?"

She obviously did, because the child tried to eat the whole swirl in one bite. Summer had to leave her milkshake unattended and use both hands to feed Spring. She was making a hell of a mess of it. Her face was smeared with vanilla on both cheeks.

"She sure is cute," he said.

"Ah, thank you!" Summer said.

He pulled on his milkshake straw with great intensity and was surprised to hear air sucking through it. So soon? He might as well have done it as a shot.

Several people came up to the line and smiled at the little girl eating an ice cream cone.

An older woman who walked up alone stood there and watched for a little bit and then looked at him.

"She's darling," the woman said. "How old is she?"

He felt positively startled and he leaned back and gestured toward Summer. "I don't know," he said. "You'll have to ask her for that!"

Summer seemed embarrassed. "She's two and three months," she said to the woman, who smiled like her face might split open.

The women then talked about babies for a while, and he sat there and sucked on his straw, even though the milkshake was long gone. The child kept attacking the cone in her mother's hand, now a glob of cardboard-like goodness.

CHAPTER NINE

By Sunday afternoon it was raining again. This time it came gently over the woods to the west of them, descending slowly like a down blanket being laid over a sleeping child. The rain fell on the leaves of the trees and each drop formed a soft rhythm, a million tiny heartbeats advancing through the woods. Frank cocked his ear to the open door of the barn and listened to its approach.

They always got a lot of rain in July—thunderstorms, mostly—but this summer felt more like a monsoon. He stood in the barn and watched the rain fall first on the garden, then the yard. It hammered the metal roof overhead. He'd been cleaning up the boat, and was about ready to stop anyway. Now he'd get wet on the way to the house. He shut off the lights and grabbed a piece of plywood to serve as an umbrella. With his cane in one hand and the other holding the plywood over his head, he walked out into the rain. He looked down at the wet grass and remembered how he would gather nightcrawlers for bait on rainy nights when he was a kid.

By the time he leaned the board against the house and shook off his hat, the phone was ringing.

She answered it. "Oh hi," she said. "Yes, he just got back in here. Looks like the rain drove him in."

She lowered the receiver from her ear and stood there holding it out. Their only phone was attached to the kitchen wall—its cord would not reach all the way to the mudroom. He leaned against the doorjamb and untied his boots. Finally, he got to the kitchen and she handed him the phone before swinging a chair out from under the table. He sat down, got the receiver positioned where he wanted it after considerable shuffling, and said, "This is Frank."

"What do ya know," Chub said.

"Oh, not too much, I reckon. I went out and checked fences this morning. River looks all right. Still high, though."

"Funny you should say that. Guess what I was calling about."

"Fences?"

"I don't give a damn about fences. No, I wanted to see if you noticed what it's doing outside."

"Rainin steady here."

"That's what I figured. You know they're fixin to turn on something fierce when this rain hits em."

Frank looked at his wife. She sat in the living room in her chair, reading a paperback. "Not sure I'd want to go too much past dark," he said. She looked up at him.

"Be at my house in a few minutes?"

"All right."

"All right, then."

He hung up after waiting several seconds to see if Chub was going to say something additional. Eventually, he heard him hang up, so he did too.

"Sounds like I'm gonna be spending my Sunday evening by myself," she said.

"How'd you know that?"

"I know what you're up to. Can't you leave them fish alone for a day or two, at least?"

"Not with this rain, I guess. But he ain't got nothing better to do."

She went to the window and looked out at the front yard, the driveway running out toward the road. A constant, slow rain fell.

"It's not going to storm, is it?" she asked.

"Don't feel like it. We'll just be gone a couple hours. Maybe we could do steaks when I get back."

"Well, I might wait dinner on you. Or maybe not." She sat back down with her book. He went to get his raingear from the closet. He liked fishing in the rain.

"Now, what do you suppose that son of a bitch is doing?" Chub asked. He was peering downstream, hand over his eyes. He wore a poncho and little rivulets ran down the plastic like streams down a mountainside.

"I can't tell," Frank said. "But I thought I seen him throw something in. We better float down there and check it out."

He goosed and turned the outboard so the bow cut its way into the main channel. The boat lightened and sped up with the faster water under it. They were heading downstream and the current helped.

They'd been out for an hour or so, fishing.

Six decent channel cats were swimming in the livewell. Chub wanted to keep them to eat. Frank had hooked a fish in an eddy near a big pile of rocks that felt like it could've been a really good one. It might've been a big flathead. At first the fish hadn't known it was hooked, then it surged twice so hard the rod tip jerked into the water. Before he could turn it, the cat had gotten itself on the other side of a rock or sunken tree and the line snapped. He kept thinking about it—how big it might've been, if it was a flathead or a giant channel, whether it would hit again if they stopped back by there.

But now they'd come around this bend to find another boat near the far bank. As they got closer they could see more. A man was standing in the little gray v-bottom, and occasionally he would reach down and pick something up and throw it out into the river. Then he would watch for a while. Small splashings near the boat. He didn't have a pole in his hands, and no rod tips poked over the gunnel. Nor did he seem to be running limblines or nets. They rarely saw another boat out here most days anyway, but this one was up to something. Frank turned his boat toward the man.

Chub sat in the front and Frank had to raise partially off his seat to see over him. The tiller was wet in his hands and still rain fell.

When they got near the other boat Frank put the motor in neutral and let the current drift them downstream. The man watched them come and sat down, the small boat rocking. He stared at them, eyes hard. Dripping black hair, long like a lion's mane, hung around his neck. He was almost bald up top.

"Howdy," Chub called.

The man raised his hand a little. He was shirtless and his nipples and chest sagged like he wore borrowed skin from someone bigger and you about expected to see a zipper running up the back. There were dark blotches on his chest that must've been tattoos. All of this wet from the rain, his blanched skin waterlogged. An anchor line came off the stern of his little metal boat, the current piling and pushing and pointing the bow downstream.

"You catching any fish?" Chub asked him.

"Ah, I ain't fishin," the man called. His voice sounded high-pitched and off.

"We seen you throwing something in the water, thought maybe you had a new way of fishing," Chub said. He laughed a little like he had shared some kind of joke. Raindrops dimpled the river's surface.

"Huh? Nah! Hell, I ain't fishin. I just got too many damned pups."

"You got too many what?" Frank asked.

"Pups! An old bitch dog a mine dropped about ten pups. She ain't got enough milk for em. That, and I ain't feedin em all."

Frank looked downstream, not sure if he'd heard correctly. He could see nothing—only the ripples made by the slow current and the occasional log or limb sticking out of the water. He put the outboard in reverse to keep them near the man, and pushed the hood of his rainsuit back off his hat so his ears were exposed.

"What did you say you was doing?" he yelled.

"You old sombitches are hard a hearin, or something. I told you, I been throwing out some pups. Not that it's any of y'alls business."

"You're just throwing em in the water," Chub said.

"Hell yes. Cheapest way to get rid of em."

"What the hell's wrong with you?" Frank asked.

The man looked from Chub back to Frank. Maybe twelve feet separated the two boats. His eyes went crazy. White showing all around the colored centers.

"What the shit you care? This ain't your river!"

"Some of it is," Frank said. "I own a piece down that ways."

"Good for you, asshole! What do I care what you own?"

Frank kept the outboard idling in reverse, trying to keep abreast of the boat without getting too close or too far from it. Chub turned around and looked at him. Frank could tell he was ready to leave this crazy son of a bitch be. He was not yet ready, himself.

"You don't have to," Frank said. "But I just think it's a cowardly man that'll drown pups in a damn river."

The man stood up violently, his boat tipping and nearly throwing him overboard. He was wearing cut-off jean shorts worn to the threads. His entire person was stained black with oil or dirt.

"Oh yeah? Well watch this, motherfucker!" he yelled. He bent down and hoisted something off the floor of the boat. What he came up with was no bigger than a sack of sugar. It was yellow and squirming. He gripped it by its back legs and it cried out. "Let's see this little fucker take his swimming lesson," he said, and he swung the animal out toward Chub.

It hit the water about halfway between the two boats and sank.

"You're the motherfucker, you know that!" Chub shouted.

The man flipped him off with dirty fingers. "Get out of here, you old bastards!" he yelled, waving his arms. "Go on and get fishin! Leave me the hell alone!"

But Frank watched where the dog splashed down, and he saw its head resurface briefly, a snout pointed skyward, just the mouth and nose coming back to air. Feet churning under the foam.

The man saw him looking and looked there himself. "That little bastard already knows how to swim!" He laughed. "Well, let him swim on to shore, then."

The dog went back under.

Frank turned around and put the motor in gear. "Get the net," he said to Chub.

"Oh, you gonna save him, are ya? Well wait cause I got one more!" The man reached down and grabbed at something, missed it, took a step in the shaky boat and grabbed again.

Again he held a pup by its hind legs and tail, and it yelped in pain and surprise. "Last one," he said, offering it up like a fish in the rain. Before Frank could speak the man whipped and swung the dog hard against the gunnel. It cracked, a sound like the swinging of a stick of firewood against the metal boatside. He dropped the body into the river, watching Frank. The pup hit the water already dying. Or dead.

The two men stared at each other, the man's eyes wide and white.

Frank twisted the throttle and moved quickly downriver. He pushed the tiller a little to the right and kept his eyes on the water. The river narrowed just past where the boat had been anchored, sweeping into a bend. The current ran faster here.

"Where'd that dog go?" he asked, barely able to maintain his voice.

Chub looked at him and then back to the river. "I think it's long gone," he said.

Frank didn't know how far downstream to look, how quickly the current would take the pup away.

But then something just ahead caught his eye—a piece of driftwood, no bigger than a muskrat. He turned toward it, slightly, careful not to run too close and risk overtaking it with the bow.

His eyes had focused on the river and its currents for some many nights and days he knew how to read it. He saw the slight ripples undulating from this piece of driftwood. It was swimming.

"Net, right there," he said, pointing. Chub saw it too and held the big catfish net over the side of the boat as they approached. The pup could barely move its paws, paddling instinctually against the current. It had lost that fight and was being pushed in small circles. Its tail flowed behind it, a useless rudder. The brown nose sucked and sputtered at the surface. Frank looked down and saw the whites of the dog's eyes, peering upward from under the water.

Then, with one fluid stroke, Chub swooped the net forward and down before swinging it aboard, just as he had a thousand times with hooked fish. In the space between them, on the ribbed floor of the jon boat, he lowered the net.

It was hard to see what he had through the folds of the mesh. But Frank put the motor in neutral and crouched forward, on his hands and knees now, pushing aside and untangling the net.

The dog looked dark as wet cardboard. It whimpered and paddled its feet. It was wild-eyed and frantic, the whites still showing around the dark circles of its irises. Not unlike those of the man who had thrown it. It scratched against the net and Frank's hands. Finally he had it clear and he scooped the pup against his stomach and cradled it to his rainsuit. He held its feet so it couldn't struggle. Still it cried out and coughed and gagged. He unzipped his jacket and pressed the dog to his shirt. He could feel the river water soaking through and the wild beating of its heart.

"Hey, we're about to hit," Chub said.

They had drifted with the current against the far bank, and now overhanging limbs raked across the boat. With one hand, Frank reached back and flipped the outboard into reverse before giving it gas. The boat pulled back into the main channel.

"Let's go sink that asshole," Chub said.

They had drifted around the bend, the other boat no longer visible.

"I sure as hell want to. But let's look for more of them dogs first."

Chub shrugged. "If you think any is still alive."

In the rain they continued downstream then, Frank instructing him to look here and there as he spotted things that could've been pups.

Eventually they found some, but they were all dead and floating, their bodies caught against logjams or in eddies, spinning slowly and silently in the current. Pink bellies rolling up with lifeless paws.

When they finally gave up and returned to find the man, he was gone.

"You ever see him before?" Frank asked.

Chub said he had not.

"Well, he must live around here somewheres."

The men rode along quietly, now going against the current, upstream. Frank held the dog against his body. It hadn't stopped crying.

"You reckon we'll ever see him again?" Chub asked.

"If we do, he better know how to catch bullets with his teeth."

"I hate to see a bastard be mean to them powerless animals."

Frank said nothing, only felt the heat rising in him again.

"You gonna keep that dog?" Chub asked.

"You want him?"

"Nah. I don't want no dog."

Frank looked down at the pup. It was shivering, face pushed down into a fold of his shirt. He could feel its ribs under its wet hair.

"I'll keep him for a while," he said. "I reckon you gotta keep a dog like this, borned already knowin how to swim."

And so they motored back to the truck like that, going slowly to avoid ripping out the propeller on a deadhead or rock, Chub sitting in the bow, the catfish still thumping against the sides of the livewell, and Frank steering the motor with one hand and holding the pup with the other. A light rain fell on everything.

CHAPTER TEN

By the time Summer finally reached for her milkshake, Ollie thought, enjoy your warm milk. Watching Spring go after her miniature cone was like seeing a possum turned loose on the buffet tables. Ice cream was smeared on her hands, face and hair, and he'd watched as a dollop flew from his finger over his head. Summer about had to make napkin-handling a full-time job. He sat across from them and played with his empty cup. At least the crowd had gone and they were alone at the tables.

"Darn. I think it's going to rain on us," Summer said, looking out at the sky over the Dairy Queen parking lot.

"Nah, not today," he said, examining the clouds.

"So, if you're named after a tractor, I guess you grew up on a farm?"

"Yeah, pretty much. My folks still live out there. It's north of town a good ways. My dad, he don't do the work anymore though."

"Do you do it?"

He snorted. "Hell no. They rent it out." He looked at the baby. She was getting fidgety. "What's your dad do?" he asked.

"Something far away."

"Is he a trucker or something?"

"I don't know. He left my mom when I was real little. Anymore, I don't hardly remember him. I don't think he even knows I got a daughter."

Ollie looked at the cup in his hand. A cartoon ice cream cone with a face was holding a spoon, apparently ready to eat itself. He was hungover and tired and having a hard time processing all of this.

They stood up to leave. By the time they were halfway back to her house the rain was falling.

"You could be a weatherman," she said.

He felt like an ass until she smiled, the skin around her eyes wrinkling in tiny creases. He stared at her. He supposed he was used to dumber women but then maybe the prettier ones were also smarter. Granted, she hadn't said much yet, but this one seemed whip sharp. Christ, she was about ten years younger than he was yet she seemed to be out in front of him on everything. It wasn't just the rain, either. She had a way about her that made him think she'd experienced another world outside Logjam, or lived in another time dimension, like a cyborg or some crazy shit he'd seen on TV.

They dashed into the house, Summer using her body to shield her daughter from the rain. He caught a glimpse of the skin above her waist as her shirt pulled up. Inside, the house felt too cool now that it was raining.

"You want to stay for a little bit?" she asked.

"Okay. Since it is, somehow, raining and all."

They sat on the couch and watched Spring slam her toys together on the floor. They didn't say much, outside of commenting on what she was doing. Finally, Spring's eyes kept closing and Summer took her down the hallway. He stayed on the couch, inspecting her different toys. Summer came back and sat next to him again.

"She missed her nap earlier, so now she'll sleep for a while before she decides to keep me up all night."

"Really? Damn, that's rough. Don't you have work tomorrow?"

"Sure. Sometimes I go in there so exhausted I about want to put a phone book on my desk and use it for a pillow."

"I feel that way at work sometimes, too. Like if I go out on a Thursday night or something. Cept, if I get too sleepy at work I could cut my fingers off."

She laughed. "Yeah, I just answer the phone most the time."

They sat without talking for a while. She pulled her knee onto the couch and turned toward him. He looked once and could see the inside of her thigh but knew if he looked again she would bust him.

"I am glad you called," she said.

"Me too."

"I know you got freaked out up there, but I think I can understand why. It's not easy for people to get."

"I didn't get freaked ou—"

She touched his arm. "No, you did. I get it. Nobody wants to take on the girl who can just barely get in bars and her kid."

"Well."

"You know what sucks, though? I feel guilty about it. Like earlier, when I told you we could go out sometime without her? Then I feel guilty about that."

He looked at her. Once in a tavern he'd talked to a woman for fifteen minutes about the difference between Bud Light and Miller Lite. Then he'd taken her out into the alley and she'd blown him. He kept silent.

"But the thing is, you know, if I don't do that—do something by myself once in a while, then all I get is this"—she motioned to the toys strewn about the room—"and work. And work is so boring sometimes I talk to telemarketers just to have something to do."

"I see your point."

"You know, though? It's like you're supposed to put your kid first. And I totally do! But they don't say a thing about putting yourself up there. Like my mom, for instance. All she tells me about is how to take care of my daughter. She's full of advice on that. And I'm like, uh Mom? What if my life sucks?"

He knew it was time to say something heartfelt and meaningful and he wanted it to come to him but it hadn't yet. If she started crying he'd panic for sure.

"I don't want your life to suck," he said finally.

She let out a small laugh. "Thanks, Ollie. I appreciate that."

"You do deserve to be happy, though. Even if you got a kid and you're young and all that." She seemed to be listening so he went on. "My parents acted like they owned me for a long time, but I still got a right to my own happiness, you know? I think everybody has that."

He could tell she was really looking at him and he held her stare.

"I have to admit," she said. "There is something about you. I mean, you're like a thirty year old teenager, but something in there intrigues me."

He started to tell her he wasn't a teenager but she was leaning in and it almost seemed like she intended to kiss him. Then it was clear she did and he just went with it. He felt her breath on his cheek and tasted the moisture of her mouth. She had a hand on the back of his head and he turned his upper body toward hers and felt her breasts press against his chest. Their bodies were touching at various points and he was conscious of every one. He smelled her hair and maybe some perfume and now he knew what they meant when preachers talked about feeling God in the room. Then she stopped and jumped up.

"Whew! Oh boy. You want something to drink?"

"Uh, no. Well, maybe a beer?"

"I don't have any beer, boy. Plus it's Sunday."

"Right."

She looked down at him, sitting on the couch. "Don't take this the wrong way, okay? But that may do it for today."

He stood up and was surprised how dizzy he felt. "I got ya. No sweat. I'll just take off."

They walked to the door together and he went to kiss her again. She turned her face and hugged him. "Get on out there, horndog."

"Maybe I can call you this week?"

"I hope so."

And even though he was getting kicked out into the rain it somehow seemed all right. He had a good feeling he would see that couch again. Then he was in his truck and backing up, waving to her like some kind of kid, jerking the transmission into drive and honking for good measure. He drove home like he was drunk. Going too slow and then too fast, swerving into the fescue along the roadside, running stop signs or sitting at them for five minutes. He had driven drunk, many times, but this felt better. He wasn't coming down off his buzz or getting sleepy, as he often did when he drove home from the Depot or a party in someone's pole barn. This time he was right on top of the buzz. He rode it. And he liked not having to watch out for the damn cops for once. And she'd been sober, too! She kissed him without even being drunk!

"Hell yes!" he kept hollering. "Hell yes!"

Man, was he glad he called her! What if he'd come home, watched a little TV, drank some beer, and gone to bed, like he usually did on Sundays? Instead there he was, kissing a girl obviously out of his reach. Or was she? Suddenly anything seemed possible. The speakers popped and shook in their mounts, playing a Motley Crue tape at full volume. He kept thinking about her smell, her hair brushing against his face, his hands.

And that ass! Man, he couldn't stop thinking about her body! Her skin fit her muscles so tight it was like hugging a dolphin or a sea animal or something. He didn't even want to think about her body now. But he couldn't stop! The kid thing had been a downer but kissing her had erased all that.

The windshield wipers slapped back and forth on the wet glass and every time he stopped at an intersection he peeled out and threw gravel pinging around the wheel wells.

His trailer was dark when he pulled in. Suddenly, his place appeared to him as it would to a stranger: a saggy-ass trailer sitting low in the weeds. He pictured the dirty dishes in the sink and on the counter, dust everywhere, girly magazines on the couch. Tomorrow, some of that shit would get cleaned up. Yes sir, he was going to make it ready for a visitor. He figured if he wanted to see more of that body—don't even think about it! he scolded himself—he would need to turn this place into a little lovers' nest of sorts.

He went inside the trailer and turned on some lights. His hands were so excited they wouldn't stop jumping. He looked at the clock: just after five. Man, it was early. Not even dark. In the fridge were three beers he'd brought home from Coondog's and he took one out and opened it. It tasted ridiculously good.

"Hell yes!" he yelled again, toasting himself.

The whole thing was too much for him to bear and he went into the bedroom and closed the door. He pulled a magazine off the shelf in his closet, scanned it, and put it back. Pulled out another one. Oh yes, this one was good. Opened it up on the bed and did his business.

There. Now maybe he could calm the hell down.

He went out and turned on the TV. Some show where the people apparently all lived in one building and screamed at each other before slamming their respective doors. One blonde woman looked a whole lot like Summer. He thought about going back to the bedroom again. His blood felt like boiling hot motor oil, fresh from the pan.

But instead he stayed and watched. Drank another beer. Then the last one. He considered going out for more but remembered it was Sunday and no one would sell. The weekend was catching up to him, and he had work tomorrow. After three beers, his mind had slowed enough that he could think about going to bed.

Maybe he'd swing by his parents' place tomorrow after work and borrow the weed-eater. Knock down some of the brush outside the trailer. But he hadn't seen his folks in a while, which meant they were going to toss a guilt layer of shit on his happy flower field.

The last time he'd been home was to go drishing in the river back in the woods with Coondog. Drishing was Coondog's idea of combining drinking and fishing. They'd barely talked to his parents, although his mama had made them sandwiches. They didn't want the bread to soak up the alcohol, so they threw them in the river.

Look at Coondog's folks—they were still in their fifties and living the good life in Florida. Coondog's dad owned a Harley and before he hit the lottery he used to sit in the garage and get drunk with them. His mom was cool as shit too. She'd worked as a waitress at the bowling alley over in Hapgood and if the boss was gone she wouldn't charge them for games or beer. Never had Ollie heard Coondog's parents ask him why he hadn't settled down or what he did all day. Sure, Coondog lived at home, so they knew what he did all day, but they still bitched a lot less.

Ollie figured his parents rode his case so hard because they didn't have any other kids to worry about. He'd never met his grandfather Tarif but now that he'd been with women he wondered why you'd ever let your dad live with you once you got married. He used to think that's why he didn't have brothers or sisters—because his mom's old man lived with them and they could never do it for fear of getting caught. Then later he was told his grandfather lived there for only the first three years. So it was more than that, because they'd been married for almost fourteen years before they got pregnant with their masterwork.

All these years later and look at how far they'd come. Not long ago he and his dad had swung on each other. The old man had been calling the trailer for days, trying to get Ollie to come out and work on some damn busted thing. But he'd been putting in extra hours at the sawmill and when he got home all he had the energy to do was lift the can to his mouth. And then the phone would ring.

After two days of putting him off, he finally drove over there, already pissed. He barely said a word to his mom and went out to the shed, where his dad was working, trying to put the cutting bar back into his old hay cutter. The bar was a piece of steel, about ten feet long, with triangular blades attached along its length. Like a row of Great White shark teeth—sharp and serrated. Each one was bolted to the bar separately, and over the course of a summer some of them broke off on rocks. You had to pull the bar out to replace the blades, but shoving it back in was a pain because it would snag and hang up.

"I didn't want your mom to have to do this," the old man said.

His dad was at one end of the cutter bar, which lay across the top of five-gallon buckets. Ollie could see three or four new teeth, still shiny and silver. The hay cutter was covered with dust and clumps of molding hay.

The John Deere was parked in here, along with the combine. Gravity beds lined one wall and the planter was tucked into the back corner. Near the front Frank had built a workbench with a vice bolted to it. In the other corner stood a welding machine and tanks for the cutting torch. He could fix most things out here, but apparently he couldn't get this cutter bar back in without Ollie's help.

He stood there and looked at it while his father adjusted things and oiled the bar.

"Why couldn't you get Chub to do this?" he asked.

"Because Chub don't move around too good no more and it ain't gonna hurt you to do something once in a while."

"I do something once in a while. I call it working a job."

"Is that what you call it? I thought you might call it helping that pecker Doug Sellers get rich."

"What the hell you care? You don't know nothing about what I do out there!"

His dad had told him not to work there, but Ollie took the job anyway. How many jobs did the old man think were lying around? Besides, he hardly even saw Doug.

"I know plenty about what you do out there," Frank said. "Now get down there and help keep this bar from binding while I push it back in."

They placed the near end of the bar back in its groove on the cutter and Ollie supported the middle as his dad pushed from the far end. It slid several inches, then stopped. When he pushed again, the section Ollie held in his hands bent up, but did not slide.

"Help it, dammit!" the old man yelled.

"By doing what?"

"Jiggle the thing! Move it along!"

Ollie took the bar up and down a little and it slid into the track maybe another inch before getting hung up again. He'd hoped to do this job—whatever it was—and be home in time to head out to Coondog's and go shoot some pool. Now it was already almost six and this looked like it might take forever.

"Watch yourself. Them blades are sharp."

"Whyn't you give me some gloves then?" Ollie asked.

"Go get some damn gloves, if you need em! There's some over there on the workbench."

He walked by his dad, glaring at him. Frank was an old man even back then, with a head full of gray hair. But his eyes would burn into you. Coondog used to say, "Man, I wouldn't want to fuck with your dad."

But Ollie was hot. By God, he hated doing this shitwork. He found some leather gloves on the workbench and pulled them on. Someone had worn them baling hay, and chaff was worked down into the fingers.

"Get down there at the front this time," his dad said. "Push it in right by the cutter."

Ollie did as he was told and it did seem to work better. But forty minutes passed and the bar was still out about four feet. Now they knelt side by side on the concrete floor, trying to jimmy the blades the rest of the way in.

When the bar went into the cutter, it passed into a track lined with protruding steel fingers. With the power take-off on the tractor engaged, the bar slid back and forth rapidly, and the hay would be cut between the teeth and fingers. But now, if one tooth got caught up on a finger, the whole thing would shudder to a stop. Burning sweat ran into Ollie's eyes.

The last remaining blade out of the cutter got jammed, and the bar would move no farther. Without thinking Ollie reached into the mouth of the cutter and pushed down on the tooth. It popped loose and slid into the finger, taking part of his glove with it. The blade sliced through the leather.

When he jerked his hand back and held it aloft, blood was already running out of the glove and over his bare wrist. With his other hand he threw the glove free. Now it seemed the tip of one finger was gone. Blood covered it and the meat of his hand darkly, like he'd dipped it in used motor oil.

"Goddamnit, what'd you do now?" Frank yelled.

"I cut myself, you son of a bitch!" He watched his hands shoot out and hit his father in the chest. He was as surprised as Frank to see it happen. A smear of blood was left on the old man's overalls.

Frank pulled back and punched his son in the neck, a blow that felt heavy but somehow padded, like being hit with a sack of feed. Ollie felt the shock and anger surge through him, and his arm went back to swing. But his right hand was the cut one, and when he saw the blood fly off his moving fist he lowered it and headed for the house.

Inside, his mom kept shaking her head and saying oh dear, oh dear while she darted around. She poured hydrogen peroxide over his finger and into the toilet, where it splashed pinkly and stained the water. She then bandaged the finger with gauze. Even the nail was cut straight. He knew he probably should go in for stitches but he wanted to make the old man feel worse by leaving it. He halfway hoped it would get infected.

"And what happened to your neck?" she asked.

He looked in the bathroom mirror. There was a red blotch on his neck under his ear. He wondered if his dad had meant to hit him there, or only missed his face due to his old age. The old bastard. I should've punched him after all, he thought.

But he said nothing of this to his mother, only left the bathroom.

She followed him out.

"Are you going to go help him finish it?" she asked.

At the door he said, "Hell no I'm not."

"Then how's he gonna get it done? He wants to cut hay tomorrow."

"Then you'll have to do it, ma. Or he can do it his own damn self."

"Oliver, don't say that."

"I'm done, ma. I'm out of here."

He got in his truck and left without looking at the shed.

At the road, he spun the tires and threw gravel in what used to be his own driveway.

Ah, the good old days, he thought now, as he sat on his couch in the trailer his parents had provided for him on the land they still owned. There had been other fights, but he remembered that one on account of the blood. Well, and the fact that all he had to do was look down at his hand. The finger he used to flip people off on his right hand was just barely longer than the ones on either side of it. The nail was a little sawed-off thing.

They had talked since then. He'd even helped the old man on a couple of jobs. But lately the time between seeing his parents had grown. He used to go over there after work most nights, then dinner on Sundays. Soon those dinners were enough. But then Sundays became good days to stay on the couch all afternoon, napping off a hangover. Any more, he might go several weeks without seeing them.

He sat on the couch and watched TV like a blind man. He thought more about Summer. What was she doing? Was she still wearing the same thing? She had said she didn't even know her dad anymore. He wondered what that would be like.

It would probably serve him well to go to sleep but he kept thinking about things. Sundays didn't always give you much but this one kept him awake.

CHAPTER ELEVEN

It was not yet five Monday morning, the window still faintly lit with predawn light, but already she lay alone in bed. She wondered how he'd managed to dress without waking her. Then again, after all the commotion yesterday afternoon, it was no wonder she'd slept through it. She doubted he'd slept at all, as wrought up as he was. She knew why he was up so early, and why he'd been so chatty last night. She remembered the little yellow face with its wet-looking brown eyes, and those tiny ears that hung like pieces of soft cloth. My goodness, this is going to change things, she thought. She took her glasses from the nightstand and rose from bed.

In the bathroom mirror she took notice. Her hair was overdue for an appointment. The skin under her eyes drooped, and a fold of skin looped from her chin like something she might see on one of her chickens. She examined her face, looking for moles that had grown or changed shape. They all looked familiar. Today she didn't lift her nightgown to inspect her back and chest. Young Dr. Mulferd had told her to do this every day, so she usually did. She was also to examine her breasts for lumps. This morning she gave herself a little less time to self-examine. She used the toilet and got dressed and hurried downstairs to the kitchen.

She saw her husband seated at the table, his back to her. She walked in and turned toward the coffee pot. There it stood, empty. She'd added the ground coffee last night and poured in water, and he couldn't even turn it on? For the love of God. She started to scold him when she noticed the boards.

In the corner between the refrigerator and stove, two pieces of dirty, worn plywood formed a box against the two walls. The boards were about two feet high. The sugar canister—the sugar canister! Right there on the floor next to dirty boards!—and some magazines kept the boards standing upright.

She looked over the boards and there lay the puppy, curled up and breathing in short puffs. Under him was the Indian blanket, bits of straw still clinging to it. A bowl of water sat in the corner. Next to it was the clock.

Frank sat turned in his seat, watching her over the back of his chair.

"I didn't make the coffee cause I didn't want to wake him up," he whispered.

At the sound of his voice the puppy straightened his legs and stretched.

Sunday afternoon she'd been inside reading a book and watching it rain when she heard the squeaky springs on the boat trailer coming down the drive. A sound she'd heard, coming and going, even in her sleep. By the time she rose and went to the window, the truck was pulling toward the house, and she could make out two shapes in the cab. Why in the world was Chub coming home with him? She didn't want to fix dinner for him, just because he had for her Saturday night.

She was thinking through what other ingredients she would need to feed him as they got closer and parked the truck. So he wasn't even going to back the boat into the lean-to? This must be a big fish, indeed. She put on her jacket and went outside.

"Well who caught it?" she asked.

The truck door swung open and she caught it in her hand. The puppy was asleep in Frank's lap. It didn't look up, even when the engine died and there was no sound. Its body lay between Frank's legs, its head propped up on his knee. She stared at it for several seconds, trying to place what it was and how it had gotten in the truck.

"Oh heavens to Betsy," she said.

"Wife," Frank said, "I want you to meet Catfish."

She gave the puppy pieces of bread soaked in milk until his belly swelled, and the evening passed with all of them out in the lean-to, watching him perform little tricks and feats. He sniffed around the lean-to and the barn and took forays out into the yard, even in the rain. On wobbly legs he went across the lawn sniffing dandelions. When Frank moved his cane tip in the dirt, the pup pounced like a cat. When Catfish peed he squatted.

They sat on lawn chairs, Chub on a bale of straw, and laughed at every antic. In the fading light Frank and Chub took turns telling how they'd found him, how he rode home in the cab of the truck, and how they decided to name him.

"Just don't tell me any more about that man, and what he was doing," she said, and they had not, although they continued to think about him.

The men told the story of the name over and over.

"So here we was with this pup, right?" Chub said. "And he asks me if I want to keep him, and I says no. So he decides to keep him himself—"

"Because what else could I do?" Frank asked her.

"Right, right," she said.

"Cause we ain't had a dog around here for several years," Frank said, "and the coons is getting bad again."

"I heard you," she said, motioning for Chub to go on.

"And so I ask Frank, I say 'what are you gonna call him?' and he says, 'well, I always liked Wendell for a dog,' and I says —"

"Wendell?" she asked. "Wendell!"

"See? That was my reaction, too, Ethel," Chub said. "I was like, 'what kinda sissy name is that?' and so I says—"

"It ain't a bad name for a dog, though," Frank said.

"But I said, 'he's gotta have a river name, on account of he come from the river.' And that's when I thought of Catfish," Chub said. He looked over at the dog. "Hey, looky there," he said, pointing. "See how he's a-rollin in the grass? He likes that cool feelin it gives him."

"I think it's a great name," she said.

"That, or Flathead," Chub said. "Or Channel. That's if you wanted to stick with the catfish family."

"I think you got the right one," Ethel said.

"Catfish works," Frank said. "But Wendell woulda worked, too."

Chub laughed, his whole body shaking. "Jesus, buddy. No dog ever got pulled out of a river to be named Wendell."

Chub stayed for supper, and she cooked another steak in the oven on the broiling pan. They left the pup outside, but he sat under the storm door and whined, so they ended up going back outside after dinner.

"Let's make a spot for him in the barn," she said. They had never allowed a dog into their house, and there was no talk of this being the first.

They found a place for Catfish in an old granary long since emptied of corn. Built out of heavy boards against an inside wall of the barn, the granary was nothing more than a box to store a heap of grain for the cattle. Frank had scooped the corn from there and poured it in long rows in the mangers for the steers he fed out. In the winters it meant not having to walk in the snow over to the grain bin, carrying heavy five-gallon buckets of corn back.

They cleared the cobwebs and swept it out. Frank put some loose straw and an old Indian blanket in there to comfort the puppy as he slept, and she went to the house and came back with an old alarm clock that she wound and placed near the blanket, because she'd heard that the ticking of a clock would remind a puppy of its mother's heart.

After they fed the puppy again from his new bowl (an old serving dish that was chipped, anyway), it was almost nine. They lifted Catfish into the granary and made their way to the door. Frank flipped off the light switch, which cut the power to the cobweb-covered light bulbs mounted to the rafters here and there. One such bulb was over the granary, and when the lights fell off a silence took over the barn.

"Goodnight Catfish," she called into the darkness.

Immediately the puppy began to whine.

Frank shut the door and slid the bolt. The dog could be heard outside the barn, his tiny frantic pleading.

"Oh," she said. "The poor little thing."

"He'll get used to it," Chub said.

"Yes, I'm sure he will," she said.

"Let me unhitch the trailer, and I'll run you home," Frank said to him. "It's getting late enough as it is."

She said goodbye and went to wash the supper dishes. Frank walked to the truck and backed the boat into the lean-to, where they lowered the jack and left it. The puppy whined and whined.

When Frank returned, Ethel was drying the silverware from dinner. They changed into their bedclothes and brushed their teeth, one after the other, at the old iron-stained sink. She turned on the little transistor radio she kept by her side of the bed. The Reds were down by three runs. She was too tired to see if they could pull it out and turned it off. She took off her glasses and left them on the nightstand. He sat on his side of the bed.

"You don't reckon he'll climb out of there, do you?" he asked.

"Out of where? That granary? The sides are three feet high."

"I know it. But I wonder if he will just wear himself out, climbing against the walls that a way."

"If he does, he'll finally go to sleep."

He smiled. "The little feller just climbed in my lap and slept the rest of the way home."

"That was so cute, him sleeping on your lap like that."

They pulled back the covers and got under them and lay down on the high bed. The smell of the cool sheets rose to them. The bed felt soft and worn and cool, even now, in the heat of summer. He reached over and pulled the string that turned off the light. Their window was open behind the white curtains, because it seldom rained in on the east side of the house, and the moon was visible out over the pasture and the woods. It cast a bluish light across their bed. The smell of the rain-soaked grass and trees beyond came through the window. He could smell the river. She reached over and put her hand on his chest.

"Do you think a coon will get in there and hurt him?" he asked.

She sighed and removed her hand. "No coon ever got Ranger." Ranger, their last dog, had also been kept in the barn as a pup, in a corner near the mangers. Frank had nailed those boards in place, because the granary was then being used for corn. Even though he'd built the pen for Ranger almost sixteen years ago, he remembered the boards he'd used. Later, when Ranger got older, he used them again to patch a hole in the back wall of the barn.

She lay quietly, listening to the night. The crickets whirred without pause or interruption outside their window. The rain had excited them. After a while she said, "But you know we still had cows then. Maybe the coons are less afraid now."

He rolled over and lifted himself partway. He looked at her for a time.

"Do you really think a coon will get in there and eat a dog?"

"No, I guess not. But he's not very big."

"No he isn't. Not very big at all."

Silence returned to the blue bedroom, save the sounds of the crickets and nighthawks calling. She moved under the covers.

"But it could scare him real bad," she said. "If all of a sudden there the coon was, looking down at little Catfish asleep in the straw. What if he woke up and saw that?"

"I thought you said he'd be asleep on account of crawling the walls all night?"

"I never said that. You said that."

"Well, a coon better not get in there after him. Not after the day he's had."

Frank woke later and looked at the clock. Half past midnight. He lay listening to the house. Ethel slept in regular rhythms next to him. Even the crickets were quiet. He lifted up on one elbow and looked out the window. He couldn't see the barn, only the yard, the tool shed, and part of the chicken coop. And the roof of the grain bin, over the tool shed. Nothing moved in the moonlight. The buildings looked gray and soft.

He rose and found his overalls at the foot of the bed. The wood floor was cold on his feet. He dressed, trying to miss the creaking spots, and took his cane from the bedside.

The house was dark and still. He moved through it like an intruder, albeit a fairly slow and clumsy one.

At the door he found his cap and the flashlight he kept by a pile of gloves. He turned it on to test it and the light hit the room. He opened the door with two hands to silence it, but his cane swung and tapped the door. He listened, but didn't hear her call. He went outside.

The grass was wet with dew and he wished he'd had the foresight to pull on his rubber boots. His leather shoes were getting soaked. He played the flashlight's beam across the grass and looked for nightcrawlers. He saw several—saw them jerk and slide back into their holes.

He gave a wide berth to the chicken coop so as not to get them squawking. That would wake up the wife for certain. Walking by the pumphouse, he saw something dart along the base of the foundation and then disappear through a hole in the concrete. It had been in his vision for such a short time he doubted seeing it at all. A rat. He would need to put out more poison tomorrow.

He paused to listen near the door of the barn, his head cocked against the chipping white paint. No sound came from within.

But there was no noise to suggest something was alive in there, either! It sounded as quiet and dead as it would have before any of them knew Catfish existed.

What if the little pup had been forced to fight a big ol boar coon? What if he was lying there now, ripped open and gasping?

He worked the bolt and the door dropped a little on its hinges as the greased bolt slid free. He turned the flashlight off and swung the door open. The barn was black dark. The musty smell of straw and hay came to him. The barn would smell that way until it was torn down or burned.

The granary was to the right. The plank floor was higher than the ground outside, and as he stepped up, a board creaked. He stopped and listened. No sound came.

He stepped again, and again the board creaked. The boards made much more noise now than they ever had in the daytime. Suddenly the door behind him, which he had left open for light, fell back against the frame. It hit with a thud and the fastening chain that hung on the inside of the door jingled.

All of his night fishing prepared him for darkness, but somehow being somewhere this familiar made it more disconcerting. His palms sweated against the flashlight and cane. He still hadn't heard a rustle from the granary, and now only a little moonlight seeped through the dusty window near the door.

He flipped on the flashlight, and the artificial beam hit the floor with a burst of white. The light reflected up against the walls and the cobwebs that hung in dusty streaks from the rafters. Something moved in the granary, the sound of straw moving against itself, and he walked quickly just to see if his dog was still alive. He shined the light over the boards, and the beam reflected back from the half-lidded eyes of the pup. Catfish, trying to walk on legs wooden from sleep.

Frank could see a little swirlhole in the blanket where the puppy had bedded down. He reached over the wall and touched the pup's warm side. Catfish licked his hand. There was nothing wrong with him. Frank petted him for a while and then walked away.

Catfish began to whine, the same sad cry.

There was only one thing to do.

He wondered if the old plywood boards he lay on when he changed the oil were still against the wall in the tool shed. He figured they would work. Just because it was something they had never done didn't necessarily mean it couldn't be done this time. Maybe she wouldn't mind so much.

He hooked his cane over the side of the granary and lifted the pup, sliding him up along the wall. He took the cane and the flashlight in one hand and cradled the dog to his chest with the other. This time the pup was dry and full. Together they left the barn and went about getting the things they needed. After he had the boards positioned in the kitchen he went back to the barn to grab the blanket and the ticking clock.

CHAPTER TWELVE

At six-fifty Monday morning Ollie parked his truck in the gravel lot in front of Sellers Sawmill. Even though it was still chilly he rolled his windows down so when he came out at lunch the cab wouldn't be burning up. He knew it'd already be eighty on the sawmill floor and by three it might reach a hundred. Despite that knowledge he looked at the pole barn that housed his employment and smiled. When he'd left work on Friday he hadn't even met Summer yet. If, say, some little kid asked him for a pearl of wisdom, this is one thing he'd learned about life: A good weekend makes all the damned difference.

Ray Jackson pulled in then, his minivan jerking to a rest next to Ollie's truck. Even seeing Ray didn't dampen his mood, and he waited for him so they could walk in together. Ollie couldn't stop smirking. Ray climbed out of the van and reached back inside for the giant coffee cup he always hauled to work.

"You look like you spent the night hammer-jacking twin Olympic swimmers," Ray said.

"Remember how I told you I was going to the demo pits?"

"Let me guess: you and Coondog won it."

"Not quite. Better. I met this new chick who just so happens to be hot as hogshit and we went out yesterday."

"Well, she musta known what to do, cause you look like you ate the icin offa twelve Kroger cakes."

Already Ray was trudging toward the sawmill, head down. Ollie knew how he was. If Ray had a good weekend, get ready to hear about it all day. If he didn't, don't try to tell him about yours. Screw it, then. Ollie would tell him about her later, once he was ready for it, or he wouldn't tell him at all. Just thinking about her dripped adrenaline into his veins. The second he got home he'd be ringing her phone.

But work was still work. By seven the blades were spinning, and by seven-thirty sawdust covered his face and arms. He felt the pieces of dust in his mouth and he chased them around with his tongue, trying to spit them. There was always too much of it. As the day passed you got to where you just accepted the sensation, like you'd spent the day licking two-by-fours.

From the back of the sawmill the logs were brought in on front-end loaders and dropped onto a conveyor that carried them down to the blades. Two men worked down on the main floor, helping to line the logs up and cut them to customers' specifications before removing the boards. He'd been one of those men for about ten years now, although there was no way it could've been that long. Nobody said time flew when you were working fifty weeks a year in a sawmill, but it sure as hell did.

Each man wore a hardhat. Connected to the hardhat came their ear protection—little padded bowls of plastic that cut out some of the constant sound. Regardless, the saws penetrated your head and the growl of wood being cut reverberated in your mind all week long.

In between logs, Ollie and Ray could talk a little bit, yelling so as to be heard through the ear guards.

"You ain't gonna believe what Danny done last night," Ray yelled before they brought in a big hickory some farmer was having planked for a hay wagon bed. Ollie stared at his mouth. It helped to be able to read lips. Close but not too close, since Ray constantly threw bad breath.

"What'd he do this time?" Ollie yelled back. Danny was the only son of Ray, and the youngest of three kids. To hear Ray talk, you'd assume his little girls didn't exist.

"He come out in the room, where me and Lacey was watching the race, and he's got this shit-eating grin on his face. I looked at Lacey, and I was like 'you better go see what he done,' cause he come out of his room, and you could just tell he'd been back there doing something."

Ollie stared at his mouth, saying nothing, nodding.

"So I asked him, 'what'd you do, son?' and he says 'Daddy, I gotta go potty.' Bout that time Lacey come out, and she starts yelling at Danny. I said, 'what he do this time?' Well, turns out the little shitter took a shit in his room, in the corner!"

Ollie laughed. He carefully mouthed the words, "Guess he done did it."

"Whassat?" Ray hollered.

"I said he done did it! He done took a shit, then he told you he had to!"

"Yeah he did! He sure did! She went back there and cleaned it up. I said to him, 'Bub, we got to work on your potty-training.' He set down there and watched the rest of the race with me."

"That's some funny shit, man!"

"I know it! You gotta have some kids, man. I guarantee they will crack your shit up!"

Ollie said nothing, only interlaced his fingers and shoved his gloves on harder.

"Hey!" Ray said. "I knew I wanted to tell you something Friday! Why'nt you get with Charlotte Hershfield?"

"Why the hell would I do that?" Ollie shook his head. Had he even been listening this morning?

"Cause I heard she's free again. Scott caught her with Jason Beard, of all the dirty bastards!"

"Well, sounds like she's with Jason Beard, don't it?"

"Hell nah. He's still married! Got two kids."

The loader brought the hickory and dropped it on the steel rack, where it slid down to the conveyor. An old tree about four feet around. A man named Donny Haslip drove the front-end loader. He was about ten years younger than they were, and a little too cocky for his own good. Supposed to have been a good football player a couple years back, but now he spent his days as a loader jockey.

Their boss, Doug Sellers, sat in an operator's booth above the saw, and he pulled the levers to move the log down the conveyor. He didn't care about them talking on the job, and he couldn't hear what they said. He was an alcoholic and came in most mornings in bad shape. Ray predicted Doug was going to run the business into the ground within five years and put them all out of work. Doug had inherited the sawmill from his father but he had no natural inclination to make money.

"You ought to call her up!" Ray yelled.

Ray was one ugly son of a bitch. He shaved his head, but left a little buzzed-hair circle on top. His nose went crooked off to the left, the result of too many jabs that had landed on target, and his tiny teeth slanted inward, as if they too had been punched. He held his neck like a box turtle, and spent all day looking up at you like you'd just come across him on the trail.

His wife was another gem, blessed with the curves and personality of a refrigerator. Her main ritual and desire in life was to smoke pot in the basement every night after the kids were asleep. Once she'd slapped a teacher across the face at a parent/teacher conference and called her "a prissy little misfit whore." But Ray was married, and had been for twelve years, and Ollie hadn't even been engaged. So he felt qualified to tell Ollie what to do.

"Charlotte always was a slut!" Ollie yelled. "I ain't callin her."

Ray shrugged his shoulders, like he was saying suit yourself. Ignore this chance at the good life.

The clamps came up around the log and Doug lined it up, rechecking his papers to see how the customer wanted it cut. The big blades, which spun on their own sliding track, began to whine as they got back to cutting speed.

"Besides, I got something going!" Ollie said.

Ray perked up and grinned his little slanted-in-teeth smile. "Who's that?"

"That girl I met at the fair!"

"Oh yeah! You said something about that. Did you do her?" Ray held his arms up and jerked them wildly, like he was driving an out-of-control garden tiller.

Ollie shook his head no.

"You got a smoker!"

Ollie shook his head again.

"Then what the hell you got going on?"

"I don't know yet. Maybe nothing. Maybe something. I'm fixin to call her tonight."

Ray shook his head in disappointment.

Doug cut the sides of the log off first, shaving off mostly bark and waste wood. They gathered and pulled the debris clear. The blades rendered the log a giant square tube—a twenty-five feet block of soon-to-be boards. Ollie and Ray pulled the boards off to the side and stacked them. They worked for a while without talking and Ollie wondered how Summer was doing at work today, whether she was asleep on a phone book or not.

At noon, they drove to the Hawesville market to buy chicken dinners. The old woman behind the counter, Mrs. Hubbard, liked to talk to them every day. Her son had been killed in Vietnam, and she always told Ollie how much he reminded her of him. He didn't know what to say about that. He usually asked her about the food before she had a chance to get started.

They returned to the sawmill and ate in the little break room, which consisted of a pop machine and a couple of tables. Ray kept asking about Summer. Their ears rang and they talked too loudly.

"The thing is," Ollie said as they were eating dessert out of the Styrofoam containers, "she's already got a kid. I don't know how I feel about that."

"Well, that means she ain't a virgin, that's all," Ray said, shoving his peach cobbler-laden fork into his mouth.

"I'm not sure I want to be a dad to some other man's kid, though."

"Man, single mamas are horny! You gotta think of it thattaway. You should be getting right in there!"

"I guess you're right."

"I know for a damn fact I'm right!"

Ollie was pretty sure Ray had been with only one woman in his life. And there were persistent rumors the first of his wife's three kids had been sired by four high school boys lucky enough to attend the party Lacey hit like a wet squall after a fight with Ray. No wonder Ray only talked about little Danny. He looked just like a chip off the old block—no doubting his paternity. Ollie stood up to throw away his Styrofoam. He'd much rather take advice from Coondog, but there were friends and there were work friends.

By mid-afternoon the metal roof of the sawmill was broiling all of them. To make four o'clock get off its ass and get there, Ollie started planning the perfect date. You couldn't really count the Dairy Queen and he wanted to impress her the next time around.

Actually, he hadn't gone on that many dates—mostly just what could be called bar dates. That meant going into the Depot or the HollyWood Tavern, often with Coondog, and leaving with some drunk woman. He might end up back at her place—socks on the sofa, a sink full of dirty dishes, maybe some kids' toys—and he'd loiter for a few hours. Once in a while he'd bring someone back to his trailer. But he liked going to their pads so he could leave whenever he wanted.

And he liked seeing into their lives during those brief and sweaty encounters. You never knew what you were going to discover. One time a woman he'd met a few times invited him back to her apartment. They rode out together in his truck, and he was too drunk to drive. But he hadn't picked up a woman in a month or so and would've driven with a sack over his head if it meant popping his rocks.

Her name was Melinda and when they got to her apartment it was no more than a room over a fried chicken restaurant in Pennytown. She unlocked the door, the whole damn thing so flimsy and ill-fitting he could've kicked it in with sock-feet, and said, "welcome to my home. Sue casa, you casa."

It was a shithole, all right. A couch took up most of the room, facing a tv set in a big wooden cabinet. On top of the console was a glass half full of brown soda and a goldfish bowl filled with water and blue gravel but no fish. The water looked like it was starting to get thick. There was a doorway to the bathroom, and another to what must've been the bedroom. You walked into the kitchen when you opened the main door.

On the ground, one piece of carpet covered the area directly in front of the couch, but the remaining floor was a patchwork of bare wood, linoleum, and even some green outdoor carpet. When Melinda came back out of the bedroom, he asked where the fish was.

"Oh, he done died two weeks ago. I just never got the bowl emptied."

"Damn, that's too bad. Did you give it too much food?"

She laughed. "No, I went to stay at my mom's and I never gave him none. I stayed with her longer than I figured I would, and when I come back, the fish was floating his ass on the top."

"Oh damn, you murderer! You killed it."

"I know it. I felt bad! I did! Please forgive me." She was looking at him in such a way he knew they didn't need much more small talk.

"I apologize for my place, it's a mess," she said.

"That's okay, I'm used to shitholes."

She looked at him with shock and hurt on her face. "What the hell do you mean by that?"

He could feel the night turning. Why hadn't he just shut up after the fish? "Oh, no, I didn't mean this is a shithole," he said, gesturing. "I meant that's what I got! I live in a shitbox! I'm used to my own, see?"

She still looked a little doubtful.

"This," he said, motioning with his hand, encompassing the couch, the patched floor, even the deserted fish bowl, "this here is nice."

Well hell, no one would've bought that, but she let it go. They went into her bedroom, which was also messy and dirty, and screwed around. They hadn't done it all, but they'd done enough he could leave satisfied. He could leave feeling like he'd had some kind of weekend.

Today he recalled those nights with something like warm nostalgia, because they were surely things of the past. They should take a replica of Melinda's apartment and put it in a museum next to the dinosaurs. Moving forward, he wouldn't be running around shabby apartments at three in the morning. No more talking his way into a handjob that took all night anyway because he was so drunk. No more saying the wrong name on the way out the door. Starting today it was going to be picnics in the grass and sweet, sweet daytime love. He began thinking about the kind of love he might be getting from Summer sometime soon—my God, even this week!—and his left leg started hopping. He wanted to take her on a real date to speed up the process. He just needed to plan it.

"Get your head out of your ass," Ray yelled, "and pick up that board like I told ya."

Ollie grabbed the other end and together they moved it to the stack. He stole a look at the watch he kept in his pocket. Still another hour.

"Damn, you got it bad! I know how that is," Ray said as they watched the blades burn through another log.

CHAPTER THIRTEEN

Frank knew the sounds of most of the vehicles likely to pull into his driveway. He was familiar with the pitch of their engines, the way their leaf springs flexed when they hit the dip in the driveway out by the mailbox, the range and timbre of their exhausts. The imported car of Hattie's whirred like Ethel's sewing machine coming up the lane, while Chub's Dodge coughed and roared. Wayne Shipp's truck sounded like money, because it was new and always brought the land rent check. Ollie's pickup had been quiet, too, until he paid for louder pipes. He hadn't been by in so long Frank had almost forgotten what they sounded like. But Frank definitely didn't recognize the sound of the vehicle pulling into his driveway now, waking him up from his post-lunch nap. Either someone had a new truck or someone was lost.

Getting up from his chair took too damn long, so he hollered for Ethel, but she was outside working in her garden. They had said it would only get hotter as the day wore on, and she wanted to pull more weeds. He figured she went back there in part just to get away from him. He couldn't begrudge her that.

They'd spent the morning watching Catfish play in the yard, until the pup grew so heavy-lidded he curled up next to Frank's boot and went to sleep under the lawn chair. She'd driven the car to town to get dog food and with it Catfish swelled like he'd ingested a giant tomato. When they went inside for lunch, she carried the puppy back out to the granary. This morning, after she discovered Catfish in the house, she made it clear he would try the barn again tonight, and this time Frank was to leave him there. But she hadn't been upset for long.

He'd asked her to get the puppy out of the granary and let him sniff around the garden, since one day he'd be in charge of guarding it. And now with some stranger here, he worried the fool might hit his dog. He rose with difficulty and grabbed his cane and made his way over to the window. Only the bed of a white pickup was visible from where he stood.

He took his cap off the shelf and pushed open the screen door. There stood a tall man in jeans and a tan uniform shirt talking with his wife, who was wiping her hands on her gardening apron. Around his feet the yellow puppy was sniffing the man's legs and wagging his tail. The man held a clipboard and a gut like a sack of chicken feed hung over his belt. The Ford four-wheel drive behind him wasn't marked, but it looked clean, white, and official. Ethel was nodding and gesturing and smiling broadly, in the way she did with strangers, whether they deserved it or not.

Frank finally reached them and Catfish scurried over and jumped on his feet. Frank pushed him away roughly with his cane. He knew the instinct was misplaced, but he had a feeling low in his chest he understood what this was about, and the anger rose in him like a river swelling and lapping at its banks after a hard rain.

The man stopped talking and looked at him. He was younger than Frank thought he'd be.

"I was telling her," he said, "I'm here as part of the project."

"We don't need it, whatever it is."

"He says he's here to appraise the farm," Ethel said. As if they'd just won something. Frank shot an iron glance at her. God as his witness, she couldn't help but to be kind to every human walking the earth.

"That's it," the man said. "I'm here to appraise the property value—"

"We didn't ask for this. Get going," he said, pointing his cane toward the pickup.

The man towered over them like they were of another race entirely. Or maybe not yet fully grown. "I been sent out to appraise every property in the redevelopment project," he said.

"Well, I don't give a shit. You're not doing this one."

The man looked at him and then at her. "Can I just tell you folks something?" Like he was ready, against his teachings, to share some of the inner workings of the machine trying to crush them. Frank had heard similar conspiratorial tones the last time he tried to buy a used truck.

"The best way for y'all to get a decent price is to let me put a fair value on your place here."

"It ain't for sale!"

"I'm not like those outsiders from Louisville," the man said, holding up the clipboard. "Hell, I grew up over near Green City. I'm one of you all. But I work for the Corps of Engineers, and I need to appraise all these properties—"

"We got that part."

"...and if I don't get to appraise this place, they're gonna give you what they think it's worth, instead of what I think it's worth. Instead of what it's truly worth."

Frank stared hard at the man. He felt his wife looking at him. Catfish sat on the grass behind him, chewing a dandelion.

"Well, you or nobody else is appraising this farm. Not now, not ever. So you might as well get the hell on down the road."

"It don't take me long," the man said. "I just gotta walk around, take some measurements."

"How clear do I have to make myself?" Frank asked. He was starting to yell.

"Y'all seem like nice enough folks. It'll be a shame to see them take advantage of y'all like they will."

Frank again pointed to the truck with his cane. It shook in his hand.

"Well, all right," the man said. "I can go. But I'll have to put it down that the landowners refused to allow the appraisal to take place." He motioned with his clipboard.

"I don't give a shit what you put down!"

"All right then."

He took a pen from his breast pocket and made a big show of writing a note on his clipboard before walking around the front of the pickup. He got in, wrote some things down while looking at his lap, and started the engine. The sound Frank had heard through the walls of his house returned.

"What the hell did you say to him before I got out here?"

"Well, honey, I never told him nothing," she said. "You know that. I'd only begun to talk to him when you came storming out."

They both watched the man reverse down the driveway. He pulled onto the road and headed toward Dwight Pearson's place. He didn't look over at them again, standing in what had been their family's yard for almost seventy-five years.

"I'm gonna need to put a chain across the driveway," he said.

"Whatever for?"

"There's gonna be more of them bastards comin. This is just the beginning of em."

"Well, maybe they'll leave us be now."

He stared at her, his eyes hard as potatoes. He shook his head and looked away. Somewhere in the yard, birds called.

"No. They ain't gonna leave us alone."

"He was here for the lake, wasn't he?"

"Yes," he said.

"How come you knew that and I didn't?"

He said nothing.

Catfish stood up and barked at a tree for no reason. She walked away, heading for the house.

He looked down his long driveway, figuring out the best way to chain it off. Let them drive through a two-inch log chain, he thought. He'd surely like to see them try it. They'd find a shotgun waiting, by God.

Hours later, she stood over the sink in front of the windowsill, washing a glass with a rag worn as soft and dingy as faded snow. It was her custom to wash the breakfast and lunch dishes shortly after eating at noon, and then she dealt with the supper plates before it got full dark and the ballgame came on. But here she stood, only now getting to the morning dishes even though it was late afternoon. There'd been days when she washed the dishes with a smile falling unceasingly on her mouth, and times when she literally cried into the sink. Today was closer to the latter, although she was no longer crying. She'd cried earlier, upstairs in the bedroom, alone, where she went to gather the worn laundry.

Out the window she could see him again. She watched him cross the yard with his dog trailing and wondered how he'd take the loss of the farm, if it came to that. How defiant he would get. He kept turning and looking back on Catfish, who ran in tight circles, nose to the ground. The yellow puppy ran near his feet and his cane and she worried he would fall. He'd spent the entire afternoon hanging a giant chain between two posts on either side of the driveway.

She'd wanted to see Hattie today, just to talk, but after the appraiser's visit she knew she needed to stay here in case something else happened and he needed her. Maybe she could run over there tomorrow, before lunch. She'd say Hattie was doing her hair again. He wouldn't notice it'd been done just last month. She needed to talk to Hattie about all of this.

Ethel knew the river came up fast in the spring, and more than ten times it'd come so far out of its banks that they'd worried about moving the animals somewhere else. Even with the barn almost a mile from the river! But that was Mother Nature and they'd dealt with it. Her father had carried this farm through the Depression and God knew what else, and he'd left it in her care and now she was going to be the one who lost it. But she understood that even worthwhile things ended, and that this might be one of those things. Her life had not been one that cultivated a belief in dramatic rescues and happy endings in general.

The sink stood about half full with soapy water, and she washed slowly, her fingers following the paths they'd traveled for a lifetime. She'd cooked hamburgers and baked beans for lunch and the plates and the bowl had already been washed and dried. Only the silverware remained.

She'd been born in the bedroom at the top of the stairs. Her father had owned this land even then. Her first memories were of this place. She'd stayed in the other little room upstairs, first with her brother John, and then by herself after he moved downstairs and then out of the house altogether.

She still remembered her mother, May. Dead now some fifty-seven years. She used to stand at this sink and wash dishes just like this. Almost everything Ethel could see out the window she attributed to her parents. May and Tarif had built this place from a wooded floodplain. See the fields beyond the barn? They didn't used to be there. The garden? Tarif had laid it out and plowed it with the horses the first time. Even the barn had been raised when Ethel was a little girl. May washed dishes by candlelight because they hadn't yet wired the house for electricity.

Frank wasn't anywhere near as good a farmer as her daddy had been, and they had to tell him often when he first came into their lives, cocksure and angry.

But by the time that happened, Ethel and Tarif were living in the farmhouse alone.

She remembered her brother. In those days they picked the corn by hand and come those fall evenings they would gather and shuck the ears by the light of the burning wood in the fireplace. That was work they got to do together. Fall was about given over entirely to the harvesting of corn. But even during that time there was still wood to be gathered. Everything revolved around trees. Some of the trees they felled for boards that built the barn, the chicken coop, the house—all of it. They took down still more just to burn in the kitchen and in the living room. All winter long, the trees on their land would be their only source of heat.

In the fall of 1926, Ethel was only seven but she looked forward to harvest season because she'd get to work alongside John in the house those evenings, pulling husks. But before they'd picked the first ear, John and their father sawed a tree that got caught in another tree's fork as it fell. For hours they worked on it, trying to get it to drop. They hooked three horses to the base, and even they couldn't jerk it free, sweating and lunging against the straps. But when John went back under the tree for some reason, the horses spooked and their sudden burst of power dropped the tree and no man could've moved fast enough.

They refused to let her go back in the woods to see where he died. When they buried him she couldn't see him either. They left his casket closed the whole time, and then he was laid to rest outside of town in the little cemetery. They'd discussed burying him on the farm, but they worried the river would rise and take him out of the ground. She spent years trying to recall the look on his face the last time she saw him.

The woods where he died were still there, even now, and she'd gone back there many times, just to sit. He'd been killed near the edge of a field, just in far enough where you could look out through the trunks and see slices of corn ready for harvest. She went back there after the funeral—stole out of the house, away from the open misery of her mother and the quiet sadness of her father—and found the spot on her own. She examined the saplings where they'd been pressed down or broken. Where the horses' hooves had gouged into the black earth. She sat out there often that winter after he died.

Her father left the giant trunk where it fell and it eventually rotted back into the soil. She watched its gradual progress of decay. She rarely went to the grave but she visited the tree for years. Sometimes she sat on its trunk and spoke to John.

She remembered the morning he died. She'd been in the kitchen, making a rhubarb pie with her mother. They'd been canning everything out of the garden, too. It was a busy time for everyone, but John had started seeing a girl from down the river a ways, and he hated being asked to work all day when he really wanted to go see this girl. The whole idea of John dating was new, and Ethel was jealous.

The cooking fire had made the kitchen especially hot that morning, even though it was October, and John came back into the house and drank a glass of water in a hurried way. He had a smear of grease on his arm and sawdust sticking to the sweat of his neck.

"How's it going back there?" their mother asked.

"Terrible."

"Is your dad staying calm?"

"No, he's not. He wants it all done before tonight and we can't do it. Not all of it. But he won't listen to me."

Ethel sat at the table, flattening out the crust with a rolling pin, and she said, "You just want to go see your girlfriend, instead of work." She'd only been teasing.

"Shut up," he said. "What do you know about working?"

And he left the house without saying anything else to his sister or mother, and later that morning he knew both about working and also what happens to a person after he dies.

Two years later, when Ethel was nine, her mother got relentlessly ill with pneumonia and died in the little bedroom on the first floor. May, victim of multiple miscarriages and the loss of her only son, lived her last two years like someone absolutely steeped in grief. She hadn't known a happy day after her son's death, and for several years after her mother died the same could be said for Ethel.

That left only her and Tarif, who'd worked himself into a crazed oblivion by then. He was hard to live with. She tried to take the place of John, and she worked like a man for most of her childhood. She enjoyed school over in Hapgood while it lasted, but eventually she stopped going altogether. She took care of her father and worked and then a man named Frank Withered came into their lives.

She looked out the window, and the same man was coming back across the yard toward the house. It was about time he thought to get out of this heat. She knew he hated not being able to do real work around the farm, but he couldn't do it anymore, it was as simple as that. She knew it burned at him. She'd seen it happen to her father first.

Catfish was calmer now, walking along in a straight line at his heels. He was a cute puppy but she didn't want him in the house. Not one more thing to clean up after. She wondered if it would bring good or harm for her husband to have a dog at this point in his life. Frank was already twenty-three years older than her dad had been when he died. He was fifty-eight years older than John had been when he passed on, and forty more than May. He was getting too old to be running around with a little dog under his feet. She thought it was a miracle either of them had lived this long, working as hard as they had.

She finished washing the silverware and dried the last fork and placed it on the dishrag spread on the countertop. She would tell him not to bring that dog in. Better to nip that in the bud right now. No more Catfish in the house. He should've left him out in the barn last night, anyway.

She did not want to talk about the appraisal or the farm. Not anymore today. She was worn out from thinking about it.

He was standing in the yard now, watched the pup sniff around. Over his head she could see the barn and the field and woods beyond it. It was hard for her to believe that they could make water come over all of this. But she knew they could. They could do anything. In her time, she'd seen the development of cars, televisions and space shuttles. What was a little dam across a river to them? They could flood the whole world, if they wanted to.

So the lake was coming. She wondered how long it would take, if they would both be alive to worry about moving. She didn't want to leave, either. No she did not. Not after all that had happened here, and it had been her land first. But she couldn't stay angry and fight like he could. She wanted to, but she couldn't. She felt today like she had when her dad burst into the house, screaming about John and the accident, and the way she felt when her mom passed away in the night and Tarif had told her that, too, in the cold morning. Some things you just couldn't do anything about. Some things just happened, as bad as they were.

She sat down at the table to rest before he came inside. She would deliver the news that the dog stayed outside and wait to see what he said. She hoped he wouldn't get too angry. She felt certain this day had already brought enough anger and pain.

CHAPTER FOURTEEN

Ollie turned left at Peterson's Market and drove toward her house. Was it really smart, coming out here without calling first? He wondered about that. On one hand, no one liked being surprised in her own home. On the other hand, he'd showered after work, thrown on a clean shirt and two splashes of cologne. It seemed like a waste of a shower if he turned back now, and what if she was just sitting around, thinking about him? She had kissed him, unprovoked. Wouldn't that be an amazing thing, to suddenly appear as if her thoughts alone had conjured him?

He decided to drive by her house first. If it looked busy he'd go home and call, not mentioning that he'd been out driving past her mailbox. If it appeared calm maybe they could all go get something to eat. He hated to revisit the Dairy Queen, but driving to the next closest restaurant would take over forty minutes, round trip.

Her house would be coming up just beyond this cornfield, and he slowed to look it over. He glanced down her driveway, back to where she parked her Omni under the trees. But there were two vehicles parked there! Mouth open, he looked at the road and then back, quickly. Sure enough—a big Ford pickup with a construction bed, an orange water cooler in a rack on the side.

His gut dropped. No woman drove a big work truck like that. Oh, what in the hell was this shit.

He kept driving and eventually the road T-d and he took a left. He'd been on this road once before but he couldn't remember why and he wasn't sure where it ran. He'd drive until he knew what to do next.

It'd been understood that she wasn't seeing anyone else. So was this the ex-boyfriend? The asshole himself! Damn, Ollie hated him right now. Parked at her house in broad daylight, like he still had business there.

I oughtta bust in there and whip his ass, he thought. Or get Coondog and bust up in there together and lay some serious hurt down. He fantasized about punching him out, but it was hard because he hadn't seen him and couldn't picture the face before his fist crashed into it.

A gravel road intersected the one he was on so he took another left. This lane so narrow fescue in the ditches brushed both sides of the truck. He drove too fast. There were hills he couldn't see over and he sped up them. It would've been easy to have a head-on at the top of a rise. It happened often enough. Everyone drove like they'd never see another car, and most times, they didn't. Sometimes they did, up close.

He tried to recall if Peterson's had a pay phone. He'd see who answered.

He took another left and drove past a nice farm with a big horse barn. Two girls were out riding in a fenced-in pasture and he watched their hair bounce with the horse's rhythm. But really he wasn't thinking about that. He was thinking about Summer.

Four miles later a stop sign startled him and he stood on the brakes and slid through the intersection, gravel flying. He backed up and took another left. Up and down hills, the road carved through the woods. He popped up by Peterson's Market, back where he started but completely different. This time he'd drive even slower and really scope the place.

But the work truck was gone. Her Omni sat there by its piece-of-shit-lonesome. By the time he noticed the truck was absent he'd missed her drive, so he turned around in the next driveway, rehearsing different things he could say. He could act like he hadn't seen the truck. Or should he be all pissed about it?

He drove up to her house like a beat dog trying one more time to lick the hand that'd smacked it. He parked and turned off the engine. The sun was still up and it was hot, so he wiped his face with the front of his shirt. Then he saw her standing behind the house. He'd never seen her behind the house before, and he realized how little he really knew about her. He couldn't read the look on her face.

"What in the world are you doing here?" she called.

He got out and walked toward her, head down. "Yeah. I thought I might stop by and see ya." So much for driving in a giant square, thinking of what to say.

She came forward and put her arms up. He hadn't hugged her except that one time when he tried to kiss her and he knew better than to try that now. He wasn't used to a hugging woman, but it was obvious she was into it. Her hair brushed his face and all he could think about was the work truck.

"Come on in," she said.

They went through the front door and it felt like stepping inside a refrigerator.

"I come by here earlier, but there was a truck in the driveway," he said, focusing on a giraffe left akimbo on the couch. He felt his face growing hotter.

"Yeah, that was Todd. He come by to pick up Spring."

He glanced around and suddenly noticed the conspicuous absence of the little girl. It was quieter.

"Where's he taking her?"

"Where's he taking her! Well, to his house, I imagine."

"Oh. Well, I didn't know." He stared at her, and she seemed to fear that an argument was coming on. Like she knew what one looked like as it approached.

"I told you we was never married," she said. "But we still split time with Spring. I want her to be able to see her Daddy."

Ollie couldn't identify or cope with the feelings in his gut. How had something so sweet turned spoiled so soon? What the hell was he supposed to do with some other man coming around here all the time? When would it stop? Well, it never would. He knew that. It's not like this son of a bitch was going to stop being the little girl's dad all of a sudden. He'd planted the seed—it was his crop forever.

She reached out and touched his arm. "Hey. What's wrong with you?"

"Nothing. I just don't like knowing some other dude is coming here, that's all."

"He don't come to talk to me! He comes and gets her, and he leaves. Tomorrow or the next day I'll go over there and get her. That's all there is to it."

"Where's he live?" He didn't really care.

"Up in town, over near the feed mill. He's married to some bitch and got a little boy."

That was something right there! Why'd she care about his wife? Jealousy. He liked knowing the asshole had moved on but it seemed like Summer was trying to replace her. He sighed and made a big production of putting his hands on his hips.

"Ollie, look," she said. "I'm sorry this bothers you, but that's the way it is right now. He's got to be able to see her."

"I know it. I got that part."

"Well what are you so upset about?"

"I'm not upset."

"You sure act like it." She stood there, arms crossed over her chest. "I'm going to get me something to drink. Do you want something?"

She turned and he followed her. He'd never been out of the living room. But he knew that this other guy—had she called him Todd?—had been in every room in this house. Sleeping in bed with her. Watching her shower. Eating breakfast together. Hell, he probably put in some of these light bulbs.

The kitchen was small and cramped and painted light green. Some fake fruit sat on the little table. It smelled like something familiar in here, but he couldn't name it.

She poured lemonade out of a pitcher into a glass and then remembered him and got down another glass and filled it, too. She handed it to him and they both drank. She put the pitcher back in the fridge.

"Well," she said. "I ain't got nothing to do tonight, so if you wanna go ride around we could."

She smiled and in that second it hit him that the house was empty. The little girl wouldn't be around all night. There was a time to fight and a time to love. It'd been the former but he could move to the latter pretty quick.

"You want to take a ride?" he asked. Not that he meant it that way! He tried to smile.

She put her glass down on the counter and took his half-full glass out of his hand and set it next to hers. She put her arms up on his shoulders.

"I like you, boy. But you can't be the jealous type. I done been down that road. And you don't want to mess with him. Just focus on me, all right?"

She kissed him and he felt like a cartoon firecracker with its fuse lit. He could almost hear the hissing sound of its burning. But even as he kissed her, he wondered about the guy. She said not to mess with him. What did she think? That he couldn't fight? Did she think her ex was tougher? He doubted it. He seriously doubted it. But then he followed her advice and focused on her. His fingers found the line on her lower back, the little riverbed over her spine. He traced it and thought about grabbing her ass, but she didn't seem ready for that.

After a few moments she said come on, and they got in his truck. As he cranked the motor she reached up and pulled down the seatbelt. That meant she wouldn't be sliding over. He always thought his girlfriend should sit right next to him.

Well, he thought, it's not like Rome was built in a day. He put his seatbelt on, even though the motion was foreign to him.

They drove until the air grew cool and bats starting swooping across the road. They looked at different things—some cows in a field, a pretty lake with two people fishing around its edges. They drove through a valley that she said looked like something in the Legend of Sleepy Hollow, because the tree branches overhead connected, forming a tunnel.

He wondered how far he should drive.

Dark and secretive places kept presenting themselves to him—spots where they could park and make out. A logging trail leading into a woods. An old deserted farmhouse alone in a field. He was tempted, but couldn't risk it. Instead, they talked about different things—what Spring had said that day in regards to a show she'd watched, how hot it was at work, what Summer'd been like in high school four or five years ago.

"I sure wish I'd known you back then," he said.

"I didn't do much, though. I was a cheerleader and senior year I got prom queen. That's about it. My grades weren't very good, but then I never cared, either."

"You were a cheerleader?"

"Yeah. It sucked. We bout froze our asses off at football games."

He drove and thought deeply about that.

"A lot of them girls still live around here, but we don't see each other much anymore," she said. "I guess everyone's just too busy."

He was still thinking about her in a cheerleading skirt.

"What about you?" she asked. "You still see your high school buddies?"

"Just one. Coondog. You'll have to meet him sometime. He's crazier than a shithouse rat."

She laughed. Ollie was getting over the work truck. He might be able to forget all about it. If he couldn't, he'd kick that guy's ass. Simple as that.

It was getting harder to see. The woods at the backs of the fields looked black and deep. He couldn't see the deer that suddenly materialized in front of the truck. He didn't see it until she screamed and then it was too late.

The deer standing there had just a moment to look at them—their own human faces open and white with surprise—before it tightened its leg muscles to trigger a leap it would never launch. Ollie saw the deer look at them but it was a moment frozen. An instant later the deer seemed to rush into the truck, hitting the front left corner and coming against the windshield, where it hit the glass with great force before flying up and over the cab. Dense sounds of metal bending. After it passed over them he realized the truck was sideways and sliding across the narrow black-topped road. The tires squealed against the pavement. He tried to turn the wheel to keep them from sliding into the ditch but they slid into it anyway, and the truck lurched to a stop and stood rocking on its shocks, off-kilter. Part of the hood was bent skyward at a crazy angle.

Everything registered and stored in his peripheral mind came back to him then. He remembered her screaming and grabbing his arm. He remembered seeing her body go forward as he braked. He remembered the thick sound—the whoooomph—as flesh hit metal.

He looked at her and the blood on her face didn't panic him because he didn't believe it was really there. He wondered how long she'd had a bloody nose before the deer ran in front of them. Why hadn't they noticed?

"Oh my God," she kept saying. Over and over. Her hands flew up to her face, gathering the neck of her T-shirt. It was a gray shirt, blood already staining the front.

"What happened to you?" He couldn't touch her face, but his hands were on her back, her arm.

Her nose bled from both nostrils. She kept lowering her T-shirt to look at the blood collecting there. Her upper lip was swollen, too, and there was blood in the spaces around her teeth.

"What else?" he asked.

She looked at him, eyes panicking.

"What else is hurt? Can you move?"

She nodded. She reached down for the buckle on the seatbelt.

He shut off the engine, opened his door and ran around to her side. She stood on the blacktop, pointing back down the road.

It was so quiet, the air cool. There was just enough light left in the sky to see the road and the weeds in the ditches lightly blowing in the breeze. The deer lay on the road, so far back he thought for a second maybe they'd hit two deer. But even from this distance he saw the animal struggling. It jerked up and down frantically. The deer had one leg up, so thin and angled it looked like a bent coat hanger, but its body lay crumpled on the blacktop. The front legs and chest faced them—the white of its belly visible—and the hind legs lay pointing back from whence they'd come. The head lifted in weak spasms.

"We didn't kill it!" She sounded like she had a bad cold, although the blood on her face was drying. "What can you do with it?"

He looked back at the deer. It lifted and fell, lifted and fell, lifted and fell on its one good leg. Each time the body fell the deer's head struck the ground. Somewhere in its brain, perhaps it was running, a flat-out sprint across a field. But the tendons and bones could follow the brain's impulses in only the most rudimentary fashion. It was like a machine trying to run with a broken part, a gear with missing teeth.

He didn't know what to do. Watching the deer made him feel cold.

He'd shot deer before back in the woods at the house, but he'd killed his last one about ten years ago. The farm was just about overrun with them. But he'd never gotten into hunting, and every time he'd gutted an animal his dad had been there to guide him. Besides, there was no gun in the truck, and only his pocketknife in his pocket. He felt for it now, and it was there. Maybe three inches long, unfolded. He looked around. There was a cornfield on this side of the road, stretching for miles in both directions. Soybeans filled the field on the other side. He'd seen a farm back down the road a ways.

But the truck would run. He thought they could back out of the ditch.

"Do you need to go to the hospital?" he asked.

She shook her head no. She had begun to cry.

"You stay here then. Maybe you wanna get back inside?"

"What are you gonna do?" She held her shirt up over her nose and mouth, her stomach exposed.

"Go see if it's all right," he said.

"Ollie, it's not all right! I can tell you that!"

"Kill it, then!" he said, louder than he intended. "Put it out of its misery."

She got in the truck. He started walking, black skid marks under his feet.

When he got closer to the deer he could see the dark blood on the road under its body, blood on the white hair of its underside. Its mouth hung open, tongue protruding, and now he heard the wheezing sound of its sucking breaths. Its eyes watched him and its motions grew even more frenzied as he approached. He stopped walking without realizing it and stood in the road.

He thought he might puke and he felt so cold his hands shook. He wondered if there might be a big rock or stick in the ditch. It would be under those tall weeds, though, and he'd never see it. He looked at the cornfield. The stalks were about waist high. There was nothing more useless to him than that cornfield right now.

Except maybe the soybean field, which offered him even less to kill an animal. The deer's hooves made scratching sounds as they scrabbled across the pavement. There were no antlers, and he couldn't remember when the bucks grew theirs back. This was probably a doe. It wasn't very big. He watched its head slap the road as the lone working leg churned.

We could drive back to that farm, he thought. Get a gun. Or call someone.

He thought about calling his father. He'd know what to do. The old man would kill the deer and be shut of it. He'd skin it and butcher out the meat himself. Then he'd cook it and serve it to Summer and him for lunch.

He was struck suddenly by the knowledge that his parents didn't know Summer existed.

He felt again of his knife, still in his pocket. He could pull it out and swing the ridiculously little blade. He could pin the deer's head under his knee and slit its throat. He could hold its thrashing body down with his own until it ceased struggling. He thought about what that would feel like.

Instead he looked one more time at the doe and jogged back to the truck.

He jumped in and she asked, "What'd you do?"

"We need to get you to the hospital."

"I don't need to go all the way out there! It's already stopped bleeding. I'll clean up back at my house."

He turned the key and the engine started. It took him several times of going back and forth, but he got the truck straightened out on the road.

"We can't just leave it." She kept looking back over her shoulder, trying to see if the deer was still alive.

"We're not. I just need a gun, is all."

"Where you gonna get one?"

"I don't know. We might stop somewhere. I could go get mine, but it'd be too far."

He drove slowly now, but still the first house was behind them before he said he hadn't seen it. Then he passed another house because he said it looked too dark.

"I don't want to wake some folks up for this," he said.

"We can't just leave it!" she cried out. He looked at her in alarm and saw the tears running down her face.

At the next farmhouse he pulled in, immediately setting off about five dogs that burst forth from their sleeping places howling and barking, their sounds amplified. He parked at the end of the drive in front of the big white house.

"I'll run in here and explain," he said.

But the dogs surrounded the truck and two of them—German shepherd looking dogs—barked up at him from outside his door. He waited, and finally a porch light came on and a tall man walked out wearing pants and no shirt. The man yelled at the dogs and they instantly stopped barking and gathered around him on the porch. Ollie walked over there and told him the story, pointing back down the road.

"Is your wife okay?" the man asked, looking over Ollie's shoulder. "Looks like she's pretty upset."

Ollie turned and saw that she held her face in her hands. Her shoulders hitched. "I think she hit her nose on the dash. She's all right, though, I guess."

The man said he'd call the sheriff and went back inside. He didn't offer to let Ollie in, so he stood there while the dogs circled him. Some of them growled. He looked back at Summer and made a motion to say everything was fine. She glanced at him and looked away. Bugs swirled around the porch light.

When the man returned, his wife came with him, already in her nightgown. A heavyset woman with gray hair.

"I called him," the man said. "He said he'd come out this way and take care of it. He said he'd shoot it, if'n it was still alive."

Ollie thanked him.

"Let me turn on that outside light, so you can see to miss my dogs," the woman said.

Ollie walked back to the truck and a light snapped on overhead. Now, by the glow of the utility pole light, he noticed how deep the dents were in the front quarter panel. The grill was busted up, too, all the way across. One headlight looked like an empty eye socket. He couldn't believe the deer hadn't shattered the windshield.

She said nothing when he got in.

He told her the sheriff was coming and that it'd be taken care of. He offered again to take her to the hospital, but she said no, she wanted to go home.

"I need to call Spring," she said. "Make sure she's all right."

He wondered why Summer needed to call her, since she hadn't been the one in the wreck, but he knew not to ask why.

Just a weekday night after work, was all it was. A night trying to build a foundation with a new girl. Now his truck was screwed up, a deer was dead, and she was mad with blood all over her face. Why did this shit have to happen to him? What, was he cursed?

He paid for insurance, but he knew it wasn't the kind that covered his own vehicle. That cost too much. So now he'd drive a dented truck until he got enough saved to have it fixed. It sure as hell wouldn't be cheap, either.

Summer hadn't said much by the time they got back to her house, and she jumped out and went to the door without saying anything. He sat there and wondered for a second, then killed the motor and followed her. She'd already gone inside.

After thinking about it some more, he opened the door and stepped into the living room.

She was in the bathroom—he heard water running in the sink. He walked down the hall and knocked lightly.

"Everything okay in there?"

"It sucks."

He waited and finally she came out. She'd put on another shirt and washed the blood from her face. Her nose looked red and swollen, but it wasn't knocked to the side or anything.

"You was wearing your seatbelt," he said. "I don't understand how it happened."

"I think maybe it hit my arm."

"Your nose did?"

"Like this." She demonstrated. He didn't see how her arm could've flown up like that, but he had no other explanation. The main thing was she was all right.

"You look just like normal," he said.

"It hurts like heck." She went toward the living room and he followed her.

"I am sorry about all of this," he said. "I hope you know that. I shoulda been watching better."

"That poor deer. I wonder why she did it? Why'd she run out in front of us like that?" She turned on the lights and sat on the couch.

"Who knows? They ain't very smart."

"She was smart! It wasn't her fault."

He stood there and looked at the open area next to her on the couch.

"I just hope she didn't have babies," she said, and it was like the idea had just occurred to her. Her eyes got wet again.

"Now hold on," he said, sitting next to her. He put his hand on her knee.

"I gotta call my daughter," she said, standing up. She went into the kitchen.

He said he'd go outside and check on his truck. He went out the back door and studied the damage to give her time to finish talking. There wasn't much light out here but it seemed like he'd hit more than a deer.

Then he saw a shadow move across the wall of the living room and was struck by the sudden odd realization that he could watch her through the windows. He felt ashamed of it. He went back inside. She'd changed again, this time into another T-shirt and sweatpants.

"She's all right," she said.

"Good. Well, I guess I better go." He laughed a little. "I reckon I impressed you enough with our second date."

"You can stay for a while and watch TV if you want. It's only 9:30."

He pretended to think about it. "If you don't mind, maybe I will."

They sat on the couch and she poured two pops in plastic cups. A night like this called for something heavier than soda but he knew she didn't keep any liquor in the house. He watched the stupid shows but kept thinking about the deer. He didn't think he'd ever forget the way it flopped on the road. It'd been broken in so many places.

He wondered why he hadn't been able to kill it. And would she have liked him more if he had?

But she didn't want things to die—she'd made that clear. So he wasn't sure if killing it would've helped or hurt him.

She sat next to him and touched her nose often. She watched TV with red eyes and didn't say much. He thought he'd stay a little longer and then take off. He didn't want to screw up any more than he already had.

"You know what the thing is," she said during a commercial, "it's been a long time since I killed something. I really don't like to do it."

"You didn't kill that deer. If anyone did, I did."

"I know you didn't mean to. But I mean, I even sweep up spiders and carry them outside. And this was a deer. It was as big as me!"

It really had looked like a human dying on the road, but he wasn't going to admit that to her now. He intended to say something to put her at ease. "You're not a killer," he said.

"You're not either. I know that."

"If anything, I guess you could say I kill hopes and dreams, but that's about it."

She looked at him, puzzled. "What?"

"Well, that's what my folks would say. That I killed their hopes and dreams, maybe."

"Your parents think you killed their hopes and dreams?"

"Nah. Forget it." It hadn't come out the way he thought it might. He'd meant to make some kind of joke. But what else was new. He'd tried to do something funny and it only made things worse. Insurance companies called things like tornadoes and deer accidents Acts of God, and that was the way his life was shaping up—like some kind of Act of God. But with his life shit just got screwed worse.

CHAPTER FIFTEEN

The yellow shreds of scrambled eggs swirled and made their way down the drain. He usually ate everything Ethel put in front of him, and she worried about his health as she finished the breakfast dishes. She'd already washed the lunch plates. It was early afternoon, and she'd been working on a crossword puzzle while he sat at the table, reading an Indiana Prairie Farmer. Before she could ask him about the eggs they both heard the combine coming down the road. He perked up at the sound—the diesel engine, the low hum of big tires on gravel. He stood up, too quickly, and fell back against the table. "Slow down! Watch what you're doing!" she exclaimed, but he ignored her and went to the living room window. It was Wayne all right, coming to get started on the wheat. The orange lights blinked atop the green machine. The combine, hulking and otherworldly, looked as foreign as the space shuttle itself on the narrow country road. And this was just the combine—the wheat head would be trailered in later, because it was too wide for even a two-lane highway. He'd been wondering when Wayne was going to run the wheat.

Frank had farmed this land with his own hands until he was near seventy. And for a long time, he'd been the neighbor with the best yields, the most uniform fields, even in years of drought or flood. He set the mark for what the soil could produce around here if everything was done just right. But there toward the end he was the last one in the county to get his corn planted, and the last one to bring it in, waiting for winter to freeze the ground solid so he could finally get his ancient Massey-Ferguson combine out there to harvest the rest of the corn, most of it collapsed and wind-torn by then. She finally got him to give it up.

Tarif had stopped farming gradually, ceding more control over the decisions to Frank and letting him do more of the work himself. But now there was no gradual cession, no ancestral hand-off, because Ollie didn't want it. He'd baled hay and straw when he was younger, and disked fields and planted soybeans and corn behind the John Deere, but when he graduated from high school and started working at the sawmill that was the end of it. When Frank got the house trailer to stop the constant bickering, they stopped seeing him almost altogether, and they surely didn't see him when there was work to be done.

So they needed someone to rent and farm the land. Frank had called Wayne Shipps, because he'd known Wayne's father back when he was alive and he trusted Wayne to do it right. It'd been three years now, and Frank had almost gotten to the point where he could stand to see someone else do it. The first year or two it felt like watching another man with your wife.

After Wayne brought in his first crop, and it became obvious that it could be done a thousand times faster and more efficiently than Frank's old equipment allowed, they admitted that Wayne could handle the task. They held an auction, invited a bunch of strangers to come and poke around the place like it was theirs, and sold off the combine and the bigger John Deere tractor. The disk, the plow, the planter, the cultivator went, too. So did three gravity beds, the baler and four hay wagons. Frank sold almost everything— the equipment he'd spent much of his life with. Steel he'd pulled around fields, driven, maintained and repaired countless times. He kept the utility John Deere to keep up on the bush-hogging and such. Everything else was gone—some implements sold to local guys he knew, but others went to different counties, sometimes two or three counties over. He might drive by a farm and see some of his old equipment. Dave Pittz still used his John Deere 4030 tractor.

Now she kept asking how Wayne was going to get the combine through the chain across the drive, and he told her that Wayne would just pull into the wheat field off the road, since the ditch was shallow along there.

As he said this Wayne slowed the John Deere and turned into their yard at the end of the field. The top of the machine scraped the branches of the trees overhead. Frank's Massey Ferguson combine had been Tarif's. Wayne's was almost three times the size and inside the cab were computers and electrical gadgets Frank had never seen the likes of.

A John Deere tractor, itself bigger than anything he'd owned, followed the combine into the yard. The tractor pulled a grain hopper—a big two-wheeled wagon capable of holding a thousand bushels of wheat. Wayne could almost load the whole field into the hopper. They were tracking up the yard, but they'd move into the field as soon as they got the wheat harvested off the end.

"I'm goin out there to talk to Wayne," he said, coming back into the kitchen.

"I figured as much."

"Will you watch Catfish?"

The puppy lay curled up like a ball in the makeshift pen in the corner of the kitchen. Somehow he'd spent the night inside again. She'd forced Frank to rebuild the pen using only magazines this time, though—her sugar canister was back safely on the counter. Catfish had eaten breakfast, gone outside to do his business, and then Frank had let him back inside to sleep on the kitchen floor while he ate his own breakfast.

"Watch it do what?" she asked.

He stood over by the door, putting on his hat.

"You know," he said. "Just take care of his needs."

•   •   •

Up in the combine, Wayne sat like some kind of pilot or god, adjusting the levels and knobs. The roar of the diesel engine was muffled by the glass cab but deafening to Frank, who stood on the grass and waited. The tractor pulling the hopper had parked behind the combine. Eventually, the combine's motor made a sound and shut off. Wayne waved a little from within the glass cab high above.

The door swung open and Wayne climbed out and smiled down at him. They'd always gotten along. Wayne was a young man—thin and strong yet, and the mustache he wore barely made him look old enough to have kids. In fact, he was a few years older than Ollie, and his sons were old enough to help run the equipment.

"Whatta say there Frank!" he called out.

"Looks like you're gonna run the wheat, huh?"

Wayne climbed down the steps and shook his hand. "I figure we'll wait a bit, let the sun dry her off a bit more, then see what it does. I need to wait for Toby to bring the head, anyway." Toby was Wayne's hired hand.

"I wondered when you was gonna do it," Frank said, looking out across the field. Here and there some of it had lain down from the wind.

"Oh, you know how it is. Been runnin over there at Stumpy's Corner some, and then a chain broke on the head, so we had to fix that, then my son's got summer league ballgames I got to go to. And always waiting on the rain to stop for once. And so on and so forth. Here I am, finally. How you been?"

"I reckon we been all right."

Wayne waited for Frank to say more, but he kept his eyes over the field and said nothing further.

Wayne's son had been in the tractor, but Frank heard it shut down and the boy came walking up.

"Frank, you remember my boy, Matt?"

Frank said he did and shook the young man's hand. The boy was old enough to have acne and he wore jeans and a T-shirt stained with oil.

"You helping your dad out?" Frank asked him.

"He works me hard," Matt said, smiling toward the ground. He was a good kid. He wasn't yet old enough to drive a car but Wayne let him drive the tractor. The sheriff would never stop him and Wayne needed the free help.

"Well, I reckon we better get this thing set up and run this field," Wayne said. "Toby'll be here any minute with the head."

"You gonna come bale the straw tomorrow, then?" Frank asked.

"Well, I don't know about that." He was beginning to look distracted, eager to work on his combine and get going. "I may have Charlie come out here with his baler and run it."

Somebody with animals would buy the straw and use it as bedding. Frank had used all the straw his wheat produced, back when he had cattle.

Wayne didn't own livestock, so straw wasn't a huge concern to him. He'd find someone who wanted to buy it, and that was enough. He wanted to get the wheat out of the field, though.

"I might want some of them straw bales," Frank said. Even then, he didn't know why. He had no real use for straw.

"Well, you bet," Wayne said. "You could talk to Charlie if he comes out."

Wayne was a church-goer at the Methodist church in Hawesville and a patient man. But when it was time to farm, and it was now—who knew when it might rain again?—it was time to farm. He was responsible for over two thousand acres, and he couldn't spend all afternoon jawing with the guy who owned this forty acre field, even if he did deeply respect that man.

"What's wheat runnin now?" Frank asked.

"Oh, I got sixty bushel at the last field. I reckon this'll do fifty or better."

"That's pretty damned good, ain't it?"

"Yeah, it's all right." Then he looked at Matt and told him to move the tractor farther away from the field so it'd be clear of the auger when he made his turns. The boy trotted off and soon the John Deere started again.

"These fields always did produce," Frank said, louder.

"Yeah, it'll be a shame if'n they all get flooded."

Frank shot a look at him. "That ain't gonna happen."

"It's not? I thought I heard—"

"There ain't nothing been settled," he said, shaking his head.

"Well, I hope so. I'd hate to lose these fields. And I'd surely hate not being able to rent off you."

Frank felt his face getting hot and he stood there, looking up at the combine, unsure of what to say next.

"You and Ethel, uh, you got plans if they do go ahead with it?" Wayne finally asked. "I'd like to help, if I could."

"We plan on stayin right here," Frank said.

They were silent and Wayne watched his boy re-position the tractor and grain hopper. Then the pick-up came down the road, pulling the trailer with the wheat head.

"I guess I better get started, huh? It won't run itself, with me and you standing around talking like a couple of old women, right?"

"Yeah, go ahead and fire her up."

Wayne said he'd talk to him later, let him know what the wheat ended up running, and then he climbed back into the cab. The engine jumped to life and the sound seemed to shake the very ground Frank stood on.

He walked back and stood under a big oak tree. Toby parked the trailer in the ditch, and Wayne drove the combine to it. Frank watched as the men positioned the head on the combine, and in no time at all, it was ready. Toby got back in the truck and turned around. He waved to Frank once and was gone, off on another errand.

Wayne backed the combine up and angled it toward the edge of the field. He would cut across the end first. The big spindle on the head starting spinning like a giant paddlewheel on a riverboat and the combine began to move through the wheat, the stalks getting swept into the head and cut off several inches above the ground. Clouds of dust rose in the air and floated off on the afternoon breeze. Frank could smell the thick dust and was close enough to see the chains and belts moving on the machine, the head pulling the wheat in, cutting it clear, and sending it up into the combine. Wayne waved as he went by the oak. Matt was still in the tractor cab down the way, no doubt listening to the radio. Frank wondered if they didn't have TV's in them nowadays.

He stood there until Wayne cleared off the end and started on the outside row, moving down the length of the field. Chaff spurted out of the rear of the combine, ready for the straw baler.

Frank wondered how many more times he'd watch wheat being harvested. He wondered how many more times he'd see wheat harvested here, on his land. He liked watching Wayne work, but sometimes he let Frank ride along in the cab. This time he hadn't offered.

CHAPTER SIXTEEN

Tuesday after work Ollie drove over to Hapgood, a pilgrim in a dented truck seeking Coondog as one might go visit a sage. If it were possible for one man alone to figure out this current situation, he felt certain it'd be done by now. He'd sure as hell given over enough man-hours to thinking about it. When he was a lot younger his mother had asked him to sort chickens by breed and age, and Summer was turning into something like that. When he got a thought chased into a corner he went back for another one and the first one shot between his legs or squirmed out a hole in the boards. He felt like he had loose feathers floating in his head. When he pulled up to the house, Coondog was out in the yard, his legs sprawled underneath the giant bucket truck he used in his tree trimming business. The hood was up. Ollie walked over and nudged the leg with his foot.

Coondog recognized the boot of his only true friend. "What say, stranger? Long time no see, you bastard."

"You could say I been real busy."

"Oh, I know what you been busy doin, you ol dog!"

"Not all what you might think."

"Bullshit." Coondog churned his legs and wiggled out from under the truck. He didn't use a creeper because he didn't have any concrete for it to roll on. He changed the oil in his many vehicles after parking them under his walnut tree, where at least he could lie on his back in the crabgrass.

"Bullshit!" he said again, grinning. He got to his feet. Oil smeared one cheek and down his neck, and his hat had been knocked off. "I know what you been doin! And her name is that little blonde thing from the fair."

Ollie laughed, surprised to feel his blood run three degrees warmer at the mention of Summer. It felt good to have something someone else wanted. If he even had her.

They shook hands and then Coondog wiped his palms. Ollie looked down at the oil on his hand. He grabbed the rag away from Coondog and wiped it off.

"What the hell's wrong here?" Ollie asked. He leaned over the grill and studied the engine.

"Nah. Just servicing it. Damn thing runs like she's got somewhere to go and all day to get there."

Ollie looked at him. He wasn't sure if that'd been praise or criticism. Coondog seemed happy enough, so he figured the truck was working out. "How's business?" he asked.

"Shit. Slower than granpappy with his buckskin rubber. I need some more storms to hit, knock some damn trees down."

"I heard that."

"I did cut a tree down today for some old woman out by Bergman's Small Engine Repair. I went driving by, and I seen it. I stopped and told her it was fixin to fall on her garage."

"Was it?"

"Sooner or later." He laughed.

"Shit me. You mean you lied to an old woman?"

"I never lied, exactly. That wood sucker was tiltin, and when a big storm hit just right, it woulda crushed the shit out of her garage."

"What you get for it?"

"I charged her four hundred. I told her, that car of yours inside the garage is worth a lot more'n that."

Ollie laughed and shook his head.

A variety of tools lay spread out in the grass and on the engine cowling. There was a ratchet, a set of sockets, an oil filter wrench, a case of oil, and a small paper sack holding an oil filter.

Coondog looked at him. "Seriously. Stop jerking me around. Tell me what you're doin with Miss Goldy-locks."

"Well, let me put it to you this way: I seen her about three times since that night."

"No shit." His greased face bore the look of a shipwrecked sailor listening to a man talk about drinking a cold glass of fresh water. Or maybe drinking it right in front of him.

"But it ain't all easy. Thing is, she got a kid."

Coondog hit him on the shoulder. "So that talky horse girl was her kid. I knew she was lying to you about that."

"What? No, not that one. She got another one."

"So? How old is he?"

"The kid? She. About three years old, I guess. Two, maybe."

Coondog held up his arms. "So what? Not like she's like, 'Mommy don't date him.' Or, 'I don't want a new daddy!' A kid that little barely knows what's going on around 'em. Trust me on that one. One night I banged a chick in her house and her kid seen me, and the chick said, "Santa Claus is here. Go back to sleep."

"I remember you tellin me that one. I know it. But it's still weird. I mean, she's got this guy around somewhere, and he's still coming around."

"The kid?"

"No, you dumbass! Summer! The one I'm seein."

"So that's her name. Summer. I've been wondering about you, man. I was wondering if you'd been getting mud for your turtle. Let's go get a beer."

When they got closer to the house Coondog stopped and stared.

"What the hell did you hit with your truck?"

"Deer. I was riding with Summer and the damn thing run right out in front of me. I killed it. It was nasty, man."

"Holy shit." He bent and inspected the damage. "This is gonna cost ya bigtime." They discussed what needed replacing, and what could be hammered out and repainted.

After that Ollie followed him into the garage, which held a three-wheeler, an old Pontiac GTO on jacks, and the black pickup he drove most of the time. An old rusted-out refrigerator stood against the wall. Coondog got out two beers and handed him one.

"Where's our demo car?" Ollie asked as he opened it.

"That damn thing? I got rid of it. I sold it to Coffee's junkyard. He went out there to the fairgrounds and loaded it. I never even had to see the shittin thing again."

"Man, that reminds me. Whatever happened that next day, when we was supposed to go out there and help pick up trash?"

"What happened? Well, I never went. Did you?"

"Hell no. I got up and called Summer."

"Then what the hell do you think happened? Somebody else picked all the shit up!"

They laughed.

"Hey, there was something else I wanted to tell you about that other guy," Ollie said. "You can do something for me, if you get a chance."

"What's that, lucky man?"

"Find out about this dude named Todd who lives in Logjam near the feed mill. Works construction or something."

"He the ex?"

"Yeah, the little kid's dad. He's showing up out there again, and I wanna know who he is. She told me he's married now."

"I can do that, sure. I'll ask around. I know people. Wouldn't hurt me to drive up there and look at people's trees, either."

Ollie helped him finish changing the oil in the bucket truck. Then they drove it down the road and back. Inside the cab, on the ripped seat of the bench, lay leather gloves and harnesses of different kinds and uses. The cab was mostly steel and smelled of sawdust and sweat. It smelled familiar.

"Ain't it funny how we both ended up cuttin trees?" Ollie yelled over the sound of the diesel.

"Yeah, it's a damn hoot."

The road ended at an entrance into a trailer court and Coondog did about a five-point turnaround to head back to his house. The bucket truck had a huge steering wheel like an eighteen-wheeler, and he cranked it and rocked back and forth, working the clutch and the gearshift with his other hand.

He got them pointed in the right direction and opened the throttle up. The big engine roared. "I just wanted to blow it out a little," he said, but Ollie knew he was showing off.

Back at the house, Coondog parked the truck in the driveway. They walked into the yard to get the tools and the empty quarts of oil they'd left lying.

"You got work to do tomorrow?" Ollie asked.

"Yeah, I got to trim some trees over by Peter's Switch. But it ain't a full day's work. I hope somebody else calls."

"Word'll get out. Just Saturday I told the woman up there at Fix-It to call you."

"She need tree work done?"

"I told her if she did, to call."

"Thanks man. You got so much good luck coming out your ass, you just givin it away, ain't ya?"

"Hey. I'm just trying to give you a hand, man."

Coondog jerked the socket off the ratchet and hammered it back into its case. "Yeah, well, fuck it," he said. "I'm already thinking of what I'm gonna do next."

"Yeah? What's that?"

"Well, when this lake comes through I been hearin about, all this is going to be a tourist resort area. And I'm set to cash in on it. See, everybody'll come here to camp and shit. Well, I'm gonna open a little bar and grill. That way, when people come here, they got a place to eat."

"Shit. That lake. I'm sick of hearin about it. They ain't never gonna do anything."

"I heard they are, this time."

"Well, you got a plan, anyway."

"Hell yes. It's gonna be a family place, cause they got the damn money, but don't worry—in the back there'll be a bar with live bands for people like us to hang out in. Chase tail."

"Sounds fucking great."

"Oh, it's gonna be. I'm gonna be the first to cash in on this new lake. Mark my words."

"When's all this happen?"

"Shit, I don't know. Right now, I gotta keep this tree trimming thing. By then I'll have some money saved up. So whenever. Whenever the damn lake comes. Whenever the water comes up and this place becomes a damn lakeside resort."

Ollie nodded. He wondered why Coondog hadn't asked too much about

Summer. He'd come out here looking for some answers. But he'd figured something else out instead: any problems or concerns he had with Summer were problems and concerns Coondog wanted. He hadn't dated anyone seriously since he'd written MARGIE on that helmet. And as much as Ollie needed help with Summer, he knew the alternative was to spend his evenings changing oil in the yard or throwing horseshoes drunk. He'd done those things.

CHAPTER SEVENTEEN

In the middle of the week, there'd been the excitement of the straw baling. Two days after Wayne had combined the whole wheat field in several hours, Charlie Wolfing baled the straw with the help of five gangly high school boys. They'd started in the morning and worked all day while Frank watched them from a lawn chair set under his oak tree. Catfish stayed with him and barked at the boys as they rode the wagons around and around the field. Charlie drove the tractor and baler while two boys stacked the load. Three others hauled the full wagons back to Charlie's with a pickup, where they unloaded it onto an elevator and stacked it in his hayloft before bringing back the empty wagons. Frank sat in his chair and counted the loads. Every hour or so Ethel brought him another glass of iced tea. The field was now an even blanket of wheat stubble, marked in regular patterns with tire tracks where the combine and the tractors had flattened the stalks. So there'd been that, and now he wanted to call Chub and head for the river. He wanted to see if it looked different—see if those government assholes had been driving stakes down there. But then the green beans came on and he spent inordinate amounts of time helping Ethel snap them.

And here she came with another brown sack filled. Over the barn the sky had darkened and she reported hearing thunder out over the woods.

"I brung this many in, before I got wet," she said, although it was clear to him that to bring any more she'd have needed another sack. And if there'd been more to get, she'd have gotten wet picking them.

Her skin fit the muscles in her arms. They'd both been out in the sun so much their skin looked like tanned deer hide. His arms were starting to show red and black blotches, but hers looked fine yet. Weathered smooth but still strong, like a board on the west side of a barn.

She put the sack next to the chair at the kitchen table and went to the sink to get a glass of water. She drank half, refilled it, and stood there looking out the window. From the cabinet over the sink she then took a large bowl and set it on the table. She unfolded a newspaper there and spread it flat. Finally she got another paper sack and placed it on the floor, open.

He watched her from his chair in the other room. From this vantage point he could see both the tv and the kitchen. He watched her more than she knew. She'd stopped for almost two minutes while she drank her water and looked out the window.

"You gonna help me with these ones?" she asked.

He stood up, and when he did the little dog lifted his head from the rug. Frank motioned for him to come on and the pup stood up and followed him. He was a smart dog, Catfish.

Frank walked into the kitchen and pulled out the chair next to hers. For two days now they'd been sitting here snapping beans, putting the middles in a bowl and dropping the ends in a paper sack. They'd used this system not only this week but for about the last thirty summers. He didn't like kitchen work but damn—the TV hit its slumps in the afternoon and he got so disgusted he could hardly watch it. Golf and such crap on.

"This about the end of em?" he asked.

She looked under the table at the pup, already asleep on the linoleum floor. "I still want to know why that animal gets to come in here all the time."

"Who, Catfish? He comes in because he's smart enough. He don't hurt nothing."

She grunted. "We never had one smart enough, before. Course, we never let em try, either."

He reached into the sack and piled some beans on the newspaper. He said nothing. She looked at him over her glasses.

"Well. He lives in here practically like a human," she said.

"Human bean?" he asked, holding one up. "I said, 'is this about the last of it.' You never told me."

She sighed. "Next week some may be ready but not so much. This is the last sackful."

"You gonna can it today?"

"You know I will."

Outside it started to rain, tiny splashes hitting the window. He watched it for a while and shook his head. It smelled like the garden in the kitchen. He picked up a bean longer than his finger and broke off one end and then the other. He broke it in the middle and tossed the two pieces in the bowl. He dropped the ends in the sack his wife had placed on the floor. He looked at it. She'd rolled down the top edges of the sack, like always. Damn what a careful and deliberate woman.

"I've been thinking about Ollie," she said.

"What about him?"

"I wonder what he's up to. What he does all day."

"So drive out there and see him."

"I hate to bother him."

"Bother him?" he said. "How could you bother him? He ain't doing nothin."

"Well, he's got his life and I don't want to meddle."

He didn't say anything. Sometimes while fishing at night a big flathead would smash a bluegill you'd hooked as bait and the monster cats were so smart they'd wrap the line around the hundred-year old stumps where they lived. And there it'd stay, still hooked, sawing the line back and forth. When this happened, you'd still feel the flathead. You couldn't see it, couldn't get it netted. Yet the line remained fast—you on one end, not wanting to cut the line, and the fish on the other, not quite strong enough to break free. Once in a while the flathead would jerk to remind you it was still hooked. Once in a while you tugged to wake it up and make it jerk again.

He thought that Ethel had the same kind of relationship with their son. Ollie was nothing more than a big stubborn flathead living in a dark hole somewhere under swirling muddy water. And she was somewhere above, trying to lure him to the surface.

Frank thought he'd done enough for the boy. What he'd done was buy that trailer off of Peggy Goodpastor after her father died in it. Peggy had put her dad in a new trailer next to her house about fifteen years ago, and when he finally died, she wanted to sell it so she could put her garden back there and look out the windows on that side of the house and not see the trailer all the time. So Frank bought it and hauled it to the backside of the farm on 450 North. And he paid to get it hooked up—had a well dug and a septic tank buried.

It was understood that Ollie would pay rent, and he did. But he did it on his schedule. At first he paid monthly. Then he had to work a bunch of overtime at Sellers and he paid for two months at once. But then on the third month he was late. Once he'd been two months behind. Anymore, he paid by dropping a check in the mail. It pissed Frank off that his own son mailed the rent check to him. Of course, it really hurt Ethel, and that angered him more.

But he never called Ollie and asked for the rent. He never told him he was hurting his mother. He just let him do whatever the hell he was doing out there in the trailer.

He realized she'd been speaking again and made an effort to listen.

"Do you?" she asked.

"Right," he said. "Wait. What?"

"I said, maybe we should go over there sometime. Take him some groceries or something to eat."

"You don't think he eats? Chub told me he saw him at the store buying groceries just last week."

"Did he talk to him?"

"Which one do you mean?"

"I mean, did Chub talk to Ollie. What else could I be meaning?"

"I don't know. Some talk, I guess. Asked him how he was doing, that kind of thing."

She sat there, thinking about that.

"You ought to go over there," she said. "You need to apologize to him."

"What the hell for?"

"Well, you yell at him. And then that time you hit him, when he was helping you with the hay cutter."

"I ain't apologizing for that. He tried to hit me. And besides, we done talked to him since then."

"Not enough, we haven't."

"If you want to see him so bad, just call him up and tell him to come over here. I ain't driving all the way out there just to find out he's probably gone anyway."

She remained quiet, shaking her head a little.

The bastard, Frank thought. What good was having a son, if he turned out like this?

They continued snapping the beans, and she rose occasionally to empty the bowl. The sack of ends was growing, too. It was still raining. Before long they finished. That would be it, for another year. The last big batch, she'd said.

Chub answered the phone like he'd just pulled his head from a bucket of water.

"What's wrong with you?" Frank asked.

"Who the hell is this?"

"You know who it is. You wanna go to the river?"

There was silence on the other end, and he assumed Chub was mentally checking his calendar, which should've been as clean as a hospital sheet.

"Who the hell are you?" Chub asked.

For the first time since he'd dialed the numbers on the rotary phone Frank got nervous. Chub wasn't the kind of guy who played a clever joke.

"It's Frank, dammit! Time's wastin. Let's take my boat out."

More silence.

Ethel walked through the kitchen with a basket of laundry and she heard enough to stop and listen, watching the expression on Frank's face.

When Chub spoke again, though, he sounded more like himself. "Frank. Jesus," he said. "You woke me up and my mind went fuzzy on me."

"I wondered about you there for a minute."

"Me, too. I was wondering who was callin me."

"Well, I was wantin to ask you about going to the river."

"Whenssat?"

"Today. Right now. We can get lunch at the diner if you was wantin to eat something first. Wifey was gonna fix me something, but I can eat at Lila's."

"Oh, today?"

Frank wasn't a speedy man, in motion or in wit. But damn, this was beginning to test even his ideas about how rapidly a conversation should evolve. "Hell yes, today!"

"Well. I don't know if I oughtta do that, or not."

"Why in the hell wouldn't you? It's rainin, ain't it."

"Yeah, but I heard they's callin for storms," Chub said.

"So?"

"Maybe I better not today. Tomorrow, for sure."

"You all right?"

"Oh sure. But I don't know that I better fish today."

"If I stay home, the wife will fall in love with me all over again, you know."

He laughed. "That sounds right."

"I'll call you first thing tomorrow then."

"That's better."

"Bye."

"Hey Frank! Wait on something here. You think you could still go eat at Lila's? I ain't got much around here."

"I'll come by there and get ya. Just be ready."

He waited for the sound of Chub hanging up, but it wasn't there. He listened for a while longer.

"Bye then," Chub finally said.

"See you in a minute."

"See ya."

He hung up and looked at Ethel, who'd been standing there with the laundry basket on her hip the whole time.

"He was sure screwed up this morning," he said.

"It sounded like it. Didn't he know who you was?"

"Not for sure, he never. And it took him about forever to find out."

"Maybe he'd been drinkin."

He looked at her angrily. "No, he wasn't."

He was glad to see Chub outside, doing something in his garage. As he parked Chub turned and waved. Rain drizzled on the windshield.

Frank walked in and peered over his shoulder to see what was in front of him on the workbench. A baitcasting reel, sideplates off. He had cotton swabs and a can of WD-40 nearby, cleaning out river sand.

"Howdy partner," Frank said.

"Hello back." He turned to shake his hand.

Frank thought his hand felt a little clammy, but he looked about normal. He wore a green t-shirt under his overalls. Hair stuck out from under his International hat. Frank could smell him a little bit, something not entirely pleasant, but that too was normal. Sometimes Chub showered every day, sometimes he couldn't make time for it. One time he stunk so bad that Frank could smell him from the back of the boat. All day he smelled him. After a while Frank left a little shad guts on his hands instead of rinsing them over the side so he could smell something else for a change.

"Sand gets everywhere, don't it?"

"It does," Chub said. "And I ain't had no breakfast yet."

"You already missed breakfast and you're fixin to miss lunch. Let's go see em."

The café they frequented was owned by a woman they'd known since school. Lila ran the café with her daughters now. It stood on an empty stretch of highway just outside of town in a building that had housed a family in its previous life. Lila's grandmother's, in fact. Customers parked in a gravel lot that had been the backyard.

They found seats at a little table by the front window and Lila herself saw them and rumbled over. Frank hated to walk into the cramped restaurant too far on account of his cane. It was hard for Chub to squeeze past too many tables, as well. They were happy to get their favorite table and happy to have her serve them, too.

"Here comes big ol cow tits," Chub whispered.

Sure enough, Lila arrived and stood over them, notebook in hand and her bosom all but blocking out the overhead lighting.

"Well, if it ain't my two favorite fishermen!" she said, too loudly. "Every time it rains, I say to the girls, look out for those two dirty catfishers, they'll be comin!"

"You know us too well, Lila," Chub said.

"Except today we're just eatin," Frank said.

"Well they say wonders never ceased and now I believe that one. What can I get you two gents this day?"

"I want the breaded tenderloin," Chub began.

"Same as always, in other words," she said, writing it down on her little pad.

"Yeah, I reckon so. Same as always."

Frank wanted the fish sandwich and fries. She wrote it down.

"How come you write it down if you already know what we's wanting?" Chub asked. He didn't flirt often but she brought out his best efforts.

"Oh, you know," she said, quieter now. "Soon's I find a cook smarter than his skillet I'll be all right, you know what I mean?"

She laughed then, a hearty, chest-shaking laugh. Her breasts heaved. She leaned down to share a secret, and the boobs fell like giant boulders from the sky. If they'd hit the table, it would've smashed to the ground in a cloud of splintered particle board and two-by-fours. The two men looked up at them as if Jesus himself were coming forth.

She kept her hair dyed red and wore too much make-up for a woman in her sixties. Now she was closer and they could smell her perfume. It was too strong for Frank, but Chub breathed in deeply.

"I'm about ready to hire me a Mescan," she whispered.

"A what?" Chub asked.

"A Mescan. To cook." She looked at Chub, but he was politely staring at the top of her shirt, where the mounds of her breasts were visible and white.

"You gonna hire a Mexican in here?" Frank asked.

"Oh yeah," she said, glancing back and forth at both of them. "I been hearin about them and their work habits. A Mescan will work for nothing and never miss a day. That old boy I got back there now is white, but he's so screwed up with his liquor he's about half cocked when he gets here."

Her breasts retook their rightful place above them. "I'll have this food right out to you sweethearts. And two coffees, like you like it."

After she left, they looked at each other and chuckled. "Remind me to ask about the help next time," Chub said.

The restaurant was halfway crowded for once and they watched people come in and sit down. Mostly working men, a construction crew clearing out under power lines. You could hear a lot of cussing. Lila made her rounds, laughing and talking.

"You seemed kinda out of it this morning," Frank said. "You feelin all right?"

Lila brought waters, and they held the cool glasses in their worn hands.

"I know I was. I don't know what gets into me sometimes."

"Does it happen a lot?"

"Bout once a day or so I get to where I wake up and don't know where I am. I might be napping in my chair and when I wake up I swear I can't place nothin."

"You see the doctor?"

"Hell nah. He'd only say I's getting old."

"You might want to, though."

Chub took a drink of his water and nodded. He stared at the red plastic glass. There was something crusted near the lip and he chipped it off with his thumbnail. "I might," he conceded.

"Have it checked out, anyway."

"Yeah, maybe so." He looked up as a young man in khakis and a collared shirt walked in and sat down at the table next to theirs. Lila came to take his order.

"What can I get you, mister?" they heard her say. Because they were all sitting in an old living room, it wasn't difficult to overhear conversations. Once they'd listened in as a man and woman talked about her being pregnant.

It hadn't been a happy chat.

"Well," the young man said, "I'm afraid I'll need a few moments. I've never eaten here before."

"You haven't? I didn't think I'd seen you before! Well, welcome to Lila's! And that'd be me. Who are you, and what in the world brings you out to these parts?"

"Uh, Steve. Steve Dunkirk. And work, actually. I'm a Project Manager for the U.S. Army Corps of Engineers, and so I'm here to study—"

"Army! You don't look like no five-star general!" She laughed good-naturedly in his face.

Frank turned in his seat to see and hear better. The young man was blushing now, explaining that civilians could work the Army Corps of Engineers.

"Don't you worry, honey," she interrupted him, "I aim to serve all branches of the military. You sit here and think about what you want to eat and then you holler at me, kay?" She snapped off a salute and went to the kitchen through a swinging door at the back of the room. Steve looked at them.

"What's good here, fellas?"

"The tenderloin's awful good," Chub said.

"Is it? I believe I'll try that, then."

"What was it you said you was here for?" Frank asked.

He watched as Steve's eyes surveyed the room before speaking. "Well, I work for the U.S. Army Corps of Engineers," he began, "and I'm managing the project we've begun feasibility studies on."

"And what project is that?"

There were probably twenty customers in the room, almost all of them men. They were involved in their own lives and meals. Steve glanced again at them before answering.

"Well, I'm primarily concerned with flood control. That and municipal use, which means things like drinking water. This project is slated to become a State Recreational Area, providing boating and fishing access, as well. Fish stocking would be managed by your state DNR...."

Lila appeared then with their food—Chub's tenderloin hanging out over the bun, almost as big as the plate itself. She put the platters down along with two cups of coffee, steaming.

"Here you go, fellas," she said. "Can I get you anything else?"

"Ketchup," Chub said.

"It's already there!" Lila said in her loud voice, pointing down.

"Oh, I see it," he said. "I guess it got lost in the shadows." He winked up at her.

"And now you're probably ready to order," she said to Steve. "And by the way, you won't want to get too involved with my catfishers here. They're bad news bears."

"I believe I'll have the tenderloin, as per this man's suggestion," Steve said. "And a Coke with that."

Lila looked at him funny before writing it down and returning to the kitchen.

Chub tore open three sugar packets from the dish on the table and poured them into his coffee. He tipped the ketchup over his fries and tenderloin. Frank was still looking at Steve.

"So what project was that, again?"

"Well, you've probably heard of it, but I'm here to help determine the feasibility of the project—"

"Where, though?"

Steve met his stare. "The one involving a section of Big Logjam River, outside of the town also named Logjam. Near here, also in Shipley County."

"I thought so. You sons a bitches."

Chub stopped eating and looked from Frank to Steve, who had lifted his hands, palms out.

"Now hold on," Steve said. "There's a process we follow, and we ascertain where we can do what we need to do with a minimum of contingencies, and any effected landowners are compensated fairly, after public meetings, which allow for—"

"I want to ask you something, mister, since you're supposed to know. These people along here, who are out to lose everything. What happens to them? Their houses?"

"Well, we certainly hope many people aren't affected—" Frank rolled his eyes and so Steve sped up—"but those who are will have their property appraised, and they'll be compensated, but we also have real estate people who help landowners relocate, buying comparable property nearby, where applicable—"

"You'll buy it, in other words."

"Well, not me, exactly, but the federal government, yes."

"And what if the landowners don't sell?"

"Uh, sir, we intend to have public meetings for this sort of debate...."

"What's wrong with us talking a little right here?"

Steve looked around. Some of the men had stopped eating and were watching. "Well the government does have the right of eminent domain," he said quickly.

"You'll take it, then."

"Now, again, this isn't really me we're talking about here. I work out of the Louisville District office, but I ultimately work for Colonel Haverstick of the U.S. Army...."

But Frank had heard enough. He grabbed his cane and started to walk out before he remembered Lila and stopped and drew a twenty out of his wallet and tossed it on the table. Chub stood up in a hurry and knocked his chair over. He righted it and grabbed both sandwiches from their plates before following Frank out the door. They heard Lila come out of the kitchen calling after them but they went on.

Out in the parking lot, a white sedan with mud splashed on the sides sat next to Frank's truck. The door of the car bore a placard that read U.S. ARMY CORPS OF ENGINEERS. Frank spat on it before he climbed into his truck. It had stopped raining but the car was still wet and the white spit bled into the raindrops.

CHAPTER EIGHTEEN

A year or even a month ago, he would've been worried sick about his truck. The dents would rust where the paint was broken and he hated driving a banged-up vehicle. But instead Ollie spent the week planning their first real date. He'd called Summer and set it up for tonight, and if she'd been too upset about the deer, he couldn't tell it. She promised to take the little kid to her mother's house and leave her overnight so it'd be just them. All week at work he thought about the date and also what it might be like to slide those blue shorts down over her hips. There were red warning stickers on all of the dangerous equipment at work, and someone should've slapped one on his forehead.

They'd built a new movie theater over in Green City. The Shipley Current ran a photo of the building under construction. He only happened to see it because Doug Sellers left the newspaper in the toilet stall at the sawmill. He hated like hell to drive an hour each way to Green City, but seeing a movie was a real date and that's what she deserved. They'd be on the highway most of the way, but if they got stuck behind some farm equipment being moved from field to field it might add another twenty minutes. And last but not least, he wasn't going to pay about fifteen bucks to see a movie with a bunch of cartoons running around. He wanted something with people shooting stuff in it—maybe some nudity if he could get it. He intended to pick her up, drive to Green City, check out the movie times, and eat at Pizza Hut.

She opened the door Friday evening, and it was the first time he'd seen her after she'd prepared herself specifically for a date. Her shirt fit tightly and was open at the neck, the V plunging down far enough he could see her tanned chest and the valley between her breasts. Some sort of medallion dangled around her neck. She'd straightened her hair and it seemed shinier. She hugged him and turned to check the house one more time before he realized she was wearing a short denim skirt.

"Jesus Christ, you look good," he said.

She turned a light on in the kitchen. "I'm not sure how much He had to do with it, but thanks anyway. He surely wasn't with me in the shower, I know that."

"Well, He at least shoulda been looking down through the roof."

She screamed a laugh. "Ollie! Boy, do you even think before you say something?"

"Not as much as I try."

"I can tell. But I'll tell you what, it felt good to get cleaned up tonight. A lot of times, me and Spring just rent movies on Friday nights."

"How's your nose feel?"

She walked right up to him, her face only inches from his. "Look at it," she said. "Does it look crooked to you now?" She smelled very clean and her perfume reminded him of when she'd kissed him on the couch.

He stared at the freckles sprinkled across her nose and cheeks. His eyes kept sliding off her nose into her eyes. They were blue with brown specks. "I think it looks great," he said, and his voice cracked.

"It still hurts me, though," she whispered.

"I am so sorry about that."

He made up his mind to kiss her but she stepped away the second he told his muscles to move. "Let's get going," she said.

They walked outside; she left the light by the door on. By the time he'd turned the truck around in the driveway she was sitting snugly right up against him. She dug the lap seatbelt out from the hinge and put it around her waist.

As he drove she had quite a bit to say about what her daughter had been up to. Nothing was being left out, it seemed. Something about saying juice had 'gone runnin.' As in 'Mommy! Look! My ju-ju is gone runnin under the couch!' Summer had been angry about it, she said, but sometimes Spring was so cute you couldn't help but laugh. He listened and laughed when it seemed right to do so.

Nothing else was said about the deer accident, thank God. More than once, late at night, he'd seen the doe flailing on broken legs. He worried she was haunted by it, too.

"We had an incident at work today," she said. "Well, almost."

"Did you drop the phone book on your toe?"

"Ha ha very funny. Did you cut your hands off at work this week, thinking about me?"

His stomach tightened. Maybe she'd been watching him through the roof! "Yes," he said, holding up his cut finger, "I did."

"Yuck! That's nasty looking. But it looks like it healed fast, if it happened this week."

He laughed. "Yeah, no, that's older. I did that out at my parents' place a while back. Thanks for saying yuck about it."

"Sorry. I saw it earlier, when we was at Dairy Queen. I was going to ask you about it."

"What stopped you, your gag reflex?"

"Did you want to hear about my work incident, or not?"

"All right then. Start talking about work, how about?"

"Well, this guy storms in, all pissed off about his electric bill. Get this—he's got his shirt off. And I'm like, mister, I know it's hot out, but do you not put on a shirt to go into the power company?"

"Damn hilljack."

"Exactly. And the guys are out back. So he starts yellin about how he can't be usin that much power. And I'm like, sir, the meters don't usually make mistakes, but if you want it reread, fine. But he's like this can't be right. And finally I stand up to go get Hank from out back, and that's when I smell him."

"Uh oh."

"Right. He stinks to high heaven. And I'm like, okay, mister, now I know you aren't using much water!"

He laughed but he thought back to the night he met her, his confidence plummeting. Had she smelled him that night? She must've! On the other hand, she was still here, and he'd showered well tonight.

"I really want to be a teacher," she said. "This job is only until Spring goes to school, then I aim to start taking classes at Ivy Tech so I can get certified to teach."

"You don't have to move to go there, do you?"

"No, I'd drive to it. You can take classes up here in Green City, at least for the first couple years."

"Long drive."

"I'd do it, though, if I could teach."

"Did you want to go to college after you graduated?"

"Not really. Sort of. I was dating Mr. Dumbass by then and I wanted to take one year off, cause I was about burnt out on school, but then before too long I got pregnant and never got to go."

"I never went either," he said.

The sun was setting out his window but there was still plenty of light. They'd driven about thirty minutes on the highway and they came to the bridge where the interstate crossed over, connecting Cincinnati to Indianapolis. A gas station stood there, alone in the cornfields.

Someone had sprayed big, black letters on the overpass.

He slowed. "Hey, looks like somebody left us a message."

She leaned forward. JULIE HOGSETT FUCKS NIGRS it read, passing overhead.

They looked at each other, eyes and mouths wide open.

"Oh my God!" she yelled. "Did you see that?"

"Hell yes I saw it!" He was laughing. "Do you know her?"

"No I don't know her, but oh my God!" She looked back as if to read the words again.

He thought that was a pretty damned funny way to get back at a chick— paint it on the bridge for everyone to see. He imagined the guy going out there at three in the morning, hanging over the side, spraying the letters upside down. Maybe he got tired, and that's why the last word was shortened.

Or maybe he thought the cops were coming.

"Who would write that?" she asked.

"Some guy. I'd say some guy Julie dumped for some black guy."

"But the whole world'll see that!"

"I bet her daddy's done seen it by now."

"Oh no," she said, grabbing his arm. "What if her parents really do see it?"

"I guess they'll know, then. I don't reckon somebody'd paint that if it wasn't true. Do you?"

She laughed a little. "I bet they know who did it."

"Yeah. Her daddy'll see that, and he'll say to her mama, 'well, I know why we ain't seen Danny Dale round here no more.'"

They laughed. Ollie wondered where Julie'd found a black man to screw. She must've gotten on that interstate and driven for a good ways. Maybe that was why Danny Dale painted it up there—because that was part of it.

"They better get that covered up," Summer said. "Soon."

As they started through the first stoplights marking the edge of Green City, it occurred to Ollie that he didn't know where they'd built the new theater. He'd counted on finding it as he drove into town, but now they were here and suddenly it seemed like a ten-screen theater complex could be hidden anywhere among these buildings and restaurants. There were a lot of cars out, even for a Friday night. He felt a little sweat trickle down his back under his clean black shirt. At every stoplight, he went straight, heading downtown to the courthouse square. That didn't seem right but taking a right or left seemed like a bigger decision. He spun his head around, trying to see a neon sign or even a large parking lot. And he never thought he'd think this, but it was a little cramped with her sitting right next to him. He wondered if she felt the heat radiating off of him.

It was getting dark, and the headlights of the oncoming cars made it harder to see. He noticed he was low on gas, and a gas station appeared ahead on a corner. The road had turned into a four-lane street now, and there were offices, apartment complexes and fast food joints on both sides. Cars were flying by him in the left lane. He made a quick right into the gas station.

"I better get some gas first," he told her.

As he pumped, she got out and went to use the restroom. He watched her walk and ended up putting in more than the ten dollars he intended to. He stopped instead at twelve.

Inside, a woman with jet-black hair sat on a stool behind the counter smoking a stubby cigarette. He walked up and she stared at him. Summer was still in the restroom so it seemed like a good time to ask.

"Howdy," he said, laying a ten and a five on the grimy counter in front of her.

"Howdy yourself," she said and hit some buttons on her register. "That all for ya?"

"Yeah. Hey listen. Where's that new theater at?"

The drawer slid open and she lifted the catches and tucked his money away. He watched her mouth but it didn't move. What the hell was taking her so long to speak? He heard a door close somewhere and Summer walked up and stood by him. Great, now one more secret was out.

The woman stopped pulling change out of the slots and stared straight ahead, at the register itself. He assumed she was thinking of the best way to get there. Then she counted out three singles and turned to look at him.

"Son, I hope you never drove too far to see a movie tonight."

"Oh yeah?" he asked. "Why is that?"

"Cause it ain't built yet."

"How's that?"

"It ain't built yet! They ain't gonna have it done til September. That's a full month away yet."

He stared at the clerk and saw a smile creep into the corners of her mouth. Her lipstick was cracked. "Sorry about that, honey."

He looked at Summer. She giggled and lowered her head. "Ah shit," he said. "Well, what the hell is up with that?"

On the drive back to Logjam they laughed about it. They'd gone to Pizza Hut, since they knew where that was, but they couldn't think of anything else they wanted to do in Green City.

"We could go to Walmart, make you watch me buy diapers," she said. "But no thank you. I'd like one night off, at least."

"Do you always buy your stuff over here?"

"Pretty much. The big stuff, anyway. Like Walmart stuff."

"If you come here all the time, why didn't you know about that theater?"

She laughed. "Oh no, you're not putting this on me! I come here for diapers, not to see movies. You're the one who's supposed to know about movies." She made her hand a gun and poked him in the shoulder.

"You know, I'm not usually this much of a fuck-up."

"Oh, sure."

"No, I mean it. Just around you."

"I can vouch for that part."

"I coulda sworn that thing would be open."

She reached into her pocket and pulled out the roll of candy. She unwrapped one end and put a wafer in his mouth and then took one for herself.

"You were smart to get those Neccos," he said.

"Tell me about it. A reminder of my big date with Tractor Guy."

"At least I paid for them."

"True."

He glanced at her and only saw what the lights from the dash illuminated, but she was looking straight ahead and smiling. She looked happy. When they went under the overpass, they turned to read it again, but it was too dark to make it out.

"We could watch tv for a while," she suggested. "Go back to my place. Or yours, if you want. You still haven't showed me where you live."

"Let's go to your place," he said.

"I keep thinking a deer is going to jump out in front of us," she said. "Are you watching what you're doing?"

"Sure. Always."

"I saw you look at me back there a ways."

"What? Why would I do that?"

"You know," she said, putting her hand on his leg, "if you can't drive and look at me at the same time, you could stop driving."

His throat closed so thoroughly he couldn't make a sound.

"Your house?" he croaked. It was still thirty minutes a way. He'd never make it now. With his elbow he pushed down an erection so fierce he thought it might catapult the steering wheel into outer space.

"What's wrong with a little adventure?" she asked.

He swerved down the next road they came to, barreling past dark houses and empty barns. A few turns later they parked on a dirt road leading to a cornfield. It was quiet and dark and stars shone out the windows.

He kissed her and she leaned back until he was on top of her on the bench seat. She raised her left leg, sliding it up the seat and hooking it behind him and he settled his hips into the space between her legs. He stopped kissing her long enough to look down. Her skirt was pushed up and the v of her underwear was visible. Her panties were white against her dark skin and the inside of her skirt and he looked so he'd remember the sight forever. She pulled him down and kissed him and he could hear her breath quickening in his ear. He pushed his hand down between her legs.

"You gotta have something," she said.

He did and he reached up and opened the glovebox. He shook out the whole box on the floor and grabbed up a row of condoms and bit one off the end.

"Good," she whispered. "But you don't have to rush. We got all night, remember."

He tried to do everything slowly but every little detail was so much better than what he'd had before, so surprisingly improved, he found himself believing he could always do it better the next time. He rushed through every step and when he came she was on top of him, her hair falling like a shroud around his face.

She cupped her hands around his ears and whispered, "Almost makes you glad they didn't get that stupid theater done, doesn't it?"

As good as it was in the pickup it was a million times better back in her bed. When he staggered out to his truck to drive home he was amazed to hear the morning birds calling in the gray chill of dawn. Where had the night gone? But he didn't really care. You could take everything he'd ever have or stand for and put it in a giant sack and he'd give it all up for a night like this. He drove home saying her name over and over.

CHAPTER NINETEEN

The jars three-fourths full of snapped and cleaned green beans rocked back and forth in the water of the steaming pot. The whole house smelled of steam and vegetables. The windows stood open, but no breeze moved through, and Ethel felt as if she were turning green inside from breathing the scent. The countertop was lined with jars, cooling on flattened towels. She wanted to get this done yesterday, but he'd come home from the diner so worked up they'd spent the afternoon out in the tool shed, wire brushing rust off a set of old metal chairs. He didn't want to talk, but she knew he'd be better if he had tools in his hands. Today he was back in the woods on his three-wheeler and he was still upset.

While she waited for the jars to get hot enough to seal, she sat at the table and read the newspaper in snatches. They only took the Shipley Current, but she read almost every page. Sometimes she got frustrated with the surplus of nonsense in it. This time they'd printed a picture of a boy sitting on a tractor with his father. The caption read, "Ride to School! Little Woods Carter, a student at North Shipley Elementary, got picked up by his father, Ralph Carter, in order to get a ride to school on an old Oliver tractor." She smiled at that, remembering how Frank had picked their son's name.

Mandy Mayfield's column recorded local events and sometimes offered recipes. Today she'd written: "The Petersons were visited by their grandchildren and daughter last Saturday. The visitors came from Columbus (IN), where their daughter Sally works for Cummins Diesel. Chet Baker is feeling better this week, and he thanks everyone who stopped by the convalescence center to wish him a speedy recovery. Keep coming! He says. Little Lucy Baker fell off her bike and scrapped both knees. She's alright, her mother says. Within two weeks, the Stumpke's (Barb and Dick) should be graced by their first grandchild. Goodluck! Barb and Dick! Maybe Dick will get a grandson to help with the farming!"

She read Mandy's column every issue, but Ethel never saw her name in it, nor Frank's. One time it made mention of someone's cat having kittens. Why, they had batches of kittens in their barn every week in the spring! And now it felt like the world was conspiring against them out here and her column was the same as always.

When the phone rang it startled her, as it almost always did. She stared at it while it rang two more times before she answered.

"Hello darling. This is Hattie."

"Oh it is you, Hat. I called your house this morning but never got no answer."

"And how are you on this fine day?"

"I'm canning green beans and waiting for Frank to come in off his three-wheeler. He's all wrought up."

"Are your green beans on already? Is that right?" There was the snap of a lighter and the sound of Hattie sucking on a cigarette.

"Oh, we must've got about two bushel," Ethel said. "We snapped them two days this week."

"You know I love green beans!"

"These turn out, I'll bring you some."

"Well honey, that's why I was calling," Hattie said, pausing to exhale. "Next week we may have to do our usual hair appointment another time."

"I hadn't even thought that far ahead yet." Ethel held the phone and looked at the pot on the stove, the jars shuddering in the heat.

"You know why? Well, Rufus and I may take a little trip down to Gatlinburg."

"Oh, I see."

"That's right. For three days and two nights. Just the two of us. We got one of them cabins in the mountains down there. And, as you can tell, I'm just a little bit excited about it." She coughed.

Rufus Blaylock had been married twice. The ink on his second divorce was not yet dry. He'd been carrying on with Hattie for some time now.

"Now what do you think of that plan?" Hattie asked. "Darling, you are not usually this quiet."

"I'm sorry. It's just that, well, it's been a rough week for us, what with these lake people coming around and all. Frank's about beside himself with it."

"Oh that lake thing. I hear people talk about it in my salon, and I tell them, 'shut up now about that lake. They been saying it for years and nothing's come of it yet!' I want real gossip, you know, not some idle chatter bout some resy-for we ain't seen yet."

"Well."

"Oh honey, this trip is just what we need. I think it might lead to something grand."

Hattie had married three times. Her first two husbands died and left her a widow, though, so people gave her the benefit of the doubt. The third one was a drunk and got arrested four times for driving under the influence. People forgave her for divorcing him. And now she acted like she wanted to marry Rufus. It may get to be too much to even let her do her hair, Ethel thought. Much less be friends with her.

Ethel sighed. "Have a wonderful time. I always wanted to go down there myself."

"Whyn't you make Frank take you now? He ain't doing nothing."

"Oh, Hattie, we're too old. Plus, you know how he is. He likes to make sure

Wayne knows how to farm. Especially now."

"Wayne Shipps, the man that rents your ground? Now there's a lucky woman. His wife, I mean."

"And we can't leave now, what with people coming around here like they are."

"Well, honey, you make him take you to Gatlinburg. This fall yet, when the leaves is pretty."

"We'll see." She could see the next batch of jars were ready to be taken from the heat. It was unfortunate that she'd caught Hat right before a trip like this. Like most hairdressers Ethel had known, Hattie always wanted to talk about herself, but if you caught her when something was happening with one of her men you were better off talking to yourself.

"How long you gonna let him fish the river like that?" Hattie asked.

"What do you mean?"

"Well, how old is he?"

"He'll be seventy-five in December."

"Darling! Think about it. What if he were to have a heart attack out there? No one to save him or call for help excepting for that worthless piece of manflesh Chub Peters? What would you do then?"

Hattie knew husbands could die when you least expected it. One of hers had been shot while hunting deer. He'd been sitting up in his tree stand at the time. The other one went walking on a train trestle and a train came unexpectedly and left him with no choice but to jump into the rocky creek far below. It'd been late August, with not enough water in the creek to hide a salamander.

"I don't know what I'd do. How could I know such a thing?" Ethel asked.

"Well, you could make him stay home. Tell him not to go. Make him fish there on your place, where you can watch him better."

"I can't tell him what to do. He's set in his ways."

"All men are, honey. But that don't mean you don't try. Ethel, dear, I hate to be the one to tell you this, but we ain't gonna live forever. That's why I'm heading to Gatlinburg. I am gonna live whilest I can."

"That's all we can do. I guess that's all God wants us to do."

"Sugar, don't go getting all Jesus on me." She blew smoke into the receiver. "You know I about done lost my faith when my second man was taken from me and the one God sent to replace him was as dumb as a door tack and drunk as a skunk living under a bar."

"I need to tend to my beans, Hat."

"Well, now call me later and reschedule your perm appointment. If you're lucky, I'll have my Gatlinburg pictures made by then. We can sit around and talk and I'll fill you in on the latest. Because let me tell you, Rufus does know the latest. Techniques, that is!" She erupted in a cackle that ended in coughing.

Ethel said goodbye and hung up. She took the beans off the stove and looked out the window to see if Frank was back yet.

They came into the house together. Catfish still had a hard time getting over the biggest step into the house, but Frank would put a boot under his little yellow rump and boost him over the doorframe.

It was already lunchtime and she sat in her chair in the living room, folding the towels stiff from the clothesline. Frank walked in and lowered himself down in his chair. As soon as he took his weight off his legs and settled his butt into the familiar groove in the cushion, Catfish scampered into the center of the room and squatted on the rug. Before Frank could yell at him, a dark shadow rolled out from under the dog's rear. The puppy looked around, eyes half-shut in thought.

"Hey!" Frank called out. "Catfish! Quit that!"

She looked up and saw what was happening.

"I told you to get this dog out of here!" She swooped down on Catfish and hoisted him up, holding the surprised pup away from her body. She darted out of the room. Frank saw one drip fall from the puppy as they went by.

"Hold on," he yelled after her. "He can't just be outside by himself!"

He stood up and went to look out the kitchen window. She had her hands on her hips, looking down at Catfish. The dog was sniffing the grass, oblivious. He saw her lips move, scolding him.

Frank couldn't laugh when they returned but there was something comical about seeing this. Ethel hadn't even scolded Ollie, really. She'd rarely raised her voice against him, even when he started getting into real trouble. Frank remembered when the sheriff had called after he picked Ollie up for his DUI. She'd answered the phone and stood there and listened, hand across her eyes. It was almost two in the morning.

When they'd gone to get him out of jail over in Green City perhaps she knew it was too late to yell at him. He was already in his mid-twenties. You couldn't ground him, or take away his truck keys. Frank had been okay with yelling, that night and other nights. He'd walked his family out of the jail, put them inside the car, and turned around in the seat and faced his son, alone in the backseat as he'd been in the squad car. Oh, Frank had yelled at him. He told Ollie he wouldn't live in their house any longer.

But she'd just sat there in the passenger seat. When they got home and pulled the car into the shed, he could see she was crying, tears running unchecked down her face.

Now she scolded this little Labrador, who didn't seem to be listening. Frank knew he should gather paper towels and start cleaning up the puddle before it soaked far into the rug. But it was hard for him to bend over like that, especially after riding the three-wheeler all morning. He sure as hell couldn't get down on his hands and knees. He started to move toward the sink, where the roll of paper towels hung under the cabinet, but instead he chuckled as Catfish pounced on her feet.

The county newspaper lay on the table, partially opened. He failed to notice the little box in the corner of the page beneath him. Inside the box were words announcing the public meeting—the one hosted to give locals a chance to speak out concerning the new reservoir proposal.

Fifteen miles away, Norman Fisk got in his Dodge dually and prepared to leave his cabin in the woods. Because it was Saturday, he allowed himself a rare pleasure: he sat still for a moment and looked over this piece of property. Here he was, ten miles outside the closest town, on land he owned outright— almost a hundred and fifty acres, mostly wooded hills with old trees. Carved into the middle of it sat his cabin, two stories of whole cedar logs stacked so perfectly a wisp of air-conditioning couldn't slip out. It was his dream home, and he'd built it when he was thirty-three, eight years ago. The pole barn tucked behind the cabin against the bank of trees held his equipment and the stall for his daughter's horse, Mr. Pickles.

Inside the cabin, his wife Brandi carried around their third child in her womb while Cheryl and Jake watched TV. Brandi might've looked out the window to see him sitting in his truck in the driveway, gazing toward the cabin and the woods beyond it. If she had, she would've wondered what he was up to, because it was against his nature to rest. But she wouldn't have gone outside or even stepped on the porch and called to him. When he was on his way to visit potential customers the rule was to leave him be.

And he allowed himself just a moment or two to stop and reflect over what he'd accumulated. Somebody might be walking up to a landowner right this very instant—a deal might be on the verge of being struck. The early bird got the worm in the land development business, he liked to say, along with the second house and the boat tied to the dock below it. If he could acquire enough future lakefront properties, he'd not only keep the pick of the litter for himself, he'd make enough to build a lake house and buy a ski boat. He cranked the big diesel over and drove out the winding lane. It'd cost a mint to blacktop the mile-long driveway, but it would've been a lot more if he didn't have a partnership with his buddy who owned a paving company. It was strictly a scratch-your-back, scratch-mine kind of deal.

He'd done a little research on this guy he was going to see, but still didn't know quite what to expect. Clarence Peters. Widower. Had one son who lived out of state. Owned three acres of what would someday be prime lakefront real estate, but was now your average, seen-better-days shitty lot with a wood house and a dilapidated detached garage. AKA Chub Peters. What the hell kind of name was Chub, anyway?

But there was a nice little lot down the road from Chub's place, and he'd already driven out there. If everything went well over the next thirty-six hours, he'd own that property. He'd overpaid, probably, since the owner, an old woman not four feet high who seemed to be alone in the world with the exception of her lapdog, admitted she'd been waiting for a reason to check herself into a nursing home. She'd taken his first offer readily, and then tried to keep him around all afternoon. That poor old lonely bat couldn't've cared less about making money—she just wanted someone to visit her. He'd lowballed her, sure, but she might've taken even less.

If he got the same kind of luck today with this Chub character, he'd be a millionaire in a rivertown whorehouse. These three-acre lots on the outskirts of Logjam weren't crap to look at, but divided into half-acre lakefront lots, they'd turn from a pig that had rolled in shit into a pig that had rolled in shit and then been sprinkled with diamonds. He didn't know who would sprinkle a shitty pig with diamonds but the metaphor was clear.

The "PETERS" on the mailbox confirmed that he'd come to the right place. He drove in and parked behind the garage. The overhead doors were up. The place looked like hell—an old boat sat there, dented and faded. A pickup parked nearby looked even worse. The paint was peeling off the cinder-block garage.

The house itself looked pretty tight yet, but it was obvious no one inside could take care of it. Or no longer cared to. Weeds grew up alongside it; the shrubs almost reached the gutters, from which little maple trees sprouted. He parked and went into the backyard. An old picnic table sat empty and leaning. There was a big tub at the far end of the yard for some purpose, and a board nailed to the fence with dark stains on it. Serial killer, he thought. Victims in the basement. He always left his pistol in the glovebox but this place almost made him second-guess his policy.

He knocked on the flimsy storm door. The metal rang and echoed in the house. No one answered.

Someone was home, because the wood door stood open. He'd already noticed the storm door was unlocked. He knocked again, louder. This time someone yelled.

When the man came stumbling to the door, clearly just up from a nap, Fisk was surprised at the size of him. Most old men shriveled up, but this guy had swollen like a deer tick in a dog's ear. A big old blockhead wearing bib overalls and no shirt. This, Fisk thought, could make for an interesting afternoon.

"Howdy," the man said from the other side of the door, making no effort to open it nor invite him inside.

"How you doin, friend?" Fisk asked, eyeing the door latch. He relied on his handshake, and now he wasn't able to use his best weapon.

"Tired. You woke me up."

"Well, I ain't sellin nothing, if that's what you think. Which I wouldn't blame you if you was, what with someone comin to your door and all."

The big man raised his eyebrows.

"I'd like to talk to you about your place here, if I could. Maybe I could come inside and tell you what I had in mind? You got a real fine place here. I'll just be a minute."

The man thought and then pushed the door open. "It ain't very clean in here," he said.

"No worries about that."

Now that they were on the same floor, Fisk could look him in the eye. He was a big man himself, but he wore cowboy boots and this giant was still in his socks. Fisk shook his hand and introduced himself.

"I'm Chub Peters," the man said.

"You live out here alone, Chub?"

"Yeah, for about eight years now." He rubbed his eyes. It was clear to Fisk he'd been dead asleep and was having a hard time placing what was happening.

Chub turned and went into the living room, and Fisk followed. The room was sunlit and bare. The curtains to the sides of the windows looked as transparent as plastic sheeting, and there was little in the room besides the TV, a dusty armchair and a big recliner that seemed well broken-in. The house smelled strongly of body odor.

Chub dropped into the recliner and motioned for him to take the only other chair in the room.

"Nice house you got here," Fisk said. "They don't make em like this anymore."

Chub looked around as if noticing it for the first time. "Yeah, it's stood up all these years, anyway."

"Well, I'll tell ya why I come out here and bothered ya, Chub. I been out looking for some houses to buy. I got a daughter who needs a place to go, and I promised her I'd drive around and look for a well-built house like this one."

"They still put signs in front of the ones for sale?"

Fisk chuckled a little. "Well, I believe in going right to a man who's got something I'd like. I hate dealin with them real estate types. All they do is take their cut and they don't know nothing about the house they's sellin."

"You got that right, I suppose." Chub yawned, his mouth opening like a bear's.

"Well, this one is right where she and her husband would like to live. And this place looks about perfect for them."

"You'd offer to buy a house without checking it out first?"

"I know a good house when I see it. Plus, I do a little plumbing and construction myself, so I figure I can help em get it ready."

"Yeah, well, I ain't really interested," Chub said. "I ain't got nowheres else to go, and I don't feel like getting out and looking. I reckon I'll just stay here for a while yet."

Fisk sat forward in his chair, hands out in front of him, elbows on his knees. He stared at the carpet between his boots. A thin, industrial carpet worn even thinner by decades of traffic. It looked like it had sand ground into it.

"The thing is, I'm prepared to offer you cash for this place. Maybe more than you thought you'd get for it."

Chub stared at him, waking up now. He looked like he might be getting excited. Or pissed.

"Look, mister, I ain't never even thought about selling this place, and now to have you come in here and—"

"Whatta got, about three acres here?"

"Yeah, about that."

"I could give you a hundred thousand for it right now. All of it, right now."

Chub stared at him, then laughed.

Fisk could tell that the amount had surprised him. It was two times what the property was worth, and the big ol sleepy bastard knew it.

"Well," Chub finally said, "I'm happy for ya, that you can go around paying folks a lot of money for their places. But I'm at the point in my life where that kind of money don't really mean shit to me."

"Well, think it over, anyway," Fisk said, standing up. It was the answer he expected. A little stronger than most, perhaps, but doable. Right on schedule. "I'll get outta here and let you get back to what you were doing. It's just that my daughter really wants a place like this, and I'd like to take care of her."

"No problem," Chub said, still sitting.

Fisk had business cards but you couldn't give those out on a trip like this. Not after the story he'd told about his daughter. "Why don't I give you my number, and that way you can call me after you think about it?"

"I don't see why not."

"You got a pen and paper?"

"No. Not handy, anyway."

Fisk stood by the recliner, looking down at him. "I got some in the truck.

I'll go get it and come back and give it to ya."

"Tell you what, write it on there and maybe leave it under a rock out there on that picnic table. I'm fixin to head out that way, anyway."

Fisk stuck his hand out and Chub took it.

"Nice talking with ya, Chub."

"Same here."

Fisk walked out the door. You couldn't expect a home run every trip to the plate. But he'd come back. Next time the big dude would know who he was, and he would've been thinking about the offer. Fisk knew how it went. People thought about getting some money in their hands and starting over. Suddenly they wouldn't need to mow the same old yard again, or paint the damn fence one more time. All the problems they'd been staring at for years would disappear—the toilet that wouldn't flush right, the leaning basement wall. It was the chance they were all waiting for, and he gave it to them.

This Chub, he'd take it, too.

Fisk scribbled his name and number and left it on the table as instructed. The old bastard, he thought, too good to let him back into the house. He had to hand it to the fat sack. Oh well. He'd be handing it to him again when he hired his dozer guy to knock this house and garage down.

CHAPTER TWENTY

The ringing phone woke him up Saturday afternoon but he came to with a smile on his face. Ollie wasn't a religious man but he'd thanked God so many times last night he half expected to hear His booming voice on the other line saying, "Glad you liked her, my favorite son." He tugged himself free of the tangle of sheets and slid along the wall toward the phone, which rang on, patiently. Maybe it wasn't God at all but the Devil, fussy like some collection agent, telling him he owed his soul for last night. Whatever. Now that he'd met her, it was like the difference between living in a house without electricity and one with. She lived so close—why hadn't he found her sooner? He'd ask whichever omnipotent being was calling.

"Don't tell me you're still asleep," she said.

"Summer!"

"Who'd you think it was?"

"It seemed like it coulda been anyone." He sat heavily on a stool at the kitchen bar and put his face in his hand.

"Nice, sucker. Just how many girls call your house?"

"Not as many as you think."

"Now I know why they don't."

He opened his mouth but couldn't say anything.

"Ha! Totally got you there. Just playing with you. Well, get ready to go hiking."

He was still stunned.

"You roger that? Get ready to go hiking, I said. Get over here and pick us up. We've been ready for hours."

"Hiking? Where?"

"At the park. It's a perfect day for it."

He looked up without lifting his head off his hand. Indeed, a warm glow came through the dirty curtains hanging over the living room window.

"Well, I guess we'll have to come pick you up, then," she said. "Give us directions to Oliver's House of Love Slaves."

"Wait." He'd caught enough of the pronouns to know her daughter was back in her possession. He pictured the toddler sliding around his floor on Playboys and 4-Wheel Drives. "I'm on my way there. Just let me put on my hiking boots."

He hung up the phone. It wasn't the Devil after all, but he'd just been told what he owed for last night.

Of course he didn't own hiking boots, nor any other piece of gear that invited exercise. Working in the hot sawmill kept him thin and wiry enough, but he had to admit his body wasn't what it once was. He'd tweezed out white hairs and beer seemed to settle around his gut more. Just last year his favorite jeans got noticeably tighter, so for two nights he did sit-ups in front of the TV. Then he said the hell with that.

But he was going to have to do something, because Summer was twenty-two, and kid or not, she was in shape like he couldn't believe. As he showered he fantasized about time travel—he'd be twenty-two and so would she. Course, if he could go back in time he'd prevent the pregnancy from ever happening. But that led him to thoughts about the conception, which infuriated him. So instead he fantasized about selling the kid and buying a new house with the money for Summer and him.

He drove there after showering and brushing his teeth, wearing his work boots. She met him in the backyard in green shorts and little hiking boots with red laces. What, did she do this all the time? He was in trouble. As he walked up he looked at her tan legs and remembered last night and leaned in to kiss her. She blocked it by putting her hands on his shoulders. He was surprised until he heard the door open behind her.

The little one stood there, pushing on the screen door. She wore matching boots—hers no bigger than coffee cups. Her shorts were puffy from the diaper underneath. Damn, kids were funny. She looked like a shrunken version of her mother.

"Hi!" Spring yelled.

"Hi there," he said.

"Hi!"

"Hi there, little hiker."

"Hi!"

Hell if he knew what else to say. He looked at Summer and grinned. "She's so cute."

"Are we ready?" she asked. She was either legitimately excited or faking it well.

"I know I am."

"Just let me grab a few things and we'll leave."

He followed her inside, stepping over the girl, who continued to play with the door. On the kitchen table sat a cooler and a big bag that looked like it carried all the baby stuff. He wanted something in his hands, so he grabbed both and turned to take them to the car.

"Hold on a second," she said. "I just remembered something. I wanted to put some more juice in there for her, but I'm out."

He stood there, his hands full. "Is that something we could get at the store out here?"

"Well, yeah I imagine Peterson's oughtta still have some juice laying around.

Unless a whole pack of toddlers busted in there last night and robbed them of their ju-ju." She laughed.

He smiled. Kid humor.

"Spring! Quit playing with that door and get in here," she called.

The little girl bounced by him and stood in front of her. He expected Summer to ask if she could live without her precious ju-ju for a few hours.

"I gotta run to the store, sweetheart. You wanna go with me, or stay here with your toys and Ollie?"

"I'll go!" he shouted.

"Stay wif Ah-ee," the girl said. "Stay wif Ah-ee!" She looked up at him with her little imitation Summer eyes.

"That settles it, then," Summer said, grabbing her purse off the counter. "See you in a little bit." She looked at him and winked.

"Hold up a second, now. I don't see why—"

She walked up to him and pinched his lips shut with her thumb and forefinger. "Just go in the other room and play with dolls for five minutes, big boy," she said quietly. With that she went out the door and he heard her car start. He was still holding the cooler and diaper bag. The little girl looked at him.

"Doll time," he said, dumping the stuff back on the table.

She ran into the living room and he followed her. Hard to imagine he'd walked through here at five this morning. And now he was back, settling down on the floor, a doll with a puckered mouth in his hand.

"Hey there, little girl," he made the doll say in its ridiculous doll voice. "What're you doing today?"

She looked at his face and then the doll standing there and smiled.

"How was work this week?" the doll asked.

She laughed.

"Hey kid! Does your mommy like this guy holding me?"

More laughter from the girl. The doll danced back and forth.

"Cause he sure likes her! He got it on with her! He thinks she's hot as balls!"

She squealed as the doll gyrated up and down.

He knew it was wrong but he didn't know how to handle kids and never claimed to. He knew if he checked the fridge, it'd be about half-full with juice.

Spring laughed until she suddenly became fixated on a wooden spoon. She poked and scratched the carpet with it, jabbering nonstop. He lay there on his stomach, doll in hand, and watched the little girl's face as she played. Her tiny nose looked just like her mama's. And of course her blue eyes and blonde hair. He wondered what she'd gotten from her daddy. She really was a cute kid, but he knew they said that about all babies, and they sure as hell couldn't all turn out cute. If every cute girl baby became a good-looking woman, how could you explain all those women he and Coondog picked up at the Depot?

A million years later, Summer pulled back into the driveway. What if something had gone wrong? He wouldn't have been ready for the smallest crisis.

The back door slammed. He waited for her. She walked in carrying a little box of juice pouches.

"Ahhh, look at that. Now that wasn't so hard, was it?"

"We got along famously!" the doll said.

"Great! Well, now we're ready," she said, and went back into the kitchen. He followed her, leaving Spring her spoon and an empty room.

Summer threw three juice pouches in the cooler and he carried it and the bag of baby gear to the car. They came outside then and he loaded the stuff into the dirty trunk of the Omni while Summer strapped the little one into the baby seat.

They'd need thirty minutes to get to the state park. He'd applied to work summers there, back when he was in high school, but no one even interviewed him. You needed to know someone to work there. It was a cherry summer job, they said, because the work was easy. Even if you were just a weed whacker, you got to work along the fence, and then you were getting paid to look at the girls tanning by the pool. So the story went, anyway.

As she drove they laughed about their date and the closed theater. They alluded to the bridge saying, but he knew not to say any of the words in front of the baby.

"Thanks for coming along today," she said.

"Hey, no problem. It gives me a chance to be with you and her both."

"Spring," she said. "Just try it. Sp...r...in...g." She drew it out, exaggerating the sounds.

"Hi mommy," she said from the backseat.

"Sure. Spring," he said. "I know her name."

Summer drove with two hands on the wheel, eyes straight ahead. "She's an important part of me, you know? We're a team, like I said."

"Hey, what's this about? It's not a big deal."

He knew he'd chosen the wrong expression when she looked at him. "Well it's a big deal to me!" she said. Then she added, whispering, "You need to know that last night is not something I make a habit of. Like, never. So. Just be aware of that."

"Well, I don't either."

"Right."

He looked out the window. A dog was lying in front of a house, chewing on the leather of an old ice skate. He looked at her again. "I am fully aware of the situation," he said.

"I'm just telling you. I don't want to be making a mistake here."

He started to ask how he could be a mistake but then decided not to. It was clear he needed to do something right today. No more mistakes or screw-ups. Last night showed how much progress he'd made, but he knew she was holding part of herself back. And the way to that part led through the little one, the child seated behind him, who was amusing herself by blowing air through her lips. Without turning around, he could imagine the spit all over her face, the mess she was making.

They parked at an open-sided shelter, where several families sat underneath the roof laughing and eating fried chicken from a paper bucket. Balloons swayed and bounced from the four-by-fours of the shelter. The sun shone brightly and the humidity was building. Beyond the shelter lay the woods and although it looked shady he knew it'd still be hot.

He put the strap of the diaper bag over his shoulder and lifted the cooler. Summer took Spring's hand and they walked by the shelter to the trailhead, marked with a board wood-burned to read Trail 3. As they walked, Spring kept her head held sideways, her eyes locked on the families with the chicken. He thought she was either really hungry or just wanted to hang out with the other little kids. Summer had to urge her along.

The dirt pack of the trail was worn smooth and they went up a ridge deeper into the woods. He led them up the trail, carrying the gear like a pack mule. But it wasn't very heavy and they weren't going very fast. They'd left the clearing of the shelter behind and now they walked surrounded by the trunks of hardwoods, the canopy over their heads shading them. Spring spent as much time bending over as she did walking, studying every leaf and stick. They'd hiked maybe fifty yards before coming to an area where the state had cut a swath of trees for an overhead power line, and here the sun could reach the ground. Wildflowers stretched away from the trail on either side, an aisle of purple and white.

"Look at the butterflies, honey!" Summer said, pointing. They flittered all around them—Monarchs, swallowtails, thousands of millers, all drawn to the sun and meadow flowers.

"Look at butt-flies," Spring said, her neck tipped all the way back.

He laughed and lowered the stuff. Far down the way a red-tailed hawk sat on the hulking metal frame of a power line pole.

"There's a big hawk," he said to Summer.

"Oh cool, I see it. Show her."

He knelt down to point it out. They'd mowed where the trail cut across the linear meadow, but as he got down by Spring's side he realized she could only see the weeds.

"You'll have to pick her up," Summer said.

And so he did, unsure of how to hold her. She weighed next to nothing but he knew there was a right way to do it. He held her against his body with his right arm and pointed at the bird. She stared at his face instead.

"See the big bird?" he kept asking. "Over there. See the big bird?"

She never took her eyes from the side of his face and he finally put her down. "I guess you'll have to go back to watching buttflies," he said and Summer laughed.

"Well, you tried," she said.

After a while they moved on down the trail. He thought for sure Spring would tire before he did but three hours later they were still out there, messing around in the woods. Spring had torn into two juice pouches and he'd downed two Mountain Dews. Together they'd found and lost about ten walking sticks for Spring, each one more important than the last. The longer ones Spring started bringing to him so he could break them down to her size over his knee.

The rain hammered against the roof above and he lay there and listened to that noise for a while. Thunder boomed in the distance. It sounded different over here. In his trailer, he could almost feel the raindrops plink on his skin as he lay in bed under that thin metal roof. Sometimes he half expected the sheets to get soaked. Now that he lived in a trailer, he knew why they always got demolished by tornadoes. Even a hard rain seemed to threaten his.

But over here, in Summer's house, with an attic, insulation, wood joists and two layers of shingles overhead, the rain sounded farther away. More rain. It seemed like it'd come down every day this summer. He rested on his back and imagined it running across the shingles and dripping into the gutters before flowing away. If he listened closely, listened under the rain, he could hear her breathing. She breathed as quietly as a kitten, each breath in and out as softly as if someone were dropping cotton balls on your cheek. That sound was something he could get used to every night. He stared at her face, watched her eyelids shudder as she dreamed. There was some bruising around her nose but not much. He noticed how perfectly the little hairs of her eyebrows lay against her skin. He'd never seen her asleep before. He checked the clock. Almost two a.m.

Suddenly he heard lightening rip through the air outside, bringing with it a tearing burst of light. The striking bolt hit something and reverberated, thunder shaking the house. He felt her jerk awake and put a hand on her shoulder.

She sat up. "Has she come in here yet?"

"No."

"This storm'll scare her to death. Get ready to hide behind the bed if she comes to the door."

"Okay."

They listened to the rain and thunder.

"I thought for sure she'd be crying by now," she said. "That was loud as heck." She lay back down next to him and put her arm over his chest.

"I guess she's wore out from hiking all day," he said.

They'd left the park and picked up some food at the Dairy Queen. All of them ate at the table in the kitchen. He hadn't eaten at a kitchen table in months, not since the last time he'd gone over to his parents'.

"I might as well get outta here, huh," he said.

"I hate to make you go home in this storm, but yeah, you better."

He didn't think she'd fall for it, but he lay still to allow her time to object. She didn't. She'd been nervous about this from the beginning, letting him back into her bed with Spring in the house. They'd watched TV after eating and when Spring went to bed they'd watched some more before wandering down the hall. But tonight nothing had happened. She'd said they could get under the covers but she was going to keep on her sweatpants and a T-shirt. And she had. She'd also set the alarm for five, so he could leave before Spring woke up. He was surprised Summer had fallen asleep at all, as anxious as she was. He stood and pulled on his jeans, which were wadded on the chair next to the bed. She sat up.

"You don't have to get up," he said. "I can let myself out and lock the door behind me."

"Are you sure?"

"I'll call you tomorrow."

"Okay." She lifted her arms to him and he kissed her. Her body was warm from being under the covers.

"Thanks for coming over today."

"I had a good time. I really did."

"If she hears you leaving, don't say anything."

"I won't."

In the front room he sat on the couch and pulled his boots on. The lightning made funny shadows across the carpet and TV screen. As he stood up, he looked out the window of the front door and waited for a strike to light up the lawn. He wanted to see how hard it was raining. He didn't have to wait long.

But when the flash came, his heart jolted as the lightning illuminated two trucks in the driveway next to the Omni. In the same burst of vision his brain registered both the strange truck and the fact that someone was standing outside the door, looking in.

CHAPTER TWENTY-ONE

Frank first thought, after being awakened by the horn, that the appraiser or someone like him had returned, and his initial idea was to grab the shotgun from where he'd recently leaned it in the corner of the coat closet. But when he got to his feet and peered out toward the end of the driveway, he recognized the truck and the giant shape behind the wheel. He took the padlock key from where he'd hung it on a nail by the door and let Catfish outside.

It was a long way to walk, this driveway. When they'd gone somewhere this week, like when Ethel took the car to get groceries, he'd driven out to the chain in his truck. Today the sun was shining, although they were calling for more storms tonight, and he decided to take the long walk to let Chub in. Maybe Catfish wouldn't pee in the house again if he had even more time to run around outside. As Frank walked the dog ran in widening circles across the yard. The truck waited for them, idling, front bumper near the chain and rear end still out on the gravel road.

Frank bent over the padlock without acknowledging his friend. The dog hunkered down by his feet, made nervous by the sound of the engine. He dropped the heavy chain to the gravel and bent over to grab Catfish's collar. Chub drove over the chain, the steel links clanking and popping under the off-road tires. He got past the chain and stopped. Frank picked up Catfish and jerked open the door with a screech.

"Give ya a lift," Chub said.

Frank pushed the pup across the seat and laid his cane on the floorboard before climbing in. Chub patted the dog's head and drove toward the house.

"That's a long way to walk," Chub said.

"Damn if it isn't. I about give out by the time I got there."

"You just put that chain up?"

"This week, I did. After that appraiser come out. Sorry to keep you waiting out there."

Chub nodded. He parked in the shade by the barn, not the house. They got out and Catfish jumped to the ground and scampered around the yard like he'd just been released from the pound.

"What brings you out this way, pardner?" Frank asked. He leaned against the bed and Chub did the same on his side. Inside the rusted-out bed were wadded-up wrappers from Dairy Queen and empty quarts of oil.

"Oh, I got some things on my mind I wanted to hash out in the open air."

"Not havin more dizzy spells, are ya?"

Chub shook his head no. His eyes scanned the yard for the dog and finally found him and watched him for a bit. "No, I had some prick come visit me. Offered to buy my place, right out of nowheres."

"Wanted to buy your place?"

"Hell yes, he did. Not three hours ago. Offering to pay a hundred thousand for it."

"While you were just sitting around there?"

"That's correct. I ain't shittin ya. Wanted to pay with a check."

They heard the sound at the same time and looked up to see Ethel come out of the house and walk across the grass toward them.

Frank looked back at him. "That's a high price."

"Too high, for my place. He knew it, too."

"Hi, Clarence," she said when she got closer. She stood there, uncertain.

"Howdy," Chub said. "He knew it was too high, but he meant it. Left his name and a phone number. Fisk was his last name."

"Never heard of him," Frank said.

They didn't act like they were bothered by her presence so she stayed.

"I hadn't neither. But here's the thing—I went down to Sickel's to see if anybody there'd work on that tiller's carburetor, on account of it still ain't runnin right, and he and another guy were talking about the damn lake. Said there's something in the local paper about it."

Ethel heard this and went back toward the house to get the paper. She knew right where she'd left it—down in the cellar, where she stacked the read papers to use as firestarters when she burned the trash.

"I'm just wonderin," Chub said, "if this Fisk might somehow have something to do with that man we saw at Lila's yesterday."

Frank leaned against the truck bed and looked back over his shoulder. His dog was sniffing the bushes on the far side of the yard. He whistled and Catfish looked up, stared at him for a moment, and then came bounding.

Chub waited. "It's gonna take all these river places, ain't it, Frank."

He said nothing.

"Ain't it though. They gonna need all these places long here to make room for the lake. They say the dam'll be downriver by where the bridge is."

Frank bent over and rubbed the pup's head, Catfish wagging his tail hard.

Chub couldn't see him. "Damn it, Frank. Ain't you even gonna do something about it? What if you—"

"What if I what!" Frank stood and yelled, his face red. "What the hell you want me to do? Put a chain cross my own damn driveway? Shoot the bastards when they come out here?"

It grew so quiet the chickens could be heard clucking over in the lot behind the coop.

She hurried from the door, newspaper in hand. "Here it is!" she called.

"Here's something about a meeting!"

Chub later asked for a glass of water, but he never went inside the house. They stood there, all three of them, leaning against the truck.

"I best be getting on home," Chub said when the first firefly lit over the yard. He climbed in his truck. "You want me to stop and put that chain up for ya?"

"Yeah, go ahead. Save me the walk." Frank and Ethel walked around to his side.

"You thinking about going to that meetin, then?" Chub asked him.

"No."

"Might be good to yell at them people a bit. Let em hear ya."

Frank shook his head. "I got no use for them things."

"I'd go with you all. Maybe say something myself."

Ethel nodded. "That'd be good," she said, and meant it.

"I might be willin to go, if you was goin," Frank said. "We'll see."

Chub started the engine, which roared to life with a burst of black smoke. Frank hated that he'd yelled at him. He reached out and patted Chub's meaty arm as it rested on the door of the truck.

"Thanks for comin out this way tonight."

Chub nodded. "I still can't figure why that guy wanted my place, though."

"Maybe it ain't connected. Who knows."

"Maybe they can be stopped, yet."

Frank looked at him. Ethel turned away and walked quickly toward the house.

Chub watched her leave. "It ain't gonna be easy on anyone. Well, goodnight. Catfish out of the way?"

Frank bent and took hold of his collar. Chub nodded again. He turned around in the barnyard and drove down the driveway. In the fading light Frank stood and watched his friend stop on the road and get out to padlock the chain between the two posts. The sounds of steel against steel floated over the yard.

Catfish absent-mindedly chewed on the leg of his overalls just above the boot. Frank kicked out violently, yelling some angry utterance, then immediately picked the cowering dog up. He held Catfish to his chest and stared at the road where the pickup had gone.

The door slapped the frame as his wife descended into the darkening yard and stood behind him.

"Don't worry about it," he said.

She stood with her hands over the lower part of her face, fingers pushed behind her glasses. Her shoulders heaved up and down. She looked small.

Catfish tensed and leaned out from his arms, peering at the strange sounds emanating from her.

"Stop, now."

"It's all gone," she said into her hands. "My daddy's land is gone."

"It's mine, too. And it ain't neither gone."

She dropped her hands, her eyes red and wet. "Don't you understand anything anymore? How do you think you can stop them? You can't."

They stared at each other, a couple forty-five years into it together in front of their old farmhouse at the end of an early August day in Indiana. Fireflies appeared over the grass. The dog shimmied to be let loose. The planet continued to revolve.

"I'm not gonna let it happen," he said.

Years ago, they'd gone to the feed mill in town for some chicken grain and the old proprietor, Fred Whitling, had erected a display of cedar bird feeders, some of them multi-leveled and elaborate. A local furniture maker had retired and turned to birds, since his hands couldn't get used to a day without tools. They were priced high, since Fred needed his cut, too.

They'd never put up a birdfeeder before. They didn't need to attract birds— the rafters of the chicken coop and the barn swarmed with sparrows and barn swallows stuck nests of mud to the ceiling joists. Bluebirds lived along the fringes of the pasture and goldfinches sat in rows along the fences. Quail ran on the ground and hawks dotted the sky. Frank had never felt the need to feed a bird on purpose, unless it was a chicken.

But Ethel stopped and admired the feeders. She examined the different models and features, softly muttering to herself. He picked up a sack of chicken grain from the back of the store and carried it past her to where Fred waited at the register.

"Frank, look at how nice these are," she said.

"I seen em," he said.

"A fella by the name of Hezekiah Johnson made them bird feeders and houses," Fred offered. He stepped out from behind the register and walked to where she stood. He was talking to Frank, though, who didn't want to hear any more about the damned feeders. He had things to get done today.

"Look at how nice his joints is. See where the sides come together? He's quite a carpenter, ain't he?" Fred asked.

"They look real nice," she said.

Fred ignored her. He looked at Frank, who remained standing in front of the register.

"Real cedar boards, too, which means it won't rot," Fred said. "Not like we get any rain, anyway, huh, Frank?"

"Yep. We better get this feed and be outta your way, Fred."

Fred nodded and walked back. It was a fifty-pound sack of feed, but it came to almost seven dollars. It kept going up. At least they got their eggs for free. Frank paid, took the change and put it in his overalls pocket, hoisted the sack of feed, and turned to the door. He looked back, and she was still standing there, eyeballing the feeders.

"Let's go," he said.

She finally moved from the display and said goodbye to Fred.

They were driving their old truck back then, a blue and white Chevy. Frank lowered the grain into the bed and climbed in the cab.

On the way home, she said, "I was thinking about putting one of them bird feeders outside the kitchen window. That way I could watch the birds as I did my dishes of an evening."

"You don't need it."

She huffed and sat silent for a while.

"I may not need it, but I wouldn't mind having it. Specially with winter coming on. I'll be in the house a lot more."

"Winter? Hell it ain't September yet."

"Well, you know what I mean. It'll get here."

"Plus then we'd have to buy food all the time for it. And what would we get from them little birds? Nothing. At least we get eggs from the chickens. That feed is up again, by the way, to almost seven dollars."

"Sometimes you just get enjoyment from things, you know."

Ollie lived at home then, and Frank had been yelling at him a lot. Sometimes he let himself yell at her, too. All three of them bristled at the sight of each other. They'd sit down to eat and she'd flinch at the first thing one of them said. Sometimes a look alone would get them rising out of their chairs and lunging forward like two dogs fighting on their hind legs, jaws snapping.

"I reckon I could just build a damned feeder," he finally said.

She didn't answer.

When they got home Ollie's truck sat in the driveway. So did Coondog's. They hated to see those two together. All they did was drink and get into trouble. She shook her head.

Two nights later the sheriff called, saying he had Ollie in his jail.

The following Monday morning while she was getting her hair done Frank drove to the feed mill and bought the best feeder Johnson had built. He brought it home and coated it with some water sealant. He took a piece of rebar, heated it, and bent it into a curve at the end. He drove that into the ground and hung the feeder from it. He'd bought cracked corn for seed, and he filled its reservoir.

That evening Ethel was doing dishes when he heard her exclaim. She came into the room where he'd been watching TV.

"You sweet old thing," she said.

"You and your foolish birds."

She stood by his chair and put her arm around his neck. He leaned over until his head rested against her side.

Night was falling in the yard now and it grew cool. Down in front of the kitchen window the same feeder hung from its hook, although it was too dark to see it anymore tonight. Catfish whined at Frank's feet, waiting to be fed.

"I don't know what we can do," she said. "A lawyer, maybe."

"We don't know no lawyers, though, do we?"

"Well, not yet, we don't," she said. "Or maybe Ollie could help us."

He grunted. "What the hell can he do? He ain't no lawyer, that's for damn sure. And he don't give a shit about this place, anyway."

"But he will, once he finds out what they're gonna do to it."

"If he cared, he'd be here. Isn't that right?"

"Not neces—"

"Isn't that right, though?"

"Oh Frank, I won't say that."

"Don't, then. But you know it's right."

"No I don't," she said. "I won't give up on him, just because you have."

"It ain't about him, anyway. This is a whole sight bigger than he is."

They stood in the yard for a while longer. Finally he said, "I gotta go feed this dog," and they all went up the steps into their house.

CHAPTER TWENTY-TWO

Seeing the face in the door's window, Ollie involuntarily yelped and fell backwards, kicking over a toy. Some tall, freestanding thing, it clattered against itself, making a tremendously loud noise in the black house. He gained the corner and hid behind it, his arms shivering and his heartbeat shaking the wall he leaned against. It was impossible to think.

The lightning continued to illuminate the house in irregular intervals, throwing odd shadows and pale blue angles around the rooms. From where he stood, he could see into the kitchen, the back door, and down the hallway leading to the bedrooms. The darkness hid much of this and suddenly he thought there might be more of them already inside.

When Summer touched his arm he shouted again.

She jumped. "What's wrong?" she asked, her voice hissing and tight. She pulled up against him along the wall.

"Someone's out there!" He sounded scared, even to his own ears.

She tried to move around him, peering into the other room. He pulled her back.

"Don't! Some fucker's looking in the door window!"

They heard the doorknob twist back and forth.

His hands knew then they needed something solid and heavy in them.

"Gun. Gun in the house?"

She shook her head no.

He scanned the dark corner of the kitchen. He'd have to cross the opening of the living room, but she'd keep knives there. He needed a big knife. Something someone could see in his hand. The house creaked from the wind.

His mind hit then on an image. He remembered seeing a big flashlight on top of the fridge. A black Maglite. He imagined the metal heft of it in his hand. He could feel himself swinging it.

He darted across the mouth of the living room and ran to the fridge. He reached around on top of it, knocking boxes of cereal and rolled up bags of potato chips to the floor. They exploded with noise as they hit.

His hand struck the flashlight, and he wrapped his fingers around its cold hardness. It was lighter than he hoped, but he gripped it and turned back toward the bedrooms.

She no longer stood in the hallway.

"Jesus Christ," she said.

Her voice came from the living room.

The next sound he heard was the creak of the hinges and the suck of the rubber seal around the door. The noises of the storm grew louder and the pressure in the house changed. He felt the wind blow into the kitchen.

"What in the world, Todd?" she asked. "It's the middle of the damned night. Are you trying to scare her to death?"

Ollie came around the corner then, flashlight in hand. And there she stood, silhouetted in the dark room, looking tiny next to this man. Todd stood dripping on the carpet.

"Who's that parked out there?" he asked.

"That's me, fucker," Ollie said, stepping forward. He held the light along his leg, his muscles rehearsing the motions needed to bring it up and swing it hard.

Todd turned. Summer stood between them.

"Stop," she said. "Todd, just leave. It's too late for this."

"Not too late for this jerk," Todd said.

"That's none of your business." She put a hand on his arm. He was tall enough to look right over her head and lock eyes with Ollie.

"Since when you having fucking dudes over here, Summer?" Todd asked.

"No fuck you!" Ollie yelled. His nerves jangled. He was tweaked out from adrenaline.

And then it started. Todd swept by her and Ollie rushed forward with the flashlight raised. Summer screamed and all three bodies collided over the coffee table. Ollie felt his head rock back with a dull flash of pain. He swung the Maglite, but something hit his elbow and absorbed the blow. He came up with his left hand and clenched a fistful of Todd's wet jacket. Summer's hair flew up and hit his face. He saw Todd's arm lift again before his right eye exploded with a white light and he felt himself falling. The backs of his legs hit something and he went down flailing.

Summer heard her first. Ollie scrambled to get to his feet and heard nothing. He'd dropped the flashlight. But Summer heard her, and a second later the sound registered with the father, who was coming around the fallen chair, fists cocked, to get at Ollie. Spring's white pajamas almost glowed in the light from the windows.

"Mommy!" she cried.

"I'm here baby," Summer said, moving to her. Spring let loose then, sobbing, sucking to get air, and sobbing again.

Ollie kicked the chair aside and got to his feet, panting. The door opened and shut with a blast of humid air. Todd was gone.

Summer knelt by her daughter, hugging her, rocking back and forth. She didn't look up.

He stepped around the upended coffee table and went to the window. Todd's truck started and its lights came on and sped down the driveway. Ollie looked around for his flashlight, intending to go after him.

"What the fuck, Summer!" he yelled.

"Shut the hell up!" she screamed. She picked up Spring and disappeared around the corner.

He stood there in the suddenly quiet room, bent over at the waist, trying to slow his breathing. Lightning continued to pop.

He drove home through the storm feeling like a madman. Or a wild animal, a raccoon maybe, trapped in someone's garage, frantic and crazy. At nearly four in the morning the roads were deserted. His headlights illuminated the pavement, almost white with the splashes of rain coming down hard. Here and there sat frogs, some of them hopping and moving in the headlights. Some of them the tires missed; some of them they did not.

Every house he drove by was blacked-out. Even the farmhouses remained dark yet. He went by the little market, so lonely and forlorn it seemed like it'd never been in business, like the owner had died right before it was set to open. Lightning lit the road and fields like a strobe.

He knew for a fact he'd been punched. Once, maybe twice. The skin around his eye was raised up on his cheek. He kept looking at himself in the rearview mirror, but it was too dark in the cab to see anything. After a few moments, he'd forget he couldn't see anything and look again. His hand kept returning to his face, like a little dog returning to a food bowl it knows is empty. Each time he was surprised to find the swelling there. The tissue was beginning to ache and his head felt bruised. He'd already punched the dash as hard as he could. Now his hand hurt, as well.

When he got to the trailer water had puddled on the linoleum where the roof leaked. Luckily it dripped over the kitchen and not over the carpet. But the carpet looked like shit anyway.

He got a beer, sat on the couch and stared at the blank TV. He'd never been so angry in his whole life. He wanted to kill Todd. He wanted to kill Summer, too, for having been with him. He was able to drink half the beer before he stood and launched the can against the wall, where it exploded in foam.

It was over with Summer.

Yet, already, he felt a pull in his gut, like a fish that'd swallowed a hook. He couldn't imagine not going back to her house, or not seeing her again. Not being in her bed again.

He sat on the couch and tried to make a mental list of the things he needed to do. First on it was to find this guy and kill him with his fists and maybe a crowbar. He might even take Coondog along to do that. Second was to go to Summer's and tell her and her kid to go to hell.

CHAPTER TWENTY-THREE

The corn out this way had grown even in the last week. Now it reached the hood of the truck, and the last time he'd come out here it was barely as high as the wheel wells. Corn lining the ditches on both sides of the road like armies of uniformed and muted soldiers. A breeze through the humid air would've been enough to move their leaves but there was none. The crop companies were adding more chemicals to the seed anymore, and corn was tougher as a result. Drought? Floods? The corn could withstand it all, they told you. But when everyone's corn looked good the prices fell. Sometimes the prices went to hell no matter what the fields looked like. Last summer this road had been flanked by soybeans, and they'd turned out pretty decent. Every season you rotated the crop and waited to see what the world thought of your plans.

Frank drove between the fields of corn and thought about nothing but the fact that they aimed to take his land. He was aware of the corn, the road, and the big pothole coming up on the right the way a bear was conscious of its winter den after sleeping in it for months.

The groundhog crouched in the shade of the ditch, chewing down the stem of a clover, and it heard the truck approaching. As the vibration grew it rushed for its den and felt the sudden heat of the blacktop and the sunlight warm on its back even as it sensed the looming metal frame bearing down on it. Frank swerved to the right and stood on the brakes. Normally he wouldn't have tried to avoid hitting a groundhog, but this one scared the hell out of him, driving in a trance like he was. The truck nosed downward and Catfish pitched forward off the seat and onto the floor with a surprised yip.

The groundhog scampered to the other side. By now it was safely back in the darkness of its hole. Frank turned the wheel straight and reached down and pulled the pup up onto the seat.

"Sorry about that. I should've hit the little bastard," he said.

Catfish turned a circle on the bench and lay back down. Frank put a hand on the pup's back. There he rode, right next to him, like the girlfriend of some farm kid taking the truck out on a Friday night, still dusty from the hayfield. Sunlight shone through the open window, illuminating man and dog both. The dog did not know the difference between this day and the one that'd come before it. To his owner there was no comparison.

He pulled in and parked behind Chub's garage. There sat the Dodge, so he knew he was around. The garage doors were down so he was probably in the house or backyard. Just thinking about some asshole trying to buy this place was enough to get Frank worked up again. He shut the truck off and took up the lead from the floorboard, the short length of rope he'd cut and tied to a metal clasp. He clipped it to Catfish's collar before opening the door. He grabbed his cane from where it hung on the side of the bed, pulled the pup across the seat and into his arms, and lowered him to the ground. There'd been some things to pick up at the hardware store, and now he wanted to see if Chub could look around the river.

It was hot. Any cooling effects of last night's storm had been baked away. Chub's house looked like it'd settled even deeper into the earth.

He hollered for Chub but heard nothing. Catfish tugged on his rope and sniffed the new ground under him, the unfamiliar gravel. Frank yelled again and waited. The old boy must be asleep in his recliner, he thought. He took the dog and walked toward the backyard. A little rickety gate hung there and he pushed it open with his cane. Once he gained entrance he followed the trail Chub's heavy feet had carved. He used his cane foot to knock on the shaky storm door, which vibrated and shuddered in its frame. They waited for a little bit.

Holding the lead and his cane with one hand, he released the little catch on the handle and pushed the door open.

"Hey Chub! Get your ass out here."

Some sparrows called from a tree in the backyard. He looked there and saw the picnic table and the catfish tub. A white butterfly flitted across the yard in the sun. He let the door slam shut and turned toward the garage. Catfish saw the butterfly and jerked against the lead, the base of his ears perked.

The side door to the garage was closed, but not pulled to, and Frank pushed it open with his cane.

"Hey there, Chub."

His voice echoed off the block walls. It was hotter than hell and a terrible stink rose and met him. He wondered how Chub could stand to work out here in the summer. He was blinded while his eyes adjusted to the dimness.

"Damn, at least open them doors up—"

And then he saw the tipped-over stool in front of the cluttered workbench and the fallen form of his friend. Chub lay on his back, his eyes shut and his mouth hanging open.

"Lord Christ," he said, rushing forward to the body prone on the concrete.

He grabbed Chub about the neck and arm but it was obvious to anyone that he'd been dead for some time. There was a bluish tint to his face and dried vomit around his mouth. One leg lay folded underneath the other, and it looked like maybe he'd just leaned back on his stool and toppled over. Down where he lay. But there was no blood behind his head and the tanned and leathered skin had blanched white.

He heard someone chanting Oh Jesus and he realized he was saying those words aloud as he grabbed and shook his friend's heavy body.

They'd both known for several years that his heart would take him, but they'd managed to hide the idea away so completely that now it felt both predestined and otherworldly. As if this were a warning to be heeded—an example of what could come to pass if they didn't change their ways.

Chub's eyes remained shut below the thick eyebrows and his bluish skin fell slackly about his face. The backs of his arms look bruised where they'd rested against the concrete. The fluids of the body dropping toward the center of the earth.

Frank knelt there, his knees on the hard floor, and looked up into the rafters of the old garage. He knew he should call for the ambulance but there hardly seemed to be a use in it. He could call the coroner as well. He felt of the thick neck for a pulse and of course there was none.

He hadn't cried in years but now he cried without pause. The garage was stifling hot and stunk but he stayed on. Chub's arms splayed out from his sides. He hadn't tried to slow his fall or brace his weight. Perhaps he'd been dead before he fell. His body had let go of his bowels and piss and brown liquid stool lay puddled between his legs and around his rear.

"I gotta call somebody," Frank finally said.

Chub's DeKalb hat lay not far from his head, and Frank placed it over his friend's face. Chub wore the tennis shoes he used around the house, the white ones from Walmart. He'd been angry when he got them home because the insides declared Made In Taiwan. Frank remembered him saying, "What the hell. I thought Sam Walton was all about Made In America. These here shoes come from Taiwan." But he wore them anyway.

"Chub, you old bastard," Frank said. A fly buzzed against a window pane on the other side of the garage. "We're gonna lose our river, buddy. Me and you coulda fought em."

It was time to call someone, time to let somebody know Chub Peters was gone.

He rose slowly to his feet and picked up his cane where it'd clattered to the floor. He hadn't heard the sound of it hitting. He glanced around the garage and didn't see his dog.

Before he turned to leave he looked down at Chub's body. So that was his death. There was nothing dignified about it and it seemed like this man deserved more.

"Good fishing with ya," he said. "You were a good man."

When he stepped outside the sun felt like a gift from God and the air smelled clean and cool. Catfish was back by the fish tub, dragging his rope, his nose held to the ground. Perhaps he smelled the river water and the fish themselves. Perhaps he was remembering he'd almost died there until these two men saved him. Catfish didn't act like he understood one of those men was now dead.

Frank watched his pup from this distance and felt defeated. Even Catfish would outlive him. Would outlive Ethel. What was the point of fighting when you got this old? You were so close to gone, what good could come of any single day?

CHAPTER TWENTY-FOUR

Somehow Ollie lived through Sunday. Normally he wouldn't have heralded such an accomplishment, but considering how many times he studied his black eye in the mirror and how many minutes he thought about Summer, he felt damned lucky his head hadn't exploded. And he'd done it without calling her once. He planned a speech to deliver over the phone when she called, but she didn't. That surprised him, but if she wanted to play hardball, she was messing with the wrong guy. He'd gotten drunk all day and listened to his heavy metal tapes. He practiced conversations with her, delivering his lines to the walls.

When he woke the next morning, his neck was bent over against his shoulder, and he was still on the damn couch. It was twenty after six. He stood up, said shit twice, and went into the bedroom to put on his work clothes. As he walked outside the grass was wet with dew and that was one more thing that pissed him off.

Ray Jackson said something about his eye right away, now even more swollen and as purple as eggplant. It hurt like a bitch. Ollie let on that he didn't feel like talking and Ray dropped it. He'd bring it up again at lunch, but for now they were content pulling and stacking boards, letting the morning fall slowly around them. It was going to be a long enough day as it was. The dust flew into their eyes and mouths. Ollie felt like he'd eaten an old T-shirt for breakfast.

When work ended what seemed like eighteen hours later, he got in his truck and drove out of the little gravel parking lot. Without really deciding to, he took the county roads out toward the old home place. It was exactly the wrong time to do that, but part of him wanted to shove his black eye in their faces. Maybe he'd make them feel a little guilt for once.

Funny how familiar this road was. He recognized everything, even though he hadn't driven this way in weeks. Fescue clumped up around the stop sign, reaching so high it almost covered the message, and he thought about how it always did that in late summer. Those big orange flowers were blooming in the ditches again. The silver maple tree in front of the house this side of his parents' still bent its branches in the same pattern. Shade fell in the same places.

He slowed to turn into the driveway of what had been his home. If he'd been more careless, if he'd been in more of a routine, he might've driven right into the chain. But since he was looking closely at everything again, he saw the barrier before he smashed the bumper into the heavy links. Not that the front of his truck could be screwed up worse.

He assumed that the chain was meant for him. "Oh screw you," he said.

He sat there and stared at the chain and posts. Pretty heavy duty—six by six posts set in concrete and a logging chain as thick as his wrists. The old man sure as hell intended to keep him out. Now Ollie really wanted to shove his face into theirs. Sure, it'd been a while, but who put up a chain to keep his only son away? He pulled into the ditch along the road and killed the engine. They could stop him from driving, but a man could still walk.

He noticed the old man's truck was gone. Out fishing, probably, running around with Chub. It'd be better for everyone if he saw his mom alone. If he wanted pity, that's where he'd find the purest dose.

The driveway was soft with putty-colored mud, the gravel smashed under decades of truck tires. He'd done his share, coming and going. The old house needed a coat of paint, and the front porch sagged a little. He'd never noticed that before. Why hadn't his dad kept up on stuff around here? It'd been a good-looking farm, back when he was growing up.

Still he walked. Damn, he didn't remember the drive being this long, but then he rarely walked it. The late afternoon sun was strong and hot on his back.

He touched his face. He'd had other black eyes but this one hurt more. Only when he pressed on it, but still. That was one asshole with a whupping coming to him. He might swing by Coondog's after this to rally the troops.

It didn't look like anyone was home, anyway. No one had come outside, no one had welcomed him back. He stood and looked at the house. He'd lived here almost his whole life and you would think you'd really get to know a place. But somehow it looked smaller now.

He remembered playing with his toy tractors in the dirt in the corner by the front porch. The tractors were still around somewhere—probably upstairs in the attic in a box. His were mostly John Deeres and Internationals. But he'd had one Allis-Chalmers. Those things were probably worth some money. He'd taken care of them—his dad made sure of that. Each night, Ollie had to bring them in and brush the dirt off before lining them up along the wall in his bedroom.

Funny how you got old so fast. Thinking about playing with his tractors damn near made his eyes water. The corner where the bush had died and left the patch of dirt was overgrown with weeds now. You could hardly see the tiny field where his tractors had churned and turned the soil so many summer days. The porch wood looked soft as butter.

Well, no need to go to the door if no one was home. He turned and walked back down the driveway.

He got in the truck and turned around on the road. The old man and his damn chain. Ollie didn't know what he'd been looking for, anyway.

•   •   •

Back in his truck on this road both familiar and foreign, he was glad he hadn't been forced to deal with his parents. As he drove he thought about how this was a good time to head for Coondog's place, to tell him about the fight and see if he was ready to go find Todd, but instead he seemed to be taking the turns that lead him back to Summer's house.

She'd be home by now, since it was almost five. He knew when she got off work, what time she picked up Spring from the sitter's, when they'd sit down to eat. He thought about that—how he'd moved from not even knowing her to knowing what kind of frozen pizza she'd soon be placing on the middle rack in the oven with the missing knob. He'd paid attention.

Sure enough, her car was there. He pulled into her driveway, knowing she could hear the gravel crunch from her spot on the couch, and knowing she would've walked to a window by now to see who was coming. He parked and thought again about what he'd say to her.

He knocked on the door. She opened it and stepped back without any form of greeting, although he saw her eyes stop on his busted one. Spring sat on the floor, watching television.

"Here he is. Ah-E," she said, looking up. Then she too noticed his eye and stared at it. She looked scared.

"Hey there, Spring," he said. He bent over to touch her hair but she leaned away. The room had been set right, of course.

Summer walked back into the kitchen, so he followed her. She resumed washing dishes. He noticed the oven light was on, illuminating a cooking pizza. The little TV on the counter was making noise and he turned it off so they could talk. As soon as it fell silent he could hear the TV Spring was watching in the other room and the ticking of the timer on the stove.

"What'd you turn that off for?" she asked.

"I figured we need to talk about Saturday night."

"Your eye looks terrible, by the way. Really nasty."

"Yeah, great. Thanks. I can tell you it hurts, if that makes you happy."

"You being hurt doesn't make me happy."

"It doesn't? I thought it might. So tell me why it happened."

"Why? What's the sense in talking about it, when you don't understand anything anyway?"

He leaned against the counter. "I might be able to understand why some guy comes to your door at three in the morning," he said. "Then again, I might not." He felt pretty good about the way that'd come out.

She threw a plate into the drying rack. "Look. Todd is Spring's father. He's got a right to stop by and check on her sometimes. He saw your truck out there and worried about her. He came in here to check on us, that's all, and then you two fight like a bunch of animals."

"Like we fought like animals!" he yelled.

She jerked her eyes toward the other room, her face hard and angry.

He added, his voice only slightly quieter, "when we fight, he's gonna know it."

"See that? Right there. That's why this is already gone too far. You can't understand it, just like I said."

"Oh, bullshit. I think I understand too much, if anything."

She continued washing, her hands buried in soapy water. Every so often, water splashed over the front of the sink and against the flowered shirt she wore. She was still dressed from work.

"You said he was coming to check on Spring, but I think he was coming to check on you," he said.

"So."

"So? See, there it is. You still like him! And how am I supposed to be around here if he's coming around here? Especially then. What the hell was he doing out so late?"

"I don't know what to tell you, except that he was out for a friend's bachelor party," she hissed. "And I can tell you he told me that when he called on Sunday, which is more than you did!"

The little girl walked in then, looking scared and sad, her lips all pouty. She leaned against Summer and pressed her nose against her thigh.

He felt the blood rise up in his face. "You know what I was thinking?" he asked. "I was planning on all of us heading down to South Carolina for a little break—just the three of us. But now? That's off."

He was making it up on the spot. He'd never been to South Carolina or seriously considered going there during this lifetime.

Summer looked down at her daughter, revealing no hint of excitement or disappointment now that the vacation had been ripped away from their grasp.

He came up with more: "But no big trip for us! Why? Because I don't think we'd want to take him, that's why! That'd be too many for the car, what with all the suitcases and all!"

Summer sighed and turned back to the dishes. "Ollie, I don't want to fight with you in front of her right now. She's already seen enough of it."

"Well, there ain't gonna be another time, I can promise you that," he said.

He wanted that one to bring on the tears, but when she turned to Spring and started talking about getting cleaned up for supper he knew he'd been dismissed. She put a hand on her daughter's back and the two of them left him alone in the kitchen. The timer on the oven dinged, signaling the pizza was done. He thought about kicking the door of the stove in, or throwing the TV into the sink. He heard them come out of the bathroom and go into the living room. The back door was right off the kitchen, and he could be gone in a second.

But walking out the front door would take him past Summer, and he wanted her to see the look on his busted face as he left her. He wanted Spring to see his eye again and start crying. So he took one last look around the kitchen with his good eye and started out.

Neither mother nor daughter looked up at him as he walked through the room and opened the door. He stepped outside and reached back for the doorknob. He wanted to slam it in their faces, but Spring was playing on the floor close by, so he showed restraint. He watched Summer as he jerked the door closed but she wasn't even looking at him.

In the truck, he said, "Fuck it, then. I'll go by my own damn self." He'd never traveled that far south, and in fact had only gone into Ohio and Kentucky and once to Illinois. But Ray at work had vacationed with his family in South Carolina last year and talked like it was heaven here on Earth. Women in the hotel hallways walking in their bikinis. A woman on the beach with a thong showing off her whole ass.

So he knew what he needed to do. Make a long trip of it and show her what life would be like without him. Go down there and run wild with some hot women. Ray said if he'd been there without his wife he would've been the king sheep in a herd of ewes. Now Ollie would be, because he was a free man, was he not? Of course he was. Hell yes he was.

He looked at the house again, but Summer wasn't coming out the door, waving her arms and begging him to stay. The house sat there like no one inside even knew he was still parked, waiting to be stopped.

CHAPTER TWENTY-FIVE

L oss," the preacher said, trying to look him in the eyes, "this is not something God meant for us to understand infallibly." They sat on the hard pew in the little church on the edge of Logjam. The preacher's eyes were magnified by his glasses and any time Frank tried to look elsewhere the preacher would touch him on the knee and affix him with a fresh stare. Frank had never spoken to this man and he'd barely set foot inside these walls. There'd been a few weddings and funerals—only funerals over the last ten years—and this particular preacher was new. He'd served elsewhere, though, because he was older than Frank. The sanctuary looked the same: chips of plaster had fallen off the low ceiling and Jesus hung from a cross on the wall. It was not an astounding likeness, Frank assumed.

He sat there and examined the curve of his cane handle, held upright between his knees. Metal worn smoother than any machine could sand it. Only a leaning hand could do such work, and only over years.

"Let us refer to the Book of Job. God threw a great many things at that man. Boils. Great hives. Loss of family." The preacher leaned forward in the pew, wearing brown pants and a thin sweater worn almost threadbare in spots. White hair sprouted like tiny saplings from the outer edges of his ears. He seemed to get a jolt of energy then and his voice became louder. "You're a farmer, right? Well, so was Job. And then God sent the Chaldeans to take his camels. All three thousand of them." The preacher sat back, pleased with himself.

Frank clenched his cane and exhaled. Where in God's name would a man run three thousand camels? And what in the hell were they good for? He turned to the casket and said nothing.

"But do you know what Job did, Mr. Withered? After God burned his sheep and had his camels carried off?"

Frank didn't even acknowledge he'd been spoken to. The preacher edged closer. "Job said, 'the Lord gave, and the Lord hath taken away; blessed be the name of the Lord.'" He sat staring at Frank's face, lightly rocking as if he would hypnotize him. "See, Job understood that while God is so very good, He must also—"

"Chub died because he was too fat and his heart give out," Frank said. "And he died too damned soon."

"It was God's wish to take him home. Just as God took back Job's camels. Can you appreciate that?"

"No."

"God wanted him. To be part of His flock now."

"So you want me to believe that Chub is now in a flock with a bunch of camels? Come on, mister."

The preacher tried a small smile. "There's room in God's heaven for all of His creatures."

"Chub won't be of much use. He never was down here, although I will admit he was hell on channel cats."

"Yes, well, he lived God's plan."

Frank looked at him. "No he never. Chub never lived nobody's plan. Not many cared if he lived or died, most days. Now these people come out here"— he motioned to the small clot of people near the door—"and they talk over him like they cared. Hell, most of em barely knew him at all."

"He was loved," the preacher said quietly. Frank's voice had grown louder and the preacher tried to counter that by whispering. "Jesus loved him."

"What lets you say that? What part of you is convinced you know enough? I fished with Chub most of my life, and I never heard him mention Jesus at all, less he was saying, 'Jesus Christ, I got a good one!'"

The preacher's face reddened and he looked down at the faded and splintered pew bench. His eyes flexed and narrowed. He focused on something over Frank's head.

"Like our Lord did for Job, He blessed the latter half of his life more than the beginning. Job ended up with twice as much as he had before."

"But you didn't know Chub," Frank interrupted. "I'd wager you don't know hardly anybody around here."

"I try to reach out to the communities I serve," the preacher said, finally. He stood and laid a mouse-like hand on Frank's shoulder before walking to the rear of the church, where a few people remained.

Ten feet in front of the pew, raised on what could've been sawhorses under a white blanket, sat the casket that bore Chub Peters. The casket was bigger than most. Funeral arrangements had been made by Chub's only son, who'd arrived yesterday, the day after Frank found the body in the garage.

Charles had landed in Indianapolis after departing from New York City or somewhere else on the east coast. He hadn't brought a wife or anyone else. Frank hadn't seen him in probably ten years, and when they found themselves standing close at the beginning of visitation very few words passed between them.

After leaving the garage that day, Frank had gone into the house with his dog and dialed what he thought was the number for the volunteer firehouse. Nothing happened. No beeps, no busy signal. The phone hung on the wall in the kitchen, with no phone book in sight. He tried to call the operator, then the firehouse again. They had yet to install a 911 system in Shipley County. Finally, after swinging his stiff finger around in a myriad of combinations, he heard a woman's voice.

"Can I do something for you?" she asked in an exasperated tone, as if she'd been watching his frustrated dialing from a little room somewhere.

"I need a rescue unit," he said. "My friend died out here in his garage."

After giving her an address and some more information about Chub's state, the operator offered to call the ambulance for him.

He sat in the backyard with Catfish until they heard the siren's wavering call as it completed the long drive from the hospital at Green City. Even with the lights it'd taken close to an hour. He'd found that to be a long hour sitting at the picnic table, knowing what his friend looked like on the garage floor. The ambulance pulled into the driveway in a swirl of noise and flashes.

He walked out in front of the garage to meet it, and the driver cut the siren but not the lights, little mirrors spinning around in globes of glass.

"He's in there," he said as a man and woman climbed out. They wore blue pants with matching tops and rubber gloves.

They rushed past him and were inside the garage for several minutes. Later they came out, and the woman asked him questions about Chub as the man got a stretcher out of the back of the ambulance. Yes, he'd been like that when he found him. No, he hadn't really moved him. Yes, he did check for a pulse. No, there hadn't been one. No, not even right after he found him.

And now Frank sat in his only jacket and tie, which clipped onto his shirt collar with a little metal bracket, and waited for Ethel, who was speaking to her dippy friend Hattie near the back of the church. He looked at the casket, but he didn't feel much anymore. He felt what Chub would've felt—he just wanted to get out of here.

Ethel finally came back to the front and touched his arm.

"You ready to go home?" she asked.

He nodded and lifted himself off the pew with his cane. His ass hurt from sitting on the hard wood bench. He looked over again and saw Chub's swollen face and neck in the opening of the casket. They hadn't done a very good job with the body, whoever did it.

She kept his arm and led him down the aisle between the pews. They'd stayed for the entire three hours allotted for visitation. Maybe twenty or so people had shown up. He understood how it was. Many times he'd skipped a visitation, too, if he was in the middle of planting or something. You could always go to the funeral, which was in the same church until the mourners moved out to the graveyard for the burial.

When they got into the truck, she said, "I seen you was talking to Father Collier. He's a nice man."

"He's an asshole," he said, starting the engine.

When they got home she went out and fed and watered the chickens
and disappeared to check the garden. He got Catfish from the granary and
released him into the yard. Since the sun had hit the grass all day it seemed
like he could probably mow, but he didn't feel like starting that now. The
dog did his business over near the tree like he usually did and came back and
started biting at Frank's feet. Catfish took a piece of pant leg in his mouth
and chewed it while rolling on his back. Frank stared down at him. He'd
gotten used to having the little sucker around. The ears that flopped around
like slices of velvet bologna. The tiny hairs that covered his face and muzzle.
The miniature eyelashes over his brown eyes. They'd done the right thing,
pulling this dog from the river.

He'd need to put these pants on again tomorrow, but still he stood and
watched the dog gnaw the fabric with his sharp teeth. Before long he lost
focus on the dog's face and his vision grew blurry.

He wiped at his eyes when he heard her coming back from the garden. She
was yelling something.

She shuffled up next to him. "I said, 'the deers got some of the tomatoes
last night.' I seen their tracks." She looked down. "Hey! Don't just let him
bite holes in your pants like that!"

Frank pulled his leg away and Catfish jumped up and ran furious circles
around them, looking for something he could retrieve.

She walked over and picked up the sock stuffed with rags they'd been using
to entertain him. She threw it maybe ten feet. Catfish, who'd seen her reach
for the sock, had already run far beyond it. He stopped thirty yards away
and turned, body cocked. He saw the sock and raced back.

"Funeral's at ten tomorrow," she said. "You need to hang those pants over
a chair and put your tie somewheres you'll find it."

He reached for his tie, but it was no longer clipped to his collar. He'd taken
it off as soon as they got in the truck. He'd have to find it before morning.

"Well, Hattie come to the church today," she said. "I don't know if you saw
her, but she's not going to Tennessee like she thought."

He took the sock from Catfish and threw it.

"Remember I told you she was going with Rufus?"

"No."

"Well, she was going, but now he's not going to take her."

"If he had any sense, he'd take her and leave her ass down there."

She laughed. "Maybe so." She watched the dog and looked around the yard
before saying it. "I want you to call Ollie and make sure he knows about the
funeral."

"You call him."

"No, you call him this time. I called him yesterday and he never answered."

"He couldn't a known it was you! Besides, he ain't gonna answer when I call him, neither!"

"Then we'll just have to drive over there."

He said nothing.

She moved over next to him and put her arm around his waist. He leaned forward on his cane and watched the dog.

"I'm so sorry about old Chub," she said. "I know he was your good friend."

He felt the moisture wick into his eyes. He grunted a little to let her know he'd heard and understood.

Catfish ran in circles with the stuffed sock in his mouth, one end dragging the ground. With his eyes, he asked them to throw it again.

When they went inside Ethel set about fixing something to eat. Once more she asked him to call, and rather than listen to her complain, he walked to the phone and dialed the number.

He let it ring a dozen times before hanging up and walking into the room where his chair waited for him. She followed.

"He still never answered?" she asked.

"No, he was out."

"You think something's wrong?"

"No more than usual."

"I mean, do you think he's okay?"

"I reckon he is. Just working late, probably."

"Well, we better go out there. He needs to know about Chub's funeral tomorrow."

"There was notice of it in the paper."

"I don't know that he takes the paper, though. He might not've even heard about it!"

"We can run out there in the morning, if you want. Before the funeral."

"But he'll be at work!"

"He don't leave that early. I ain't goin out there any more tonight, though, so don't ask."

She stood there and watched him for a while before going back into the kitchen to finish supper.

He turned on the news, which down here came out of Cincinnati. The newscasters acted like they didn't know Indiana existed. He didn't think Ollie had any business going to the funeral. What he had business doing was going to work, since it was a weekday and all. That way he could keep his job and stay out of trouble. He didn't need to go to a funeral for some man not even his friend.

But Frank would have to attend, and already he was dreading going back to the church and shaking that preacher's hand. He didn't want to see those people again. He didn't want to see Chub in his oversized casket again. They'd dressed him in some suit they must've gotten from the church, because they couldn't have found it in his house. If there was one thing he knew about Chub, it was that the man hadn't owned a suit in his entire life.

CHAPTER TWENTY-SIX

Ollie hadn't gone to the sawmill Tuesday morning. Instead he woke up at the normal time, called in a vacation day, and slept two more hours. Then he filled a duffle bag with three pairs of jeans, a stack of T-shirts, socks and underwear. After some thought he tossed in three Playboys he hadn't read completely. By read he meant looked at. At the bank he withdrew the little bit of money his checking account held. If he'd kept a savings account he would've drained that, too. Should he encounter a dry county along the way, he bought two cases of beer. He also bought a map at the gas station where he filled up. He'd thrown all of this, along with a sleeping bag and his pillow, into the truck. Now he felt so liberated he thought he might never go back to work.

Driving on the interstate was not something he'd done a lot of. He drove along in the left lane until he got enough angry stares from people passing on the right that he remembered the right lane was home. He knew it was one or the other but had forgotten. The duffle bag sat on the seat next to him, over the pillow and sleeping bag. The beer rode along on the floorboards. He'd emptied the truck bed of trash and drove with the tailgate down to decrease wind resistance.

He only had two vacation days left, so he'd asked for today and tomorrow off. There were a few sick days to use after that. His other vacation days had been spent puking bile. He was one for working through a hangover and he'd done so most of his life, but some mornings got just too ugly. He planned on puking some down south, too, because once he got to South Carolina he sure as hell intended to party.

Coondog knew he was gone, but no one else. Not his parents, not Summer. They'd miss him when they finally figured it out. Especially Summer. He pictured her weeping long into the night, unable to go to work or even care for her daughter. As far as she went, it was like the song said: "You don't know what you got, til it's gone." She would sure as hell learn what she'd had, once she called his trailer a million times and never got an answer. Thinking about her put him in the mood for that song so he fed the tape into the deck and cranked it up. Why, he was heading into Kentucky even now. The sign came up alongside the interstate and he drove by it with a little wave.

He'd gone to Coondog's to tell him about the trip right after leaving Summer's house, and he'd found him in the dank nastiness of the basement, stapling red Christmas lights to the floor joists. Under the web of lights sat a twin bed. There was a lamp with a naked blue bulb next to the bed on a cardboard box. The mattress was bare.

"Don't let me interrupt you, whatever the hell you're doing," Ollie said, coming down the steps.

Coondog jumped. "Dude, you scared the shit outta me. What the hell's up?"

"What's up with you? Moving your bed down here?"

"Oh hell no. You know I sleep in the master suite in my big-ass queen. This is for something else entirely—dude, what the hell happened to your eye?"

"Yeah, well, I wanted to talk to you about that. Remember Summer's—"

"Holy shit, that chick hit you that hard?"

"No, you damn fool! Her ex! The one I told you was still comin around? Well, he jumped me late Saturday night over at her place. Totally blindsided me, the fucker."

Coondog nodded, studying the bruise. "Well, it looks like he got you a good one. His name's Todd something-or-other, by the way. He lives with his old lady and little kid on the first floor of a rented house across from the feed mill. I seen his place—it's got gray steps leading to the second floor."

"All right, man. Good work. You ready to go pound his ass?"

Coondog kept studying his eye. It took him a while to answer. "Yeah, sometime. Supposed to be some kind of hard ass, though. This guy I useta work with told me he wasn't really one to fuck with."

"He ain't that damn tough. I bout whipped his ass myself, if he hadn't jumped me in the dark like he did."

Coondog looked away and went back to stapling the string of lights to the dusty boards. "Yeah, well, check this out, anyway," he said. "You know what it's for?"

"For keeping high school girls locked in a sex dungeon?"

He laughed. "I wish, dude. But yes and no. This is for increased sense perception."

Ollie looked at the bed. It stood on the dirty concrete floor surrounded by seeping mildewed walls. On a shelf nearby sat a bunch of canned vegetables no one had touched in twenty years. The whole cellar was no bigger than a one-car garage and smelled a little like septic.

"See what I mean?" Coondog asked.

"Not yet, dude. I don't get it."

"Well, you can't just give a chick the same experience everyone else is. Or even every time you're doing her. She needs variety. So, say she's at my place, getting good and liquored up. Ready to party a little. But instead of taking her upstairs to my bedroom, I take her hand and lead her down here. I already got the red lights on and some incense burning. She comes down and her shit is about blown."

"No, yeah, it would be," Ollie said, pretending to look around with amazement as he pictured the elegance and fantasy.

"You gotta imagine it dark, with only the colored lights on."

"Right, right. I totally can."

"But it's more than lights. Under the bed, I aim to keep certain trinkets. Things like whipped cream, handcuffs, ice cubes." He reached over and picked up his beer and took a long drink.

"You mind if I get one of them?"

"Sure. Let's go upstairs. I about got this place ready, anyhow."

They walked up the shaky wood steps together.

"I wanted to come see you before I leave," Ollie said.

"You going somewheres with that chick?"

"Nah, man. Me and her done broke up, just tonight, in fact. That fight ruined it, and I told her off."

"So where you going?"

"I'm thinking about headin down south. Maybe all the way to South Carolina. Get to the coast, anyway."

"What the hell for?"

"See the beach, man! Look at the hot women! What the hell does anybody go to the beach for?" He sat on the couch and Coondog went into the kitchen. When he came back he held two beers and handed one over.

"You want, you can go to Florida and crash with my folks some," Coondog offered. "Me and you was talking about goin down there anyways." He'd gone to Florida several times, but Ollie hadn't made it. How his parents lived didn't much sound like the scene Ollie was after.

"Instead, I was thinking of asking you to come with me to South Carolina," Ollie said. "Run em as a team, beat the bushes. You flush em one way, I'll be flushing them another. Hunt em like deer."

Coondog laughed. "I ain't got enough money to help you with even gas," he finally said.

"I ain't exactly loaded myself. But I aim to find work once I get down there."

"You mean to stay down there? Like for a long time?"

"Hell yes. What's here for me now? I ain't plannin on coming back."

Coondog sat on his couch. He tried to stifle a yawn, but finally let it out. He yawned big and loud and his eyes watered. "Sorry about that," he said. "I been up late, getting that basement ready."

"You coming with me or not?"

"Ah shit, man. What about my truck? I gotta make payments on it. I can't just take off. I'm tryin to get this business goin, you know?"

"They got trees down south, I reckon."

"And what, drive a damn Ford bucket truck down there at forty miles an hour? Leave the damn house locked up?"

Ollie hadn't thought about that. He intended to leave his trailer deserted.

Coondog tipped his beer up and finished it. He sat the empty can on the coffee table next to a magazine about cars, a TV schedule and a candle, the wax inside the glass jar covered with dust.

"I can't figure you," he said. "First I figure you about to get hitched to some chick you meet at the goddamn fair, of all places. Then you get your ass punched and you tell me that's over and you movin to South Carolina. I guess I could call what you're going through a midlife crisis."

"Damn, man! I just think it's time for a damned change! This shit is getting old around here."

"What'd your folks say?"

Ollie stood up and walked past the television over to the window. Outside in the moonlight he could see the giant bucket truck and the oil-changing tree. "I ain't telling them nothing," he said.

"You're just gonna take off and not let em know where you gone or nothing?"

"Pretty much."

"When the hell did they piss in your Cheerios?"

"Ah shit, man. They been doin that."

"By the way, are they gonna lose the farm? People been talking to me about cutting down trees, since they're gonna be flooded out anyways."

He walked over and looked at Coondog. "I don't know nothing about that, one way or the other."

"There goes your inheritance, I guess, huh?"

"See that? See that shit? That's what I mean. I don't want nothing from them no more. They all but cut me out, anyhow. I'm such a disappointment to them, they can keep my inheritance."

"Well, where they gonna go?"

"Hell if I know. I ain't talked to em in weeks."

"But I mean if they get flooded out. Where they gonna live?"

Something like genuine alarm and interest was rising in Ollie. "You don't think the whole place will get flooded?"

"Logjam?"

"Their farm."

"Oh yeah. I mean. Well, that's what they're saying, anyway. All the farms along the bottom there are going to be in the lake. Your parents' place'll be the first under."

Ollie reached down, grabbed his beer up from the table, and drained it. "Well, anyway. I'm headed south."

•   •   •

Interstate driving had its allure, he saw that now. The truck would only do about fifty, but the traffic was light and he felt at ease with the road. He drove with one hand and looked around him. Here and there a farm, a barn with a silo rising. Groups of houses in cornfields. A cement mixing plant. A golf course, with several people out walking around on it. What the hell was that good for? Once in a while, an exit off the interstate with gas stations and fast food restaurants.

He'd bought the beer warm, so there was no concern it might get skunked now, with the sun coming in through the windows. But he wished he'd iced some in a cooler. It was a damn nice day to be drinking a beer. But he knew he shouldn't do that, anyway, at least not out here on the interstate. It was a heck of a nice day, though: sunny as could be, maybe eighty, eighty-five. He'd put on his sunglasses and they barely fit over his swollen eye, but he hadn't let it bother him. He wondered what kind of weather to expect in South Carolina. He might need to buy some shorts. A swimsuit. When he was little they'd played in the river, but he'd swum in cut-offs.

So they meant to flood out the old river. He imagined the swimming hole back in the woods getting bigger and deeper until it swallowed the trees, then the pasture, then the barn. It couldn't come up that high, could it? To cover the damn barn? What about the house? No way. When he was ten or so, he and Coondog built a fort from old fence posts on a little rise in the woods. They'd spent hours back there, playing G.I. Joe. But later that summer the river flooded and when they walked back to the fort, they couldn't even get close before the water was sloshing around their knees. When the river dropped the fort was covered in mud and stank. They'd knocked it down. He'd seen the river that high, but didn't think it could get any higher.

The road rolled forward, the engine hammering along. Soon he'd need gas. He was hungry, anyway. He saw a sign for a Burger King coming up and felt his mouth water. Where was he? Somewhere in Kentucky. Sure was pretty down here, what with their big-ass hills, green and round like giant wooded boobs. He laughed at that idea. He didn't know the name of the nearest town, but that wasn't what was important about traveling. Traveling was about putting some distance between you and where you were coming from. And he was definitely doing that. He'd burned through a whole tank of fuel already.

He'd been surrounded by hills his whole life but by God, these here must be mountains. They rose up from the interstate on either side as if the road itself was a river turning and carving its way down through the rock. He'd gone mudding in some tight spots, but these cliffs were making him sweat through his shirt. Nobody talked about Kentucky having mountains, but he hadn't seen a sign for Tennessee yet. He thought if he stopped and went home right now, he'd be able to claim he'd seen real mountains.

Heat from the motor came through the dash. He'd never driven it this hard. Checking the oil the next time he stopped would be a good idea. If the engine died right here he didn't know what in the hell he'd do, or even how he'd get off the road without ramping off a mountainside or plowing right into the side of one. Especially now that it was getting dark. In spots the trees were cleared away and he stole glances out over valleys that looked like they knew no end.

The map lay in a crumpled pile atop his duffel bag. He'd consulted it again at lunch and he knew to stay on 75 through Kentucky and into Tennessee. It'd seemed like he could do all that in a day, but now he was tired and his arms were sore from wrestling with the steering wheel. The off-road tires had a tendency to wander.

Going through Lexington had been a little too intense for his liking, too. He'd hit the city around lunchtime and the traffic swarmed him like a cloud of hornets, passing him on both sides, gesturing and waving. He'd locked onto the steering wheel and kept his eyes straight ahead. Thank the stars he was supposed to stay on 75, so he didn't really have to read road signs.

Down here in southern Kentucky the traffic was thinner, and it wasn't even full dark, but he thought about stopping somewhere and sleeping. He figured he'd park somewhere and crash in the bed of his truck. He didn't think anyone would mess with him—after all, he'd barely seen a house once he got into the mountains. He'd buy a sack of ice and a Styrofoam cooler, then knock back some of those beers as they got cold.

He wondered what Summer was doing tonight. What she and Spring were going to eat for dinner. He thought about stopping at a pay phone and calling her, but then he caught himself. Calling her the same day he left? Before she really learned her lesson? No thanks. He might as well call and admit he was whipped, and then drive home with his tail wrapped up under him, covering his genitals.

The trees down here were so thick he wondered if a man could even walk through them. Sure looked like bear country. Bear and mountain lion country. And of course coyotes, but they had those back home.

When he was in junior high school, about seventh grade, he'd camped with the old man back in the woods by the river. They'd done this right after school let out in the spring. In a week, the report cards would be mailed home and he'd be in serious trouble. But that hadn't occurred yet. He recalled how the trees had leafed out, the treetops overhead blocking out the sun, except where little daggers of light came through the canopy and lit the ground. He thought about those days and tried to remember himself before he'd driven a car, had sex, drank hard liquor. It was like seeing a kid riding a bike and trying to guess what he was thinking. Ollie had no idea who he'd been.

But his father was different back then, too. And that spring the crops had gone into the ground fairly quickly, due to a long dry spell in April and May, and with the hay not quite on yet, there was time for a night in the woods. The old man wanted to fish all night, so they camped on a sandbar on the inside of a river bend.

His dad drug branches and logs down from the woods and soon a fire burned in a pit carved into the sand. Ollie hadn't seen how he'd done it so quickly. His own job was to whittle green branches down to a point to skewer hot dogs. When enough wood lay piled, the old man cast out the lines and propped the rods against sticks in the sand. He fastened little bells to the tips, so they could hear a fish thumping the rod.

Ollie wanted to remember now what they'd talked about, but he could only see quick images and hear snippets of sound. Surely they'd talked some. The night came on slowly, the mosquitoes thick once you got out of the smoke of the fire. His dad caught a little bullhead, and they both looked at it before he tossed it back into the river. Later the old man yelled that there was a bite on the pole Ollie was supposed to watch, but when he got there, the fish had stolen the bait. They were baiting up with a bluegill Frank had cut into strips.

At some point late at night his father caught a giant turtle, and Ollie held the flashlight's beam on it. A softshell—its shell as big around as a five-gallon bucket—hooked in the snout of its pointy nose. Its mouth, white inside, popped and snapped. With the hook out, they set it on the bank, where it hissed and slid into the water faster than Ollie would've thought.

They hadn't brought a tent, and when Ollie couldn't stay awake any longer he unrolled his sleeping bag under the smoke of the fire and climbed into its coolness. He saw his father's silhouette against the shiny, moonlit water—sitting on a bucket, waiting for the fish.

Much later, he jerked awake. The coyotes called again. He'd heard them through the walls of the house but this time they seemed to be right in the camp. Snarling, yipping, barking to each other. They could sound like dogs, and a breath later they'd sound like women screaming in the woods.

"Hear them coyotes?" the old man whispered.

The air was heavy and dark and it felt to Ollie like they'd never been inside a house in all their lives. Eventually, the sounds moved off down the valley and his dad stood up to feed some more wood to the fire.

Looking back on it, he probably hadn't done that sort of thing often enough. He didn't always know it as it was happening, but those were pretty good times. But what could you do? Once you got a little older, you started running around, drinking and chasing girls. There were so many different kinds of girls and so many ways to get drunk. Then you looked up one day and you weren't a kid anymore and you were living in a trailer all alone. If you could go back in time you'd do more of it, more camping and fishing with the old man, but you couldn't, so what was the use in thinking about it?

He drove on and started thinking about finding a place to get some food. A diner or truckstop or something. Then he'd find a place to park and get some sleep. If he decided not to sleep in the truck bed he could always sleep across the seat. He didn't think a bear would come after him over the tailgate but what the hell did he know about bears.

CHAPTER TWENTY-SEVEN

When Frank woke the next morning, his first thoughts were of fishing. Even before he was fully awake his mind formed lists of things he'd need to fish with Chub today. Then he opened his eyes and took in the bearings of the old familiar room, the same one he'd woken in for the last forty-five years, and the cold and certain knowledge that his friend was dead returned. There was the funeral to deal with. Ollie. These facts visited him one after another and he left his head on the pillow, eyes closed again.

Eventually he rose and drew on his clothes. In the kitchen he lifted Catfish, tail wagging, out of his corner pen, and the dog followed him to the door. Frank let him out, poured some coffee, and sat down at the table. There was an empty plate at his place. In a minute or so the pup would scratch at the door and he'd serve him a bowl of food. Ethel sat at the table, drinking coffee and reading the paper.

"Howdy," he said to her, quietly.

She looked up at him, eyes tired. She looked ten years older today than she had yesterday. "There's something in here about his funeral," she said.

"I figured there would be."

She read it to him—a list of facts he already knew. Where the funeral would be held. What time it started. The notice didn't say anything about the man himself. He listened only partly as he waited for the sound of Catfish's scratching.

"But there's something else in here about that town meeting regarding the lake," she said, and he watched her while she turned pages. She looked down through the reading lenses of her bifocals and studied each page before licking her finger and flipping. "Here it is. This says they plan on moving the public hearing next month."

He poured a little milk from the small glass pitcher into his coffee and picked up a piece of toast from the plate in the middle of the table. She'd already buttered it. He took a bite and chewed, looking at the rest of the piece in his hand.

"I said they aim to move the public meeting," she said.

"I heard you."

"Well, you never said nothing about it."

"We ain't goin to a public meeting."

She stared across the table. "Well, now it's gonna be at the grade school. Not the high school. On account of some conflict or another." She waited for him to speak, but he only chewed his toast. "So now it's gonna be at the grade school, and not the high school."

Still he said nothing.

"Well, I just thought maybe in the meantime we could talk to somebody," she said. "Somebody who knows a little something about this."

"You mean a lawyer, then."

"Maybe. Or someone like that. Somebody who could tell us about our rights."

He dropped the rest of his toast on his plate. "We ain't gonna talk to nobody! We don't know no lawyers! And if we did, why would they help us over them? Jesus, why can't you figure that out?"

She stood unsteadily, pressing her hands against the tabletop, and took her coffee to the sink. He turned in his chair to watch her. She threw the cup against the enameled steel and broke her first dish in over ten years with a loud clatter.

He stared at her. It was just after five in the morning. Chub's funeral was in five hours. There was one thing to suggest that'd make her stop talking about the damn meeting.

"Let's go out to Ollie's," he said. "Fore he gets up and goes to work."

Catfish scratched at the door, whining.

It was already eighty degrees when they walked outside. There was no fog but the heat surrounded them like that, hammering down their chests and pulling their air out. There were still shards of her coffee cup in the sink.

It didn't take long to drive there, of course. Just several left turns they didn't usually take, and the trailer came into view in its little field of weeds.

"He lives so close to us," she said, as if she were surprised.

Already they could tell something was wrong. The light burned on the pole in the yard, even though the sun was up fully now. When they got closer to the drive, they could see his truck was gone.

"He's out for breakfast," she said.

He almost laughed. He felt like saying, "Yes, and he's probably also helping the Amish way out west of town prepare to go to the moon." But he kept silent and parked in the driveway. The grass hadn't been cut, and around the base of the trailer the weeds grew tall. Lights on for no reason. So this is how he meant to repay them for providing a place to live.

They sat in the truck without speaking, studying the trailer. Catfish perched on the seat between them, watching his face. Any time Frank looked down at him, his tail beat against the seat or her ribs.

"Whyn't you go knock on the door?" he said. The dog's eyebrows went up and his tail thumped.

"He ain't home, though."

"It doesn't look like it. But maybe his truck's in the shop or something." He didn't want to drive home yet, where there'd be little to do except wait for the topic of the reservoir to come up until it was time to dress for the funeral.

She wanted to go—she'd only been waiting for him to ask her. She wanted more than anything to go to her son's door and find out who he was now, why he hadn't spoken to them nearly all summer.

So she got out and went down the beaten path to the front door. She noted the ripped screens, the crooked shutters. The places where the skirt had fallen away to reveal the cavern beneath the trailer. She could smell the place.

She knocked on the screen door first. After doing that twice, she opened it and knocked on the wood one. Her muffled thuds echoed out the windows on either side of her. Then, using all the courage in her, she tried the doorknob. She was relieved to find it locked.

But there was a little window in the wood door, and standing on her toes on the small steps, she could peer into it. Through the dirty pane she made out the TV and the counter that marked the beginning of the kitchen.

He honked then, and the jolt that traveled through her spine felt like it'd kill her. She turned, let the screen door slap, and hurried back down the path. She jerked open the door.

"You about scared me to death, you dummy!" she yelled.

"He ain't home, then. No use in dawdling."

He started the truck and she clambered in, pushing Catfish aside.

"I'd like to know why the fool left his light on, though," he said. "I'm glad I ain't payin his lectric bill."

They drove home in silence.

When they got back to the house, he parked the truck and lowered Catfish to the ground, who wheeled across the grass in exultation.

"You gonna mess with the chicken coop today?" he asked.

"It's too hot even for this time of morning. I'd about croak in there today. Besides, we don't have much time fore I got to get ready."

"You want to check the garden?"

Together they walked behind the barn and through the rows of vegetables. More tomatoes were ripe, and they'd eaten a bunch already. She'd can the rest. The sweet corn was about there—another week or two and they'd start shucking the fullest ears.

"I wonder where in the world he went," she said.

"He probably just slept over at Coondog's." A little while later he added, "If you want, we can go out there again after we get back from the cemetery."

She bent over to pick a tomato. "No, he never. He went somewhere else, somewhere farther. A mother knows."

"Where in the world could he go?"

"I don't know! That's why I'm worried weary over him."

"You got other things to worry about first." He made his way down the row, his cane leaving pocked holes in the soil.

And so, although he hadn't gone into any church for years, Frank walked back into this one for the second time in two days. Ethel was next to him, wearing the black dress she always wore to funerals. He wore the same jacket and pants he'd worn to visitation. Again the tie, which he'd found in the truck, was clipped to his collar. They passed through the tall wooden doors and immediately the casket was visible at the front of the church, under the cross with the likeness of Jesus hanging on it.

Then a young man appeared in front of them, holding out his hand. Frank stared until he recognized the boy—Charles, Chub's son. He'd seen him only yesterday but it'd been so long before then he remained a stranger. Frank shook his hand.

"Good to see you again, Frank," Charles was saying. "I mean, all things considered, of course."

Frank nodded and Charles moved back and shook Ethel's hand without saying her name.

"I still can't believe how grown up you are," she said. "I'm glad you're home."

This time there was a woman standing behind Charles. He turned slightly and put his hand on the woman's shoulder.

"This is my wife, Sarah," he said. The woman smiled weakly and kept her hands at her sides. "She couldn't make it in for the viewing, but she flew in this morning."

Frank nodded at her. Ethel said, "How do you do."

Sarah was thin and pale, making her seem younger than she must've been. They stood there, a wan couple. Charles put his hands in his suit pockets and pursed his lips and nodded. His eyes went to Frank's tie and stayed there for a moment, registering it away.

"Well, I know you were close to my dad," he said.

Frank looked at him. "I was."

"His fishing buddy, right?" Charles seemed to alight on this subject. He looked at Sarah. "This is the guy Dad was always fishing with!"

The look on her face made it clear that she was hearing this news for the first time. Still, she nodded and smiled.

Frank looked to the front of the church, where several people stood around the casket. A few more sat in the pews. The church no more full than it'd been during visitation. The preacher stood off to the left of the casket.

"—this year?"

Frank looked at him.

Charles waited for a while and then asked again, "I said, did you and my dad catch any of those big catfish this year?" He turned to his wife. "These guys would go out in their boats and catch these giant catfish. You should've seen these fish! They were huge!" Charles wore glasses and seemed to want some kind of beard around his mouth.

"I guess we did catch some this year," Frank said, looking away.

"And what is it you use for bait, to catch those big ones? I can't remember what my dad used to tell me. Was it chunks of cheese or something? Maybe hot dogs?" Charles wasn't exactly loud, but he didn't seem to remember where and when this conversation was taking place.

Frank glanced down at his cane handle. Christ, he knew he'd have to talk some, but he hadn't thought it'd be this bad.

"Are you two expecting children?" Ethel asked, looking at Sarah.

She was visibly surprised. "Not yet," she stammered. "Well, not for a while, anyway."

"That's good," Ethel said. "LuAnne always wanted grandkids. She would've liked that, God rest her soul."

At the mention of his mother's name Charles's face grew even paler. "Well, we'd better let you find your seats," he said. "I just wanted to say thanks for being such a good friend to my dad." He held out his hand again.

Frank looked at him until Ethel grabbed his arm and then Frank shook hands. Without saying more Frank and Ethel moved past them and sat near the front in a pew.

The preacher approached them cautiously and shook their hands. Neither Frank nor Ethel stood. The preacher said a few words of vague condolences, his giant eyes full of rehearsed sympathy, and let them be. A few neighbors and friends from long ago stopped and said some things. Save Charles and Sarah, there were no young people in the congregation. No crying babies, no freshly-scrubbed farm kids with cowlicks. Only old and stooped citizens, practiced at funerals and grieving.

Later, the preacher rose behind the pulpit and said his piece about death and Clarence Peters. He quoted relevant scripture, again touching on Job and his struggles. He said the names of Charles and Sarah, as they were the last of the immediate family. Charles, seated in the front pew across the aisle, cried effectively and efficiently, although his wife, who had only met her husband's father a few times, couldn't even manage that.

Still later, they all stood and the women sang "Amazing Grace." And only then, with the collective sound of their old and thin voices warbling and rising to the ceiling, did Frank need to reach for the handkerchief he carried in his back pocket. He lowered his head and wiped his eyes while the preacher closed the casket's lid.

He had stopped looking at his friend's face during the service, because it hadn't seemed like him. But when he realized the casket had been sealed, and he'd never see Chub's face again, he gasped and wept. Ethel rubbed his back, her own face wet with tears. He wanted to believe that Chub was in a better place, as everyone said, and that he'd find rivers there full of catfish for him to catch and fry. At the same time, Chub was never one for fishing alone and Frank hoped some other catmen who had gone first would take a third partner into their boat until he got there. And they'd better not carry on about his size or smell, either.

Because of his cane, they hadn't asked Frank to be a pallbearer. And there wouldn't have been enough friends and relatives, so instead workers from the cemetery moved the large casket to the waiting hearse after everyone filed out of the church. It took ten of them. None of them knew the man inside the casket, and later, drinking beers at a tavern in Hapgood after the grave had been shoveled shut, they'd joke about how heavy the bastard was.

Norman Fisk sat in his log cabin and stared at the name in the paper for several moments. Clarence Peters. Funeral to be held today. Why was that name familiar? Only survived by one son, Charles. He didn't think he knew the son. The notice claimed Clarence died at age seventy-two, but still, he knew the name meant something.

He read the funeral notices in the Current to keep up on property and see what was suddenly available. Most died in a nursing home, having long since given up their property, or maybe they left behind a small house in town that could be rented or torn down and replaced with a duplex. Most people, he noticed, didn't leave much behind by way of land. Or the kids would take it for themselves. But you never knew when a heart attack or car wreck or some freak accident would KO some young fucker and all of a sudden a widow would be left with a big painted farm and a broken heart. He checked every week, often consulting his plat map to see where the dearly-deceased had owned land.

So it didn't take him long to place Clarence Peters. Man called himself Chub. Big old dude living out there in that ranch house by himself, sitting on what would someday be close to the edge of the lake. Chub Peters, who refused to sell his three acres, worth about fifty if you didn't know about the lake, for a hundred grand.

Well now he wasn't around to say no. Fisk grabbed his keys off the kitchen counter and went into the den, where his two kids and pregnant wife lay watching a movie. He hated to see them wasting the day but he let it slide with Brandi being so far along.

"Gotta go check some property out," he said.

"Dad," Cheryl began, "don't forget you need to take me school shopping soon. School's almost here, and I'm gonna need some new jeans, shoes, a purse—"

"We're going. But not today and probably not tomorrow. So chill, all right?"

"But Dad, the thing is, with—"

"Brandi." He looked at his wife.

"Cheryl," she said. "Dad's busy now. You can tell me your list later."

"See you all later," he said, but they had resumed watching the movie.

He stood there, but they didn't look up. "Cheryl, clean that stall out before I get back, okay?"

"Fine, Dad."

He remembered, of course, exactly how to get there. When he pulled his dually into the drive, he saw a slight, dark-haired woman coming out of the house with a box in her hands. She wore shorts and he checked her out thoroughly. Not bad. Little pale and thin for his tastes, but not too shabby. She put the box into a tiny car—a rental, he noticed—and stood there like she was scared to death.

"Hello there," he said, climbing out of the cab.

"Hello," she said. "You probably want to talk to my husband. He's inside."

"That'd be Charles?"

"How'd you know that? Did you attend Charles's school or something?"

"I don't believe I did. Although I did graduate from over at Green City."

"Oh. Well, he's inside."

"Ma'am, I am awfully sorry to hear about your loss. Chub was a fine man." He was now close enough to reach his hand out. She took it and shook it once, timidly.

She turned and he followed her into the house. It was even more disorderly. Boxes sat open, overflowing with papers. Cabinet doors hung open.

"Honey," she called. "Someone's here to see you about your dad."

From the moment Charles came up out of the basement, sweaty and dirty but still wearing his collared shirt, Fisk knew he had him. The chump looked like he was drowning. It took a lot of work and perseverance to go through someone's home after he died, and this guy clearly had already done enough to last him.

They moved out to the old picnic table in the backyard. It was too hot and dusty in the house. Out at the table, in the shade cast by the big oak tree, they sat and talked. Fisk couldn't help but smile as he recalled leaving his name on a piece of paper on this same table just last week.

"So, did you know my father pretty well?" Charles asked.

"I sure did. He was a good man."

Charles glanced at his wife. "I don't recall seeing you at the funeral."

"I know it," Fisk said. "That's partly why I'm here. I was out of town on business for all of last week, and I just got back an hour ago. Hated like heck to miss it. I came over here soon's I got back. Glad I caught you all."

No one said anything for a while.

"So, you're flying out soon, I guess?" Fisk asked.

"Yeah, Friday. We need to get back. I wanted to get some of this taken care of first, I guess. Sarah needs to get back, though, on account of her job."

Fisk nodded in her direction. It felt like the picnic table might collapse under their weight. When one of them shifted, the whole table settled.

"What will you do with all of Chub's things?" he asked. "Since you're flying out and all."

Charles looked back at the house. "Yeah, there's a lot of it. In the garage there, too. I guess it'll all go in storage, until we have time to come back out here and go through it more carefully."

"Tell you what, I got a big closed trailer I could lend you to help move his stuff. I'm not using it this week."

Charles's eyes brightened, but then dimmed just as quickly. "Thanks, but all we have to pull it with is that car."

Fisk looked around the yard like he was mulling some things over. Damn I'm good, he thought.

In the inside of an hour Fisk had offered to not only lend them the use of his pickup and trailer, but to help them load it. He'd drive Chub's things to the storage unit they'd rented over in Green City and he'd pack up the garage himself. Charles allowed that he felt a little weird in there, so Fisk would do that part. It was the least he could do, missing the funeral and all.

For the rest of that day and all of Thursday, the three of them worked hard. Fisk called someone he knew and had a Dumpster hauled out there for trash, and as time passed and the work grew, Charles kept suggesting more and more things just be thrown away. No one would want that chair, right? What about the television? It's so old it hardly works. The fridge was nasty—did Fisk think he could get it into the Dumpster? All right then, go get the Bobcat skid loader. Fisk was a big man, and more used to this kind of work. Charles and Sarah told him repeatedly they couldn't have done it without his help.

As they worked, they talked. They would've caught Fisk in his lies about Chub if they'd known him better themselves. And Fisk kept asking about their careers back East, instead. He wanted to know about them, not talk about the deceased. He was so friendly and interested in their lives!

Eventually, the issue of the house itself came up. And Charles spoke about how difficult it would be to deal with a realtor in Indiana when he was home in Boston. But that became a moot point when Fisk told them about his daughter. She'd love a house like this, he said. Did he look too young to have a daughter that old? Well, he explained in a way that meant they should move on to something else, she was getting married young.

By the time the plane left Indianapolis Friday, bound for Boston in a direct flight, what remained of Chub's possessions were either in a storage unit in Green City or on their way to the dump. And the house, garage, and three acres had been bought, for sixty thousand dollars, by Norman Fisk.

When they settled into their seats on the plane, Sarah elated to be leaving Indiana, and Charles less so but still relieved, they talked about what a godsend Fisk had been.

"He certainly made that job easier," Charles said. "Now we won't have to fly back out next month."

"Can you believe Norman has a daughter old enough to get married? He didn't look past forty, himself."

He laughed. "I told you! That's how they do it out here."

CHAPTER TWENTY-EIGHT

It'd lightly rained at some point during the night, and now Ollie's sleeping bag felt heavy and moist. The sun was just strong enough to heat up the damp bedding and make it stink like wet feathers. His back ached from sleeping on the steel truck bed, and his eye throbbed. As he pulled himself out of the sleeping bag, everything he touched was wet. Soon he was chilled and miserable.

When he looked around, things appeared as they had the night before—he was near the entrance to some sort of park. While it seemed public enough, there was no gatehouse and, apparently, no patrolling rangers. He'd been seeing signs for the Daniel Boone National Forest, and he thought he was close to it, if not smack-dab in it. The only other thing in this small clearing off the road was a dumpster, and he'd heard something bump against it in the night.

But he'd slept all the way through and survived his first night on the road. He knew the open road was a bitch and that he'd be forced to earn her respect. Last night surely earned him some, although he'd paid dearly for it. He stepped to the ground in his sock feet and felt the moisture soak through them. His dry clothes were in the cab, but it'd be tricky getting dressed in there. He'd done it, of course, and his mind went to Summer. By now she'd be missing him. He hoped she was, anyway.

He was sure as hell noticing her absence.

It seemed like breakfast might help the way he felt. He pulled on dry clothes and his boots. He got out and took a leak near the dumpster, then lifted the plastic lid and peered inside. Nothing much. One black trash bag and a brown paper sack with a bottleneck sticking out of it. He thought about looking inside the trash bag and then decided against it. He did, though, find a big rock next to the dumpster, so he used that to weigh down the sleeping bag.

The truck started and he realized he hadn't checked the oil. He'd do that later. He drove back out to the main road, but turned away from the interstate and cruised into a little town. The sign on the highway read "Welcome to Lewisburg—Home of the Indians," along with other claims, but he had no time to read them. It was a town not altogether unfamiliar to him, looking quite a bit like those back home. When he reached the downtown area, he noticed a red awning that said "Mary Lou's Diner," so he parked across the street from it. He grabbed the damp sleeping bag from the bed and stuffed it into the cab.

A few people outside the restaurant seemed to be waiting for others, so he walked past them and went into the diner. It felt a little too warm and the place was clouded in cigarette smoke. Immediately to his right was a counter with a row of stools, and one or two of them were open, so he went and plopped down. A man to his left wearing a cap glanced up and looked him over and then nodded, satisfied that he didn't know him. There was a woman on his right who sat next to her husband, and she didn't look up at all. Ollie got the suspicion that he might smell a little too strongly to be sitting right by people, but he could leave one stool open between him and the woman, anyway. That would have to do. He didn't know where he might go to take a shower.

He turned the coffee cup in front of him over and instantly a heavy-set woman stood across the counter from him, filling it. She said she'd be right back to take his order, and handed him a sticky plastic-coated menu. He opened it and decided he'd have an omelette with about everything in it. Thinking about it made his tongue dart to the corners of his mouth.

The big woman came back and he ordered. She wrote it down without saying more than she had to.

The man next to him listened and then turned a little on his stool.

"You from outta town?" he asked.

Ollie looked at him. He was probably as old as his dad. His mustache had a piece of bacon or something in it. His skin was as worn as the underside of an old belt.

"Yep, from Indiana."

The man made a sound with his throat. "Where ya headin?"

"I'm trying to get to South Carolina."

"That right? Well, you got a long way to go."

"I reckon so. Bout how long it take from here?"

The man thought on this. He sipped his coffee, which had just been freshened, and it was hot and burned him. It registered on his face. "Not sure I know," he said, touching his napkin to his tongue.

"You never been there?"

"Nah. Now, my sister and them went several times, and they said it don't take too long."

Ollie took a drink of his coffee. He poured a little sugar into it from the glass container sitting there. The little trap door on the top opened as the sugar poured out in a thin stream.

"You leaving your wife at home?" the man asked.

"I ain't married."

The man looked at him again. "That right? How old are you?"

"Thirty-one."

"Shit, boy, by the time I was that age I had four kids and was on my second wife on account of I wore my first one out."

"That right?"

He nodded. His plate sat empty in front of him, but he didn't seem in a hurry to leave, either. "You're probably better off," the man said.

Ollie said nothing. He looked up at the wall behind the counter. An opening into the kitchen and a framed snapshot of little kids in baseball uniforms.

"I mean, my kids bout put me in the poor house. Some of em couldn't stay out of trouble, neither. Now most of em's settled down, though. Got fifteen grandkids."

"I was datin a woman, she had a kid," Ollie said, almost before he knew he was going to speak.

"Uh-huh. My second wife, she had two kids of her own, and I had them two of mine from my first wife."

"But I don't know if I'm seeing her no more or not."

"My first wife, me and her didn't get along too good. We got married young. Then when Lincoln Plastics shut down out here, and I lost my job, she decided she'd had enough of that and me altogether. "

Ollie looked down the counter. People were smoking. Some were bent over their food. Some were talking to those sitting next to them.

The waitress brought his breakfast then—a half circle of scrambled egg, pregnant and mounded over everything he'd ordered inside it. She poured him some more coffee. He picked up his fork and began to eat. He found himself to be much hungrier then. The omelette was good and he wondered how they'd cooked it so fast.

The man next to him continued talking. Now it was more about his old job, it seemed. Ollie nodded once in a while and forked the hot food into his mouth.

Moments later, the man paused. Ollie looked up at him. "What's that?" he asked.

"I said where bouts you from in Indiana?"

"Southeastern part. Near Green City."

"I had a cousin move up that way once. Ever hear of Vevee or something like that?"

Ollie said he had.

"Yeah, she moved up there. Talk about a wild one. She put a tattoo said 'Ride Me' on her arm. Meant it, too. That was a cousin, on my mother's side. Them ones, they was always crazy. One of em's in the pen now."

The omelette came with a side of toast and Ollie grabbed one piece and sopped up the yellow cheese and egg that had pooled on his plate. Christ, this food was good. He felt a lot better already. The ticket was under the edge of his plate and he picked it up and looked at it. He decided to leave four bucks and that'd cover the tip, too. It wouldn't leave much for the waitress, but she hadn't done much to deserve it.

It was unbelievable that the man should still be talking, but he was. Ollie reached for his wallet. He knew he was close to Tennessee, and he was anxious to see what that was like. Day two of driving. He needed to take a shit now, but he thought he'd get down the road a bit first.

"Well, I wished I coulda told how far you had to go," the man said. "You don't mess around when you eat, do ya?"

Ollie put the four singles out in front of his plate and drained his coffee. "Don't worry about it," he said, standing up.

The man reached in the front pocket of his flannel shirt and pulled out a lighter and some cigarettes. He took one out and lit it. He blew smoke down onto his plate. Ollie watched it hit the plate and blow upwards again.

"See ya," he said.

"Yeah, take her easy," the man said.

Before Ollie turned to leave, the waitress came over and took his plate. "You okay, hon?" she asked.

"Yeah, I'm fine," he said. "That was good, thanks."

She nodded and walked back down the counter. She left the plate in front of the other man. He looked down and smoked.

Ollie walked outside. The sun was up pretty good now, and it was warm. He reached in the truck and threw the sleeping bag into the bed, up against the cab, and set the rock back on top of it.

He headed toward the interstate. Even when you stopped, the road was a lonely place. At least he had Tennessee to look forward to. Still, it was starting to feel weird being so far from home. He didn't know anybody down here.

What he'd thought were mountains in Kentucky were replaced by sheer glaciers of rock so large it strained the truck just to drive up them. And then, once he'd labored up one, he'd come roaring down the mountainside into a curve that threatened to throw his old Chevy off into the abyss. And now the radio, which he'd come to rely on greatly, gained and lost reception. A song would be playing clear as mountain air and then the radio waves would bounce off a cliff or something and he'd be left with static.

He'd survived Knoxville traffic and even lucked his way onto Interstate 40, so he aimed for Asheville, North Carolina. He was driving by a bunch of big signs meant to lure you to Gatlinburg when Johnny Cash came on the radio, and for once the station stayed steady. Johnny played "A Boy Named Sue," and a melancholic mood settled over him like seeing a graveyard procession and he drove slower and thought about his old man.

"All he left me was this old guitar and an empty bottle of booze," Johnny sang.

What would his father have left him? Hard to say, since the old man had lived in the same house and slept in the same room for as long as Ollie'd been alive. He tried to imagine Frank making decisions about what to leave behind, running off like the guy in the song. Ollie guessed he'd have left the farm itself, because he couldn't pack that up, even if he wanted to.

Damn, how far along was the old man, anyway? Was he seventy-five already? Maybe only seventy-two? The song ended then, and he'd been thinking and zoned out on his favorite verse—the part where father and son fight out into the street, and eventually reconcile after trying to kill each other. "Cursing and a cussin through the mud, the blood and the beer." He loved that line, but he'd missed it.

But what would the old man leave? Well, the truck and the boat, for sure. That boat was the first thing somebody thought of when they thought of his dad. The truck was newer than Ollie's—he guessed he might keep it. Still, it'd be weird driving around his dad's truck. He could always sell it, though, and use the money to replace this one. The boat he'd sell. The thought of making money off his dad's death excited him a little, as much as it shamed him to feel it.

And what about the farm? Over two hundred acres, owned free and clear under the family name. That'd be his, and although he didn't know what an acre was going for these days, it was worth a hell of a lot more than a truck and an old boat.

His mom would be in charge, of course. He assumed she'd outlive the old man. She'd stay on the farm, too, since it'd been hers even longer. Not to mention he'd heard horror stories about the nursing home in Hapgood, and he didn't want to see her go there. But he couldn't see taking care of her in his trailer. Would he move back into the house, then? Maybe so.

He drove without looking around. He'd already driven more in the last two days than he usually did in two months back home. As another eighteen-wheeler passed him, he wondered how they sat up there and drove all damned day.

Starting tomorrow he'd need to call in sick every morning. That stood to be a pain in the ass, especially once the partying got under way. He calculated the amount of work he might miss on this trip. He hoped to be in South Carolina today—he was already almost in North Carolina, and how much farther could South Carolina be? But then it'd be Thursday morning, and he'd call in sick. Fine. When he stopped and really thought about it, though, it kind of seemed like he only had one sick day coming to him. He'd lost track there during the spring, when he'd gone on a little tear. Beginning Friday morning, then, he'd be using vacation and sick days he didn't have.

He'd be shitcanned for sure.

When he left, he hadn't worried too much because he didn't plan on returning. But if he ended up going back, he didn't know where else to work. He needed that damn sawmill job.

So he wouldn't go back: problem solved as quickly as it'd come up. He drove even deeper into the mountains. He'd slowed way down to better handle the treacherous curves, but cars were stacking up on his ass. Just when it seemed like the worst was behind him, up he'd go, ears popping. Signs kept warning about a big tunnel ahead, too. They'd hung chain-link fencing on the mountains to keep the rockslides off the interstate. What the hell kind of place was this?

It was proving to be harder than he'd thought, this trip. Granted, he wasn't in South Carolina yet, and that was where all the hot women were supposed to be. Ray didn't say anything about hot women in Kentucky or Tennessee, or even North Carolina. He said they lived in South Carolina.

But how could he meet these women by himself? What was he supposed to do, walk around and introduce himself? Sure, he'd talked with that desperate loser in the diner, but he knew from past experiences, there was a whale of a difference between talking to some old man and a hot ass chick!

And then he thought to himself, I already got a hot woman back home.

She'd be at work now, processing the bills and answering the phone. He visualized her mouth near the receiver. Her straight, white teeth behind her lips.

God, he missed her.

He touched his fingertips to his eye. Still sore, but the swelling had gone down considerably. Maybe he'd been wrong to take so much of that out on her. Suddenly, the desire to talk to her overcame him. He needed to say some of this to her, not just in his head! But there were no exits up here in the mountains.

He replayed the conversation where he'd yelled at her, telling her she'd never get another chance to see him. That seemed a little harsh, now. She'd been as caught off-guard as he was that night Todd appeared. But he'd blamed her. No wonder he was down here in the mountains alone. No wonder she let him leave.

But he could call her house later. By now she knew he was gone. She was probably worried to death about him—maybe she'd gone looking for his trailer, seeking him out, just driving around aimlessly in the country in her shitty little Omni, crying into a tiny wad of toilet paper. Poor thing! No doubt she regretted that fight even more than he did.

Yes, one phone call might make a difference, he allowed. He climbed the next mountain. Sooner or later he'd have to come down—and sooner or later they'd have to let people exit off this crazy road.

CHAPTER TWENTY-NINE

The public place best suited for this kind of meeting would've been the high school auditorium over in Green City, but they'd been remodeling it all summer. Although it only lacked drywall and paint, no one wanted to postpone the meeting. Locals had been discussing this lake over coffee, family pitch-ins and church dinners for years, and were desperate for something official. The U.S. Army Corps of Engineers couldn't reschedule due to some contractors lagging behind, anyway. So they held the meeting in Green City Elementary. After the day's food remnants had been scrubbed off the tables, and all the trays and silverware washed, they brought down the silver metal doors that covered the window bays where the little kids dropped off their plates heaped with uneaten food and locked the doors to the kitchen. The staff left the tables open and unfolded this time, and were told not to stack the chairs against the far wall. This is where the public meeting would commence.

The people of Shipley County started to wander in an hour early. In the front of the room, on the same tiny stage where the students had watched a version of the 'Three Little Pigs' in the spring, a few men milled about. They'd set up a row of chairs, as well as a podium and a white screen.

The guests wondered where they were supposed to sit. Their only option seemed to be the tiny chairs meant for six through twelve year olds.

"Sorry folks," a man kept saying from the stage. "This building doesn't have any bigger chairs." The seats were no higher than the knees of even the shortest men and women. No one would sit. Beaux Silvers, who ran a nearby gas station, said, "Oh the hell you say," loudly and stood against the back wall, arms folded across his chest. Those walking in behind him followed suit.

Fifty showed up, followed by another wave. Many members of the crowd had white hair, but younger people turned out, too. A few lead little kids. The children were astonished to see so many adults in their lunchroom. They gazed about, wide-eyed, and tried to tell their parents about events that'd transpired in this very place until they got shushed quiet.

When Frank and Ethel entered, the place was almost full. The walls on all three sides were taken, and people stood in clusters throughout the expanse of the room. He walked in wearing his clean pants and a newer hat, and she wore a cotton dress. A younger couple they didn't know saw that he carried a cane and moved off the wall to give him a place to lean. Ethel thanked them. They stood to the right of the stage, near the entrance.

She'd called Ollie for this, but he hadn't answered. They didn't know where he was.

They'd come anyway, without Ollie and without Chub, and they leaned against the wall of the school lunchroom and waited for the men on the stage to begin speaking. With so many people standing, they couldn't see much. The tiny chairs had been stacked, and they stood in towers throughout the crowd.

Four sheriff's deputies filed in then, wearing their tan uniforms fully geared, complete with holstered pistols. They positioned themselves one on each wall and on either side of the stage. People moved aside for them and then stared at the various tools fastened to their belts.

With a loud buzz and then a pop, the microphone on the podium came to life in the man's hand. He wore a blue uniform, as did three other men on the stage. "Standing room only," he said, and then smiled onto the audience, which did not laugh.

"Our apologies, folks, on this situation here with these chairs. The high school is being redone—there's your tax dollars at work—and this is the only public room we could get that was big enough. And you'd be surprised how hard it is to find people-sized—you know, big people—chairs in an elementary school."

Some talking broke out in the crowd. Some of the women laughed a little while most of the men stood there stone-faced.

"Well, anyway, I'll get started. My name is Steve Dunkirk, and I'm a Project Manager for the United States Army Corps of Engineers. I'd start by providing a little overview: the USACE consists of about thirty-four thousand civilians and over six hundred military members. Basically, we are engineers, scientists, hydrologists, natural resource managers, among other titles. In a word, we oversee federal engineering projects. With regards to this particular project in Shipley County, we're overseeing the possibility of a reservoir project, which includes feasibility studies, construction, and maintenance, for the purposes of municipal use and flood management, specifically concerning the Big Logjam River and its upper tributaries. To that end, I represent the Louisville District, which covers five states, one of those being Indiana, encompassing three hundred and six thousand miles."

He paused and looked around the room. The townspeople of Shipley County stared at him. He took a small sip from a cup hidden on a shelf in the podium, itself bearing the county seal—a nondescript collection of images too small to be seen clearly unless you stood inches away.

"At this time, I should introduce those who share the stage with me tonight. As I said earlier, my name's Steve Dunkirk, and I'm the Project Manager. Everett Schutte is here, and he's in engineering design." A man on Frank's side of the stage raised his hand. "Walter Shain is an attorney with the USACE." A white haired man stood from his seat on the stage and then sat back down. "Bill Lewis is a real estate expert." Another man raised his hand. "Finally,"

Dunkirk announced, "Colonel Haverstick is here from Washington, D.C." A man stood, wearing the full dress uniform of the U.S. Army, complete with badges and ribbons of color and striation. A tall man with a nearly shaved head. Frank hadn't seen him—he'd been hidden behind the podium.

The audience shifted from foot to foot and shuffled along the walls. Already they'd been met with things they hadn't expected.

Dunkirk gripped the sides of the podium. "Now, our policy has always been and will always be to involve the public in a discourse regarding projects that affect them and their region directly. As such this one does. With this public forum, which will be recorded, transcribed, and made public record, we intend to invite the public to voice their feelings regarding said project."

The people sat there, as mute and still as midnight mice caught by a flipped light switch.

"Areas that stand, in particular, to be involved include properties near the town of Logjam and, specifically, the areas northwest of the town limits, marked approximately by 100 West out to 600 West going west and up to 300 North, north of town. This project calls for the damming—that is to say, build an artificial structure that will reduce the flow of—Big Logjam River, which will reduce flooding downstream of that structure, including properties near town and farther downstream, up to and including the Ohio River."

Again small chattering sounds rose and Dunkirk took another sip from the cup.

"Now what is the over-arching purpose of this project? You ask. Why dam this little river? Well, as some of you know all too well, this waterway is prone to flooding."

Some members of the audience turned and said a few quick words to others standing near. Heads nodded and shook around the room.

"This dam will help us manage the waterway more efficiently, and certainly that's first and foremost our top priority. Also provided with flood control will be the municipal use of the water itself, that is to say the impounded body of water, which will provide a source of drinking water. Our studies show that currently, a good percentage of you rely on dug wells and such, and while that is certainly fine, this project will provide a more reliable and steady source of water, which should prove beneficial also with regard to trying to lure industry, in an effort to provide jobs to the people of this county. That is to say, to all of you."

He took another sip from his cup. "With a reservoir of some size in the vicinity, factories will be able to locate here due to the availability of water. The surrounding towns will also have access to a dependable water supply. And the reservoir will provide recreation in the forms of swimming, boating and fishing and the like."

The men seated on the stage nodded solemnly and watched the crowd. The engineer looked at his notes and glanced up from time to time.

"Now, most of you have heard some things about this project, probably, because news travels fast, doesn't it? Our intention with this forum is to eliminate some of the miscommunication and misintelligence that can accompany such a project, and to further that the USACE will display maps, charts and things of that nature tonight that should provide clarity, both in terms of what will be provided and how citizens will be affected. We also intend to allow citizens a chance to speak."

There was a ripple across the audience and a sprinkling of hands went up immediately.

"You ought to tell us first where it's gonna be, exactly," a man yelled out.

Dunkirk raised a hand. "Now, our intention is to give all of you a chance to speak and ask questions, but there are some experts up here who'd like to address, first, topics like environmental issues, the kinds of permits we're required to file, financial impact—"

"But we need to know where the water's gonna be!" the same man shouted.

Dunkirk nodded, glanced at the engineer behind him, and said, "that's right, and we will do that, but first, our chief engineer on this project, Everett Schutte." He left the podium and sat in a chair behind it.

Schutte stood and turned on an overhead projector and the screen on the stage lit up with a white light. "Could we lower the lights on the stage please?" he asked into the microphone. Some minutes passed before the lights over the stage fell dark, brightening the screen. He placed a transparency on the glass and everyone could see the shadow of his hand on the screen before a map snapped into focus.

He stepped again to the podium and cleared his throat. "My name is Everett Schutte, engineer with the USACE," he said. He held a long pointer.

On the map, a wavering blue line was clearly evident down the middle. This was the river in question, but everything else was scarcely discernible. There were brown squares that looked like fields, and green areas that might have been woodlots, but the audience was too far away to see much. Black lines intersected the map.

With his pointer, Schutte jabbed at a spot where a black line ran across the blue wavy one. "To give you all a point of reference, this is 600 West, or what you all might know as or call Smith's Hill Road. This line represents the bridge over Big Logjam River, in the vicinity of 150 North. Some of you might remember there used to be a covered bridge or something of that nature there until about ten years ago when the Indiana Department of

Transportation, or INDOT, had to tear it down to build a new bridge, which is what is out there now. At any rate, about one mile upriver of this bridge is the proposed site for the earthen-dam structure, marked by the green line here."

As he drew his pointer upriver, murmurs spread across the crowd as they surmised and speculated on whose land would be closest. A few voices rose.

"How far will it back up?" someone shouted, and it was too obvious and plain to ignore.

"At this time, we figure the body of water to be about nine hundred and fifty acres in size, which is not really a big reservoir, by most standards," Schutte said. There was considerable crowd noise at this. "A minimum of people will be affected, but we figure a lake of this size will provide ample flood control while also meeting the immediate and short term needs, as well as most of the long-term needs, of the municipal base here."

"But where will it go?" someone yelled.

Those looking closely at the map had already spotted the thin red line across the river, far upstream from the bridge.

"Here," Schutte said, pointing to that mark.

Noise grew in the auditorium.

"By our estimation," he began, "about one hundred and sixty-two landowners will be affected directly . . ." then someone on the stage said something and Schutte stopped talking. The crowd reverberation had grown such that it was hard to hear him at all.

Frank leaned against the wall. He felt like he was underwater, some massive flathead catfish watching the surface of the river from far below. He lay hidden under a big sunken oak tree, its trunk shading him, tentacles of moss clinging to the rotting wood swaying overhead. He had the firm and current-swept bottom beneath him. He sensed commotion on the surface, but was protected and safe here. Little fish swam around him, seeking the log's shelter but afraid to venture too close to his cavernous mouth. It was daytime, and for the biggest catfish, a time to rest and recuperate. Sounds came to him in distorted waves.

He'd already placed their farm on the map. It lay almost exactly halfway between the green line representing the dam and the red line marking the upper end of the lake. Their land was certain to be flooded. If these people stopped the water's flow, if they built their green-line, everything on his farm—the fields, the trees, the buildings, the house—would be swallowed up by the dammed and angry river.

He lost his naturally sound sense of time as the meeting passed. What in the hell was this guy talking about now? Rates of flow over the dam? Cubic feet of water? Displacement of pressure? It became clear their intention was to make the audience wait—numbing them all the while with their scientific talk—until some of them cooled off or got so mad they walked out, punching the doors of the school. Meanwhile, people shouted questions, ignoring all requests to do otherwise. Some woman in the back asked if they intended to make a state park of some sort around the lake, and if so, would there be both primitive and RV camping available?

The frustration built in the room with its ridiculously small furniture. The anger swelled and heated the air, like a front bringing with it a hot electrical storm.

Frank raised his hand then and suddenly he felt the atmosphere in the room shift. The room seemed to grow quiet. Dizziness swayed him. He thought his ears might explode from the pressure but he kept his hand up.

"What are you going to tell them?" Ethel whispered, tugging on his shirt.

He didn't turn to her. He stood and faced the stage. His ears and neck felt like they were glowing with heat.

For another hour those on stage lectured. First one spoke, then another. More monotone voices delivering exposition about procedures, forms and policies. Around Frank and Ethel a few individuals stormed out in protest, waving their hands dismissively at the stage. Others wandered in late to occupy new spaces along the walls, eventually leaning over to ask their neighbors, 'what's this guy talking about?' to which those asked could only shrug. Frank stood with his hand in the air. When one arm got tired he switched.

Finally, Dunkirk allowed that they would be pleased to take questions from the audience. But they wanted a twenty-minute break first. And they wanted everyone who wanted to speak to sign up during the break, providing a name and address. Speakers would then go in the order they'd signed up, and would be limited to three minutes each. When he said all this, the crowd erupted. Dunkirk tapped the microphone and said, "People, please. We know from experience we must maintain some kind of order here."

A stack of forms had been piled near the stage, and already people were lining up to fill out the required information.

Still Frank stood with his hand in the air.

The USACE men exited through a door off the rear of the stage.

"They're saying we got to sign up to speak," Ethel said, gesturing toward the line. "They ain't gonna let you just talk."

He stood, staring straight ahead, arm raised. The stage was now empty, save the podium, the projector and chairs piled with notebooks and papers.

"Well, I gotta use the restroom," she said, and left.

The crowd never fully dispersed for the allotted break, but after twenty minutes the sheriff's deputies gathered the lists and put them in order. A microphone was placed on the floor, facing the podium. Gradually, the men returned to their seats on the stage. The crowd grew a little quieter. Ethel returned to find Frank in the same position. Dunkirk walked to the podium.

"All right, folks. This officially marks the beginning of the portion of this public meeting where your opinions will be heard and recorded. Again, you will be called to the microphone, standing right there, and you'll state your full name and address for the record. You get a maximum of three minutes, although certainly you don't need to use all that time. I'd ask you to remember that the U.S. Army Corps of Engineers is here to work with you, and I ask that we keep this meeting civil in nature."

He paused and shuffled some papers. "The first name on the list is Mabel … Mabel…Mabel Thompkins, it looks like?"

By then a wild-haired woman in sweat pants was making her way down to the microphone. When she reached the stand she grabbed the microphone and a loud popping sound resonated throughout the cafeteria. She jerked her hand back like the thing had burned her.

Dunkirk was still at the podium and he asked her to state her name and address, for the record, before she spoke.

"Well, then. My name is Mabel Thompkinson, not Thompkins, like you said. And I live by myself, ever since my husband died, over on county road 25 East, just outside of town. We been there going on thirty years. All's I want to say, is that I do see the river flooded sometimes. Once I seen it come over the bridge. So I can see what damming it would do some good. But my thing is, can it be a smaller dam? Maybe it don't need to be no nine hundred acre lake, or whatever it is he said. That seems too big for people around here. Thank you."

She turned and made her way back toward her tiny seat.

"Ma'am, I thank you for your question," Dunkirk began. "But, to really reach optimal flood control, as well as municipal use, that is, to reach full achievement of the municipal use side of things, our engineers think it would be best for this impoundment to be of that size, roughly. And, again, this is also to achieve best success with the prevention of floods."

He looked down at his notes. "Kenny Williams?"

A young man no older than Ollie strode through the crowd. At the microphone, he said, "I'd like to give my spot over to this older gentleman back there, who's been standing with his hand up waiting to speak for a long time." He gestured toward Frank, and suddenly the whole attention of the room shifted toward him. Ethel grabbed his arm, alarmed at the sudden peerings of hundreds of eyes.

"Well, now, hold on," Dunkirk said. "Again, following procedure, anyone wanting to speak ought to have signed up when they had the chance."

"Well, it's my turn, but I'm giving it up. That seems fair," the young man said, and he left the microphone standing alone. As he returned to his spot on the back wall, he motioned for Frank to step forward.

Frank lowered his hand for the first time in over an hour. He took his cane in his right hand and made his way to the center and front of the room.

Dunkirk watched him approach, as did the others on the stage. "You, sir. Go ahead with your question, then. But you'll need to leave your name and address with us in writing before you leave. And state your name clearly now."

He got to the microphone and studied it for a moment. Little wires criss-crossed over a ball. He'd never seen one up close before. He looked up at the podium and Dunkirk over it. He recognized him from Lila's café, but if Dunkirk recognized him, he didn't show it.

"My name is Frank Withered," he said and paused as his voice echoed back to him. "Me and my wife own 237 acres on this river you all are talking about damming up. My wife's family had it before me, and they had it since 1910. I been working it myself since 1940. That's a long time to be in one place. I reckon you all are talking about my land, because I live right smack on that river, up from that bridge you got marked on your map there."

The room grew silent. Those few who were seated could be heard creaking the chairs. No one so much as coughed now.

Frank's ears were ringing and his hands shook. But he had no trouble being heard. "So I guess I want some of you fancy fuckers to tell me: how can you take a man's land out from under him when he don't want to give it?"

Many of the crowd broke into applause. Dunkirk's face grew red and he tapped the microphone on the podium angrily. "Sir, you will not speak like that in this public forum," he said, but people were clapping and no one could hear him. Ethel looked at the floor between her small white shoes. The USACE men glanced at each other quickly. The two sheriff's deputies nearest the stage rocked back on their heels, arms crossed. Eventually, the room quieted down.

Dunkirk nodded at the podium. "I'm going to ignore the tone of that question, even though it was highly inappropriate, sir. I see that's a fair question. But we will keep this civil, is that clear? What I would like to do now is turn this over to my associate, who will handle all the legal issues connected to this project. This is Walter Shain, an attorney for the Corps of Engineers."

No one clapped as the large man stood and walked slowly to the podium.

He hadn't spoken yet.

Shain stood like a tree and his hair was snow white and closely cropped. His eyebrows and mustache were of a darker shade, and his eyes were dark. All of these features drew attention to his face, which he now held steadily above the podium. He looked at individual members of the audience with neither smile nor frown. He looked upon them with the countenance of someone studying a loaf of bread. He did not look at Frank, who continued to stand before the stage.

"The Fifth Amendment of the United States Constitution gives the government rights of seizure," he began. His voice was as deep, slow and solid as the Ohio River itself. "This means that the U.S. Constitution, of which all of you undoubtedly support wholeheartedly, supports the notion that this little river can be dammed for the municipal use of the community and the government, both State and Federal."

The crowd remained silent and stalwart.

"This action will require some displacement of landowners, which is always regrettable. But it happens from time to time, and this will be one of those instances. This project will necessitate community involvement, and this will include relocation for some."

The crowd grew restless and he waited for the din to quiet.

"Mr. Bill Lewis, whom you were introduced to earlier, is one such real estate expert in the Corps who will help displaced landowners." He turned and motioned toward the man seated on the stage. "And each landowner will be paid a fair value, of course. Each landowner will receive a certain amount per acre to be settled by the property values of the surrounding area. You are merely selling your property to the United States government. If you choose not to sell, then the rights of eminent domain will be invoked." He turned to leave the podium.

"I ain't sellin!" Frank shouted into the microphone. His voice boomed against the walls.

"Me neither!" another man yelled.

Shain stopped and fixed his stare at Frank. "You might recall I mentioned the U.S. Constitution," he said. "It gives the Corps of Engineers the power to claim your land, using the rule of eminent domain. This is history; this is fact. You can challenge this procedure in a court of law, with court costs accrued being the plaintiff's responsibility. Let me notify all of you—" and with this, he scanned the crowd with his eyes "— that challenging the U.S. government in a court of law is both an expensive and time-consuming effort. Now, it is your right, of course, as citizens. But I will tell you that these cases have very seldom been decided in favor of the plaintiff."

A thick, squatty man began speaking from the side of the room. He wore a green plastic jacket with the Pioneer Seeds logo on it. Frank knew him as Harris Peas, a farmer from down the river.

"Like Frank, I too own land along this crick," he yelled, stubby finger pointed at Shain. "And I don't intend to sell it to you or anybody else. Now I fought for this country, and I love it. But to hear you all saying you can come and take my land whenever you want, I say to that, you all come on and try it."

Some shook their heads and whispered at this.

"Then you, sir, will need to hire legal representation, and pursue the matter through the proper channels," Shain said.

"Those ain't what I'm talking about!" Harris yelled. A deputy walked toward him, and Harris stepped behind others and slid back against the wall.

Shain stood there and scanned the cafeteria. His expression hadn't changed; his complexion hadn't colored. He looked like a man who'd faced this kind of crowd before. None of these landowners would hire attorneys. And if they did, they'd be small-time hacks with no experience in eminent domain rulings. Let this passion wilt into frustration and finally bloom as surrender. There weren't many ways to beat the government, he knew, and he also understood these people in front of him would find none of them.

The room felt like a dying animal.

Frank stood at the microphone and stared at Shain. He'd kill this man, he thought, if they'd let him reach him. Or if he had a gun in his belt. He'd shoot the son of a bitch where he stood with that smug expression on his face. But none of that was possible.

Dunkirk replaced Shain at the podium and called another name. Frank walked back to Ethel. People looked at him and sadly shook their heads from side to side.

Someone asked about the price offered to landowners and got a long answer about market value and fluctuating worth.

Another asked about the timetable and Dunkirk replied, "The whole process—the building of the structure, the preparation of the land, all the various procedures and so forth—takes years. But we are prepared to move on this right away. We expect to begin contacting landowners to notify them of their offers to purchase as early as next week."

Again the room lit up with voices. "Next week!" someone yelled.

Dunkirk said nothing. He stood there, as still as a statue of a great man, one erected in a town park or square. A founding father, perhaps. "Within one year, all of the necessary property will be in the hands of the U.S. Army Corps of Engineers," he finally said.

The crowd was explosive now—some yelling toward the stage, others talking to those around them. Every mouth in the room worked up and down.

Except for Ethel's. She stood against the wall and pushed her fingertips to her eyes.

And then Colonel Haverstick rose and took his place behind the podium, his carriage erect, his chest decorated and his eyes magnetizing. The crowd hushed. The Corps of Engineers had just played their trump card, and the effect was immediate.

"Ladies and gentlemen, please," he said. "On behalf of the United States of America, I ask that you trust the Army Corps of Engineers to do their job for the betterment of this community..."

But Frank was already walking out, Ethel behind him. He hadn't joined no goddamn army.

CHAPTER THIRTY

Tennessee didn't look that big on the map, but it took about forever to cross it. Ollie had celebrated his transcendence as he crossed the borders into Kentucky and Tennessee, but now he drove past the sign proclaiming he'd just entered North Carolina with a furrowed brow and rigid claws clamping the wheel. It still seemed likely that his truck might go careening off the mountainside any minute now, but he could no longer bring himself to care. He'd always planned on dying in his home state, but if it happened down here, surely someone would box him up and send him north. He just wanted to talk to Summer before he glanced over and saw the Grim Reaper riding shotgun.

When he saw the exit for the 'Welcome to North Carolina' rest stop, he pulled onto the sloping ramp and followed the path to the parking lot. He shut off the motor and listened to its furious ticking. It smelled hot.

In front of him was a little park area, laid out with picnic tables and grills set in concrete. Over there was a building with restrooms inside, and vending machines lined up along the outside wall. His knees creaked as he stood on solid ground again. Standing made him realize how badly he needed to take a leak. He locked the door with his key, and then realized he'd forgotten to throw the sleeping bag in the cab. He just left it in the bed. Who'd steal that stinky-ass thing anyway?

Inside the building, a man sat with a small boy on a flat wood bench. As Ollie walked in he overheard the boy ask, "But why can't Mommy pee where we do?"

The man wore brown shorts and a pink collared shirt, his skin mayonnaise white. Shittin kids! Ollie thought. They don't have any sense of what they can and can't say out in public. The father started explaining how mommies were different in a patient and careful tone. Ollie heard him say something about little boys standing up before he went into the restroom and out of earshot.

He finished pissing and washed his hands in the sink. His good eye stared back at him like it belonged to someone else entirely. The swelling was down enough to allow sight out of the black eye, but it still looked like a bruised and purple lump of meat.

He walked into the common area and the little boy and his dad had moved outside and were visible through the windows. They were with a pretty woman now. Ollie thought about how the man might tell his wife later what their son had said and they'd laugh. Three pay phones hung on the wall next to a giant map of North Carolina. He felt of his pockets. He hadn't switched jeans, and all the change he'd accumulated on the trip rode in a little fist in his pocket.

Now his courage failed him, though. What would he say to her? What if someone walked in and stood there listening to him talk? He didn't want to talk to her for the first time in several days with somebody judging every word.

He picked up the receiver and put it to his ear. How much change did he need to reach Indiana? He dropped a quarter and dialed her number.

A loud beep jolted his ear and an artificial voice told him to deposit more money. He slid in another dime and then a nickel. There was a pause, a few more beeps, and then, before he'd totally prepared himself, a ringing tone.

He expected her to pick up after every ring. Three, four, five times it rang. He waited, muscles taut as leaf springs. After about twelve or fifteen rings he put the receiver back on its hook and the coins fell against the metal door of the catch. Of course she was at work.

Outside, he put the money in a vending machine and got a soda. The picnic tables were empty. He sat on the top of one and sipped his Coke. It hadn't come out very cold.

Beyond the parking strip for cars and trucks was a larger lot for tractor trailers. Several semis sat there, and he couldn't tell if they were running or not. He didn't see any movement about them. A tanker had curtains drawn across the front glass.

An RV was parked among the big rigs—the kind retired couples bought to tour the country. His grandparents hadn't lived to an age where they could do that, of course, and it didn't seem like something his parents would do. He was staring at the RV, wondering what it'd be like to ride in a moving house, when the door swung open and a little man stepped out. He was still a good ways off, but Ollie could see he was indeed a senior citizen, wearing khaki shorts and black socks. On his head sat a hat with a brim all the way around. Giant sunglasses. Holy shit he'd called that one on the nose.

The man came toward the building and Ollie watched him stroll across the pavement.

The old fellow took notice of Ollie and veered right toward him, walking across the grass with sure, small steps. Ollie watched him approach and was not alarmed by it.

"Now this is the kind of weather I could get used to," the man said. He gained the table and sat down. His face was marked with black moles and freckles, his eyes hidden behind the sunglasses.

"Yeah, it sure feels nice," Ollie said. He'd always heard the south was hot, but today was balmy. A slight breeze drew across them.

"We came here from Virginia and the nation's capital, and I'll tell ya, I like this ocean heat."

"Yeah. I do too." Ollie thought he noticed his bruised eye registering on the man's face.

"Where you headed, young man?" he asked.

"I think South Carolina, but I never been before."

"Well, you're in a world of luck, because we just love it down there. Some of the prettiest coast you're likely to see. In fact, we intend to spend some time near Hilton Head, but we had to take a detour over here to see my wife's cousin."

Ollie looked at him. The old dude reminded him of a crawdad or maybe a praying mantis. The fact that he was talking to such an odd man, a man no one back home had ever met, made him feel good. That was a big part of traveling, right there.

"Are you driving that truck?" the man asked.

Ollie looked where he pointed, although his was the only pickup in the lot. He nodded. "Yeah. I hit a deer with it back home."

"And where do you call home?"

"Logjam, Indiana."

"That near Indianapolis?"

"No." The man seemed to want more, so Ollie said, "It's southeast of it a couple of hours." He'd only been to Indianapolis a handful of times. None of them recently.

"Well, my wife and I went through Indiana once, on our way out west. We went across Indiana, Illinois and Iowa before we headed up into the Dakotas."

"Uh-huh," Ollie said, like he'd made that exact trip many times.

The man looked around at the trees. There was a squirrel now on the ground near one of the grills and his eyes must've found it. He looked in that direction for a little while.

Ollie said nothing, just watched the squirrel with him. He hadn't traveled much and didn't know what he might volunteer.

Finally the man said, "Well, I wanted to get a diet soda, but why don't you come back and say hi to my wife? We really delight in having company in the motor home."

Ollie hadn't expected such an offer, but he said yes without thinking and followed the man to the vending machines, where he carefully counted out exact change from a little purse thing he produced from his pocket and received a Diet Coke.

They walked across the parking lot without speaking. They went through a little median of grass and onto the other lot. Now Ollie could hear the big diesels running at idle.

Approaching the RV was like walking toward a building and the man jerked the door open and stepped up inside. Ollie followed him, his eyes taking a moment to adjust to the shaded interior.

"Wife, we have a visitor," the man called in a sing-songy voice. Ollie'd never met someone so proper. It must be some kind of act, he thought.

"Oh," a woman said, and then he saw her—a pleasant looking old woman with hair piled in an elaborate bun. She was not tall and looked like her husband in the face.

She shook Ollie's hand and said, "Welcome. My name is Ellen, and it's a pleasure to have you visit us."

"Yeah, well, thanks," Ollie said.

"Please sit down," the man said. He gestured toward a table connected to the wall. There were benches on either side of it, and Ollie sat on the far side. It felt like a real table under his hands.

"Would you like something to drink, young man?" Ellen asked.

He said no thanks, that he'd just finished a Coke outside there.

The man sat down with his Diet Coke across from Ollie, and Ellen moved in next to her husband. They looked at him expectantly.

"This fella's heading to South Carolina," the man said. He'd removed his gigantic shades and now his eyes were visible. They looked cloudy.

"Oh! Well, we love South Carolina. Arthur and I are going there, too. To Hilton Head, once we visit—"

"I told him that," Arthur said, but not unpleasantly.

"Now where are you going?" she asked Ollie.

The question caught him off guard, and he sat there mute for a second. "Somewheres on the coast," he said, shrugging.

The two paused and glanced at each other. Then Arthur said, "A free spirit! I like that."

"Yes, we're like that, too," Ellen said, although it seemed to Ollie that they were, in fact, not like that.

Ollie felt the silence growing to awkward proportions, so he finally said, "This is really a nice camper you all got here."

"Motor home. Yes. We like it," Arthur said. "Been on the road in her for about five years now."

Ollie raised his eyebrows. "Is that right?"

"Over 80,000 miles," Ellen said.

"That's a lot."

"So, are you traveling alone?" Ellen asked.

He saw her husband look at her like she'd messed up, but Ollie didn't mind. He wanted to answer questions instead of come up with them. "Yeah," he said. Then he added, "My girlfriend had to work."

The lie obviously surprised them a little. It had Ollie. "What kind of work does she do?" Arthur asked.

"She's a secretary."

"Oh," Ellen said.

"So you had to come all this way without her?" Arthur asked.

"Yeah, I did. I hate that I had to, though."

"I bet!" Ellen said. "Don't you miss her?"

"Yeah, I do. In fact, I just called her from in there," he said, pointing back with his thumb. The building seemed to be behind him, but he'd gotten turned around in the dimly lit RV.

"I'm sure she liked that," Ellen said.

"Yeah, she sure did. Well, she was at work now, so I didn't get to talk to her."

The elderly couple looked at each other. Probably wondering why someone would call when he ought to have known she'd be at work.

"How long will you stay down here?" Arthur asked.

"Oh, not too long, I reckon."

"You better get back to your lady friend," Ellen said. She looked kind and old, her features soft as warm milk.

"I think I oughtta. I was thinking I might head back today, even."

"Without even going to South Carolina?" she asked.

"I might."

Arthur chuckled. "You certainly are a free spirit."

Everyone smiled. But now somehow the mood in the RV had changed. Ollie thought they were probably wishing they hadn't invited him in. He was talking himself into a damn corner.

"Well it's too bad she couldn't have come along with you," Ellen said. "Must be tough to travel alone."

"I know it," Ollie said. "Her boss can be a real bit...he's tough."

"Do you want to know my advice, after forty-eight years of marriage?" she asked.

He nodded.

"Do everything together," she said. "Do it together, or don't do it at all."

Ollie nodded again and smiled. He didn't have anything else to say but he wanted to sit here a while yet. It was air-conditioned in the RV, and clean. He wondered what it was worth. It was like being in a really nice house. The old man sipped his soda and the woman looked at him and smiled.

Ollie saw signs for all things Great Smoky Mountains and, despite the cars passing him on the interstate, he felt like an age-old explorer, seeing a country for the first time ever with white man's eyes. By now, though, he was spending so much time wondering about Summer's thoughts, all but the constant drone of driving was lost on him. He'd played the scenario of their reunion over in his head so many times, it'd grown unbearable not being able to see his movie play itself out in real time.

He saw a sign for a campground featuring a cartoon black bear on two legs and he memorized the exit number. Driving had already made him tired, and he needed to think some things through before he drove any farther. He'd camp, buy some food and drink some beer. Because he'd accomplished two things today: he'd survived these mountains and bought a cooler. Now the beer rode along chilly as could be. She'd be home from work, and he wanted to call her house again with a little buzz and let their conversation make up his mind for him. If nothing else, he needed to find a shower. A smell crept up from the opening of his shirt neck and about made him gag.

He took the exit and found the campground all right, but it was smaller and shittier than he figured it'd be. He drove under a big sign, again with a rearing bear, and through a gate in a split-rail fence. Against the backdrop of the green mountains sat a scattering of campers and tents. There were several structures anchored to the ground in some kind of earnest way, and one of these was labeled the office. When he entered the low-slung cabin, a woman with a mustache told him he was lucky, that they only had three sites left. And those were primitive.

"What's that mean?" he asked.

"No hot box. By that I mean electricity," the hairy woman said.

"So what do I get?"

"You get a parking spot for your truck and access to the campground's shower and bathroom facilities," she said, as if reading from a brochure.

He looked at her. "For fifteen bucks?"

"Plus you can use all the campground's facilities, which include hiking trails, plus playgrounds in case you brung any kids with ya."

"I don't have any," he said. He thought of Spring back home, slamming her toys together and talking nonsense.

He gave the woman his money and she handed him a tag to hang on his rearview mirror. While he filled out a form she looked at his license.

"Your eye looks better in this picture," she said, snorting a little.

"It does, don't it? Hey, where can I eat round here?"

She thought about it. He stared at her upper lip.

"I reckon most folks eat at their sites, to get the real camping experience," she said.

"I didn't bring no food or gear or nothing."

"Well, there's a camp store on the property, right next door, and you could buy some hot dogs and a long fork there," she said. "And get you some marshmallows, too—make it a real camping experience."

"Yeah, I might do that. Is there a restaurant around, though, like a Burger

King or something?"

She looked at him. "Not less you get back on the interstate and drive about twenty miles."

"Like the hell I'm gonna do that."

She shrugged and handed him a copy of the form. "You better try the store, then," she said, going back to her desk behind the counter.

The camp store was a dingy little concrete block place filled with food and trinkets, and all of it looked like it'd been on the shelf too long. He had cash left, but he needed gas to go either direction and if he made it to the beach he'd need to pop for a hotel. He walked around and looked at things. A high school kid sat at the cash register, reading a magazine. He hadn't acknowledged that Ollie was even in the store. Ollie thought he'd steal something to teach the kid a lesson. He wasn't sure what lesson that'd teach him, though.

The hot dogs were in a cold case in the back, and he pulled out a package of them and got a bag of stale buns off a shelf next to several dusty boxes of Cheerios. He wasn't used to extravagance but this was downright paltry. Sure enough, as the woman had forecast, he found a small wooden barrel with metal wire forks in it. He lifted one out. That's when he realized he had nothing to make a fire with. But they'd expected that, too—the bags of charcoal were right there.

Now he had too much to carry, so he took an armload to the register and piled it on the counter. "Hey," he said to the kid. The kid glanced at him and started to ring up the items. Ollie went back for the briquettes and that's when he saw the bears.

Several little stuffed black bears stood on the shelf there, across from the insect repellant. They each wore chains around their necks with little medallions that read Great Smoky Mtns. He looked at the price tag. Almost ten bucks apiece.

He'd come so far as to enter the world of souvenirs with place names on them. He picked a bear up, thinking of Summer. Its paws had made imprints in the dust, and he rubbed the animal on his chest and shook the dust free. Holding it, he realized it'd be a better match for Spring. He froze there in thought. If he went home with something for the little one and had nothing to hand to Summer, what the hell would that be worth? He hadn't planned on coming home bearing gifts, but women loved stuffed animals and he took that to be universal fact.

The kid made a sound with his throat and Ollie realized he'd already put those things through the register. He grabbed two bears and carried them along with the charcoal to the counter. The kid added them into the machine and said nothing as the total came up on the little screen. Thirty some bucks. Bullshit. Ollie paid, the kid made change, and he left the store with two sacks' worth of possessions.

The campsite was nothing more than a roughly-cut piece of yard with a post sticking out of it. The post bore his assigned number, so he parked next to it. There were tents and pop-up campers all around him. He felt like he'd parked in the middle of someone's backyard barbeque. Not too far away stood a brick building that he guessed held the showers. He could see the back of the office and the camp store. Behind him the mountains rose.

With the sun setting, he opened his first beer and carried it to the shower. There were little curtain things meant to give you some privacy but they were alive with black mold and it was still like bathing in the open because they only came to your chest. Luckily no one walked in, save some man who carried a newspaper into a rickety stall and read to himself out loud. Ollie'd remembered the soap somehow but had forgotten shampoo, so he lathered his hair with bar soap. The water was no warmer than piss and he'd pissed in a harder stream. Still, it felt good to get clean and when he walked out of the restroom he noticed a phone bolted to the wall there. Now all he needed to do was eat and get a little drunk.

He didn't have any matches, but he scrounged around and came up with a lighter in the glove box. Of course the condoms were still in there and those made him homesick. After piling the charcoal about a hundred different ways, he got it burning without starter fluid. The fire had to be built in a metal box about three feet off the ground.

He cooked a hot dog on the fork over the heat of the metal box and decided he'd never in his life felt more like a jackass.

The hot dog tasted good, but he had nothing to go with it, no ketchup or bag of Cheetos, so he drank beer and cooked eight hot dogs and ate them. He hadn't realized how hungry he was.

The light faded and noise surrounded him as he sat on his tailgate—kids ran up and down the lanes dividing the campsites, and adults laughed and shouted. Three kids raced by on bikes. You could look across the campground and see odd lights—lanterns and strings of lit plastic objects hanging from awnings of pull-along campers. Those were parked some distance away— over where the hot boxes were, he guessed. Hot boxes, she'd called them. He smiled, thinking about that woman and her mustache.

He got the bears out of the sack and held them in his hands. So this meant there were black bears in the Great Smoky Mountains. He'd like to see one, but he knew better than to expect a bear to come waltzing into this mess.

He drank three more beers and carried a fourth back to the restroom. It seemed like every camping couple had kids. One little boy ran toward him with a plastic gun, making shooting noises. Ollie held his arms up and kept going. He walked by a couple of sites with older men and women sitting in chairs, watching other campsites. They nodded at him and he thought about Arthur and Ellen, and how he'd never see them again.

For days now he'd thought about calling her, and very little else, yet he still kept finding other things to do. He went in the restroom and took a leak. It must've been a popular time to shower, because it was so humid the tile walls in front of his face were sweating. The hot steam from the showers mixed with the smell of shit and piss. Turning around he caught a glimpse of some man's hairy ass. There was his bear. He washed his hands without the benefit of soap, because they apparently figured you'd carry in your own, and walked outside to the phone. He still had some change on him, thanks in part to the mute at the camp store, and he dropped several coins into the slot.

He'd done all this without really thinking and when her voice was there he opened his mouth but didn't speak.

"Hello?" Summer said again.

"Well, it's me," he said. His throat was nearly pinched shut.

She didn't say anything for a long time. He thought maybe she was gone when she asked, "What in the hell do you think you're doing?"

"I guess I'm in the Smoky Mountains by now."

More silence.

"I came down here a coupla days ago. I reckon I drove through about the world's longest tunnel, too, along the way."

"Yeah, I know when you left! You just took off, remember? Do you remember when you failed to tell me you were going anywhere? Do you remember that part?"

"I know it. I just needed to take off."

"Well, you did it, asshole. Congratulations! Talk to you later," she said, but she didn't hang up. He heard her breathing.

A woman with a toddler talking loudly walked into the restroom. He turned his back to them and plugged his free ear with his finger, as he'd seen done on television. Christ, he didn't need anyone listening in on this.

"Look," he said. "I know it was a dumb thing to do. I just needed ... I don't know. I thought I needed to get away for a while."

"Ollie, I'm not into people taking off all the time. We don't need a whole lot of that crap around here."

"I know it. But when he showed up that night, I kind of—"

"You will need to deposit ... twenty ... five ... cents," a voice from nowhere suddenly said. He held the receiver out from his ear and looked at it, and then at the phone itself. He dug into his jeans pocket, found a quarter, dropped it to the ground, and about ripped his head off as he leaned over to get it with the phone held against his ear until the cable jerked tight. He grabbed the damn coin and inserted it.

"Ollie, where are you?"

"Smoky Mountains," he said. Now even the phone was turning against him and he felt a sense of urgency to set his life right before it cut him off for good. "I'm trying to tell you I'm sorry about this."

"Are you coming back?"

"I sure want to. Sooner rather than later."

"You're not gonna lose your job, are you?"

"No. Well, I hope not."

"What were you saying about that night?"

"How he come over."

"What about it?"

"I need for that sort of thing to stop."

He listened as she pulled in several deep breaths. "That's funny, because you know what I need?" she asked.

"What?"

"For you to start acting like something more than a damn two-year-old. For you to put something of yourself out there and to stop beating me up for every little thing I can't change, and for ...." And then just the sound of her crying.

He'd heard her cry when they hit the deer but this time he alone had caused it and he was already so lonesome he thought he might start crying, too.

"Summer?" he said. "Are you listening to me? All right. I think I will. And oh yeah—I got you something. You and Spring both. Don't cry. I'm coming back."

CHAPTER THIRTY-ONE

They rode home after the meeting along county roads dark and deserted. The moon hung nearly full overhead and its blue hue illuminated the gravel they drove on, a ribbon of light. Ethel sat next to him in the darkened cab and he could hear her crying, a sound like kittens mewling, suddenly familiar again, although he felt sure he'd gone years at a time without hearing it.

He wasn't the kind to blame a man for working, but there were some jobs that involved killing and some jobs that one should be killed for doing. Like that bastard from the meeting tonight—that steel-eyed son of a bitch attorney. Frank kept seeing him up there on the stage, lording over them like they were so many cattle in a slaughterhouse pen. And he knew there were others, too—those he hadn't seen tonight and would never see. The governor must've wanted this lake. District representatives. But, really, some of the ones who most deserved shot were those in this county—people he'd known all his life!—who had supported this idea from the beginning and even called for it. Those fools who thought they knew the river, who thought the floods were too much to contend with, even though they weren't farmers or landowners and at most had to deal with occasional closed roads. Those who thought this county needed a big damn puddle in it. There was more blame than opportunities for retribution and he knew this, as well.

They drove in silence over roads and bridges they'd known all their lives. She'd stop crying from time to time to stare out the windows at fields lit by moonlight and the dark thickets that edged them. Houses here and there were marked with burning porch lights and maybe a few glowing windows. Some of the people inside the houses were all but ignorant of what went on in the fields around them. Some of them hunted and fished, but some of them drove to the factories in Green City and home again without stepping outside except to walk back and forth from the vehicle to the door. Some of them didn't want the reservoir, some of them did, and some of them hadn't given it any more thought than they'd give to a pair of socks.

It was funny how some could be so unaffected, he thought, while others were destroyed.

It made a man wonder about the chance of it all. What if Tarif had bought another piece of land—one just up or downstream? Or what if he'd settled in another county altogether? They'd be at home tonight, resting—one of those unaffected couples with no more on their minds than dinner.

But Frank understood there may well have been other things to worry about on other farms. Maybe Ollie would've fallen down an old well at a different place and drowned while still a baby. Perhaps lightning would've struck Ethel while she worked in the garden. Who the hell knew what could happen on other farms, in other times?

And now here they were, parked in front of the chain that marked their home. He got out and dropped it. Even though it seemed pointless, he drove across and climbed out and put it back. When he parked the truck in the lean-to, she walked toward the house. He watched her walk away, across the grass damp with dew, and then went into the other side of the barn to get Catfish out of his pen. The dog had woken up with the sounds of the engine and was startlingly awake, hurtling against the plywood walls of the granary. You could count the dog in with the townspeople who didn't know enough to be worried. He whined and wagged his tail like he hadn't seen Frank in days.

Once lifted over the wall of the granary, Catfish ran out into the yard, where he scuttled against the wet grass. He looked almost white in the moonlight. The dog sniffed around some, crooked his tail and pooped, and then returned to Frank's side. Catfish needed to be fed and he jumped against him, his paws getting Frank's good pants dirty. The cool wetness soaked through.

The food was in the house, but Frank wasn't ready to go inside. He stood in the yard and looked around. The metal roofs of the tool shed, grain bin and barn reflected the moon's light. The chicken coop huddled like a shadow and was silent. He knew the hens would be asleep now, roosting on the elevated platform. He'd nailed one-by-ones a foot above the platform and this is where the chickens lined up and slept, heads tucked under their wings. She'd fed them before the meeting, and now the little door into the fenced-in yard was blocked with a board. They'd never had a fox or coyote get inside. The birds slept in peace.

He could see the woods beyond the pasture. It appeared black now, a solid mass instead of individual trees. Just above the treetop line the sky was stone gray although it grew darker more directly overhead. He looked there and found stars aplenty. It would have been a pleasant night to fish. In the heart of the woods flowed the river.

The stars looked as they had when he was a kid. He remembered the first time he'd slept outside without a tent or tarp stretched over him. This had happened on his father's farm, a piece of land only about ten miles north of where he stood. He'd slept outside on the front porch because he had a new dog, a stray named Lightning. His father wouldn't let it come in the house, so he slept outside with the dog curled against his side. Lightning stunk and fleas bit Frank all night long as he lay on his back and looked up. He'd scared himself with thoughts about what the vastness above him meant. Two nights later, Lightning would run off and never be seen again.

The bank had taken that farm after his father died. Frank still drove by it sometimes. It'd come under someone else's care a time or two. Now the people who owned it—Thomas was their name—were building a new house in one of the fields. The barn had been torn down long ago, and they'd recently logged the woodlot again.

He recalled how his father had warned him about the life of a stray—they'd stick for a while and then move on down the road. But Frank had taken care of Lightning, giving him scraps of meat and keeping the water in the bowl fresh. He'd slept on the ground for him. All to make this particular stray abandon the rootless life. But his father had been right about some things and this was one of them.

Those were old memories. They'd remained with him, hidden away somewhere, after all this time. How could a person's mind keep over seventy years of memories like that? Damned if he knew. He stood in his yard and wondered about what was coming. He didn't really want to pray, but he recognized this would probably be a good time to do it.

CHAPTER THIRTY-TWO

After sleeping in his truck bed again, homeless man style, Ollie woke feeling blue and mean. It'd gotten hot early, the sun waking him by cooking his brain in its pan. When he jerked the damp sleeping bag away, flies buzzed his almost naked body. He lay there staring at the rusted walls of his pickup. The phone call replayed itself in his mind, but now it felt like he resided in some other country altogether removed from her world. Last night, he'd thought he could go back, but this morning stale beer was pulsing out through his pores and he didn't think he could serve anyone but himself.

He didn't know if he should push on toward South Carolina or not.

Last night he was certain he'd get up, eat breakfast somewhere, and spin the wheels until he pulled into her driveway. As he passed out in his makeshift bed he imagined hugging Summer and swinging her around before asking her to marry him. Then he'd lift Spring above his head and hug her too. She'd giggle wildly and Summer would stand off to the side crying happy tears.

But then he woke up dehydrated and sore. He lay with his arms over his eyes, knees up, ratty underwear covering his ass. The bed of this truck was hard enough to make his trailer bedroom back home look like the prince's palace. Home. It sure as hell wasn't that trailer—sure, he'd crashed there for years, but it was such a goddamned mess he couldn't even bring his girlfriend to see it.

Maybe he'd just move into her house. Even in this black mood that sounded pretty good. But how could he ever rest knowing Todd might stop by? How could he live with the knowledge that Todd, that asshole, knew the layout of the house, knew where the couch sat in relation to the TV, knew which wall the bed was pushed against? Maybe even knew how the bed sounded bumping against that wall? Jesus Christ. No thank you, Mr. Make Me a Bullshit Offer.

They'd have to buy a new house. New furniture, too.

What he really wanted to do was build a log cabin back in the woods on his folks' place. Chinked logs, smoke snaking out of the chimney, rocking chair on the front porch—the whole thing looking like some damn postcard from down here. Once in the cabin he and Summer could start fresh and it'd be like Todd hadn't existed.

But he hadn't talked to either his mom or dad in weeks and when he did they'd probably tell him to get off their property. He'd fallen so far in their eyes already and now there was this stuff Coondog had said about the lake. He didn't think it was going to happen, but they'd probably be mad he hadn't been around to listen to them bitch about the possibility. And what else made him guilty, what else had he done? Stopped coming around. Stopped putting up with the old man's shit. Stopped thinking everything they said was right.

But it was more than that, and he understood this even as he lay in the truck bed, his bladder distended with hot piss he was too lazy to empty. He'd stopped believing. He'd been given a chance to take over the farm when his dad wanted to stop doing so much, and he'd declined. He'd said, in effect, I think I'll just keep doing what I'm doing, which consists of getting drunk every night, whoring and working at the sawmill.

Funny how your own thoughts could strike in the pit of your gut and push cold blood through your veins.

Dinner. About six years ago. He'd come home from work in a bad mood, not unlike the one he suffered this morning. He'd walked in to find his mom at the stove, which was not an unusual spot for her. His father was out in the fields, and this, too, was not unusual.

His mom barely spoke to him, and he sensed his dad's angry presence lingering in the house. The air felt like it'd been witness to a fight not too many hours before.

"What's he doing?" Ollie'd asked.

"He's out in the lower woods field. Disking. Where he's been all day, just like yesterday and the day before that."

"Something break down?"

He knew immediately he'd gone into some sort of trap. She took the spoon she'd been stirring with and leaned it against the side of the soup pan.

"Did you know that your dad is almost sixty-nine years old?"

He went over and sat down at the table. Looked down at the worn wood, sawdust clinging to the hairs on his arms.

"Well, I guess I knew he wasn't twenty-five anymore," he said.

She walked away from the stove and stood over him.

"Well then, did you know he fell getting out of the tractor back by the river yesterday and almost hit his head on the step? Did you know he laid back there for over an hour with no one to help him get up?"

"No, Ma, I didn't. I was workin yesterday."

"Well, he did. He fell down and laid back there like some helpless old man. He finally climbed back in the tractor. And you know what he did, Ollie? He kept right on disking until he finished that field! And he's out there again, right now."

He got up and went to the cupboard. He took down a glass and poured it full of tea from the fridge and started to drink, standing by the sink and looking out onto the backyard.

She moved to where she could see him. "I'll just tell you, then. What I told him. I told him we need to sell this place."

He stared at her. What he felt most was anger. All day he'd worked in the hot-ass sawmill and now he had to carry this load of shit.

"He can't do it anymore, Ollie. Not all of it, and not all by himself. He's been waiting for you to take any interest, but you never do."

"You're not gonna sell out," he said, putting his glass in the sink. Resisting the urge to render it into a million particles of dust. "You've lived here forever."

"I won't keep it if it's going to kill him."

"Come on, Ma. Quit trying to lay all of his crap on me. You know I got a job. I can maybe help more on the weekends, but—"

"He don't need that kind of help, Ollie. He needs somebody to take over the place, the farming ... look at me."

He turned to her, hands on his hips.

"He's too old to do all this, and I am too," she said. "Did you think we'd just keep farming forever? Like we did back when you was in grade school?"

By God, he wasn't a grade-schooler anymore, and that'd be obvious to anyone looking at him. He'd been knocking around inside this house for over two and a half decades already. And he'd noticed how gray the old man's hair had gotten, how long it took him to stand up from his chair. Hell if he knew what to say, though.

"He's out there even now, ridin in the tractor," she said. "At least I hope he still is. He doesn't have enough sense to quit, I know that. He's gonna go at it til it kills him."

The old man had finished that growing season more or less on his own, but Wayne Shipps had been called to help with the combining because snow was drifting around the corn and his dad was so far behind it seemed some fields might not get harvested at all. Then one evening that winter Wayne came over and talked with his parents long into the night. Ollie stayed in his room, listening to records, but the next morning his mom announced that Wayne, starting in the spring, would be doing all the farming.

Laying here in the North Carolina sun, he felt it again—the icy blood coming and going from his heart. Because even though things hadn't seemed vastly different after Wayne took over—different tractors went up and down the rows, Wayne brought checks, the old man watched it all from the three-wheeler—he understood now everything had changed that winter. But what had they expected him to do? Quit his job and start farming? Live forever with them in that house?

And what the hell did they want from him now?

He knew he had to get up. He heard kids starting to talk, their excited chatter and squealings violating the morning air. He'd come too far to see only mountains and not the ocean. He'd never been this close to something that different and he might not get this close again. Or maybe he'd go to the ocean and never see the fields and farms of his past again. Maybe in twenty years he wouldn't be able to imagine field after field of corn and soybeans and wooded hills, just like now he couldn't imagine an ocean.

He pulled on some jeans that lay crumpled near the wheel well. They were warm and limp. His mouth needed something at least as strong as bleach to get the taste out of it.

"Screw this to hell," he said as he struggled over the tailgate.

He hadn't expected to wake up and think about his mom. He looked back at everything and wondered how it had gotten so fractured. Somehow staying near them had forced them all apart.

He knew Summer expected him to head back today. But did she really want him to? Somehow, even she felt tainted now. She was some other man's wife, whether she'd been married or not. He'd always be second.

And what good would it be to run home to a farm they were going to flood anyway?

He walked into the brick building that housed the toilets and showers and stood in front of the reeking urinal. He then stared at himself in the mirror and he looked like he'd slept in the bed of a truck. And he looked like he'd been punched by some guy who'd been with his girlfriend first and still laid claim to her.

Christ, with a mood this foul you could pound a case of beer and still feel as low. This he knew from experience. He went back to his campsite. He felt like he could drive north or south and no one would notice his presence or absence at either end.

CHAPTER THIRTY-THREE

Frank sat astraddle the three-wheeler and followed the forlorn trail into the woods. He drove slowly, the bumps and ruts of the path traveling up through the tires and suspension and shaking his sinewy frame and bones. It was morning and if rain were to begin falling it would surprise no one, least of all himself. Gray clouds hung over his head, pressed low by God or whomever. He studied his fields, green, growing and whistling in the early morning breeze. Seated atop the machine he could no longer look across the tops of the corn. Some of it had yellowed where rainwater had pooled but it might come out of that yet. And now into the woods, where the change felt palpable, like driving under the coolness of a waterfall. Sprouts of briars and saplings lined the trail, and leaves and soil made from centuries of dead leaves supported the tires as the three-wheeler further ground the loam into powder.

When he reached the bend in the river he slowed the engine and shut it down. He watched the current roll into the bend, eddy here beneath his feet, and then wash downstream. It wasn't hard to imagine where the fish would be. There, on the cusp of that eddy, where the water swirled back upriver past the exposed roots of the old sycamore tree. Over there, under that partially submerged pile of jagged concrete from the old back step they'd broken up and hauled down here over twenty years ago. And out there, where the ripple broke down into the deepest water of the hole.

All good spots to fish, and they'd yielded catfish more times than a man could count, but he carried no pole today.

Instead he perched on the three-wheeler parked above the steep rise of the bank and watched the river slip by, the current constantly different in its swirlings. A circling vortex might hold your attention for some time, only to disappear when you looked away. A reliable string of bubbles trailing behind a leaf-draped limb might last for minutes before the last bubble floated away without replacement. The river rose and fell within minutes, and the water went up and down in ways that humans couldn't see or understand. On the inside bend of this same hole he'd camped with his son many years ago and they'd caught a giant soft-shelled turtle. And had it been that night when the boy woke so scared of coyotes? Yes, he remembered it all. It was a damned shame he hadn't made time for more camping. He didn't know if anything would've turned out differently if he had, but it would've been a good thing to try.

Chub's house had been sitting empty since the funeral, he figured. Couldn't hurt to swing by there later today and check on the place. He wondered what Charles had done with the old boat, the truck, the catfishing rods and reels.

By birthright, all of that gear belonged to Chub's son now and that had to make sense even when it didn't.

No doubt Charles would hire someone to hold an estate sale at the house. Everything in the garage—the mowers, the fishing tackle, the damn tiller—would be sold at an auction. Then the worn-out furniture would go, followed by the house and the property itself. He thought of the bidders standing in the garage where Chub had fallen and pawing through his left-behind junk.

The more he considered this the surer he became that he should drive out there today and take those rods and reels from the garage. It'd be locked to guard against thieves, but he knew where Chub hid a spare key. No sense in letting his rods and reels go to some stranger who had no idea what they were worth. The old boy had taken care of his reels, and they'd last another fifty years in the hands of somebody who knew how to use them. If Chub had taken out a will, he would've wanted Frank to get them, anyway, so no one was going to tell him they weren't rightfully his.

It was too bad about Chub, though, dying when he did. At the meeting, he would've liked that line about fancy fuckers. Once the plan had been stopped they would've laughed about that phrase, later, maybe out at Lila's or on the riverbank some night. Frank stared so hard at the water it lost all focus and fuzzed out.

Maybe on the way to Chub's he'd go by the trailer again, too. But he'd already decided what was up with Ollie. Only trouble with the law made a man take up and leave like that. There was no other excuse for it. And he trusted his wife's instincts when it came to their son. She'd always been the one to know when he was in the deepest water, and she said he was gone far away. Hell, she could've raised him right, if he hadn't been around, screwing the boy up. She was a good mother. But he'd been too hard on him. Or too soft, he couldn't tell which.

He wondered what Ollie had done. Probably stole something—tried to find some way to get rich without working for it. He didn't think he had the constitution to kill someone. Maybe he'd wrecked his truck driving home from the damn bar.

The thought then came like a thunderclap that Ollie could've been the one killed—impaled on his steering wheel in a ditch somewhere or shot after getting caught with another man's woman. Maybe his body had been buried out in the hills among the copperheads or thrown into the river to wash downstream like an old log.

It all made his head pound. All these worries. And nothing he could do about any one of them. He looked at the river. The logs stuck in the mud on the bottom and wagging with the current, the water swirling and trying to pull them down. He started the three-wheeler and rode back through the woods toward the house. He needed to check on Ethel, anyway. He drove and looked around at everything again. His kingdom of dirt.

CHAPTER THIRTY-FOUR

A few cars drove by him at this late and lonely hour, but Ollie couldn't figure out where in the hell they might be going. Not in this quiet little place, anyway. Not here in Logjam, where the Dairy Queen closed at nine, even on a Friday night, and every other business flipped its door sign over hours before then. Of course, he'd been places that would just be getting started at this hour: Knoxville, down in Tennessee, or Asheville, North Carolina, say. He'd practiced saying these names in his head, so he could casually drop them into conversations like a seasoned traveler. Not that he'd visited either of those cities at this time, now close to midnight. But he'd driven by them on their bypasses. And no one could refute him and say they weren't exactly as he described them.

He'd grown used to interstate driving, and these cars and pickups passing him on these narrow streets moved like drips of molasses down the side of a bucket. And what were they out for? They weren't driving to the corner all-night gas station for some emergency Aspirin or a rubber from the restroom vending machine, because the gas station closed at seven and you couldn't buy condoms in this town. Some punk-ass high school kid could drive fifteen miles in any direction and not find a condom for sale. He knew this because he'd tried. No one in this county wanted to sell condoms, but they must've been all right with seeing ten pregnant girls in every graduating class of sixty kids. He smirked to himself. Damn, he hadn't seen it all, but he'd walked into gas stations at damn near three in the morning out there off the interstate.

The streetlights burned dimly on their posts above the cracked and patched roads. He drove down the streets slowly, taking it all in, as if he'd never seen his hometown before. Traveling great distances gave a man a wise perspective, he noticed. He slowed as he reached the electric company office. They'd left a light on, and looking through the front window past the painted letters he saw what must've been her desk, empty. Where she'd been working all week, wondering about him. He hadn't driven by the office since he met her and it felt weird to look at the building now. It was a nondescript little place and there was no reason to look at it before.

He drove the length of the main street and then turned down a side road when it T'd near the old feed mill. Some kid had spray painted "LSHS Football" on the side of a deserted house next to the mill. Right on the house itself. Lower Shipley High School, where he himself had attended, some fourteen years ago. He'd played football for a couple of years, too, but ended up quitting because the coach wouldn't quit being an asshole.

He tried to read the mailboxes lined up in front of the small wood houses, but not all of them were marked with names. And some of the houses and converted apartments had no mailboxes, keeping a post office box instead. There were fewer streetlamps here, and his lone working headlight cast a weak beam. But he knew the son of a bitch lived down here somewhere, and he needed to find his house tonight, before he saw her again for the first time.

He kept a tire wrench behind the seat, a steel X, and he'd planned for many, many miles the most effective way to use it. He'd decided it was the right thing to do. Yet the wrench had four ends to it, four different sizes of sockets, and he couldn't decide how best to hold the tool to deliver a crippling blow.

If there'd been a vast ocean somewhere beyond those mountains where he'd camped, he hadn't looked upon it. He hadn't smelled its salty air or sensed its wet, shifting sand under his pale feet. He hadn't felt its waves crashing against him, the undertow trying to pull his legs out to sea. He hadn't listened to its surf washing under a cacophony of crying gulls.

And now that he was back home in Indiana he probably never would. He might send a postcard to the ocean telling it to kiss his ass.

Instead, this plan had been borne to him in the steaming hot campground: he would confront her old boyfriend, the one who'd lain with her and impregnated her. He'd finally put the idea of him being with her to rest. Then he, Ollie, would emerge victorious and go forth with Summer, the only man she'd ever known. He didn't really know why it was important to feel this way, but it was.

As he tied up and weighed down his sparse belongings in the bed of his truck that morning, all of this seemed possible. He'd drive straight back, find the asshole at his house, beat him senseless, and tell his prone and bleeding shape to never come near Summer or her daughter again. His alibi would be watertight, as they said on TV, because Coondog knew he was on the road, and people had seen him down there. The mustache woman, for example. She had his name on her books.

His plan was to do this tonight and hide out all weekend. Monday morning he'd return to work and say he'd gotten in the night before. The only glitch he'd found in this plan came in a park in Kentucky where he'd stopped to sleep for a few hours Friday afternoon. Like an incoming mortar round, it hit him: he'd forgotten to call Sellers at the sawmill. He thought he had one sick day left, but he'd missed two days now beyond his vacation time without so much as an excuse. So the plan was to go back to work, if he could. If he got fired, he'd go to her house and wait for her to get off work. See how that went.

But first he wanted to see how this fucker liked being jumped in his own house late at night and hit over the head with a tire iron.

•   •   •

He'd seen all of these houses before. He saw one yard lit up under a streetlamp and his mind was flooded with a memory of playing whiffleball with his grade school buds Jeff Smith and Doug Cavins. Ollie'd spent the night there a time or two and Jeff's mother had mixed red Kool-aid that tasted better than any he'd ever had. Now the trees they'd used as bases were bigger. The streets were devoid of cars as he continued his reconnaissance.

Then he saw it—a white house with a wooden frame built against it. Gray steps going to the second floor. He slowed to a stop right on the street, his truck idling, and stared at the house. There was a light on behind the curtains in a single window upstairs. But almost every window was lit on the first floor.

He moved the truck forward, peering in the windows. He saw the blue dancing light of a television. Part of a wallpaper border. A hung picture frame. In the driveway on the other side of the house he noticed the white pickup with the attached water cooler parked next to a hatchback.

When the house next door blocked his view, he turned back to the road and looked for a place to turn around. He knew where the tire wrench was—behind the seat, against the Indian blanket he kept for emergencies or for when he picked up a girl from the bar and no beds were available. He imagined the steel in his hands.

It'd be a hell of a thing, fighting right now, after driving almost twelve hours. Sleeping in spurts in the truck, driving the mountains at night like a speed-crazed trucker.

Maybe he should go to Coondog's and crash for the night. But then his alibi would be shot, and Coondog would go down as an accomplice if they got caught. He decided it wasn't right to make Coondog risk jail for something he himself wanted and intended to keep for himself. If this needed to be done to earn Summer, he'd pay the toll alone.

The next hour would make the rest of his life with her possible. And he'd be ready soon. He just needed a few more minutes yet.

Sitting where he was, in the parking lot of the feed mill, he could watch Todd's house. The parking lot was gravel and dark and he drank a beer from the cooler. The lights were still burning in the house, and once in a while someone walked past the windows.

He wondered if that prick had done this to Summer that night: parked outside her house and watched before coming to the door. Maybe he'd gone further—maybe he'd peered in her windows first? Seen Ollie watching her sleep? Fuck him, the asshole. He probably had. Maybe he'd peeped her other nights, too, ones Ollie didn't even know about.

He sat listening to Metallica, and even turned down he felt it working. Any minute now he was going to push open the creaking door, reach behind the seat, and make his way over to that house.

A bright yellow and red toy sat on the sidewalk in front of it. Some kind of trike, resting in the glow of the streetlight. He studied it—it was not unlike something Summer would have around for Spring. A foot-driven trinket intended to wear out little shitters. What did it feel like to have two kids, close to the same age? Each one coming out of a different woman? Todd had moved on completely and left Summer with one kid simply so he could start again with another.

Which is exactly what Ollie wanted him to do—move on. But he sat in the dark truck and drank his beer and wondered how it could be done. How could Todd leave Summer and Spring like that? What was it about this new woman that made her so much better?

He didn't want this asshole to want Summer anymore, but he didn't want him to not want her, either.

If this woman in the house across the street was better than Summer, and more deserving of a real family, then he'd have to see her. Check her out thoroughly. They lived on only the first floor—would it be possible, he wondered, to sneak up and look in their bedroom window? Maybe some answers could be found there.

One more beer, he told himself. Maybe two more songs. The dash had cracked a long time ago and he stuck his finger into the fissure and broke off a small piece of plastic. Damn truck was falling apart, inside and out. Sure, he'd watch them do their business. He didn't think she could be better at anything than Summer was, but he'd see about that. And while he was at it, he'd check out what kind of equipment this loser was packing. Not that he'd be looking there! Maybe he'd wait until old Toddy was mounted on top of her to sneak in and hammer that wrench down through the back of his skull.

The second Metallica song took a long time, but when it faded out, he threw the empty can to the floorboard and shoved open the door. It let out a metal screech, as it had every time since they'd hit the deer. He stepped out, grabbed the tire iron, and pushed the door shut with his hip until it latched.

He jogged across the narrow road away from the streetlight and tried to look disinterested as he trotted along the sidewalk. The house grew larger. Now he could see in detail the wooden steps leading to the second floor apartment. Pine, standard grade. Built like it'd been thrown together in a weekend.

There was a small yard on this side of the house, and he walked bent over, holding the wrench close to his chest. There was a window under the steps, and he thought he could look in there and still be hidden.

As he crept under the steps he got a face full of spider webs. Brushing them off, he knocked his cap to the ground. He grabbed it and screwed it back down on his head. He smelled the house now—the cool scent of the yard and something like natural gas or sewer. The TV was playing somewhere in the house, and the sound of voices came through the walls.

He stood there for a while, half leaning against the vinyl siding of the house. For some reason he was panting. Finally he lifted his face to the window and looked in. A kitchen. He saw a white refrigerator and part of a countertop. Dishes and pans piled on the counter. A sippy cup for a little kid.

He wondered if Todd had a gun. Probably. Too bad he didn't intend to give him a chance to retrieve it. No doubt it'd be in a closet somewhere, or locked in his truck. You couldn't keep a weapon out in the TV room with a little kid running around. And if you were busy screwing your wife you couldn't reach for a pistol.

But nothing was changing here. No one came into the kitchen, and no one noticed the shape under the stairs. He needed to move.

He slipped out from under the stairs and ran, staying close to the wall of the house. He slid around back. Four heaping trashcans sat there, and another car was parked in the alley. A yard barn stood with its doors wide open. A lawn mower was visible in the faint haze that emanated from the utility light high on a pole overhead. There were more kid's toys scattered here, too.

The back door led out onto a little wood platform, with another window beside it. He climbed onto the platform and crawled under the back door, staying low, until he crouched beneath the window. He could hear the blood moving by his ears. This fucker! he kept whispering in his head. This fucker! The noise from the TV was louder here.

He looked across the backyard. It butted against some other yards, but there were no fences. He could run out that way, if he had to, and circle around to his truck.

His heart was hammering now. When he lifted his head to look through the corner pane, he noticed the light from the TV flickering across the ceiling. The first thing he placed was the back of a couch, halfway into the room. He kept raising and lowering his head quickly, stealing glimpses. There was a lamp standing in the corner throwing light in an upward circle.

And there the fucker himself sat. Sock feet propped on an ottoman, head back against the headrest of a recliner. The chair was tilted toward the TV so that Ollie could see part of his face, illuminated by the tube. He looked about half asleep. He didn't look as big as Ollie remembered him, especially wearing what looked like pajama bottoms. Sissy fucker. One sock had slipped halfway off his foot.

Ollie lifted his head for a better look into the room. Now he noticed the long hair hanging down from the armrest of the couch. The woman was stretched out on it, head on the side closest to Todd's chair. She might've already been asleep.

And then he finally noticed the little feet, just visible on the carpet past the couch. The little boy stretched out on the floor in front of the TV, a thin blanket covering his legs. All three of them reclining and reposing and close enough to touch one another.

So Ollie stood there, looking in on them. The more he watched, the more brazen he became in his staring. If they had a dog, it would've barked by now. They had no idea he was crouched ten feet away, examining them. As he watched his breath fogged the window in front of his face. He clenched the tire wrench tightly in his fist.

Then there was a sudden movement and he jerked his head back to the very corner of the window. The little boy got off the floor, holding his blanket like a cape, and staggered to the side of the recliner. He held out his arms and Todd bent down and helped him climb up into the chair. Then the woman sat up but all Ollie could see was her long hair. She must've turned off the TV, because the screen went dark.

Todd stood up and carried the boy to the lamp. He stood there with his back to Ollie while the woman walked out of the room to the left. It looked like she had a nice body. Ollie could see the boy's sleeping face on Todd's shoulder.

Another light came on in the adjoining room, casting its glow through the doorway. Todd turned off the lamp and Ollie watched him carry his son across the shadows and into the lit room.

Ollie was left kneeling outside the house in the darkness, save the yellowish light from the utility post. He could hear faint talking now, amid running water. He imagined them brushing their teeth, maybe washing their faces. They'd put the kid in his little bed, just like Summer did with Spring every night. She had her own rituals, and he guessed similar rituals were going on right now in this house.

He looked down at the wrench in his hand. When he stood up his knees popped. He reached for the back door and placed his hand upon the knob. It was an antique and it wiggled in his grip, but it wouldn't twist open. The glass on the door looked wavy and he thought he could break it with a well-placed scream.

He climbed off the platform and once again stole around the house. There was a lit window in the wall in front of him, but as he approached a heavy curtain was pulled over it and the light went out. He listened at it for a while but heard nothing.

In front of the house sat the boy's trike. Ollie hid behind the corner and glared at it. That damn thing. So now this big fucker had a son, a daughter, and what seemed to be a second hot woman. No one man deserved everything while there were others who didn't have much. He shoved the wrench under his belt behind his back. He ran across the yard and seized the trike about the handlebars. There was little weight to it.

Turning around, he found the biggest window on the front of the house. He knew now it was the one that looked in on the TV room. He ran toward the dark window and hurled the trike over his head. It hit the glass where it paused but a moment before it passed through with a shudder and an explosion of twinkling shards.

Before the last piece fell from the frame he was running across the street, tire wrench back in hand. He heard screaming and yelling behind him but he made it to his truck and tore off out of the rear of the feed mill's parking lot. He pushed the accelerator to the floor and roared away down the desolate and potholed streets of his hometown.

CHAPTER THIRTY-FIVE

Frank couldn't bring himself to drive out to Chub's place. Dust was settling on the reels' oiled levelwinds even as he thought about it, but he couldn't make himself go out there to save them. He wasn't ready to walk into that garage again. Instead he ran two tanks of gas through the three-wheeler, revisiting and inspecting every tree, weed and puddle of his farm.

On Sunday morning he rode into the yard and pulled the three-wheeler into the lean-to alongside the boat, its tires sliding into the grooves they'd worn in the dirt floor. Three divots cupped the tires when he stopped. He stood off the machine and leaned against the boat's side. He ran his eyes over its interior, wondering if he should bolt headlights on the bow to navigate the river at night, now that Chub wouldn't be up there with his handheld spotlight. And if he added a hand crank and a series of pulleys, could he lower the front anchor from his seat in the stern? But the boat was dusty, and it would've been clear to anyone that his plans served the same purpose as the sketches of mansions the lifer in prison draws.

Catfish wasn't in the granary and that meant Ethel had him somewhere. They weren't in the garden, though, because he'd driven by there coming back from the woods. Outside the sun hit him like stepping under a heat lamp.

He noticed the door to the chicken coop was propped open with its rock and he wondered what she'd be doing in there now, with this heat turned on the way it was. Even the chickens were outside, knotted together in the shade of the coop, cocking their heads to the side and pecking the ground occasionally. She ought to know better than to mess with that damn coop in the hottest part of the day.

He looked toward the coop again and noticed Catfish standing there, peering through the screen door.

"What are you doing?" he called.

No answer. He took a few more steps. "Hey."

The pup glanced over, but then turned back toward the darkness of the coop and whined, rangy legs dancing.

The windows on the side of the coop were angled open. Normally, she propped the outer door wide to let in the breeze. But Catfish had taken with the idea of rushing the screen door and surprising the chickens. No amount of scolding would stop him. He liked to catch them inside while they ate or sat their eggs. He'd charge the screen, barking and growling, and trigger an explosion of noise and feathers.

But this time he wasn't acting like he meant to scare a bunch of chickens.

Frank's eyes were fried from the light and he had to stand over the dog and press his face to the screen to see anything. It was too dark inside and he raised his hand to shield his eyes against the sun. Catfish whimpered and stared into the coop.

"What are you—"

He saw his wife sitting on the rank dirt floor. She was looking up into the rafters, her legs caught beneath her in awkward angles.

He dropped his cane and jerked the door open. Catfish slipped in first. Two hens were sitting on eggs in the hutches along the wall, and they immediately began to screech. They burst forth from the hutches and scrambled for the low opening that led to the yard, scratching and beaking each other in their panic. But Catfish went directly to Ethel and licked her neck. She lowered her eyes from the ceiling and looked at him, wonder and befuddlement on her face.

Frank grasped her shoulder, her thin bones under his fingers.

She looked upon him with the same expression she'd given Catfish. As if she'd never seen him before. Her face was red and filmed with sweat, hair lying damp about her ears where it'd pulled loose from the cloth tie she always wore. He noticed her glasses were missing and found them in the dust and feathers and clumps of dark shit. He took them up and placed them in his pocket.

It was over one hundred degrees in the coop and the fine dust from the floor rose in columns of sunlight and hung there. The air hot and thick like breathing dust itself in choking tatters.

She looked past him with eyes open beyond their limits, rings of white visible around the blue irises.

"Stand up," he said, lifting his hand under her armpit.

Slowly her outstretched leg churned. The other remained folded beneath her, toes pointing downward. He lifted her against him and prodded at the lifeless leg with his free hand. Finally it moved and she positioned it under her weight, the muscle still cramped and forcing her to wobble on her toes. He could smell the sweat and dirt on her skin.

"What happened to you?" he asked.

She glanced at him, eyes wide and scared. "Who are you?"

"Dammit, you know who I am. What're you doing out here? It's too hot for you to be out here now. It's too damn hot."

"My leg's locked."

He led her toward the door, Catfish underfoot and peering upward. Frank pushed the screen open with his boot and walked her through it, the pup following.

In the house, he poured a glass of water from the pitcher in the fridge and carried it to where she sat slumped at the table. She'd said almost nothing coming across the yard and now she looked around her kitchen and occasionally muttered something he couldn't understand. But she took the glass and sipped.

It wasn't lost on him that he'd recently found his friend in a similar position, and only the fact that his wife was awake kept him from cursing God through the roof of the house.

"I need to call you the doctor," he said.

Her face was still red, a driblet of water clinging to her bottom lip. "Don't do that," she said.

"I'm going to, though. You had a heat spell out there."

She lifted the cup slowly and drank. "Don't," she said, once the glass was empty. "I'll be all right now."

Somehow the sound of her voice, weak as it was, kept him from taking the phone from its catch on the wall. He'd found her to be right almost always, and her eyes were beginning to look more like themselves, the blue in them familiar again. He stood and watched her and the kitchen was so quiet he could hear the sound of a car far away on a county road and eventually it grew silent again.

"I just got too hot," she said.

"What was you doing out there?"

She stared at him. "Well, I was cleaning out the coop!"

"It's too damned hot for that. You know better'n that."

She seemed to have forgotten her reasons. "I don't think I wanted to be in this house any longer," she said finally. "I think that's what it was."

He led her to the couch and helped her recline against a pillow placed over the wood armrest. He took her canvas shoes off—the sides and soles marked with dust and chicken dirt—and drew the curtains closed. He refilled her glass with fresh water from the fridge and set it next to her on the end table. The outside of the glass sweated in the humid air. They'd never had air conditioning and until now he'd never wished for it. He laid his calloused hand across her forehead. It felt hot but so did everything else.

He sat down in his chair then. He looked at the TV but didn't turn it on. Instead he stared at his wife and watched her eyes close as she drifted off. He knew he should get up and call the doctor soon, but it seemed smarter to stay where he could watch her rest.

Later, he did rise and make the call.

"Dr. Mulferd's office," a young-sounding woman said.

"Yeah, I need to talk to him. My wife suffered a setback out in this heat."

"Beg your pardon, sir?"

"This is Frank Withered, out here by Logjam. My wife's suffered some kind of setback out in this heat."

"Does she need to go to the hospital instead?"

"Well, no. I don't think so. She's sleeping now."

The receptionist grew alarmed. "Sometimes they need to stay awake! Did she suffer a heatstroke?"

"I'm not sure what you'd call it. She was out in the chicken coop, and when I found her, she was collapsed. I'd really like to talk to him about this."

"Hmmmmm. He's with a patient right now. Can he call you back? But you might need to go to the emergency room instead."

"Let me give you my number then. It's—"

"Sir, I'm going to need your name."

"Frank Withered, I done told you. The doctor knows me."

"I'm sure he does. Your number?"

"717, 1490."

"Is that an 812 number?"

"What?"

"Is that area code 812?"

"What the hell? Sure it is."

She said the doctor would call and hung up.

It didn't take long for Dr. Mulferd to call back. Frank tried to get to the kitchen as quickly as he could, but still the ringing woke her.

"Who's calling?" she cried out.

"Nobody. Rest," he said as he picked up the phone.

"Frank, it's Dr. Bob. What's wrong with Ethel?"

"Yes. Doctor, um, hello. I wanted to ask you about my wife. She collapsed out in the coop today." He'd stretched the phone cord along the interior wall of the kitchen, but it was his custom to talk loudly on the phone. She was saying something in the other room, but he plugged his open ear with his finger to better hear the receiver. The doctor had been talking.

"...is she in the house now?"

"Yes, she's restin on the couch."

"She's conscious? I mean, she's awake and alert?"

"Seems to be, yes. Part of the time. She drank some water."

"Good. Let's get her drinking more. Is she running a fever now?"

"I couldn't say for sure on that, but I felt of her forehead and it seemed hot."

"And she's speaking to you?"

"Pretty much, but she's messed up on some things."

"All right. Let's go ahead and take her over to County Memorial, Frank. Let them check her out, to be on the safe side. I'd rather they do that there, instead of having you bring her out here."

"Take her to the hospital now?"

"I think so, yes. As soon as possible."

Of course the hospital was over in Green City. It took the better part of an hour to drive there, not to mention the traffic. He looked out the window at the barn. There was still plenty of daylight left, but he hated to set out on that trip this late in the day.

"Frank? Are you still there? Can you take her now?"

"I guess we could. I'd have to drive her myself, though."

"You're still driving, aren't you?"

"Oh sure. I just almost wish this didn't call for a hospital. Maybe I could still bring her in to see you, there in the office?"

"No, we'd better not. Do you want me to call you an ambulance?"

"No! I can't see where we'd need that. We'll get there, if you're sure we need to go for this."

"I'm going to call them and tell them to expect you. They'll let me know what they tell her. I imagine she's all right—probably heat exhaustion. And I'll call you back at home this evening."

"Will do."

Frank hung up the phone and went into the living room. Ethel sat propped up on the couch, her hair clumped on top of her head.

"Was that the doctor?" she asked.

"He said we oughtta take you over to Green City."

"Whatever for? I feel fine now. It was just a spell."

"He says they need to check you out. I don't know. Maybe he's right."

"I hate to make that drive," she said.

"I know it. Much as I hate to."

An hour later, the signage for the different entrances confused them. One was marked Emergency Room, and that seemed correct, but underneath it said AMBULANCES in red, and they knew that couldn't be right. Another sign was marked General Visitors, and they'd gone that way once before when Hattie was laid up with a kidney infection. Frank had brought Ethel over to see her, but he'd stayed in the truck. Still, it didn't seem like they were merely visitors this time, so they hesitated out near the entrance, Frank behind the wheel, gazing up at the signs and studying the different parking lots. They were both talking at once. Suddenly a car pulled up behind them and honked. Frank looked up and saw a man gesturing wildly.

"Son of a bitch!" he called out and drove forward, taking the first parking spot he saw.

They were forced to walk a ways across the still-hot pavement to reach the nearest door. She kept saying they didn't really need to be there, but he told her they weren't turning around now.

When they walked through the big glass door of the hospital, a blast of cold air met them. It was an old sand-colored building, but the interior brandished new carpeting and smelled as if it'd been painted recently. In front of them stood a curved desk, built off the ground, and a woman with glasses sat up on the throne. She looked at them expectantly.

"Yes?" she asked.

"We're gonna need to see a doctor for her," he said, pointing toward his wife.

The woman looked at her.

"I'm fine," Ethel said, apologetically.

"No you ain't neither fine!" he exclaimed. "We're here, ain't we? Tell the truth now."

"Okay," the woman on high said. "It's all right. Now, what doctor did you want to see?"

They both looked at her.

"Oh, I don't think we know that," Ethel finally said.

"We don't know any of em!" he said. "Our doctor told us to come here, so we did!"

"Okay. And who is your doctor?" the woman asked.

"Dr. Mulferd. Over there at Hapgood."

"And he told you to come here? To the maternity ward?"

"The what? He just told us to come in here!"

The woman had experienced enough of him. She turned to Ethel. "What is it you wanted to see the doctors about, ma'am?"

Ethel didn't know what to call it. "I collapsed out in this heat," she said. "I'm fine now, but Dr. Mulferd thought we needed to get it checked out."

"Okay," the woman said. "Sounds like you need the emergency room—"

"We was trying to get there," Frank blurted out. "But we couldn't find it when we was lost in your parking lot!"

"Yes, well. It's over on the other end of the hospital. You'll need to walk some distance, I'm afraid. Or I could ask an orderly to wheel you in a chair."

"Oh, what the hell, lady."

"Sir, you'll need to calm down. This is the maternity ward. We have little babies around here. This is a happy place."

What seemed like hours later they stood in the ER, filling out registration. Actually, Ethel filled out the proper forms while Frank sat mutely in front of a television in a small waiting room nearby. The required paperwork had been too much for him and she was afraid he'd rip the pages to pieces and make a scene.

It was close to seven o'clock when they finally called her back for an examination.

"Whatever it was is gone by now," he told her as they heard her name read. "I don't know that they'll find anything at this time of day." He was so mad his hands shook. She rose from the chair slowly and stood there, rubbing her legs. Finally she straightened and turned to leave.

"You didn't tell me your legs was still hurting," he said.

But she walked away in her deliberate and quiet manner, following the nurse who had appeared with a clipboard bearing their information.

It was another hour before she returned. She looked about the same, but she was worn out. He could see it in her eyes. She carried a slip of paper.

"What'd he say?" Frank asked.

"They said it might've been a heat exhaustion. I'm supposed to take it easy for a while. Stay out of the heat. Drink lots of water."

"Heat exhaustion?" he asked, still sitting. He wasn't going to leave until she'd been cured all the way.

"That's what he called it," she said. "He had a nurse put a needle in my arm here and put a bag of fluids in me. Gave me some pills for my legs cramping. Come on. Let's go home. We got a long way to go yet."

It took him a while to stand up, and then they began the precarious journey back out of the hospital.

"How in the hell are we supposed to find the truck now?" he asked.

"I think I'll recognize it when we get outside."

"Recognize it? Course you will. I reckon I'll recognize my own truck, too, once I find it."

"That's not what I meant, dear. I meant the parking lots."

"Well, you ain't walking all around, looking for it, I'll tell you that. I'll go find it. You wait here, in this entryway. I'll go find it and come back and pick you up. Be ready."

So she paused there, in the brightly lit entrance to the emergency room. He walked off, leaning over his cane, across the smooth pavement of the parking lot. She watched him make his cautious progress. The sun was down now, and the lights on the poles above the cars swarmed with moths. The lights made it bright enough to give the appearance of daylight. She knew it was already way past dark, though. They'd be home late.

She hated to have caused so much trouble. She knew he hated to come into the city like this. And for what this doctor had said, acting like he didn't even care who she was or what was wrong with her? And now her arm was sore from the IV drip. The doctor said there was nothing else he could do for her, just told her to stay out of the heat, drink water all day and rest. Like she wasn't trying. Like someone didn't need to take care of the chickens. As long as they had chickens she wasn't going to let them die from neglect.

Ethel leaned against the door and slept as he drove, and he tried to remember the last time he'd seen her asleep in his truck. These days the longest trips they took were to Peterson's Market or maybe out to Chub's for dinner. Not anything long enough to make anybody tired. He guessed the last time he'd seen her asleep in his truck had been long, long ago, back when they'd still gone on drives to get away from Tarif. While her dad lived with them, she never really relaxed, even at night. Not with him asleep in the room downstairs. So they'd developed a signal: on nice evenings after dinner, if most of the work was done, one of them would announce it was a nice night to go fishing. Tarif was never invited. Frank'd throw a rod or two into the truck and in minutes they'd be parked down by the river somewhere. On those trips he wouldn't even cast a line. They spent their best newlywed nights in the cab of his pickup. He'd been a young man then, and sometimes after they'd finished the second time she'd fall asleep. He used to watch her face while she slept and think, even if he'd done nothing else right, he'd done well to marry her. Was in fact lucky to have done so.

But he wasn't a young man anymore and she wasn't a young woman. He glanced over at her now, head leaning against the glass and mouth open slightly, and she looked plain exhausted. They were close to home, driving the narrow gravel lane, and still she slept on. So far, two coons and a possum had crossed in front of them, but he hadn't braked hard enough to wake her up. All three of them had made it across, anyway.

It was a sorry weird thing to have friends dying off because they were getting too old to keep living. None of this had snuck up on Frank. He'd lived a long damn time, and he knew what that meant, what cost needed to be paid. But this business of having Chub die and then finding Ethel out of sorts like that in the chicken coop surprised him just the same. He'd understood every one of them was going to die sometime, but somehow he didn't think he'd be alive to watch it happen. He'd been told if you were lucky it felt like you were going to sleep, but he'd considered that and dismissed it as so much horseshit. There was a difference between sleeping and dying and anyone alive knew that.

He'd driven home from the river many nights like this, and he knew he wouldn't fall asleep. Sometimes Chub did—once he'd run the truck and trailer thudding into the ditch—but Frank never did. One gift he'd been given was the ability to stay awake. And he knew how to drive at night, when a lot of men didn't. He went even slower but he kept his eyes open.

It was damn pretty country, he thought. Day or night.

He'd always liked how the headlights reflected off the waves of fescue lining the road and whitened them. And how when you looked away from the light's glare you could see the valleys of the hilly pastures lit up with moonlight, dotted here and there with clumps of black trees. Fences lining them, the posts like black bones reaching out of the ground.

That's why he'd started catfishing. So he could be outside all night. He'd grown up around a lot of tough men, and had probably become one himself, but not all of them were cut out for nights. That river looked like one thing during the day, with sunlight reflecting off the ripples, throwing sparkles of brightness, but after the sun set it became a living, breathing creature that kept its secrets. He'd listened to the coyotes scream and slept with the snakes enough to know that not every place is the same all the time. Sometimes a place that allowed you to be brave during the day would take that away from you at night.

And now he came to their farm, his place day or night for going on forty-five years. He could see the moonlight glancing off the barn roof and the paint-peeled boards.

Somehow she sensed they were home and woke before he said anything. He stopped in front of the chain and got out. The dome light lit the cab with a sudden and obnoxious light, but he closed the door behind him so the mosquitoes wouldn't be drawn to it.

She stretched her arms a little in front of her and watched him unlock the padlock. There was a bandage over the IV hole and it'd pulled off some. She was thankful they'd made it home. If the doctor had told her to stay overnight at the hospital she didn't know what they would've done.

He got in and drove a short distance over the chain. Then he had to get out and put it up behind them. Finally that was done.

"I'm gonna drop you off at the house," he said. "No need for you to walk."

She nodded.

"It'll take me a minute to mess with the dog. He ain't been fed yet today. You think you'll be all right in there by yourself for a little bit?"

"I'll be fine," she said, her voice cracking from being asleep.

"All right then. I'll be in directly."

He stopped the truck and she eased out. They'd forgotten to turn on the kitchen light and the house was dark. When she shut the door she didn't get it all the way closed and he tried to remember to slam it once he'd parked. He waited until she'd used the key from her purse and he saw the kitchen light come on.

As soon as he pulled in the barn he could hear Catfish, barking and whining. Frank hoped he hadn't pooped in the granary, or that'd be one more thing he'd have to take care of before he got inside.

He lifted the pup out and the granary was dry and clean. Catfish ran out into the yard like he was on fire, though. There was a light with a pull string near the door to the yard and Frank leaned against the doorjamb and stood in its light, watching his dog. A bat swooped low. Cobwebs hung from the rafters and boards overhead. The cobwebs had grown soft and dusty and hung like clumps of a young woman's hair.

CHAPTER THIRTY-SIX

In his dream suddenly there came a knocking. He was on the ocean, in this big-ass cruise ship, one with as much going on inside as outside, and then something was knocking on it. He was on the boat with Spring, of all things and people. Not Summer. He hadn't seen Summer anywhere on this vessel, although downstairs he'd found a working sawmill. While he and Spring were playing tennis on the top deck, surrounded by nothing but deep blue water, Ray had walked up to them, still covered in sawdust, and said Ollie needed to get back to work. Ollie had yelled at him, said he wasn't ready to stop playing tennis yet. Which was odd, since he'd never played. He'd been riding the dream along, waiting to see what he and his little friend would discover next, when something started knocking on the ship, like they were running aground. Spring dropped her racquet and started to cry.

He was so tired it took a long time to come back from the dream. As he did, he realized with a jolt he was in the trailer. But it was still halfway dark. He remembered he had to get up for work, since it was Monday. But not even this early. The knocking! What the hell? Someone was at his door! He wasn't on a big ocean liner at all—he was asleep alone in his trailer and now someone was knocking on his door at 5:37 a.m. And then he remembered Todd's house and he jerked on a pair of jeans and felt under his bed for the baseball bat.

As he went down the short narrow hall the knocking got louder, incessant. He'd spent the entire weekend holed up like a wanted man, not calling anyone, sleeping varied hours and watching the driveway the rest of the time. Sealing his alibi. No one had come for him, and he'd begun to think Todd hadn't seen the perpetrator at all. Now it seemed he'd finally shown up to ask about his front window. Ollie had him on his property this time, though, and could claim self-defense if he beat him down with this bat.

He turned the corner and instead saw the top of his father's hat through the window in the wooden door. The same green farmer's cap he wore all the time over his gray hair.

The old man wasn't looking in—he stared out across the yard and the fields beyond. His fields. Ollie was close to the door when he realized he still carried the bat, so he shoved it behind the couch.

The wood door opened with a whoosh and the screen door jumped in its loose frame and made a metal-on-metal sound. His dad turned and their eyes met. Ollie pushed the storm door wide.

"Hey," he said.

Frank didn't say anything but took hold of the doorjamb on each side, cane held against the frame in his right hand, and pulled himself up into the trailer. Ollie stepped back. Stuff was still where he'd thrown it after his road trip. The sleeping bag was draped over the little bar that separated the kitchen from the living room. Wet, dirty clothes lay humped here and there. A chipped Styrofoam cooler sat on the floor.

"I was just fixin to get up for work when I heard you knocking," Ollie said. "Otherwise I'd been out here sooner."

Frank looked around the place. Ollie could feel the criticism with which he took in everything. Then he looked right at him.

"I guess you got yourself in trouble with the law or something, so you took off runnin like a coward."

"Don't go saying that! You don't know where I been." Ollie stood there without a shirt on, his arms crossed.

"Well, whatever it was. That ain't my business and I don't give a shit. But you better know now that your mama's worried sick about you being missing and now she's suffered heatstroke."

"What? She all right?"

Frank looked down. Put his cane foot between his toes and tapped it on the filthy linoleum. "I guess so. Doctor said she'll be all right. But I don't know for sure."

"When the hell did this happen?"

Frank's eyes snapped up. "It happened yesterday, if'n you give a damn. We been trying to call you and we even come out here once and we couldn't raise you."

"I've been on a trip." Ollie suddenly felt embarrassed of his half-assed vacation and he walked into the kitchen like he meant to make coffee or something. "I been outta town for a few days." He was behind the cabinet now and his dad couldn't see his face. It was easier to talk. He opened the cabinet where he kept the coffee. But the next sound he heard was the storm door being pushed open again. When he got around the bar the old man was already stepping down.

"Where you going now?" Ollie asked.

"I'm going back to the house to eat something. And to check on her."

Ollie went to the door and caught it before it could slam shut like it always did. "You want some coffee here? I can make some."

Frank stopped. "I only come here to tell you about your mom. You wanna live out here like some damn crazy that's your life. I don't give a care one way or the other. But I figured I'd tell you you've made her a nervous wreck."

"I'll come out there," Ollie said. "After work, that is."

Frank was already going down the uneven path toward his truck. "Get your ass to your job," he said, and then he said some other things Ollie couldn't hear.

The sun came up over the field to the east and he felt the rays on his face. You could see everything you wanted to see. Ollie stood there at the door and watched the old man turn his pickup around and go down the driveway. He didn't wave and Frank didn't look to see if he had or not.

Friday night he'd returned to his trailer full-on drunk and still high from crashing Todd's house. He was a little surprised to see the pole light burning, but he figured he'd probably left it on. He'd taken off without checking to make sure the stove was off, the coffee pot unplugged. At the time, he hadn't thought he'd ever be back. If it burned down before he got out of state, so be it.

But there it sat, illuminated in the weak light's dome. Home sweet home. A trailer in the weeds. Probably the mice had all but taken over the place in his absence. One time he'd turned up a box of cereal over his bowl and a mouse shot out and scampered right off the edge of the table. He sat in his truck and looked at the dwelling, a warrior returned from his journey. A sojourner back from a pilgrimage. A knight returning to his castle. Oh fuck me, he thought. It feels all right to be back home again in Indiana, but fuck me if someone deserves to come home to this.

Inside, everything was exactly as he'd left it. No one had even come by to notice he was missing.

He pulled into the sawmill parking lot at the same time as Ray, and all Ray said was, "Hell, you better go talk to him," so Ollie went to the little office built on the loft overlooking the main floor of the sawmill. When he knocked on the door, he heard Doug inside, talking on the phone. After a minute Doug yelled to come in.

This is where Doug sat when he wrote the checks every other Friday, and now he was behind his desk, still talking on the phone. Something about ordering parts for one of the skid loaders. Ollie had seen something move across Doug's face as he opened the door, and now Doug was avoiding looking at him. Ollie sat down and picked his fingernails, his hands shaking from the caffeine he'd drunk that morning.

Doug finished and put the phone back on the base. He stared at Ollie. Silence. He picked a ballpoint pen off his desk and started to click it.

"Where you been, Mr. Withered?"

"I'll tell you what, I got so damn sick last week—" Ollie began.

"No, we're not gonna have that shit today," Doug said, sitting forward. "Not today we're not. I got shit broken down and we're behind on the jobs we do have. Not that we got enough. So I ain't gonna sit here and hear all about how you been too sick to work." He was clicking his pen as fast as he could pull the trigger. "Ray's been out there working overtime trying to make up for you."

"Well, the thing is, I been real sick. You know I don't miss much, but this flu about—"

"Your phone broke?"

"—uh, yeah, it's out. And I's too sick to get over to dad's to call. I just wanna get back to work today."

Doug pulled a file out of a drawer and opened it on his desk and flipped through some pages. There weren't many, total. "How many days you miss on me this year?" he asked, continuing to look.

"I missed about three, all told. That's it. Before this here, I mean."

Doug looked down and nodded, seeming to verify this information. He didn't say anything. Ollie noticed his hands were shaking a little bit, too.

Ollie had been called into the office throughout most of his education and this was starting to feel like one of those times. He wasn't about to beg this drunk son of a bitch. Not at his age, he wasn't going to. He'd never kissed ass in a principal's office and he wasn't going to start living that way now. But this time he'd messed up for no real reason and Ray was going to be pissed, too. He hadn't really thought about Ray.

"You figure I can't replace you, Ollie? Is that what you're thinking here today?"

"No, I know you can. I mean, I hope you don't, is the thing."

"Damn right I can. Lots of people out this way looking for work. I myself got a nephew I just about hired last week to replace your ass. I would've already done that if he wasn't such an ignorant little inbred."

Ollie felt himself smiling and tried to stop.

Doug smiled a little himself. "I know you've been pretty good out there," he said, motioning to the door and the sawmill behind it. "I'd hate to lose you after ten years."

"I want to stay."

"Well, you better not pull that kind of stunt again. Me and your dad's been pretty good friends before, and you've been pretty good here. I ain't gonna fire you for this." He closed the file and then pointed at him with it. "But you know I could."

"I thought you might."

"Next time I will. No questions asked. You take off again like that and you don't need to come back."

"I got you, Doug."

"You say you got your shit, ready to work today?"

"You bet," Ollie said, standing up.

"Then you better get out there and punch in and get ready to go. We got a bunch we got to get through today, if we's ever gonna get caught up."

Ollie pulled open the thin door and headed for the stairs that'd take him down to the main floor, where he'd gather his gear from the break room. Ray would be sitting there, drinking coffee, getting ready to start. He'd need to apologize to Ray. He was going to make some shit up about the way things had gone down in South Carolina. He'd tell Ray about all the women—all those loose, bikini-wearing women walking on the soft sand beaches of South Carolina, big knockers swinging. And hadn't they just about fallen over themselves, trying to get at him? Yes, they had. They most certainly had gone nuts for him. Once he started in on the stories, he hoped Ray would forget he'd worked harder last week, trying to feed his paternally-questionable kids who sometimes shat on the floor.

By the end of the workday, it was as if he'd never left. Never done anything but work in this mill all day, every day. It all came back to him: the sawdust getting under his collar and down his shirt, the way the sweat formed under his hard hat and ran down his face and neck. The noise. The excitement from keeping this job had lasted about the first hour, and now he had his mom to worry about and he still hadn't seen Summer yet.

He'd gone to Todd's to settle the score and claim Summer as his own. Even if he hadn't hurt him like he planned to do, he definitely scared him. And his wife and kid. And it sure as hell felt good to hoist that toy through his goddamned window. He'd thought about it all weekend, and he was starting to feel like he and Todd were even now. But the last time he'd spoken to Summer had been in that park in North Carolina, and any more that seemed like last year. She was within miles now, but the closer he got the harder it was to face her. It was one thing to pay back Todd. It was another to figure out what he owed Summer and if she'd even accept a check from him anymore. He had the bears but they didn't seem like much when you considered what he'd done.

When work ended, he walked out to his truck with Ray. Ray, for one, seemed happy to have him back. Here came another one of his stories, now that they were within sight of their vehicles, within sight of salvation.

"Well, I guess me and Lacey gonna be spending some time in the laundry room tonight," he began.

Ollie kept walking. He wanted to get home, shower, and head to Summer's. He'd go there first and then out to see his mom. "Yeah, I need to do some too," he said. "I still got all my stuff from my trip yet to wash."

"That ain't want I'm talking about." Ray smiled his little slanted-in teeth grin.

"Yeah, well, when you live alone you gotta do your own clothes, that's all I'm sayin."

They reached his truck, but Ray leaned against the bed. Ollie didn't want to be rude now—he'd tried all day to get back on Ray's good side. He stood with his hand on the door handle.

"No, what I'm talking about is something other than laundry entirely," Ray said. "Me and Lacey got this little tradition, I guess you'd call it."

"Oh yeah?" Ollie wondered why he'd argued for this job back.

"Well, I don't know if you know this, but women get off on washing machines. By sittin on em! They like the vibration, I reckon." He waited for Ollie's reaction.

Ollie dropped his hand from the door and smiled, like he was now completely engrossed in the information. Eyebrows up, like tell me more.

"See, tonight, the kids always watch Knight Rider, right? Well, we tell em, 'you kids stay up here and watch TV. We gotta go do some laundry.' And then we go down there and get it on!" Ray squealed with laughter and held his meaty arms out in front of him, pumping his hips.

Ollie laughed. "Oh shit."

"Yeah, every Monday! I come home and Lacey'll say, 'we really need to do some laundry tonight. I been wantin to real bad.'"

"Man that sounds like a good tradition," Ollie said. He opened his truck door and it squealed. "Shoot. I better get on home, go check on my mom."

Ray grabbed his arm. "The thing is, last week it wasn't normal, the way she wanted it. If you know where I'm going with this."

"What, she'd use her mouth or something?"

He guffawed, his nasty breath shooting into Ollie's face. "Nah, it wan't the mouth, where she wanted it!" He hit him on the arm. "Guess again."

Oh my God, Ollie thought. When will it end. He shrugged.

"That's right—the ass!" Ray laughed his open-mouthed horselaugh again.

Ollie hoped the disgust wasn't showing on his face. "Oh man, and all the while the kids is watching Knight Rider. That's some good stuff, Ray."

"Hell yeah they are! Meantime, we're down there, getting it on right there on the washer! See, we do it on Mondays on account of how close our bedroom is to Tricia's. She come in on us once and I had to tell her me and mommy was play wrestling."

Ollie got in his truck and shut the door. He started it. The sun had made the cab suffocatingly hot.

Ray leaned on the windowsill, and Ollie could smell him. "See, now you know why I'm in such a hurry to get home tonight."

"You bet! See you tomorrow, then."

"See you tomorrow, buddy." Ray slapped the top of the truck. "Hey! Glad you're back!"

"Thanks, man. Sorry again about that overtime deal. I owe you one."

Ray looked at him. "Ah, who cares. It's just work, you know?"

In the shower, Ollie stayed until the hot water ran out. The plastic liner of the tub had pulled away from the drywall long ago and the whole time he stood there showering he studied the black mold growing in the gap. It was a hell of a place to go to get clean, this shower. Plus he never cleaned it.

But now he scrubbed himself pink—he wanted to wash off the trip, the weekend in hiding, the day at work, the old man's guilt-trip. He washed his hair twice. If he had any chance of Summer letting him in, he'd need to be cleaner than she'd ever seen him.

He decided not to call first. He'd planned on showing up at her door with flowers, but he didn't know where to get them. There was only the little market out by her house, but they wouldn't have something like that. He tried to think of yards where he'd seen a bunch of flowers growing, where he could jump out of the truck and pick some real quick. There were flowers planted in half barrels up at the Dairy Queen, but somebody would see him do that. Screw it. No flowers, then. He'd just show up, clean.

Wearing his coolest pair of jeans and the shirt that showed off the muscles in his arms, he opened his one bottle of cologne and spilled some on his palm and spread it on his razor-burned neck. He stood in front of the bathroom mirror and brushed his teeth and combed his hair. Only then did he pick up the sack that held the two bears. They'd been taken out and examined many times.

He drove the roads back to her house. It'd been almost a week since the night he left so mad, jerking their vacation away and taking it alone. He wondered what it would've been like with them along.

Her house looked normal as he drove by. Just a drive by first, to see if everything looked on the up and up. It did. Her car was there, but the rest of the driveway was empty. The grass had grown up quite a bit. He'd offer to cut that for her this week, if she'd let him.

In another minute or two, he stood at her door, knocking, just like old times, the bears hanging in a sack by his side. He held the screen door open with his thigh so she could jump right out and hug him if she wanted to. It wouldn't take long to gage her reaction. He'd know any second now if he was going to be all right.

When the door opened, it swung hard and fast and immediately he found he couldn't look up. Like his neck was paralyzed. He stood there, staring at her bare feet on the carpet. Her beautiful, beautiful Indiana feet. Suddenly he'd never felt so ashamed in all his life.

Spring appeared on the carpet behind her mother's legs then, peering around them like bars in a jail. Those he knew a little something about, and he could say with certainty her legs were a lot better than the real thing. He would say there was no comparison.

"Ah-ee?" Spring asked.

He made himself look up then, into Summer's face. Her eyes were angry and the lower lids were full. Her bottom lip trembled. He looked back down at her feet.

"What the hell is this?" she asked.

"I'm not sure I can say. I meant to be back sooner, but then I had to take care of something. And then there was my job to mess with. And now my mom had something happen to her. This whole trip, somehow it—"

"Ruined any chance you had?"

He looked out over the yard. He'd swear to God a woman couldn't make him cry but somehow this one had taken him to the brink of it half a dozen times in a month. He turned all the way around and faced the road, his back to them.

"You're a leaver, Ollie. I see that now. And I know what I'm talking about, because my dad was one and her dad was another one. I don't want a third."

He had an answer for that but when he started to say something he heard the door shut behind him.

He walked to the truck and was almost there when he remembered the bears in his hand. Pulling his sleeves up to his eyes he wiped each one hard one time and went back to the door. He knocked.

When she opened it this time she was invested in a full-on cry, tears running down her face. The screen door stood between them.

"I told you I got you and her something down there and I wasn't lying about that." He held the sack up. "I'll tell you right now it's not much in here. Just a little something I picked up in the mountains down where I was."

She didn't move.

"If you don't want to take them from me, I can leave em out here and you can tell her to come out later and look. Tell her Santa came early this year or something. I don't know. I ain't got no use for them, I know that. But make sure she knows that only one is meant for her."

He put the sack on the front step and turned to go back to his truck. Now the words were coming though, and he had more to say. "Because I never said I'd put her first. I always thought of you first and her second, and that one night you said you wanted that."

He heard the screen door push open and she stepped outside. "I said we're a team. I never said I had to come first."

He looked at her and motioned at the brown paper sack, top rolled over itself. "Well, then, I got the whole team something."

She reached over and picked it up. Opening the mouth of it she saw the cheap plush bears piled at the bottom. She seemed to cry a little harder then and looked at him. "Did you think about what I told you on the phone? Do you know what I meant when I said you need to do some things, too?"

"What the hell else you think I've been thinking about?"

"Well?"

"All I been doing is driving up and down mountains, thinking about you and what a damn fool I was for yelling at you like that. And about how it wasn't all your fault."

"But you're not going to take off again like that, are you?"

"Summer, look. I never even wanted to go in the first place. And then I didn't even make it to the damn ocean."

Her face was red and still she cried but he saw a hint of her smile return, a flash of white like a strobe from a lighthouse, and he sensed that it'd be all right to go to her and not say anything else for a while. He did that and felt her tears soak through to his shoulder. He rubbed her back and breathed in deeply the scent of her hair, committing it to his mind.

Outside, a branch scratched against the side of the house as the evening air blew across the yard. He sat on the couch while Spring paraded a series of toys in front of him, all of them coming out to be introduced to her new bear. Summer was next to him, holding hers on her lap, and they laughed at Spring's commentary. But the emotional hangover lingered in all of them and the air felt like it always did after a storm passed. When Spring introduced the dustpan her mother had left in her room it was clearly time to do something else.

"Let's take some lemonades out back," Summer suggested.

"Yes!" Spring yelled. "And Bear!"

Ollie and Spring went outside first and pulled chairs up to the wrought-iron table, dragging them over the uneven and lopsided bricks. Summer came out with three plastic glasses of iced lemonade. Bear sat on the table, golden medallion gleaming. The heat had died down and it was pleasant.

When the shadows from the trees grew longer and the first firefly lit, Spring jumped up and asked if she could chase it. Summer went in the house and returned with an old mayonnaise jar and the little girl went flying out into the backyard under the three big maples.

He took a drink, but the glass was already empty and the three cubes melting in the bottom broke loose and crashed to his face, spilling a little diluted lemonade down the outside of his throat. She laughed. He took the neck of his shirt and dried off. He laughed, too. He leaned in and kissed her.

What the hell, he wondered. What had he been doing down there?

They both watched Spring. She was on her hands and knees, trying to sort through the grass under her fingers. The jar was on its side next to her. There was at least one firefly lighting within.

Spring yelled then, something about some of them getting away. She wanted to show all the fire bugs to them, but not all of them could be caught. She was getting tired and it'd be bedtime soon. He thought maybe he'd stick around after she got tucked in, spend some time alone with Summer.

He was ready to help catch the remaining fireflies. Ready to cram all the lightning bugs into the old jar, all of them, all the light that container of glass could possibly hold.

CHAPTER THIRTY-SEVEN

Frank knew he needed to check on Ethel, but he was still worked up, so instead he drove around and examined his fields. He'd been as worthless as tits on a boar since the meeting and he would've admitted that to anybody. Driving aimlessly on either the three-wheeler or in this truck and just waiting for the water to rise. He felt as helpless and oblivious as an old box turtle, scratching across a barren and dry riverbed, wall of water descending just upstream. And the shame of it was now his wife needed him around more, but he was so fed up if he stopped moving he'd just break whatever got near his hands. Goddamn Ollie and his trailer. It looked like a pigsty in there: nasty clothes piled, a smell so sour he wondered if the septic tank hadn't backed up. If Ollie's mother had seen how he lived it would've about killed her. Actually, she probably would've set about cleaning it. Oh, he'd gone somewhere, that was evident enough, but wherever he'd gone wouldn't keep him. So Frank could at least go home and deliver the good news: their son was back where he started, living in his own mess like a simple.

Frank turned left instead of right at the old shot-up stop sign and many of these cornfields had low spots, too, where puddles had yellowed the stalks. In the tool shed he still had a single-blade plow he attached to the three-point hitch of his John Deere to ditch puddles. You knocked over some corn doing that, but the corn left standing grew better once you got the water off its roots. That was Wayne's decision now, and Frank didn't feel like spending his days draining puddles when they were threatening to flood the whole damn place anyway.

He wished he'd brought Catfish along, but he hadn't wanted him nosing around out there at the trailer. Who knew what kind of chemicals Ollie had lying around. A little antifreeze would kill a dog. Down in the ditch he saw a black snake coiled in the sun on an old fence post. Black shiny bastard. Just seeing him made his blood chill.

Well, he might as well head over to Chub's and pick up those rods and reels. He drove out that way and tried to steel himself against those first few steps into the garage.

When he got close enough to see the mailbox knocked over in the fescue he knew something bad had happened.

The front yard was scraped bare, the sod turned over and rolled like ribbons of peeled flesh. He hit the brake and stopped on the road. The house was still standing, but the windows were naked and he could see the empty yellow walls inside. The yard had been bulldozed flat, the bushes along the front of the house yanked. Now the house sat there exposed and meek, a kid's toy plopped down in a sandbox.

The garage was gone altogether.

In the backyard stood a small mountain of cinder blocks and detritus. Here and there two-by-fours and roof joists jutted skyward amid patches of shingles. A few yard trees that had been ripped out lay toppled with their roots clawing the air. The picnic table, the fish tub and the fence where so many catfish had hung lay hidden behind the pile. Or maybe they'd been bulldozed away.

Frank looked over the rubble. If only the boy had left it alone for a year or two. Maybe he wouldn't have lived to see this.

Ethel was playing solitaire when he returned, the stained and bent cards spread out on the old wood table. A half-full glass of water sat nearby. He walked in, Catfish following, and placed his hand on her forehead. His hand felt warm and smelled of dog.

"You don't feel too hot," Frank said.

"I'm telling you, I feel fine today. What I am is wore out from yesterday, is all."

"You drinking your water?"

"I drunk more water in the last day than a fish. I can't get two turns done before I need to head down the hall again."

"You winning your card game?"

"No."

He went into the living room and sat in his chair. The yellow dog went with him and lay down near his feet. Frank took his cane and stroked the pup's head. Catfish closed his eyes.

"Well, I seen him," he said.

"What did you say?"

"I said I been out there. I seen him. He's back from whatever he's been doing."

She rose from the table and came into the room. "Ollie?" Catfish lifted his head and looked at her.

"Who'd you think I meant? Yeah, I went out there first thing this morning, fore he went to work."

"Well, where'd he been all this time?"

"Don't ask me cause I don't know no more than you do. I almost didn't say nothing but I figured you'd want to know he was all right."

"Well of course I'd want to know!"

"Now you do, then." He picked up the remote and turned on the television.

She stood there a while before going back to her cards.

He thought Ollie probably had his old man pegged for an asshole and if he wanted to think that he probably wouldn't get many arguments. When he himself had been fourteen he'd come across his dad lying outside their barn where he'd fallen from the hayloft. When Frank found him he looked like he was asleep, except his head was looking almost backwards and his eyes were open. He was dead drunk.

It'd happened sometime during the night at the end of October. Maybe his father intended to climb into the loft to look out across the little rundown farm he was fixing to lose to the bank. Maybe he went up there to jump. But if he wanted to do that, he would've shot himself, because the hayloft wasn't that high and their shotgun worked every time.

His dad had been drunk almost every day Frank knew him, and had beaten him at various times with items ranging from a shovel handle to a corn cob. The morning Frank found him he'd crouched by the body for a while and listened for breathing. Then he went in and told his mother.

There was some relief in that he was dead. The farm lay in shambles but Frank would try to salvage it, make it turn a profit. And for several months he worked without stopping. He worked hard enough to save the place, too, if his father's drinking hadn't put them so far in the hole. Then his mother took sick and died. He lived in their little house for two months alone before the bank repossessed everything his family had ever claimed to own.

A couple of different neighbors took him in and let him exchange labor for food and a bed. For fourteen years he worked for others. He was twenty-eight when he got Ethel to marry him. He'd been watching her for a long time.

And now, here he sat, in the same house he'd moved into on his wedding night. Others had lived rougher lives and he knew that to be fact. But he thought if Ollie wanted to swap stories sometime on growing up with a knot on your head he'd be able to hold his own.

When the sheriff had shown up at the door back then with those bank papers, he'd gone into the whitewashed house and thought, there ain't no way I can do this by myself. There ain't no way. And he was young and full of fight in those days. But he'd lived a whole life since then. Look at him now: an old man watching television with his dog. There was no fight left in him.

"Where else did you go this morning?" she called from the kitchen.

"They tore down Chub's garage," he said.

CHAPTER THIRTY-EIGHT

Sleeping two hours before rising to work among saw blades after the craziness of the past week wouldn't have been what a medical doctor or some other learned person might have recommended, but it was exactly what Ollie did after finding himself back in Summer's grace. He'd driven home before dawn and slept a little and now he was back on the concrete floor, watching a giant oak get planked. The way the night had turned out, he hadn't been able to visit or even call his mama, and he hated that. But things with Summer had required immediate and careful attention. What had the old man called this thing with his mom? Heatstroke. He thought about asking Ray if people couldn't use half of their bodies after a heatstroke, but he never did. Ray wasn't no damned doctor, and he was in a shitty mood besides. Ollie figured that the washing machine had broken but he sure as hell wasn't going to ask about that. Tonight after work, he was going to see his mom. And he had another plan cooking in his head, too.

When his dad showed up yesterday morning, it became pretty clear that his parents had written off his vacation as a trip to the pen. As soon as he took a little leave of absence, something people did all the time, they automatically assumed the worst—their son had fucked up again, and this time they'd tossed him in the state lockup. He wouldn't be surprised to find out they'd called the jail, looking to see if he'd checked in. Granted, he had spent a night or two in that fine establishment. But a man deserved a chance to start over, didn't he?

Well, tonight, he'd show them what he'd been up to. Let the old dried-up man run his eyes over Summer's brown legs. By God, he wasn't so old yet he wouldn't do that. Let his mom go ga-ga over Spring's antics and long eyelashes. Hell yes. He'd shove his women in their faces, show them he could make more than shit piles in his life.

Directly after work he went home, showered thoroughly and called Summer. Told her he had a surprise for her, and to get Spring ready.

"Let me guess: you're taking us to the Dairy Queen," she said.

"Nope, that ain't it," he said. But she seemed disappointed, so he added, "Well, that's part of it. But it ain't all of it."

He hung up and shoved his keys and wallet into his jeans. Then he reached for his pocketknife and a pack of gum and pocketed them also. He was two strides down the path when he suddenly felt like he'd gulped soured milk: they would be coming within miles of right here. She'd been asking about his place since the beginning—now what could he say? He'd been hiding it like a body in a basement, but he didn't know how much longer he could maintain the secrecy.

Already on the verge of being late, he flew around the trailer and tried to tuck trash away. There was no way he was going to do dishes now, so he spread a towel over the sinkful of plates and the cookie sheet covered with dried bits of fish sticks. All of the clothes tumbled into the still-wet bathtub and hid behind the shower curtain. The rooms smelled like the inside of a laundry hamper, but he didn't have anything to make it smell better. He put a little more thought toward that and then took the bottle of cologne from the bathroom cabinet and sprinkled a drop or two on the carpet. Hard to say if that helped and it's not like they gave that stuff to you. Sometime when he got to Walmart he'd have to buy some carpet spray or maybe even a candle. But how much can you polish a turd, he said to himself as he swung the flimsy door shut behind him.

Spring wore a little purple dress and she was excited. He'd said enough to Summer to let her know that they might dress up a little. He himself wore a collared shirt with three buttons and the same jeans he'd worn the night before. Summer wore black pants and a black and white shirt. It didn't show off her boobs the way he would've liked, but she still looked good.

"I don't look like an old milk cow in this, do I?" she asked.

"You look nice," he said. "Besides that, where we're going, cows is a good thing."

In the driveway, Summer hurried toward her Omni, carrying the diaper bag over her shoulder and pulling Spring's hand. It was humid and she wanted to keep them clean. But he didn't want to drive up to his ancestral home in that damn little shitcan, riding along in the passenger seat like a ten year old.

"Uh, well, where we're going, I'd rather we took my truck," he said.

"Dairy Queen!" Spring squealed.

Summer looked at his truck. "But we'll have to move her seat over. And I'm not sure it's supposed to be in the middle. Or maybe it just can't face forward. I can't remember."

"I'll take care of that."

The middle seatbelt had been pushed under and behind the bench again, and when he swung the seatback forward to reach it he saw the tire wrench. He was relieved there weren't clumps of hair and bone sticking to it. By the time they got the child seat set up the heat had affected all of them and Spring was crying and fussy.

"Oh come on now," he said to her. "Don't you want to ride in Ah-ee's truck?"

She continued to whine as they strapped her into the seat between them.

He worried what his parents would think if he pulled in with a crying toddler. He'd imagined they'd meet the cute Spring, not the loud one with snot streaming out her nose. Now she was positioned so she stared at him as he drove. As if the radio had morphed into human form, or the heating vents had leaked out a ghost.

There was no air conditioning, so they drove down the road with wind blowing through the windows. Until Spring starting crying again, her hands held to her face.

"Ollie, that's too much wind," Summer said, but when they rolled them up her own face got red and little beads of sweat appeared on her upper lip.

"Now it's too hot. I'm sweating like a pig over here. My make-up's gonna look like Frankenstein."

He drove faster over the county roads and lowered his window an inch more. It wouldn't do to pull in with his ladies in such dejected spirits.

"So, who wants to know where we're goin?" he asked.

"Dairy Queen," Spring said quietly.

"Well, not exactly," he said. Spring looked up at him like she didn't understand what he was saying but it better not mean anything other than the DQ. He turned to Summer for help, but he hadn't told her yet, either, so she just stared at him, red-faced.

"Dairy Queen and home?" Spring said.

"Well, not home just yet," he said. "We just got started! But what say we go see Ollie's home? Where he lived when he was your size?"

Spring stared at him, her little face as unchanging as a peeled potato. But Summer brightened.

"Are we really? Going to your house?"

He stopped for a sign and turned left. They weren't far now. It felt weird to drive these roads he so often took home from her house late at night now that the sun was shining and they were all in the truck.

"Yeah," he said. "I figured it was time you met em."

"Wait—so we're not going to your house? Your trailer? Where you live now, I mean?"

He laughed. "I said, 'where I lived when I was her size!' I know you think I'm a mix of man and boy, but you surely knew I didn't grow up by myself in a trailer!"

"So we're going, right now, to meet your mom and dad?"

"Sure. Why not?"

She shifted in her seat. "Ollie, I wished you'd told me we was going to meet your folks! I coulda gotten cleaned up more."

"You look fine! Don't worry about it."

"But what about your dad?"

He'd told her enough, usually late at night, about the fights and how the old man had finally moved him out. In every story, he'd cast himself as either the hero or victim. Sometimes both at once.

"Yeah, well, him. He come out to my house yesterday morning and told me my mom is sick. So we gotta go see her, mainly."

"Baby come on!" Summer yelled. "You can't just spring this on us! Your mom is sick?" Spring heard her name and started twisting in her car seat, trying to tug on her mother's shirt.

"Mommy?" she said. "Mommy? Mommy?"

"She had a heatstroke. I tried to tell you last night, but we got in a fight, and then later I didn't want to mess anything up."

"Well, you gotta tell me that!"

"I meant for this trip to be a surprise," he said. "Are you surprised?"

"Heck yes I'm—"

"I mean, I know you're surprised. But I want them to meet you, that's all. Please."

She sat there in silence. When Spring said something else, she snapped at her, "What is it, Spring!"

"I need ju-ju."

Oh holy shit, he thought. Anymore, a ten-minute drive down back roads is a bigger deal than driving over the mountains and through the world's longest tunnel.

"Is it?" Summer asked.

"What?"

"Isn't your house close to your parents'?"

"Sort of, yeah."

"Well, can we please go there first? Just so I can freshen up and give her something to drink? So she's not crying when we get there?" He surely needed a break. And he had foreseen this enough to clean the trailer a little. Maybe if they went to his place he could get his head together a little bit before the real show began.

"Okay," he said. "We'll just run by there for a minute. But I'm warnin ya, it ain't no damn White House."

"Oh Ollie, stop it. Do you really think we hang out with you because you live in a giant mansion on a hill?"

He looked at her. She smiled.

"I don't know why you all hang out with me," he admitted.

It was a hell of a thing to be embarrassed of where you lived, but he parked the truck and went around to her side. Spring had finally stopped whining and kept trying to peer over their shoulders, trying to figure out where she was.

"This is where Ollie lives," Summer said, setting her to the ground and then turning to gaze on the place herself. He saw her take it all in: the sagging and gapping skirt, the tall weeds, the missing shutters. The whole thing tilting like a ship going down, already taking water.

"It's not so bad," she said.

"Well, I told ya, that's all I'm saying."

She laughed a little as they started toward the house. "You could stand to mow, though. You mow at my house, but you must not like to do it here!"

He huffed. "I don't really like to do nothing here."

Summer walked slowly, holding her daughter's hand, and he went ahead of them to open the door. Spring looked about like she was in a museum. Or maybe a carnival, where a tiger might jump out of the weeds at any second and lunge against a chain.

The door stuck when he tugged on it and then sprang outward with a clang.

"Watch your step, here."

They came up into the trailer and he didn't know where to stand or put his hands. He leaned back against the bar and tried to sniff the air inconspicuously.

Summer looked around. "This is cozy."

"Mommy, this is messy!" Spring said.

"Maybe you're both right," he said. "Anybody need to use the restroom or something?"

Summer took Spring down the hallway to the bathroom. Ollie stood outside the door and listened for the sound of the curtain hangers against the rod, hoping they wouldn't discover his stash of filthy clothes. He heard them talking but couldn't understand the words.

After a while the toilet flushed and they came out. With all three of them in the hallway, it was cramped. Summer looked back toward the bedroom, perhaps expecting a tour.

"Back there is where I sleep," he said. "We can see it, if you want."

The bedspread lay pulled up to the pillow, but the sheets were still knotted up underneath. They all took a quick look around. Spring remained quiet now—either her mother had told her to, or she'd been struck silent by the ambience of the place.

"You don't have any pictures up," Summer said.

"What?"

"No pictures on any wall," she said, motioning like a saleswoman. "You know, like people have."

"Oh yeah. Nah, I don't have any up."

"Why don't you?"

"What would I put up?"

"You know! Family. Or a reunion or something. A wedding."

"Oh." He shrugged. "My folks just live right over there. I could see em anytime I want. And I ain't been married, so there aren't many wedding shots." He thought about it. "I could put up one of my buddy Coondog, I reckon."

She laughed. "That guy. I gotta meet him sometime."

"Let's see how you handle today first."

"Maybe so. But you know, you could hang a picture of us somewhere."

The idea shocked him a little. "I'd do it," he said. "I would definitely do it, if I had one."

"I'll get you one. Remind me."

They walked back into the main room. He noticed how she was right—every wall was bare.

In the living room, there was nothing for them to do. They didn't even sit.

"You all want to run over to my folks' house for a second?" he asked, as if coming up with the idea for the first time.

"I wanna go home," Spring said.

Summer knelt down. "Not yet, all right." Then she stood and said, "Let's go now, before she really gets fussy. It's getting to be time for her to eat."

Supper! Damn, he hadn't even thought of that. "I bet we can find something to eat over there," he said, moving toward the door.

"Are they expecting us for dinner?"

He felt his gut tighten. She wouldn't like this part, either. "I think so. I mean, my mom's always ready for something like that."

"Ollie! She is or she isn't!"

He pushed open the door and held it. "Watch this step going down, you guys."

What else could he say? That she wasn't expecting them at all? That walking into their house moments from now might very well cause his mother to faint and his dad to swing a fist? That he hadn't called to tell them about this visit, or called them at all in months? Maybe Summer wanted to hear that his parents didn't even know she or her daughter existed?

Oh hell no. He was not about to get into that now. Better to just dump the whole bucket of water over all their heads at once.

They went down the steps and across the path. He hung behind them to lock the door, pretending someone might try to gain entry. He knew there were other ways of doing things. He knew other families held different customs and practices. But this wasn't their world. And this seemed to be the only way it went down in his world.

He got them situated in the truck again. The sun still hung above the trees over yonder but it'd cooled down. A nice evening to sit outside and talk with family. He gunned the motor and dropped it into gear. The back tires spun and spit gravel. Summer rolled her eyes and Spring giggled.

"Well, I can't wait to finally meet your mom and dad," Summer said as they rocketed down the gravel lane.

"I know it. It took me a while to get this done, and I apologize for that. But just wait. Wait til they meet you. I look for them to shit and fall back in it."

"Ollie!" Summer said, nodding at Spring.

"My fault. But I mean it. They are really going to be excited." He thought about it for a moment. "I just hope my mom is feeling better."

"Well I hope so, too! Not just because she's your mom, but because it could get real awkward in a hurry."

"Oh, baby, come on now. What in the world could be awkward about this?"

CHAPTER THIRTY-NINE

E thel heard them first. She hadn't started frying the chicken yet, but she'd chopped up the potatoes, onions and eggs for the potato salad. There hadn't been much on the table at noontime, and she wanted to make up for it with dinner. He was still in the living room, moping, where he'd been the last day and a half. There was no reason to celebrate but two half-hearted meals in a row would only make it worse. She heard something out by the road, and then that animal of his ran to the window in the living room and shook the house with his full-blown big dog bark. You didn't hear it very often, thank God. It was amazing how much the pup had grown, and when he barked in earnest it was like having a wolf in the house. It was too much, but she'd given up on teaching either of them any sense.

She laid the knife aside and walked into the living room. He was already at the window.

"I heard something," she said. So the dog wouldn't get credit for everything.

He ignored her. He was staring out past the trees to the end of the long driveway.

She looked and there it was—his old red pickup. Her heart leapt. Something had happened to the front of it, but it was his, all right. It sat on the other side of the chain. The driver's door was open.

Catfish barked again, so close and loud it threatened to break the glass, and she turned on him with a quick rage that surprised even her and shushed him with an open hand. "Don't you bark at him!" she hissed.

"He can't get by that chain," Frank said.

"Go!" she said. "Go let him in!"

When he didn't move she yelled, "Frank! Get out there and take down that chain so he can come up here!"

Finally he turned and walked across the room. When Catfish saw him head that direction he ran ahead, spinning and yipping. She stared at her husband's back.

"He better not leave," she said. "He better not. He's back, and he's come to see us."

"He ain't going nowhere," he said over his shoulder as he turned the corner.

She knew he'd walk through the kitchen and take his hat down by the door. He'd check to make sure he carried the key to the padlock. He'd get both and go outside, where he'd watch his dog piddle in the grass umpteen times. If he walked all the way down the drive it'd be another fifteen minutes.

She took off toward the door. She hadn't run in years but she thought she might be able to now. She remembered what the doctor had said, but if Ollie left again and didn't come back that would kill her, too.

When she got to the door he was just going outside, cane in hand. He looked up at her.

"If you're comin," he said, "at least wipe your face off. You ain't letting him see you like that."

CHAPTER FORTY

The chain had been up earlier, of course, but somehow he'd forgotten about it. Or maybe he just assumed it'd be taken down in preparation for his unscheduled, unannounced visit. Now they waited in the truck while he studied it, as if he could break the links with his bare hands. He glanced up and Summer was staring at him like he was the biggest dumbass in the world. A title he was definitely in the running for.

He didn't think his dad would hide a key somewhere by the road, but he needed something to do, so he searched in the clumps of fescue rising around the mailbox post. He opened the mailbox and peered inside. Running up to the house meant leaving Summer and Spring in the hot truck, and he wanted them near him when he saw his parents. He wanted their presence to make an impact.

This was some trick, now. Coming home and being locked out. He could drive out across the wheat field or cross the ditch, but it was steep and he'd tear the muddy yard up. Not that he gave a damn right now about their grass. He wondered if Spring could walk the hundred or so yards to the house. He could always carry her, but what if they went all that way and his parents were gone? No thanks! He'd pass on that game of whack-a-mole.

He was pretty much out of ideas when the gravel crunched behind him and his father's pickup came rolling along the dips and potholes of the drive. His mom sat in the cab as well. With a small wave he stood there and waited on them.

The old man pulled off into the grass and killed the motor. Now there was only the sound of one engine and a cicada buzzing in a yard tree. Ollie wanted to turn around and look at Summer, but he watched his parents' reactions instead. His mother's eyes had found her, and she stared into Ollie's truck, confused. She climbed out and walked over, glancing between her son and Summer.

"Hi mom," he said.

She came to him and reached over the chain, placing her hands on his arms. He felt her desperate squeezes. He couldn't recall the last time he'd hugged her, but he thought she might do that now if not for the chain stretched waist-high between them.

"Did something happen to your face?" She looked up at it.

"No."

"Well. I'm so glad you're here," she said. Then she lowered her eyes. "And you've brung someone?"

Before he could answer his father appeared and wordlessly began unlocking the padlock. The chain clinked against itself.

"I brought Summer along," Ollie said. "And Spring."

The door opened and Summer started to climb out, but Frank dropped the chain to the gravel with a metallic thud and said, "Bring her on up to the house. We ain't gonna stand out here and talk on the damn road." Then he added, "Just drive over the chain."

Like dogs or children Ollie and his mother turned and went back to their vehicles. He put his truck in gear and drove by his parents and down the driveway.

"I didn't know if I should get out, or not!" Summer said.

"You can up here."

Spring sat silently between them, looking around.

"I don't know what the deal is with that stupid chain of his," he said. "Some damn thing."

At the house he parked under the tree where he'd parked his first car back in high school. He went around and helped Summer get Spring free of her car seat. They lifted her out just as his parents pulled up. His dad drove right on by and stopped in his usual spot in the barn, maybe fifty yards past them.

So again they waited—man, woman and child. Finally, his mom and dad walked out of the barn and he saw them both stop and stare at Spring. He didn't think they'd seen her yet—with her car seat facing backward like that they couldn't. The old man said something and she answered him and after a while they came on. When they reached the little group Ethel looked at the ground and Frank seemed to be somewhere else entirely.

"How you all doin?" Ollie asked.

"Just fine," Ethel said. She looked pale.

"Good."

"We've been getting too much rain, though," she said.

"I heard that."

He could feel Summer's eyes burning into the side of his face. "Um, like I was saying out there, this here's Summer." He pointed her out with his thumb. "And the baby one here is her daughter. Spring's her name." The little girl stood silently next to her mother, holding her hand.

"How do you do," Ethel said, nodding. Frank glanced at Summer, nodded, and looked away again.

Catfish barked out in the barn. Ethel had insisted they put him in the granary.

"Since when you all got a dog?" Ollie asked.

No one said anything for a while. Ethel looked at Frank.

"Most of the summer," Frank said.

"Oh yeah?"

It was quiet again. Then Catfish started howling at the injustice of being kept from such an important gathering, his voice rising and wavering in the evening mugginess.

Suddenly Summer stepped toward Ethel with her hand extended, causing her to jump a little. "I'm sorry. What did you say your name was?"

Ethel took her hand lightly. "I'm Ollie's mother. I'm Ethel."

He realized then what Summer had been expecting, but before he could react she was shaking his father's hand. "I'm Summer," she repeated.

"Frank." He acted like he'd never shaken a woman's hand, nor had he ever expected to.

"Nice to meet both of you, finally. This is my daughter, Spring." Spring, who was still clutching her mother's other hand, looked to the barn. She was scared of the dog sounds.

Ethel looked down at her and smiled. "Well, she's adorable. Enough of this heat, though. Let's all go inside."

The two women turned toward the house, little girl in tow.

"Now wait one minute," Frank said. They all stopped. He stared at Ollie. "Are you telling me you got a little girl you never told us about?"

"Frank!" Ethel exclaimed. "Oh my Lord. That's not—"

"She ain't mine, Dad!" Ollie yelled. "What'd you think!"

Frank looked over their heads like he didn't believe what anyone was telling him anymore.

"Spring's mine from someone else," Summer said, standing right in front of him. "Me and him's been over a long time, though. I'm with Ollie now." She smiled and later Ollie would wonder how she did it: how her face could somehow put people at ease. How she could hide her own anger.

"I see," Frank said. "Well, I didn't know."

Ethel opened the door and Summer lifted Spring, who was pretty well traumatized, into the house. Ollie went next.

"I'm gonna go check on my dog," Frank said, and the door closed.

"Come on in, come on in," Ethel was saying now, talking constantly and quietly, clucking like a hen as she moved around. No one knew where to go. Finally she ushered them into the living room, where Summer sat on the couch and set Spring down in front of her. It was only mildly cooler in the house.

Spring looked around the room and at the old woman. She then turned her face back into her mother's lap.

"Are you bein shy?" Summer asked her, glancing down and tussling her light hair.

But Ethel had gone into the kitchen, where they heard her mumbling about chicken and getting it ready. Summer looked across the room at Ollie and he shrugged his shoulders. He sat in his mom's chair, and his head kept swimming on him. Summer whispered something.

"What?" he asked, loudly.

She rolled her eyes. "Spring needs changing," she whispered.

"Oh! Well, all right." He made no move from the chair. Even Spring was staring at him. Pots were being shuffled around in the kitchen.

"The bag's still in the truck. Will you go get it, please?"

He stood up. "Got it. You bet."

"Ollie!" she hissed.

"Yeah?"

"You didn't ask your mom how she is."

"Oh yeah. Well, I was fixing to do just that."

He went into the kitchen and his mother was placing raw pieces of chicken into a skillet.

"You feeling all right, ma?"

"I'm fine. I had a little spell several days ago out in the chicken coop, but I'm all right now. Fine."

"Did you get too hot or something?"

She stopped, a drumstick held just above the spattering grease. "I must've. I was okay even then but your dad called Dr. Mulferd and he made him take me all the way over to Green City, against my wishes."

"You gotta be careful, ma. It's been hot as ... well, anything. Out there at work, too."

"Oh, I know it. I try not to do too much." She tonged in the remaining pieces of chicken and wiped her hands on a towel.

He stood by the stove and watched the chicken pieces begin to dance in the oil. She looked old to him for the first time. Like she'd aged ten years since he'd seen her last. "Be careful," he said. "That's all I'm saying."

"I don't know if I'll have enough chicken or not. I usually fry a whole one, then keep the extra for lunches. So I might have enough. I hope you all can stay and eat?"

"Yeah, why not. We can."

"She seems really nice," Ethel whispered. "Her and her little one both."

"She is. Really nice, that is."

"I'm glad you found someone." She reached over and patted his arm.

"Me too. Well, I gotta go get a diaper. Hey, why you got boards in your kitchen?"

"Don't talk to me about that."

As soon as he stepped outside, Catfish rushed him, barking and growling, all feet and teeth. The hair on the dog's back stood up like a mohawk. Ollie raised his hands and looked up. His dad stood out in the yard. The sun was slipping behind the barn roof.

"So this is your dog, huh?" he called out. Catfish crouched and barked at him.

Frank walked over and knelt down and took hold of his collar. "Yeah, this is Catfish," he said. The dog quieted but kept his eyes on Ollie.

"Where'd you get it?"

"Me and Chub pulled him out of the river a while back."

Ollie nodded. Seemed like something they would do. "How's he doing?"

"Who?"

"Chub."

Frank stood and looked at him. "Well, seeings as how he's been dead a couple weeks now, I guess you could say he's doing about the same."

"Oh shit. Well, I didn't know that!" He kept his eyes on the dog, as if he were the one they were talking about. It didn't feel right to apologize so he asked what caused it.

"Heart attack."

"I'll be damned. No, I hadn't heard about that." Ollie bent to pet Catfish and the dog allowed it. "Well, I gotta run to the truck and grab something," he said.

Later, after he returned with the diaper bag and Summer had taken care of things with Spring in the bedroom upstairs, she went into the kitchen to help prepare the food. She'd gotten Spring interested in a coloring book she miraculously pulled from the bag of diapers, sippy cups and wipes, and now Ollie sat on the couch, more or less the man in charge, and watched Spring color.

His mom was asking Summer about who her parents and grandparents were, and he listened in. They seemed to be getting along and Spring was being amazingly good, stretched out on the floor and engrossed in her crayon work. He prayed that she'd continue to keep her cool. It felt weird as hell to have a kid in here. He thought about taking Spring out and showing her the chickens, but if that damn vicious dog of his dad's scared her the fragile eggshell that was this evening might crack.

Frank came in then and went to the kitchen sink to wash up. Ollie hoped Summer hadn't left the diaper bag out where he might fall over it. That was all they needed. But the old man walked to the table unscathed and sat down. He hadn't said anything to the women. Ollie could see his back from the couch, his gray hair pressed in a ring from his hat. At least I'll keep my hair, he thought.

Outside, the sun was down and the yard lay in shadow. They'd eat and then take off. Maybe he'd be able to hang out with Summer for a while after Spring went to sleep. This had really been a good idea, bringing them out here. Now Summer would understand why he was so screwed up.

That really was a hell of a thing, though, this news about Chub dying. No doubt that'd hit the old man pretty hard. They had hung out for as long as Ollie could remember. Chub had always been a pretty cool guy, a Coondog for his dad. Not into much except for fishing, that's for sure. And eating. It's not like he'd talked that often to Ollie or anything. Still, you hated to hear the big old boy had kicked the bucket. He'd seen him in the store not too far back.

Ollie watched his dad's shoulders as he sat bent over the table and thought about his friend being gone. The old man had really pissed him off with that crack about Spring being his, but maybe he'd evened the score by asking about Chub. He felt bad about it.

"Corn about got flooded out this summer, didn't it?" Ollie asked.

In the kitchen, Ethel and Summer paused and looked at Frank. Spring stopped coloring.

Frank didn't turn around. "You don't know the half of it."

Ethel shook her head. "Oh Ollie," she said, but so quietly only Summer could hear, "we need to talk about some things."

CHAPTER FORTY-ONE

O f course the visit was something she was anxious to converse about. She'd waited months just to see Ollie and now he'd given her so many additional things to say about his new family. But at the moment Frank was outside messing around and she had no one to talk with. She sat at the table and relived the visit—what he'd said, what the little girl was wearing. She hadn't seen too many things she'd classify as miracles, but she was considering adding Ollie meeting Summer to her short list.

Even though Frank had provided Ollie with strict instructions on how to re-fasten the chain after he headed back home, or wherever he was staying, as soon as he left Frank drove out there to make sure he'd done it correctly. In the headlamps' beams he studied it. Not exactly as he'd told him to do it, sure enough, so he unlocked the padlock and positioned it so it hung down, not up. Otherwise the key works might fill with rain and rust. That was his son right there: he could do some things, but nothing exactly right, and a lot of them wrong altogether. Redoing the lock gave Frank a chance to think about the mess Ollie'd walked into before Ethel got started.

"Well, now I know why we haven't heard from him for a while," she said as soon as Frank walked through the door. It was late, but she hadn't even changed into her nightgown. "He's been involved with her all summer."

Frank grunted to let her know he'd heard. He took off his cap and hung it by the door. He put Catfish up for the night in the corner of the kitchen. The pup sat down and looked around like he couldn't imagine why such an injustice had been done to him again. Then he spun around twice and lay down on the Indian blanket.

"And I think he was really good with that little girl," she said, following him through the kitchen.

Frank started up the stairs.

"Didn't you see him with little Spring?" she asked. "He was really good."

"Get changed. You need your rest. It's too late for us to be up talking like this any more tonight."

"Oh, I'm fine!" she said, climbing up the steps. "But this means a lot to him! And to us, too. That was one thing I could tell about him tonight."

He walked into their bedroom and turned on the bedside lamp. She met him there.

"There's a name for his kind of girl, but I ain't gonna say it out loud," he said.

"Frank! Where in the world you'd get that idea?"

"She's a loose woman, is what she is, if you're gonna make me say it. And now she's lookin to pawn off her kid."

She smacked her hand on the dresser. "I can't believe you're saying this. She told us her baby came from someone else! She freely said that. And you don't want to know what I thought about how you treated her tonight."

"Well then, how's that work?" He was seated on the bed, pulling off his boots. "So now he's got to raise it like his own? Pay for all its medical bills and whatnot?"

"If he wants to, yes! And I think he should. He'd be a good father—I've always thought that. His time just came in a different way, that's all."

"He's in over his head, the way he is. He won't stick with it long enough to finish the job, and then that girl's back out on her ass. With the way she looks, I'd say she likes it that way."

Now Ethel removed her clothes, her hands snapping in anger at the buttons. "She's a pretty girl, and you saw that. Her and her baby both. They both have such pretty eyes. You better stop your talking like that."

He hung his thin cotton shirt on the bedpost and said nothing. She stood staring at him for a while and then went across the hall to the bathroom and shut the door. The pipes shuddered like they always did when the sink started running.

The older girl had been a sight to look at, he'd admit. When he came up from the barn and saw her standing there he almost stopped cold, remembering how it felt to stare at some girl so young and well put-together. But he wouldn't give Ollie the satisfaction of seeing him admiring her. Certainly his son wanted to bring her out here and show her off like a new car—that was clear enough. But she looked good enough he wondered how Ollie had gotten her to go anywhere with him.

This baby was another matter. Oh, she had her mother's looks all right. And he'd seen and heard enough to know things happened like that, but it still felt wrong to him. Raising another man's child. Especially when that man wasn't dead. What if they bumped into him somewhere? The only thing he could compare it to was buying used equipment. He'd never in his life bought a new tractor, so every one he'd ever owned had been broken in under another man's ass. When he picked up a used tractor at an auction, first he'd wash it like a truck with the hose and soap. Then he'd drain and replenish all the fluids, even if they'd just been changed. It was silly and a waste of time and he knew it, but he had to purge the old owner. Sometimes it took a year of work before the tractor felt like it was truly his. He'd owned an International 986 that he only kept for two seasons because it never stopped feeling like he was borrowing someone else's machine.

But to come prancing over here after being gone for months with a new woman on his arm, and then not even know about Chub? No sir. He wouldn't take that shit. Now the boy's mother might look past all that, but he himself didn't plan to. He was glad Ollie had come around, for her sake. It seemed like it had made a difference to her already. But he wasn't buying in on that load of garbage.

When she came back she'd washed her face and without a word she climbed into bed. He used the bathroom himself and when he came back she was asleep, or pretending to be, so he didn't say anything else about any of it. He lay in the bed and wondered how Ollie could possibly take care of another human being.

The next morning they sat at the table and ate their breakfast.

"I think I'm going to call him later," she said. "I want them to come over again, and this time I'll have a proper meal ready."

Frank just shook his head. Later, he went to check the river on his three-wheeler.

When he got back from the woods he parked at the house and after lunch he rode out to the mailbox. Sometimes the mail lady got there as early as ten, but usually they had to wait until after lunch. Her all-time latest run had been 3:35, and that seemed entirely too late by his estimation.

The mailbox was an empty cave, and he started to turn around and head back to the house when he saw her old station wagon coming down the road. Sometimes a bunch of her kids would be piled in the back as she made her rounds, but this time it looked devoid of life except for her. He sat astride his three-wheeler in the ditch next to the mailbox and waited. He'd put Catfish in the barn so he wouldn't be near the road.

"Guess you knew I was coming," she said as she stopped in front of him. She sat on the passenger side, her leg over the transmission hump to reach the pedals. Her yellow hair was all crazy. She was close enough he could smell the liquor on her. She was around forty and didn't have a husband, nor had she ever claimed one, which made him think of Ollie. Frank hated his damn mail lady.

"You're on time, is all," he said.

"Guess what? You gotta sign for something." She was digging around in the seat next to her.

"I didn't order nothing."

"Maybe not. But this letter is official-like. You and the others around here are signing for it today. Made my morning a real pain in the patooty. I had to leave the house even earlier. Not to mention I got a sick kid."

She produced an envelope bigger than normal but gave him a form instead. Then she pulled a pen from her breast pocket and held that out to him. He signed the form against the gas tank of the three-wheeler and returned it. She handed over the letter and a brochure.

"Later, alligator," she said and hit the gas. The station wagon groaned and accelerated on down the road.

He looked in his hands: a catalog advertising garden seeds and a white envelope, heavy and thick, that bore insignia he didn't recognize. He drove with one hand and took the mail to the house.

At the table, he sat down and put the envelope in front of him. He'd gotten letters like this before, papers about property taxes, set-aside ground, information about various licenses. Letters from Uncle Sam, Ethel called them. She took care of most of that.

But this one was marked with the image of some kind of building. It said "United States Government." She heard him and came in from the living room.

"What'd we get today?" she asked.

When he didn't answer she pulled a chair around to his side and sat down. He took out his pocketknife and sliced the top of the envelope open. Inside lay a small book of pages.

It was a jurisdictional offer to purchase. It described their property in language they couldn't understand, even though they knew intimately the land it rendered. Other papers seemed to describe the reservoir project itself. There were things in there about relocation assistance. There was an offer to buy the land. For over an hour they read together and separately, barely speaking. Sometimes they'd ask questions, but those questions would float around the table unanswered. Then one of them would gasp and ask part of another question. Sometimes he'd merely curse.

It wasn't a lot of money, if they read it correctly. They'd never attached a dollar amount to the land they stood on, but now they knew what it was worth. A little over a hundred and twenty thousand dollars. In its best years the farm had brought in about thirty thousand from the crops and the feeder cattle. And most of that had to be turned around and put back into the farm. Some years, flooding years, they'd lost money on it. But now they knew what their land—their very lives!—was worth. A hundred and twenty thousand, for a place her family had cared for since 1910. About fifteen hundred per year, if a person wanted to look at it that way.

"They can burn in hell," he said.

Frank and Ethel kept trying to read the various letters and documents. He'd read them while seated at the kitchen table, his lips moving silently, and then he'd go outside for a while, only to return to the stack of papers. She read them all afternoon. They didn't carry the envelope or its papers from room to room. It all stayed right where he'd opened it, on the table where they took their meals.

CHAPTER FORTY-TWO

Here was one more thing Ollie believed about life and how to live it: when it starts getting better, you don't dare back down. Quite the opposite—you pour gas on the fire. Add a cup of water to the flood. Salt to a wound. Basically, anything you can do to make something more potent. Say it however you want. So when he got home from work that afternoon he was thinking about his truck. He'd been driving the red girl around all over the country with a busted front end, and now that things were so good with Summer, it just didn't make sense to drive a dented pickup. He had a shiny new outlook on life and wanted his truck to reflect that.

So he stood at the bar in his trailer, pawing through the contents of a seldom-used drawer looking for the yellow pages. He wanted to call Terry Barry's body shop. Instead of the directory he found an old Chinese throwing star he'd picked up at a flea market. It was metal and looked like a little saw blade. He laughed, fitting it into his hand. Once he made this call he'd go out back and throw the star at the stump at the edge of the field. See if it still stuck. He was going to Summer's later but a ninja had to make time for himself.

Damn he felt good. She'd liked his mom a lot and now she believed him when he called his dad an asshole. She thought his mom was a sweet old lady, and offered to have them over to her house for dinner. He couldn't picture his dad moving around her place, but he was just happy Summer had gotten over how unplanned the whole thing had been. On the drive home, Spring slept and Summer kept saying they needed to go back to the farm more often. He didn't really care how many times that happened in the next month, but he was relieved no punches had been thrown. And then, best of all, after she put Spring to bed, she allowed him into her bedroom and propped a chair against the door.

"I think she's too tired tonight to hear anything," she said.

Like always, he'd driven home before work, but last night she hadn't slid under the covers with all her clothes on.

Rifling through the drawer with that happy buzz in his head he didn't hear the car pull up. He didn't detect anything until the soft knocking touched the door, a little bird asking to come inside.

He jerked it open and there stood his mother. He looked down the path behind her, expecting to see his dad limping along. Not there. The silver Buick she drove was parked by his truck.

"Mom! What are you doing here?"

She'd been to his trailer before, but not for a long time and never alone.

"I hated to come out here by myself this late—"

"It's not late, Mom. It's like five or six. Come on in here. I just got home from work not too long ago."

"But I still should've called first. You probably got supper on the stove. Is Summer here?" She climbed up into the trailer and looked around.

"Nah, she ain't here. I might run over to her place a little later on. I's just checking on some body shops when you walked up."

She stood there, uncertain. He started to offer her a bar stool but that seemed too high and unwieldy. Instead he directed her to a chair in the living room.

"This place is kind of disheveled at the moment," he said.

She nodded. "Does Summer mind it? What about her daughter?"

"They don't really hang out here all that much. It's usually a lot easier for me to go to her place."

She nodded again and looked down at her lap.

"You feeling good, Ma? You want something to drink or something?"

She didn't say anything and he was frightened to see the sudden wash of tears coming down her face. He knelt on the dirty carpet beside her.

"Hey! What is it now?"

She shook her head, like she meant to say no, it's nothing, but still the tears came. He put his hand on her arm and left it there.

She cried for while yet, tears building up behind the dam of her glasses on her cheek.

"Is it the effects of the heat stroke?" he asked.

She shook her head, a little confusion showing on her face.

He thought to get her a tissue so he stood up and pulled some toilet paper off the roll on the bathroom sink. She wiped under her glasses with it.

"They're taking it from us, son."

"What's that now?"

"Our farm. It's gone."

"Who's taking it!"

"They's taking it to build their lake. We got a notice about it today. They said they might, and now they say—"

"Wait—who is they?" He was imagining one man, maybe two.

"Oh, the government. The Army Engineers." She blew her nose raggedly. "All of them."

He left her side and sat on the couch. "I heard about that lake," he said. "I just figured it was never gonna happen."

"That's what we thought, too. We went to a meeting and everything. But now I think we just weren't paying attention or something."

"But they can't do that!"

"They aim to pay us for it."

"But still! How much is it?"

"Seems like a lot, to me. But we don't know where to go to. Your dad doesn't want to have to pack up his tools."

"Well you all know you can move in here any time, even if it's just for a little bit. I can clean it up."

She looked at him, eye rims red. "Ollie, they're takin every acre we own. Every last one of them. This out here, too."

He sat back on the couch. "Oh hell no."

She began to cry hard again. "I'm sorry we lost your house, too." She choked. "But we didn't have no way of stopping it."

Her body hitched again and he went and stood by her chair. She reached her arm around him and he bent over and clasped her in an awkward hug. Under his arms, her bones felt like they were carved from balsa wood or were perhaps the airy bones of birds. He felt each breath leaving her body. She smelled like the kitchen back home and he thought she probably always would.

"They didn't even tell me," he said quietly.

She clung to him. "Maybe they don't even know you're out here."

He pulled away and stood up. "Well, now they'll see where I'm at. They done messed with the wrong guy."

"Don't you do anything," she said, wiping her eyes. "You can't, anyhow. Everything is already done and finished."

He stomped into the kitchen and back. His anger felt righteous and even pious. He'd already thought about moving into Summer's—an idea that excited him—but would his parents be forced off their farm? Not while he was alive. He simply wouldn't allow it. Whoever these people were, they hadn't counted on him. They'd planned to chase all these old people off without a fight, but they hadn't known about Ollie, living in his secret location. Now they were going to find out they'd made a serious miscalculation. He'd hurt his parents a lot, but sometimes there were reasons for things. He was starting to believe it was meant to happen this way—that he'd repay them in one big swing with the most heroic and triumphant gesture this town had ever seen.

"Where do I go?" he asked.

"Go where?"

"Wherever those assholes that aim to take our farm are. Where's their office?"

She looked at him. "How would I know? Indianapolis? Louisville. They said Louisville at the meeting."

"Well, that's where you'll find me, just so they know."

"Ollie, you can't. It's not like that. You can't change their minds now."

"Wanna bet on that?" He was almost yelling. "I was just down in Kentucky last week. I can surely go back anytime I want."

She just stared at him. No more betting. Any luck she'd carried was gone and she already knew he didn't have nearly as much as he thought.

For an hour after she left he sat there. He thought about South Carolina again and how hurricanes hit the beaches. People knew it was coming, but sometimes they stayed put, anyway. So he'd heard. This had been like that. They kept saying it was coming and he hadn't even gone to the hardware store to buy plywood to board up his windows. Now the whole place was shaking from the first blast and he felt like an idiot. He was sitting inside his trailer while winds threatened to lift the damn place off the ground.

You could walk outside and yell at the hurricane, but you'd only end up looking like a fool. And he didn't know where to go to fight this lake. After she left he finally found the damn yellow pages, but as he flipped through them on the bar he realized he didn't know what to look under. Lake construction? Just people with dozers hoping to build them for you. Reservoirs? He couldn't spell it. Government? There must've been a hundred things listed there, and none of them made sense. He called one number and got so frustrated with the woman's bitchy tone he about broke the receiver over the counter.

He called Summer's house and told her he wouldn't be over tonight. He said he had to help his mom do something and she was glad he was helping out.

Next he called Coondog. It rang so many times he forgot who he was calling when the man answered.

"Yeah!" Coondog always answered his phone this way. He sounded out of breath, like he'd run in from the garage or something.

"What the hell are you doing?"

"Me! What the hell are you doin? I thought you was down south still."

"Nah, I'm back."

"Did you get laid down there?"

"Not really. It's a long story."

"Did you kick that guy's ass?"

"I didn't need to, turns out. Me and her's back together."

"Glad to hear it. You still coulda kicked his ass, though."

"Hey—something's up."

"Oh yeah?"

"Yeah. You doing something now?"

"Just got home. You wouldn't believe what's been going on around here. I'm talking hand over fist."

"You care if I run over there yet tonight? I got something I wanna go over."

"Bring it on over."

"All right. See you in a bit."

"Hold on."

"What?"

"Swing by and get us some chicken or something from the tavern. I ain't ate yet and I'm hungry enough to eat the ass end off a horse. There ain't no food here neither."

When Ollie pulled in, the bucket truck sat in the driveway and it was filthy, like it'd been run through a pond or something. Branches hanging off the top of it, mud splashed up on the sides. There was a flatbed trailer behind it he'd never seen before. A heavy-duty trailer used for hauling serious equipment.

He went through the side door in the garage and helped himself to a beer from the fridge. He got almost into the house before he went back to get Coondog one in case he needed it.

Coondog sat in front of the television, watching some gossip show about life in Hollywood. It was apparent he'd just showered. His hair was wet and his shirt was off.

"There you are, peckerhead," he said.

Ollie tossed him a beer and held up a paper sack already greasy on the bottom. "Here's the chicken you ordered."

Coondog stood and shook his hand. "Glad you decided to come back to us Hoosiers, especially bearing chicken."

"Yeah, well. You know how it is. Who wants to go somewhere and start the hell over?"

They sat down at the little table in the kitchen like adults. Coondog pulled off about ten paper towels.

"I just cleaned that living room," he said. He opened the sack and lifted out a box. "What else you get with this?"

"Nothing. Just chicken."

"No tater salad? No chips?"

"Eat your chicken and like it, bitch."

"Shit."

They took out pieces of the fried greasy food and set them on paper towels. They pulled from their beers. Ollie was still mad and trying to decide where to start.

"You're talking to a rich man," Coondog said. "You're breaking bread with a damned king here tonight."

"That's good. Cause you're talking to someone who's fixin to lose his house."

Coondog stopped eating. He'd been down-deep happy, Ollie could tell, but he knew when to shut up. "You're shittin me."

"Nope. They're gonna take it. Mine and mom and dad's both. The government's building their fucking lake, so we're gonna lose it all."

Coondog nodded. "I tried to tell you that, way back earlier this summer. Weren't you listening to me?"

"Fuck! I didn't think they'd do it!"

Coondog bit some meat off the drumstick in his hand. With the chicken still in his mouth he took a pull off his beer. Chewing both he said, "They'll pay you for it."

"Fuck! They better! My folks is gonna lose their whole farm. You know how long they had that?"

"I hate to see em lose it. Nice place out there. The river and everything, back there by the woods? Member all those times when you and me went back there fishing and drinking beer?"

Ollie nodded.

"Well anyway," Coondog went on, "they gotta help you all find a new place to live. They have to, by law."

"How'd you hear all this shit?"

"I been talking with a lot of people dealing with it. Mostly out by where you all live. Dwight Pearson, lives out by you. Doug and Nikki Cupp, on down the river a ways. Old lady Hutch, you know her."

"Why the hell you talking to all them?"

"Didn't I just tell you you was dining with a rich man? Well, theys the ones making me rich!"

Ollie had taken maybe two bites out of a piece of breast meat. It waited on the paper towel in front of him. Coondog kept eating and talking.

"Since the lake's coming, and they're gonna lose the land anyway, people is getting the wood off it. Logging the shit out of it—I mean clearcutting it down to nothin. Everything down by the river is getting cut."

"And you're doing it?"

"Shit, me and a buncha other guys. Some real big-time outfits working in there. I had to go out and get me a skidder just to run with em. You probably seen the trailer when you come by. My skidder's out in the woods, but you gotta see it sometime. Let me tell ya, working that skidder on those hills ain't for those without balls."

"Who's buying it?"

"I bought it!"

"The trees."

"Shit. Timber companies all over. I bet you're seeing some come through your job up there. People getting some sawed into boards for themselves or whatever."

Ollie shook his head.

"Think about it," Coondog said. "You know the first thing the government's gonna do, once they get it, is log it off. Ever heard of a lake with trees in it? Didn't think so. They'd log it off first and make more money. So, what peoples doin, they're logging it themselves. Taking some money with em fore they get run off."

"So there ain't no one else gonna fight it?"

"Fight what? The government? Hell no. Why bother. They've known for a long time they were gonna do this."

"I don't know what my folks is gonna do. My mom come out to my place just tonight. This thing's about crushed her already."

"I hate to hear that. Your mama's a sweet woman. I was gonna go out there and ask them if they wanted me to saw off some of their trees. But I been too busy to ask em yet."

"Dad won't do that shit!"

Coondog shrugged. "Most of em is, along there. They either started or got somebody lined up to do it."

Ollie sat there and tried to eat some more. He couldn't tell if he had a right to be pissed or not. Coondog was only doing what they hired him to do.

"You and your fucking lakeside bar and grill, too," he said finally.

"Shit yeah! Why not? I'm making some real nice start-up cash right now. First I'll log em, then I'll give everybody a place to get drunk and eat when they come off the water from skiing. Chicks walking in still wearing bikinis."

"I'm still fucking pissed, though. It shitting pisses me off that they can do that to us."

Coondog leaned over the table. "Don't fight it, man. Do what I'm doing— make it work for you. What are you gonna lose? That old trailer? Shit, pull it somewhere else!"

"Oh shit, it ain't me. I don't give a damn—I'll just move into Summer's." He knew he'd just gotten him back for that trailer comment. Coondog might've been making money, but he still didn't see any Summers around the place.

The barb showed on Coondog's face. "Well, fuck then, what're you worried about?"

"My damn parents for one thing."

"I get that. I really do. But I'm telling you right now, it's a done deal. A flat-out done deal."

"I ain't certain about that."

"It is. Trust me. Now, you wanna talk about going in with me on this bar, you know I'll let you in on the action. Cause you're my damn man. You and me, we been around a long time."

Ollie sat around a couple more hours and got pretty drunk. He couldn't figure it out—how Coondog had gotten so far ahead of him on this one. He didn't seem like someone in the know, but somehow he'd figured out this lake thing long before Ollie had. And now he was getting rich while Ollie was lucky to still have a damn job. The same job he'd had for ten fucking years. Christ.

Here he'd been driving down south like some kind of hippie, and his only friend had been building a business. Meanwhile his parents were losing their farm, at least in part because he hadn't been around to do anything about it.

So he sat on the couch, pretending to watch some lame movie on television, his only consolation the thought of Summer back at her house, tucking Spring into bed.

And even that didn't help much.

He was still burning when the movie ended and he got up to drive home.

"Thanks for bringing that chicken," Coondog said.

"Shit. That's nothing."

"Dude, you gotta see that log skidder I got. It's used, but I'm telling you, it's nice. An old John Deere, like your pop's tractors he used to have. I swear to God, I can put a hurtin on em with this thing."

CHAPTER FORTY-THREE

B y Thursday evening it felt like it was fish or die. He'd sunk as low as he'd ever been, but he suspected that he could get even lower and probably would in the coming months. He needed to mow the yard, but tasks like that felt so pointless anymore it almost made you want to laugh. Like God was laughing in your face already. Maybe it wasn't God, but it sure felt like someone was laughing. If he'd ever needed the river, truly required it like his next breath, it was now, so he lowered the rods into the boat and took inventory. Four fishing rods, life jacket, cushion to sit on, paddle, gas tank, landing net, cast net, bucket for bait, tackle box. There were other things but he knew he had them because they stayed in the boat. He tied the rods together and strapped them to a cleat before placing anchors on top of the life jacket and seat cushion so they wouldn't blow out as he went down the road to the river.

Mow the yard! Might as well paint the barn while he was at it. Maybe put some oil on the back door hinge so it'd stop squeaking. Pour new limestone in the tool shed. Reorganize his workbench. Build miles of new fence. Oh yes, there were many tasks to be done now that the water was coming. Make it real nice for the fishes. He pictured catfish swimming around their murky kitchen, strips of wallpaper peeling and waving in the current. A big flathead playing solitaire at the table while its mate drifted down the stairs. A channel cat resting on the couch, staring at the television.

Going to Lila's café for dinner seemed right, but he didn't think he could face her giant bosom without Chub. He'd avoided the place since the funeral, and the first conversation with her was going to be hard. She'd really liked Chub. They probably deserved each other after LuAnne died, but Lila had been married to the same man for practically her whole life. He'd lost an arm when some kind of infection set in decades ago and she'd taken care of him ever since. And run the café, along with her daughters, on top of that. She would've been good to Chub but sometimes the best women were taken. Chub had gotten LuAnne, though, and she'd been a good one. It was just a shame that his final years turned out to be lonely ones. In a better world maybe Lila would've cushioned his fall after LuAnne passed.

In many ways this felt like a normal evening: getting the boat ready, thinking about eating at Lila's. Thinking about fishing and watching Chub fish. Sometimes his mind would wander on like that, putting Chub and Lila together, and he'd feel happy again. But then he'd remember Chub was gone, Lila was spoken for and the farm was, too. When your mind woke back up to the realities of the situation it was like getting the taste of catshit in your mouth.

When the boat was prepared to his satisfaction he walked inside to tell Ethel he was going. He didn't know how she planned on spending her evening, but he'd already told her she was to stay inside, out of this heat. She'd gone to the store yesterday at about this time, and when she came home she looked like she'd been crying.

Catfish ran alongside, and he considered taking him to the river. But the dog hadn't been in the boat, not since the day they pulled him over the side, and today was going to be hard enough. There were a lot of little things to worry about when boating the river, things like anchoring, avoiding deadheads, even landing fish, and he was going to do all of them by himself for the first time in many years.

Still, he'd strongly considered taking Catfish, because he feared he might not like the company if he fished alone. If not for her heat episode, he would've made Ethel go. Do them both some good to get out. Since they'd gotten the papers yesterday, she'd gone as silent as a stalk of summer corn. So sad nothing he said could reach her. It didn't help matters that the letter had arrived right after their disagreement about Ollie. Maybe it was the worst possible time to go to the river, or maybe it was the best, depending on how you looked at it.

"Hey, I'm going," he called, opening the back door. She was sitting at the table, reading the papers. Catfish slipped into the house, went to her, sniffed her hand, and trotted back to the door. She turned to them.

"I talked to Hattie about this. She heard at the salon we all only got forty days to move out."

He stood there, door in hand. He'd read that too, he thought.

"What are you gonna do while I'm gone?" he asked.

"I don't know," she said. "Get what I can out of the garden, I guess."

"Well, don't get too hot."

"I'm going to try to freeze the corn."

"You hear me? Don't get too hot I said."

"I heard you. I don't know what else to do. But this one paper makes out like we only got forty days to leave! What about that?"

It wasn't her fault, and he hated the way he'd been to her lately. But he brought the door closed and walked back to the barn. He put Catfish in the granary and got in the truck. The dog whined. Frank felt like he'd eaten something still alive, something hard and mean like a young snapping turtle, and now it was growing, clawing and biting its way out. Every day it grew.

On the old familiar road he drove with the windows down, boat trailer bumping and squeaking behind him. Near Chesterton's gravel bar the road dipped into a steep valley and fell into evening shadows cast by rows of tall maples. The lane was narrow, yet he couldn't help but build up speed as he came down the hill. He feathered the brakes and watched the boat in the rearview. He'd driven this way a thousand times.

An old van sat at the bottom of the hill, just barely cocked off the road, with its hood raised. As soon as he saw it he shoved the brake down hard and the tires locked up and slid on the gravel, the boat's weight pushing ahead. The tires squabbled, grabbing at loose gravel, and metal squealed as the trailer pushed against its hitch. He narrowly missed plowing into the rear of the van and grated to a stop under a cloud of dust.

He looked back at the van. Engine trouble or not, this guy was a damn fool for stopping where he had, the lone spot where no one could see him. Ask a farmer around here to get a tractor and pull your junker out to a flat stretch. Or turn your stupid flashers on, at least. Maybe someone was walking ahead, gas can in hand. Damn fool. If he saw him down the road he'd pull over and cuss him.

His heart had just begun to slow when a man reared up out of the ditch. He'd been under the van engine, blocked from sight, and he appeared at the truck's window like one of the dead, climbing forth from his grave. He gripped the door and thrust his reeking head inside the cab.

"You bout going fast enough, you old sombitch!" he yelled.

A wild-haired man, his sagging hairy chest covered in faded tattoos. He was stained black with grease and his eyes were wide and white.

And then Frank recognized him. That crazy man from the river, drowning those pups. Trying to drown his pup.

The man saw Frank at the same instant and took a step back. But by then Frank was out. He grabbed his cane from where it was hooked on the side of the bed and came around the front of the truck.

The man turned when he saw Frank coming and started for the van, where maybe he kept a wrench or even a pistol. Whatever he was going for, he never made it.

The first blow from the cane caught him across the shoulder and neck, and Frank could feel in his arm the solidness of the impact, like striking a burlap sack stuffed with feed. The crazy man's eyes lit up with pain and he let out a yelp.

The blow bent him down, and his spine came up exposed like a log ready for the ax. Frank lifted the cane over his head and swung it like one, with both hands. There was a sharp crack and the man dropped to the ground, clutching himself.

Frank stood over him, panting heavily.

"There was a time I wouldn't a had to use my cane on you, you damn piece of shit." His breath came in rough jags. He held the cane to his shoulder like a batter.

The man on the ground buried his face in the dust and gravel at the side of the road. His tongue darted out and retreated with dirt stuck to it, his mouth opening and closing like a broken hinge, and his eyes searched for something behind his eyebrows. He sucked for air like his lungs were collapsed. It looked like he was dying. Frank had hit him so hard the second time it seemed possible he was.

He stood there and watched him claw and scratch the roadbed.

"What you did to my dog was wrong," he said. Then, since saying it triggered memories of that morning, the puppies hitting the water and swirling down, some of them making noises as they went, he swung the cane again. It hit the man mostly on his arm, which he had cradled against his scarred chest. The blow triggered a rapid jerking, like hitting just the tail of a snake with a truck tire. The man squirmed tighter into a fetal ball, his head tucked between his arms, his face no longer visible. Black strands of greasy hair lay tangled across his back and onto the ground.

Frank walked around the truck and hooked his cane over the bed. The engine was still idling. He drove on, the boat following obediently behind, and in the dust from the gravel road remained the van with its hood raised and the fallen man, his teeth shoveling dirt and pebbles while he lay gasping for air.

CHAPTER FORTY-FOUR

Throughout the day trucks hauled in mud-streaked logs of various sizes and types and stacked them around the sawmill in numerous piles, marked and labeled on the sawn butts. The skid loaders were unloading trucks from the time he got to work until he stopped, and inside the sawmill they'd worked just as fast. He'd driven home with a sore back and aching knees. His hands felt swollen and tight. Summer had promised to cook dinner, and Spring would be at her grandmother's house, but if his plan had been less important, a little less life-changing, he might've canceled. That kind of day at work called for a couch and beer. The shower put some energy back into him, though, and he drove to her house rehearsing his proposal.

In the hours since his mother's visit, he'd accepted the fact that the trailer was a goner. That listing ship was finally going the way of the Titanic. He wondered why he'd never managed to save any real money—after paying a few bills, the rest of his paycheck just kind of slipped away every month. Who the hell knew where it went. Now one possibility involved buying land somewhere on credit and dropping the trailer on it. His parents wouldn't care if he took the trailer, seemed like. On the other hand, he was ready to be out of the damn thing. It didn't stand to reason he could afford his own house, though, as he'd never had a mortgage or anything other than a truck loan in his name. The best idea, by far, seemed to be moving in with Summer.

Not that he knew what living with a woman was like. And don't forget the kid, he told himself. He surely didn't know what to expect living with both big and little women. But everyone on the planet had kids, so how hard could it be? Moving in with Summer would bring one obvious advantage, too, and he couldn't wait to utilize that perk. If he got to sleep in Summer's bed all night, he didn't care if he had to read a bedtime story once in a while, or whatever else Spring required.

While at work he'd imagined his mind drawn out as one of those cartoons— the kind showing the brain and what someone was thinking about. Like, this much sports and this much beer, or whatever. Except his would be drawn like this: "Lake" over here. Not too big, but definitely there. "Making Money Off Lake" next to it. "Parents Losing Farm" over the eyeballs. Bigger. "Loss of Trailer": same size. "Moving in with Summer" would be in the middle of his brain. Some size to that one, for sure. And then right next to it, or maybe even all around it?—he didn't know, he wasn't a cartoonist—would be "Sex with Summer After Moving in With Her." Maybe that would be the biggest portion of his brain, if truth be told. He was glad he had hair so no one could see what he was thinking and in what amounts. Then again he figured everyone had a brain like that: filled with dark secrets no one else could see.

When he got to her house Summer was in the kitchen. He let himself in and put his arms around her waist while she stirred a pot holding what looked like green beans. She wriggled her hips and shook him off. He liked the way her hips felt against him and tried to hold on.

"Dammit, let me cook here," she said. Then she laughed and stuck out her lips. He kissed her.

"That's what the man always does when his woman is cooking on TV," he said.

"I've seen em do that, too. But I ain't a good enough cook to work with distractions. There's a pop in the fridge if you want it."

She never kept beer in the house. If he were to live here fulltime, they'd have to start. He'd bring that up later if things went really well. He leaned against the countertop and watched her work.

"How's your mom?" she asked.

"Uh, not so good, really. Something's come up with them."

She looked at him. "Oh my gosh. Is she all right?"

"She's fine, if you mean the way she feels."

"She hates me. Is that it?"

He laughed. "That's the furthest thing from the truth I ever heard."

"Well what is it then?"

"Maybe I better wait and tell you after dinner. That was my plan."

She squinted her eyes at him. "You're full of plans."

"That's not all, either."

"Exactly my point." She opened the oven and he felt the heat rise out in a wave. She reached in with an oven mitt and checked a pan covered in aluminum foil.

"So Spring's at your mom's?"

"Yep. I gotta go get her later, though."

"What time?"

"Nine or so. No later. She'll be asleep in the car seat as it is."

"You want me to go with you to pick her up? I ain't even met your mom yet. And now here you done went and met my crazy-ass folks."

"Nah, not tonight. That'd be too late to meet somebody for the first time." She seemed to think about it. "But you will before too long, don't worry."

He went to the fridge and got a can of off-brand soda. There were various things in there he hadn't seen before. A bag of miniature carrots and strawberry yogurt. "You want something?" he asked.

"Maybe you could set the table? Let me work my magic here. I need all the concentration I can muster up."

He pictured her brain cartoon—nothing but food and cooking. He couldn't imagine thinking like that, even for a second. Not with an empty house, anyway.

She'd prepared some sort of casserole with ham and other stuff in it and what she called new potatoes, which were just miniature potatoes that somehow tasted better. He even ate some green beans. He told her it was great as he shoveled it in.

"I know I'm not much of a chef," she said. "You'd be surprised how hard it is to cook around here. There's only about two things she'll eat."

"Well, I really liked it."

For dessert she brought over two little fancy dishes swirled full of chocolate pudding.

"Damn I love that stuff," he said. "I ain't had it in years, though. Maybe not since I was a little kid." He ate it all in four spoonfuls.

She laughed, barely touching hers. "Somehow I knew you'd like it."

"I better start," he said, putting his spoon down. "I've been waitin to tell you the big news, but it's not all good."

"Okay." She looked nervous.

"I told you my mom come by. All by herself. Well, she's saying they're gonna lose the farm out there. The homeplace. I guess they're gonna build the lake after all, and they're taking that land to do it."

"Oh, Ollie, that's awful! I didn't know that's where it was going to be!"

"I know it. That's what I said. Where did you think they'd put it?"

"I didn't know. But I'd heard about it, that they were going to build one around here somewhere."

"I'd been hearin stuff, too, but I didn't think it'd happen. Well, anyway. They're gonna lose everything. House, barn—I reckon all of it. She's about sick over it. I imagine he is, too."

"That poor woman. They shouldn't do that to people like her. Where's she supposed to go? She's like … how old?"

"She's—" he thought about it. "She's too old for that shit, anyway."

"Here's the thing," he said, picking up his empty pudding dish and setting it back down. "She told me they'll take my trailer, too. And I ain't even been told about that yet, except by her."

He tried to read her face but couldn't tell if she saw the next thing coming. She revealed neither great anguish nor tremendous excitement.

"I was wondering where you thought I should live," he said.

Suddenly she stood and took her plate to the sink. From there, she said, "Well, hold on. Where are your parents going to live?"

"I don't know about that. Supposed to be, they help em find a new place. Not sure if they'll help me find a new place, though. Since they don't even seem to know I live out there now."

She turned on the faucet and ran water into the sink.

"Come over here," he said.

"I'm listening." She came back and sat at the little table.

"I was wondering what you'd think about me movin in here with you all."

"Ollie," she said quietly, "hold on a second."

"What?"

"Think about what you're saying. I mean, you ain't even met my mom yet. And now you want to move in here with us? What'll that do to Spring?"

"I'm already around here all the time, baby! She's totally used to me."

"That's what I'm saying."

"I can meet your mom any old time you want. Later tonight, even. I already told you that."

"It's not just that." She sighed and put her elbows on the table before lowering her face into her hands. "It's just a little sudden, isn't it?"

"Sudden? Not really. Summer, we've been going out since the fair. And you know this is different for me. I've told you that."

She looked up. "It's just now August, though!"

He stared at her for a while. "Well, I can see you ain't ready for the idea. And I get that. It's just that I thought I'd ask, since I'm fixin to lose my house and all."

"Maybe you ought to move in with your folks for a bit and help them out."

"Where's that? What the hell. We just said I didn't know where they're going."

"Ollie, look." She reached across the table and grabbed his arm with both hands, her blue eyes focusing right on him. "I just don't want to mess with her head, you know?"

"Spring?"

"Yes, her! You know what that'd do to her, having you move in here?"

"She likes me!"

"Sure she does. But that's not living with us."

"So, what, that's never going to happen? We're always going to live in separate houses, and I drive home every night at three in the morning?"

"No, not that. Not forever, anyhow."

"Til when, then?"

"Don't rush me, all right? I can't be rushed again. Not when I got her to think about, too."

They sat in silence for a while.

"You got to remember," she said. "I haven't lived with anyone before."

"Like I have." He'd told her about his history with women, explaining how no particular relationship had advanced too far past the bar stage. When she'd asked how many women he'd slept with, he told her a couple. He was thinking, a couple over thirty, a couple under twenty, a couple with brown hair.... She'd told him she'd only slept with two, as well, but he didn't think she was lying.

"Forget I brought it up," he said.

"No, I'm glad you brought it up. I mean, it's nice to know you think of us like that. That you want to be around us."

"Of course I wanna be around you. I just might be driving back and forth from Coondog's, that's all."

He stood and carried his plate and a dish to the counter.

When he walked back to the table she grabbed his arm. "Promise you're not mad?"

"Too bad I am, though. I'm pissed off about a lot of things, still. I'm mad that they're taking our farm, first off. I'm mad that I can't just move in here, since I'm here all the time, anyway. I'm mad that Coondog is getting rich while I can't even buy my own house. I'm mad at so many fucking things right now I can't even name em."

She stood up and faced him. She put her hands on his shoulders and he left them there. "How much longer?" she asked.

"How much longer what?"

"Ever since I met you, you've been angry about something. You've wanted this thing to change, or that person to be different. I figured something out a long time ago that you still need to learn. You know what that is?"

He looked at her. "What?"

"I used to believe that the cavalry was coming. Remember them, from TV shows? Someone would be trapped in a house or something and be surrounded, but then the cavalry would ride up and save the day. I used to think they were coming to save me. Back then I think I meant my dad— he was coming back to save me from mom. Later on, it was Todd. He was going to save me."

"Oh, like that asshole could save anyone—"

"Ollie, listen a little longer yet. You're going to miss the point of my little speech here. And here it is: no one is coming. You catch that? There is no cavalry. So you might as well knock the windows out with your little rifle and start firing at those bad guys your own damn self. That's what I told myself, anyway. Cause there ain't nobody coming to save us."

She kept her hands on his shoulders, staring into his eyes. "So how much longer," she said, "are you going to wait for help before you take care of your own problems?"

His chest felt tight. She was a goddamned snake charmer. A gypsy. A crystal-ball lady. A seer from another time and place. He'd never in all his life been handled like this.

"Are you trying to say I got a little rifle?" he asked.

She laughed. "I knew you'd get my point."

"Oh I got your point, Miss Teacher. I can't move in until you get a ring. Got it. Crystal clear."

She smacked his arm. "Don't even joke around about that," she said, still smiling.

"Well, then, I won't joke around about this. You asked me at the fair what my story was, and I said I didn't have one. Maybe I didn't. Or maybe it wasn't any good yet. It hadn't gotten to the good part yet, anyway. But now I think it started right here, in this house."

He could see in her eyes that he'd hit the mark and she pulled him into a hug.

"That's right, girl," he said. "Your cavalier is here now." He felt the laughs shaking her chest.

"Cavalry."

"Whatever in the hell it is. Here I am, anyway."

CHAPTER FORTY-FIVE

Frank drove the dirt lane alongside Chesterton's cornfield, heading down to the river, the truck bumping and sliding in and out of ruts. What had happened back on the road left him edgy and tight, but in some ways he felt better than he had in a long time. He'd been swinging at ghosts for months now and finally one had stood still long enough to get hit. He understood he'd made the man pay for the collective sins of others but devils and wolves ran in packs and he'd been lucky to catch one out alone.

The corn over here looked as sodden and flooded-out as it did anywhere else in the county. Ahead lay the sparse trees that lined the river. Under them was the big gravel bar where he'd launched his boat for years. Under the river was the bedrock even the current had been slow to erode, and so it ran shallower here, and in the fall or late summer it gurgled as it rolled over beds of stone. Music of water. The air felt cool in the shade of these old trees that had withstood hundreds of floodings. The river was still high, the water brown. Not much gurgling today—more a constant thrum of energy.

He was about ten miles upstream from his place—far enough away from the proposed dam that he didn't think the reservoir would change this stretch. Just downriver from here ran a series of bends and cutbacks where the river carved nasty, deep holes into itself. Spots where the current ate away at the banks trying to withhold it. Bankside trees leaned when their roots were exposed and dislodged by the swirling water, and then the trees themselves would topple and be swept downstream until they piled on the outer edges of massive bends. Catfish country. If he rode the river the better part of a day he'd end up on his own farm. He'd done that many times, fishing the whole run, but he usually fished the piece just below this gravel bar. Sometimes he wondered about dropping a stopped bottle in the river here—how long would it take to reach his woods? In his more romantic youth he'd toyed with the idea of sending a message downriver to Ethel. Like so many things, that was an idea he'd run out of time for.

But even in times like these the river lifted him up.

He launched his boat and tied a rope from the bow eye to a tree standing above the bank. He parked his truck and trailer up by the cornfield, in case the river rose while he fished.

The outboard started fine so he levered it into gear and the boat joined the current. The farther downstream he went the deeper he got into land being claimed. He understood what would become of the river when the lake consumed it. Every dammed reservoir had a channel winding like a snake under its surface. Channels were flooded rivers. This river would always exist—even these logjams and cutbanks would remain, hidden under many feet of water.

He knew he was passing good spots to fish but still he motored on. Here was where they'd netted Catfish from the river. He put the motor in neutral and the boat drifted until the bow nudged the cliff of dirt that rose six vertical feet from the water. Swallows darted in and out of holes in this soil. Above him towered rows of corn, planted right to edge of the bank.

The stern of the boat spun around slowly and he felt it lodge against the root ball of a sunken tree. He remembered how the man had looked when they'd come across him that day, how they'd wondered what he was throwing into the water. He thought of his dog now. He felt again the cane in his hand, colliding with that man's spine.

He didn't think he'd killed him.

He didn't really care if he had but he wondered if they could trace it back to him. It'd be a hell of a thing, to go to prison at his age. Ethel would never forgive him. But as long as he lived, even if they came and hauled him away in a squad car, he wasn't going to feel any guilt. If he could change one thing, he wished Catfish had been along to see that man eating the road.

It felt odd to just float around, looking at things, but he didn't feel like fishing yet. Which in itself was odd. Instead he was thinking about guilt and what a man was capable of doing. Both to himself and to each other. To animals.

The saws had been running for a while but their sounds hadn't registered. The boat was lodged securely against the roots so he reached back and killed the outboard. Now he heard several chainsaws plainly.

Dwight Pearson owned this land along the river here. He was a decent man. Planting corn that close to the bank was a greedy mistake, but other things he did well enough. He left the river alone. Frank didn't think he even fished it. He'd never seen him down here, unless he was working the fields or bush-hogging or something. Even though they were neighbors they didn't really speak that often. They each lifted a finger off the steering wheel when they met on the road and several times a year they'd stop by the other's farm to examine things and discuss the rain or lack of it.

Frank jerked the rope to start the outboard. Using the paddle, he pushed off the root ball until the boat was pulled away in the current. The river wound back and forth sharply here, and he couldn't see very far ahead. The horizon was hidden, as well—looking to either side only offered views of the banks. It was like riding in a tunnel with the roof cut away.

For centuries, these bends had flowed between deep woods of hickory and oak. The Miami Indians had made their camps in the riverside hills under these trees, leaving behind only their stone tools and chipped arrowheads. Now the chainsaws grew louder and a stretch of river he had always known to be shaded was aglow in the evening sun.

The hillsides above him were a tangled mess of branches and logs. Leaves attached to limbs that had been cut hours or days ago wilted. Patches of dark soil remained where the skidders had spun and slid. The white meat of the revealed and broken roots caught in the sunlight, and the air thudded with the sounds of the saws.

He'd cut enough trees on his own land, and so had those before him. But this wasn't cutting old dead trees for firewood, or bucking one fallen across a fence. This was clear-cutting—turning a woodlot into a field. They meant to remove all the trees, from the oldest oaks to the young sycamores that grew along the banks.

He caught a glimpse of a brightly colored T-shirt on the hill above him, but no one seemed to notice him. He floated by the workers on the current, an old man in a small jon boat. If they'd looked down at the river right then he might've shook his fist at them, and they would've laughed about that. But they were hot and sweating and thinking about getting off for the day. They didn't look down at the river below them. They kept their eyes turned to their saws.

Ethel needed a stepladder to reach the thin rope that hung from the door in the ceiling. She got the little three-step stool they kept folded between the refrigerator and the cabinet and stood on it to pull the rope. Down came the collapsible ladder that led to the attic. She hadn't gone up there in years.

This was in the pantry, where she kept canned vegetables and big pots for cooking. Their house was too old for this kind of ladder, but Frank had redone the pantry about twenty years ago during a blizzard, back when he had more strength and a bout of cabin fever. He'd torn out a rickety staircase, too tiny to be safe, and replaced it with this funny ladder that collapsed upon itself and rested on its door when closed.

The ladder was heavy for her but she managed to get it open and resting on the floor. Above her the entrance to the attic yawned like a mouth. She set the little stool aside and went to get a flashlight. Then she rose, step after step, into the darkness.

There was one bulb up here, and it lit when she tugged on its string. Boxes. Cobwebs. The odd breeze moving in from the eaves of the house. Under her the joists groaned and moved ever slightly. They'd had a problem with bats one summer, but she threw the flashlight's beam along the rafters and didn't see any now. Thank goodness. Bad enough she climbed up here while Frank was away. If she had a heart attack due to bats he'd come home and scold her for sure. Just thinking the words made her mind wander to Chub and then her husband, out on the river now without him.

She made her way to the end of the attic, the edge of the house nearest the barn, where things had been piled in storage the longest. She crept by Ollie's old crib, folded against the studs of the rafters, and smiled. Now it looked so old! Could he really have fit in there?

Surely his new girlfriend had everything she needed like that, but she'd try to remember to ask, anyway. Maybe the little girl could use something. All of this could be cleaned up. She'd just need Ollie's help in getting it down.

Back here were fewer cardboard boxes and more wooden crates and chests, from a time when everything was made of wood. Chests heavy even when empty. She crawled with her head low—only a child could stand upright here—and shined the flashlight on each box in every stack. Some of them had writing; others were bare. This one was marked, "Ollie, 2, 3 years clothes." Here a small one read, "Dishes," although she couldn't recall what they looked like. How funny: she'd eaten off them and washed them by hand for probably twenty years. Now she could remember they were white but not what kind of flowers went around their edges.

The bulb was above the steps, down on the other end of the attic, and only some of the light made its way to this end. Looking back to it, she saw the dust floating in the air her passage had stirred. Frank had run the wire up to that bulb when he put in the steps. When the house was built none of it had electricity, of course. Or even running water.

Here was what she'd come for: the old round-topped chest. It was just as she remembered it—slats of wood holding decorated tin, marked with tiny punched holes. It had belonged to Tarif and May. Her daddy had been born in 1892, and this chest preceded even him. Now it sat near the end of their attic and they'd been careful to not stack anything on top of it.

She laid the flashlight aside and released the catch on the chest. It took a good deal of strength to raise the lid, but once there, a little length of chain kept it from falling back. She picked up the flashlight and ran the beam over the contents.

She'd been twenty-four when her daddy died, and he was still very real to her. But May had died when Ethel was only nine, and the black and white photographs that remained, now framed and displayed downstairs, had all but replaced any real images Ethel had of her mother. Still, there were a few memories.

In the chest were the artifacts of her family, nearly everything that remained solid enough to touch. She knelt on her sore knees to inspect them again. Here were her daddy's boots, the leather worn as thin as waxed paper, and she lifted them from the chest and smelled the soles. They still smelled like animals and the dirt of the farm. She'd kept some of their clothes, as well—a pair of his bib overalls and a dress, carefully folded and layered in

white paper, that had been her mother's very best. She took the dress into
her lap and lifted a piece of the brittle paper. The dress was white with lace
trimming, but it had yellowed with age. She ran her fingers over the lace. She
knew the dress was small—her mother had been such a slight woman, too
small, perhaps, to live out here like this—so she didn't unfold it completely.
She had held the dress against herself and knew its size precisely. After her
mother died she pressed it to her chest many, many times. She had done so
the night before she married Frank in the courthouse. She'd worn her own
best dress for that, although she always regretted that she couldn't have
gotten married in something of her mother's.

She'd kept John's straw hat. Years ago mice had eaten most of it, and what
they left barely resembled a hat. It would've fit in a shoebox. He'd worn it
most days, but he wasn't wearing it when he died, so she'd always considered
it oddly lucky.

Under the clothes were papers of various kinds. A few newspaper clippings,
now yellow and soft as silk. A marriage license for Tarif and May. Another
for Frank and Ethel. Here was a photograph of her father standing in a field
next to two harnessed draft horses. They are as tall at the shoulder as he is.
Her father is not smiling.

She could remember horses, and their first tractors. She could remember
the noise of the equipment working around her. She remembered the smell
of her father and brother when they came in from the fields. Their smell
around her as she ate with them. She remembered the smell of her mother
in the kitchen, the heat from the fire in the old stove making her face shine.
She remembered the sound of her mother's sobs traveling through the walls
of this house in the weeks after her brother died out in the woods.

She knelt by the chest and remembered sixty-six years in this house. On
this soil. She was older than some of the trees in the woods and even they
reached the sky now. She remembered so much and yet she remembered
almost nothing. She sat in the near dark of the attic and remembered the
feel of her mother's soft lips kissing her goodnight and the feel of her father's
hand, so calloused it felt like it had been carved from wood, petting her hair
as she lay down to sleep. She remembered them walking out of her bedroom
together every night, leaving her alone in the darkness but unafraid.

Ethel flipped through a few more photographs and clippings, but now they
blurred in her shaking hand. The wood under her knees hurt but still she
knelt, trying, trying to remember more.

Frank motored downstream with his blood boiling. Here was Pearson, a
fellow river farmer, a man who ought to know that any loss of income due
to the current would be repaid by the simple presence of the river itself,

logging his land like some kind of goddamned businessman. He understood why Pearson would do it—he'd already imagined the river underwater, and he knew the bottoms would be plucked and carved like a turkey before they brought the water over her banks. They'd take everything they could get from her and then make her disappear forever under herself.

He was heartsick and low and he'd left the sound of the chainsaws upriver, but still their echoes bounced across the ridges above him. The motors straining as the blade bit wood, then revving when backed out of it. Trees grew down here, below Pearson's property, leafed out and green and leaning over the river. But when he watched the current roll around the boat he saw specks of sawdust floating like a hatch of insects.

Now about halfway to his farm, he considered going there to check on Ethel and to say the hell with all of it. He'd get out and let his boat drift on downriver and never again park his three-wheeler where he could watch the water roll by. He'd stay inside in his chair until they came with their government-owned bulldozers and dropped the house down on his head. Or maybe he'd shove the three-wheeler, the one tractor he still owned, the truck, the tools and everything else into the current. Just haul everything he'd accumulated back to the river, say a few words, and toss it all in.

And what was stopping him, he wondered, from throwing himself in after that?

Ethel. She needed him for whatever was coming next. And he was going to help her, because he'd decided, by God, they weren't going to break her down any further. They could do what they were going to do, but he meant to protect her. Damn them all to hell, anyway. He didn't have Chub anymore and Ollie was as lost as ever, but he wasn't going to let them take Ethel from him.

His hand was on the tiller and the outboard was running, but he barely controlled the boat's direction. Suddenly the bank loomed large and he was surprised to see he'd let the current push him so close. He shoved hard to the side and twisted the throttle. The boat swung back out into the channel, but there was a logjam waiting and he didn't react quickly enough. The leading log hit the boat broadside, turning him sideways, and the river piled against the other side. For a moment the boat rocked there in tense stasis, caught between the current and the tangle of logs and roots. Water rose dangerously high on the upriver gunnel, the metal straining and popping against the weight of the river.

"Get the hell off!" he yelled. The boat slowly slid forward, the wood screeching against the aluminum. The outboard, even at full throttle, had just enough power to move him, the prop churning out a white tube under the surface. The bow swung downstream and he shot clear of the front edge of the logjam, but then he crashed into the branches from one of the same half-submerged trees.

The limbs raked the front of the boat and swept back as the current and motor continued pushing. He barely got a hand up before the first branch hit him, knocking him off the seat. He let go of the outboard and shielded his face, but he felt the wood gouging him and heard limbs breaking and snapping. Finally the stern swung outward, away from the logjam, and the bow twisted out the limbs. The boat drifted free in a slow spin.

He struggled to pull himself back onto the seat. His face burned and he knew the branches had scratched away some skin. It was his own damned fault for being so careless. He straightened the outboard and checked to see if any rods or equipment had been knocked overboard. It all seemed intact.

Ahead lay a slower bend where the water slackened and deepened. The sun was coloring the highest treetops on the ridge in front of him, and he needed to get his head straight. He came into the bend and dropped his homemade anchor overboard, the line burning through his hands until it hit bottom. The rope shuddered and held as the anchor gripped, so he secured the line to the cleat on the gunnel. The boat rested amid the bubbles and pieces of wood and weed that floated by.

He touched his hand to his face and it came away with a little blood on it. He had a towel onboard, warm to the touch from lying in the sun, and he held it against his face to staunch whatever bleeding was there. The towel smelled strongly of fish. He knew he was lucky water hadn't come over the side of the boat. You never wanted to go down the river sideways or backward, and he'd gotten careless and done both.

A shad popped the surface nearby. He looked where it had been. The cast net was in a five-gallon bucket and he decided to see if he could net any shad while he tried to get his bearings. He stood and took the net from its bucket. It too smelled of fish and river water. He looped the line over his wrist and shook the weights free. Now it looked like a blanket of monofilament mesh held up by its middle. With a twisting motion that hurt his back he grabbed the weighted edge of the net and spun it out over the gunnel. It didn't open very well. He'd gotten to where it was hard for him to lay a net out all the way. Used to be he could spin one as flat as a pancake every time. The more the cast net opened, the more shad it fell over and trapped as it sank.

But the net had spread some, so he allowed it to sink to the bottom. He jerked the line still tethered to his wrist and hauled upward. It caught on something briefly and then rose. Before it even broke the surface he saw a glimpse of something white in the folds. He lifted the dripping net into the boat. Two good-sized shad were caught, and they kicked against the mesh. Silver and oily, about five inches long. Perfect cat bait. Water streamed off the net and splashed on his boots.

He lifted the ring and the shad fell to the bottom of the boat. They flipped their tails and jumped and fell, jumped and fell. Their gills pumped. He picked them up, their big black eyes staring, and dropped them into the dry bucket. They hit like thrown mice and jumped some more.

Now he had two decent shad and it seemed like a waste to not fish with them. A big tree was sunk at the core of this hole and he knew catfish would be lying around the branches and trunk. He draped the net over the seat in front of him and took his bait knife from his tackle box. He picked up the shad and cut each one right behind the head and then again about an inch back, and again until each was in four pieces. He sliced off the tails and dropped them overboard. The eyes on the shad went dead. The pieces of cutbait went back into the bucket. There was blood on his hands and on the knife and he leaned over and rinsed them off in the river.

After he toweled dry his hands he jerked the cord to start the outboard. He lifted the anchor, and this too was something that had gotten harder. He'd taken part of a frame from an old disk and welded re-bar across it to make this anchor, and the thing weighed about twenty-five pounds. Hoisting it through ten feet of water wasn't easy. He got it up and lowered it to the floor. He moved the cast net so they wouldn't get tangled before he put the motor in gear and went downstream.

When he was several yards upriver from the submerged tree he dropped the anchor overboard again. He knew where the tree was because several branches broke the surface, grass bent double around them from the current. The anchor took quite a bit of line, so he knew it was still deep here. He left a little slack and tied it off. The boat swayed and eventually came to rest. The current kept the anchor line tight enough to tremble where it entered the water.

He took up a rod, but it'd taken a beating when he hit the logjam and he had to untangle it. Luckily none of the guides had been wrenched off. He baited up with one of the shad heads, driving the hook through its eyes and skull, and cast it toward the tree. The sinker pulled the cutbait to the bottom. He set the rod in a holder and engaged the clicker on the reel.

While he straightened a second rod the first line jumped and went tight. The clicker sang as line peeled off, the rod jumping. He took it from the holder and drove the hook home. He could feel the thudding life of a catfish on the other end.

Turning on the seat, he faced the tree and the fish swimming below him. The catfish kept diving under the branches and tangles of its lair. The line rubbed against wood and he felt this, too. If he didn't get the fish clear of that his line would break.

By lifting the rod and then cranking the reel as he lowered it, slowly he levered the cat from the bottom. This was a good one—sometimes they came up right away, busting on the surface and throwing spray. But this fish stayed down, and he knew the longer it took to see it the bigger it would be.

Suddenly the catfish made a heavy run under the boat. He stood and let the rod bend in a deep arc as the fish surged under his feet. He swung the rod to the left to keep it from running into the anchor line or getting snagged on the outboard. He should've lifted the motor, but it was too late now that one was hooked.

The fish swam out from under the bow and headed back toward the tree. He raised the rod and stopped it short of the snag and it swam back in a hurry, still hidden. The cat circled a couple of times and he reached for the landing net. He lifted the pole with one hand and got ready to swoop the net with the other.

And then the catfish rose to the surface, its giant tail slapping the water and spraying drops everywhere. This before it shot back under the boat another time. The big ones never gave up.

Again he brought it back out, and again the fish made a run for the cover of the tree. After a few more surges he slid the net under the tired catfish. He dropped the rod and used both hands to lift the dripping net into the boat, the cat filling the swell of it.

He lowered the fish near his feet and grabbed his pliers to free the hook imbedded in the corner of its fleshy jaw. The head of the shad was gone. He put his thumb in the fish's mouth and the catfish bit down with what seemed like anger and vengeance in its large, wide-set eyes. He laughed even though it hurt and picked up the catfish. It weighed close to thirteen pounds, he was sure, and as he lifted it clear of the net the big tail swung, its sandpaper mouth rasping his thumb. Now he'd been bloodied twice.

But the fish was a specimen, thick and muscled like a horse. Dark gray on the top and lighter near the belly. A beautiful fish. He examined the cat, turning it over to gaze on the other side, before lowering it into the water.

Kneeling on the floor of his boat, he held his hand in its mouth while it righted itself and breathed the river again. He looked down into its eyes. He didn't know what might happen to the fish when the river rose over its banks, but he thought this one would be all right. He imagined it swimming through the tree stumps, eating the swimming mice and squirrels. Over the years he and Chub had killed and eaten a lot of catfish from this river, but he understood you couldn't kill them all. Nor would you want to. He looked at the fish and felt something not unlike love for it. Whatever happened, this fish would adapt.

Realizing it was back in the river, the catfish bit down once on his thumb and surged forward with a thrust of its tail. He took his hand from its mouth and let it leave. Its tail splashed and water flew on his face and the coolness shocked him a little. When he opened his eyes, the fish was gone. There was a swirl living its life on the surface, but then, as he watched, it died out too. He knelt there and peered into the river for a long time.

PART II

I t rose through the trees as surely and as steadily as tomato plants growing in June. First it surrounded the trunks of the sycamores, then it came farther and slipped over the roots of the oaks and maples. They were merely stumps by then, and within weeks all the stumps were gone, their flat tops like so many kitchen tables submerged.

It crept through the fescue and the sagging wire fence. The garden, long since returned to a rectangular patch of weeds, was overtaken slowly, from west to east.

It lapped at the stone foundation of the barn before crawling up the frame, the hand-hewn timbers as seasoned and hard as iron. By the time it reached the floor of the loft, it was touching the bottom step at the back of the house. Looters had kicked the door in, and the water flowed over the threshold and across the floor. The dirty river water climbed the steps to their bedroom.

It covered everything until the only remaining mark of their existence was the peak of the barn roof. The water swirled around it, the upturned keel of a ship sinking, and then the barn roof, too, was hidden.

CHAPTER FORTY-SIX

Ollie was home now, and worn out from work, but still he sat in his parked truck and smelled deeply of the plush upholstery. What did they call this material? Who cared. It was soft, deep blue, and smelled like the factory. Damn, this thing was sharp inside and out. Driving a new pickup made a man feel like he'd swallowed about a hundred lightning bugs and they were doing their darnedest to light him up from within. He'd keep up on the oil changings and greasings and tell the women not to eat their chocolate-dipped cones in here. The guy who'd owned it before had taken care of it, for all the 27,535 miles he'd driven it. And now it was Ollie's, still under factory warranty. Pretty much brand new. If they gave him half a second, he'd come out here and wash it thoroughly after supper.

He walked onto the back patio, the bricks still uneven and lined with grass pushing up through the cracks, and paused before going inside. Even dusty, that blue metallic flake was a damn sharp color. He pushed through the back door.

"Hey, here I am," he said. He tried to be pretty quiet. Sometimes one of them would be asleep. He heard the TV.

The kitchen was empty so he walked into the living room. There they were, sitting on the couch, watching something with the volume cranked. His two blonde queenies.

"He's home!" Spring yelled as she jumped off the couch and ran to him, throwing her arms around his waist.

"Don't get that sawdust all over ya, squirt. I ain't changed yet."

She made a dramatic show of sniffing his shirt. "Yep. You still smell like trees."

"You got that about right. That's what I'm saying."

Summer clicked off the television and smiled. "Hey," she said. "How was work today?"

"Work. Got busy again."

"Spring! Give daddy some room, why don't you, girl? You're maulin him."

Spring let go of him. "Guess what? Mommy says Cheryl's going to babysit me today."

He looked at Summer, who said, "Not today, she means. This weekend. Spring, honey, I never said today."

Spring stuck her bottom lip out, then started in about having Cheryl over. Something else too, about some show or another. Some game they were going to play.

"Ray wants us to come over Saturday," he said. "Grill out or something. I hate to say no to him again. You know how that goes."

"Oh great. More fun at nasty Ray and Lacey's. Looking forward to it."

Things had changed at work. It had gotten to the point where Doug couldn't both run the sawmill and drink fulltime the way he wanted to. The place had been hemorrhaging money for years because Doug worked hard to find ways to make it fail, and you didn't have to look that hard with a sawmill. So then one day last year Doug announced he'd sold the business to Ray. Now Ray was the boss, and Ollie had been promoted to foreman, meaning he sat in the booth and ran the blades. Somehow Ray was doing all right with the numbers, too. Why Doug had gone straight to Ray and never asked Ollie about buying it was something he hadn't figured out yet. Might've still been hard feelings left from that trip down south.

"We'll see, then," he said. "Maybe I'll tell him you're sick again. He can't argue with that."

"That ain't even a lie."

"You're sick still?"

"Twice today. I about lost it at the table at lunch, sitting there with Tina. I thought I was gonna need to get in the blocks for the forty yard dash. Somehow I stopped it, though."

Spring had continued to talk, but they were used to their conversations having a constant backdrop of kindergarten chatter. "Mommy's sick," she was saying now. "And it's my brother making her sick!"

It was a lot for Ollie to digest. They'd already gone to the doctor a couple of times for various tests. He'd just started to get certain house routines and rules down: when he could sleep and when he couldn't, how much time he could spend with Coondog, and a whole list of things to always do and never do in the bathroom. Nights now, though, he'd lie awake and study the cracks in the ceiling through many blue moon hours. Christ, there was a lot to worry about.

"I hate that you're sick all the time, baby," he said.

She shrugged. "Part of it."

He thought about that for a moment. "Do I got time to wash my truck after supper?"

"I don't know. What do you want?"

"Can you make spaghetti?"

"Oh no no no," Spring said.

"Again?" Summer asked. "We just had it."

"I know. I don't know why I like it so much."

"I know what I'm going to have," Spring said and ran into the kitchen.

Summer rose from the couch. She walked over and leaned into him and he felt her belly press against his. "People'll think you're the pregnant one," she said. She laughed and her breath tickled his neck.

"I'm still not used to having a steady cook on staff."

"Staff my ass," she said.

At dinner he asked Spring why she was getting babysat this weekend.

"Because Cheryl is my friend and mom says she needs to practice babysitting."

He looked over at Summer and then back at Spring. "Ask your mom who's going to practice paying Cheryl."

"I called her after work," Summer said. "It was kind of supposed to be a surprise date night for me and you."

"Way to go, Spring," he said. She was eating a bologna sandwich because that's what she ate every night. She studied him to see if he was kidding and then giggled.

"I thought we could go out Saturday a little bit," Summer said. "I need to move around while I still can. I didn't even care where we went."

"As long as it's not Ray's, right?" he asked.

"Righto. Please, please please. Do not make me spend another night talking to Lacey while you and Ray throw horseshoes outside."

He laughed. "Yeah, I'll get us out of that. Maybe we can go see a movie or something."

"Spring wanted me to take them to the beach," she said, over the steady sound of her daughter's voice. "I told her maybe some other time."

"No doubt. I'm about beached out."

The beach was Spring's new favorite place on the planet. The parks people had hauled in truckloads of sand and roped off part of the lake. It was pretty nice. Sand got about so hot it'd fry your feet off, but they'd kept most of the rocks out of it.

"I didn't want us to have to watch two of em," she said. "Plus, I think Cheryl starts looking around for b-o-y-s when they're at the beach, instead of babysitting."

"Meantime we're payin her for that. I'm saying right now, that chick's got a racket going."

"I told you, I'm grooming her. Trust me, you'll want a good babysitter on call."

"Did you say we're going to the beach?" Spring asked.

"No!" they both said.

"But she does," he said. "Have a racket going. Rich people always know how to make more money. You ever notice that? Look at her dad. Even their kids figure it out. It's like it's in their blood or something."

"Well, you better be nice to Norman if we want to buy some land off him sometime to build us a house."

Ollie went back to eating, twirling spaghetti on his fork. He looked out the window. Still enough light to get out there and wash the Chevy. Just last week he'd sold the old one, still dented, to Coondog, who'd paid cash. Maybe there wasn't a restaurant bar by the lake called "Coondog's" yet, but the son of a bitch was doing all right. He'd been hiring two high school guys every summer to help him trim trees, and now a twenty-year old was sharing his bed—some girl who'd gone to high school around here and then hitched all the way to California to be an actress. She'd come home ahead of schedule and found Coondog instead. Somehow he fit neatly into her newly-revised life plan. Ollie didn't know how often they utilized the pleasure dungeon, but he knew for a fact they'd made tapes.

"You know he's got lots around the lake," she said.

"Who does?"

"Fisk! He told me the other day when I was picking up Crazy here. Both waterfront and not."

"Like we can afford those."

"Probably not. No, we can't. Not right on the water. But we might be able to get close."

He looked over at Spring, now taking half her sandwich and tearing the crusts off the bread. Old enough to sit at the table and talk about what happened at kindergarten. Getting on the bus every morning to be shuttled away to the primary school outside Hapgood.

"You think that's what's next for us, huh?" he asked. "New house on a one acre lot? Picket fence, with a dog in it? Two kids?"

"I do want a dog!" Spring yelled. "Like Pappy's!"

Summer grinned at him from the opposite end of the little table. Her face had broken out some now that her hormones were going berserk, a few pimples sprouting along the jawline, but she was still show-stopping beautiful. He looked at her and felt what he'd known since the fair: that she was the single best thing to ever happen to him. If she wanted a house near the lake, he'd make it happen. He was considering finding another job, but if he had to work harder at the sawmill he could do it. Over one year married and now they were saying he might have a son. That was some stuff he never saw coming, that's for sure. It wasn't the way his parents had done things, and not what he'd imagined for himself. But if there was a man whose life ran the course he'd marked long ago, Ollie wanted to meet him, because his was the first.

Summer laughed. "That's what I'm saying. Can you imagine us as the All-American family? But seriously. Norman said land prices are only going to go up. He says we need to act fast."

Act fast, he thought. If he'd been doing anything over the last few years, that was it. Ollie stood up and took his plate to the sink and washed it off and put it in the dishwasher. Then he placed his hand on Summer's head. He felt her scalp under his fingertips and he moved his fingers and watched her hair jump. She rolled her eyes up and looked at him.

"I better go get that truck washed, anyway."

"I'll help," Spring said, pushing herself away from the table.

"Well?" Summer asked.

"Well what?"

"Well what about those lots? Are you gonna talk to him about them sometime soon?"

"You know I will. And I'll tell you something else, too." He went to the back door and stood with his hand on the knob.

"Oh yeah?"

"He's not getting that much out of me. I'll be the one telling him what they're worth. And I'll get my price, too."

"I know you will," she said.

He went outside with Spring and together they drug the hose around the side of the house. They got the carwash bucket and sponges from the little shed he'd built last summer and poured some car soap concentrate from the shelf into the bucket. There was a rack there where he hung towels for drying the vehicles. He'd done several little things like that to make this property his own. To improve it for both of them. He liked the idea of them building a brand new place together. He'd learned a lot about how to keep a house in good repair.

When he started hosing off the truck, Spring screaming wildly and flirting with the spray, Summer came outside and sat at the table. It wasn't too hot, with just enough daylight remaining to wash the vehicle and towel it off. This was a nice evening for truck washing. He saw something flash in the paint then and when he looked up Summer was lowering the camera. He started to tell her to put the damn thing away and let them work, but instead he sprayed the hose at her. It only reached halfway, as he knew it would, but she squealed and shielded her face.

"Put the sponge against the tire and pose for your mom," he said to Spring, and she did with great theatrics. He was in the shot, too, holding the hose in such a way to suggest he was about to soak her. But after the flash he turned the spray toward the hood and any settled dust and grime began to rinse away in the sparkling cold water.

CHAPTER FORTY-SEVEN

He reclined asleep in his old chair, wizened ever further now by additional years and the stress of relocating most of what he'd accumulated and kept after nearly eighty years in this world. The old chair, bought at a department store in Green City in the fifties, was cracked and faded so far beyond its original condition it was as if it'd molted or transformed, like mold consuming a loaf of bread. His hat rested on the floor next to his chair and his cane was hooked lightly where the arm came to rest against the back. He slept with his head tilted up and his mouth open.

So here he dozed, in this rectangular ranch house with vinyl siding and a detached garage. Out front, the yard was still bare in patches where the seed wouldn't take in the clay soil. Several bushes had been rooted along the front of the house, but some of them stood as dried sprigs. No one had bothered to rip up the dead ones. Behind the small garage sat his old jon boat, covered with a green tarp weighted down with broken pieces of concrete blocks. One tire was flat on the trailer and weeds grew up around it.

In the kitchen, Ethel sat by herself, facing a spread of cards. She studied them for a while before moving three cards from the stack across her hands, turning up the third. She examined this new card and those in front of her before repeating the process.

A baby could be heard screaming in the house next door, high wavering sobs that reminded her of coyotes. She looked at the clock. Sometimes she thought he cried at regular times, but she'd given up on finding a pattern. They already had two other babies over there, but this third one was a cryer. The parents were nice enough folks. Sometimes she talked to them when she went out back in the evenings to refill her bird feeder. Just friendly chatter about the weather or a new car on the lane.

It was Saturday and the six houses she could see from the kitchen window all had cars parked in their driveways. On weekdays she might look and every single car would be gone. Frank had taken to sitting in a folding chair on the sidewalk in front of the house, counting the cars that drove by on the highway just visible beyond the houses across the street. He'd come in at dusk and report the tally. "Seventy-nine," he'd say. Or "only fifty-six all afternoon." Today was dark and gloomy and threatened rain. A storm seemed possible. Late in the night a storm had broken, and she'd wakened and knew he was awake, too. But neither of them spoke. They listened to the storm blow out and went back to sleep.

Ollie had helped them move in, and her brightest days were when he came by. She'd grown to love Summer, and Spring was an absolute bright spot in their lives. Even Frank watched her with a smile on his face. Sometimes they came over for dinner—it didn't happen every week but almost every month. In May, for example, she'd only seen Ollie three times and Summer and the little girl once. Certainly she wanted them to come over more often than they did, but she didn't like saying anything about it. She knew they'd come when they wanted to.

She felt tremendous relief now that her son was married, just like everyone else's. They hadn't married in the town church, though, the way she'd hoped, with the preacher Collier residing. Instead they'd gone to Gatlinburg, and let some preacher they didn't even know marry them in a place they'd never visited. It didn't seem right to Ethel but Frank didn't care. Ollie told her that was what people did when they got married the way he did, later in life. And to a woman who already had a baby.

But they were married and that was the main thing. They lived together over there at her place, in what had been Summer's grandma's house. Years ago, Ethel had known her grandmother a little bit, but had never been in that lady's house and didn't feel right dropping by now. So, instead, most days she waited, just like this, passing the time and hoping she'd get to see her son and the girls.

Her shoulders hurt almost all the time. Arthritis. She took pills for it. Her left knee sometimes failed her, too. It was an odd thing to have to think about taking a step, but that was what it came to on its worst days. She'd be forced to stop and stare down at her knee, commanding it to do what it had done all its life without provocation.

Sometimes she thought about her age and remembered being a little girl, back before her mother died. She and John would run to the river and hide from each other in the woods. They talked a lot back then. When he died he was a teenager and not really speaking to her, and it was a shame they never got to come out of that together. But earlier they'd talked like little kids do and told each other that they'd live to be at least eighty. Of course it seemed like forever to them then! She thought it was so funny now that they had talked about that, but she remembered it clear as day. Now she was almost eighty and thought she would make it. She figured John would be happy one of them had. She didn't know if she'd go much past it, but she was pretty much at peace with that.

They had moved her brother's body. And her mother's. And her father's. Their caskets had been dug up and reburied in a cornfield outside of what they called New Logjam. The little country cemetery had been transplanted, one exhumed body after another, to this place where they hadn't even planted grass yet. The government workers dug up the old stones and erected them over the new graves. As if nothing had changed but the hills surrounding.

She had gone to the new cemetery once, where she wept. She hadn't been one to visit their graves often but the thought of them being moved sickened her. If a person didn't have respect for some things, there was nothing you could do about that, but every person on God's earth ought to respect the dead.

It provided some solace to her that Frank had purchased two lots next to where her brother and parents lay.

Frank was a constant worry to her. She watched him now, sleeping in his chair in the adjoining room. She listened as he drew in a slow, uneven breath, and much later pushed it out again. Then a pause and another ill formed breath. All he did anymore was complain about one pain or another, but he wouldn't see Dr. Mulferd for any of it. Some days were fine, but other days she and Frank snapped and bickered at each other like they never had before. Each one focusing on his or her own pains and particular sadness.

If he didn't have that dog, she thought, he may not have made it this long.

She looked at the dog, stretched out across the floor of the living room, asleep. Right on the carpet. She still hadn't gotten used to that, but every night they'd been here, he'd been inside, too. And now he even slept by the bed! As old and stooped as Frank had become, the animal on the floor looked like a racehorse, leg muscles bulging and spasmodically jumping as he dreamed. He weighed over a hundred pounds, for sure. Right in the house! His tail alone knocked things off the table. Old Catfish.

But the dog kept her husband moving, since Frank took him on little walks down the lane and got up to let him outside. During the day, left alone in the backyard to do his business, Catfish sometimes scampered around the neighbors' houses and brought things back. Shoes left outside to dry, an old tennis ball. Once a doll. All of this mortified Ethel, and she ran around to the neighbors apologizing and returning things. Frank just laughed. After all, he's a Labrador Retriever, he'd say. She suspected Frank was telling him to do it.

When Ollie came over, he threw a ball for Catfish to fetch, and later, inside the house, Spring would climb all over the dog, sometimes riding him like a bull. Catfish tolerated these things, but did everything with one eye on Frank. He was Frank's dog forever, and when he tired of their antics he would go and sit by his chair, and all games would cease.

Sometimes Ethel wondered who would go first among them. She didn't want to pass before Frank, because she hated to think of him in a nursing home. It was hard enough for her to take care of him—no way he'd manage by himself. If Frank went first, she feared what would become of Catfish. She thought the animal might die of a broken heart, his big head resting in Frank's old chair. But she understood absolutely if something were to happen to the dog, Frank would surely follow, having lost the one thing that kept him going. She dreaded the day when Catfish would get sick, but he was so big and strong she couldn't imagine something hurting him. He seemed to gain strength every day while they lost more of theirs.

She looked at the clock. Almost ten. Ollie might come for lunch, but lately it seemed they kept other plans for the weekends—things she couldn't or wouldn't do, like going to the new beach. She liked hearing of the fun things they did with Spring, but it was a shame they couldn't bring her by more often. What a talker that little girl was! Ethel had always wondered what it was like having a sister or a daughter, since she'd been surrounded by males her whole life. When Spring was in the house the whole place came alive. When she left the whole place felt quieter than ever.

The money part of it was the least of their concerns. The government had given them enough to buy this place outright, and they still had some in the bank they intended to leave Ollie's family. The government had also helped them locate this little house, only about ten miles from the farm. At first it was all right, but then the other lots around theirs sold and the new neighbors made the house feel altogether different from the homeplace.

All this after their struggles: Frank's refusal to sell, the days in the courthouse, the judge finally telling them it was done, it was over. The government invoking their God-given right to take. Not once had they said yes to anything but here they were, having taken the money forced into their hands. They never sold their farm but they accepted money for it. Those had been darker days than they thought possible, packing up what they could and piling the rest, old furniture and magazines, calendars and rugs, and burning it all in a bonfire in the backyard, right where both Ollie and Catfish had played. Frank grew so despondent he refused to speak for whole days.

She couldn't find anyone who wanted the chickens, so she sold them all to the locker plant for a dollar a head, where they were butchered and donated to the volunteer firemen for fundraising chicken dinners.

Now, in this new house, neither of them did anything, so it didn't really matter what waited outside their door. They could have been in a house on the river Styx in hell, and it wouldn't have changed things. Some days he acted like that's exactly where they were. But then, if they had been on a river, he might've appreciated it more.

The sound of the TV startled her and she turned to see Frank holding the remote, his hair pressed awkwardly to his head where he'd slept against it. He was awake to watch his game shows. Catfish stretched his legs and relaxed again, all four feet splayed out in front of him. Something about the morning made her so blue and melancholy she didn't know what she was saying until she said it.

"You gotta get out the house today. Take your dog and go somewhere for once."

He looked over at her, surprised and angry.

"What?" he yelled.

"I said I'm going to Hattie's. You ought to go somewhere too. We need to get out." She hadn't thought of going to Hattie's until now, but she knew she needed to. Hattie had been calling, urging her to come to the salon and look at photographs she'd taken on her trip to Canada. A different man this time, one not much older than Ollie.

"Where the hell do you want me to go?" he asked.

Catfish lifted his head up, yawned noisily, and stared at her, as if he were asking the same question. It was almost creepy how he could understand what she said.

"I don't know! Take your boat out somewhere."

She couldn't believe she'd said it. He hadn't taken the boat out in years—not since the move, really. He'd just pulled the boat to the new house and covered it up. Once in a while he still went somewhere and fished from the bank, but he never messed with his boat anymore. If someone were to stop by and offer to buy it, she thought he would consider it—and for most of their lives it'd seemed like he might be buried in that boat.

Frank turned back to the television but she could tell he was thinking. He changed channels and listened to some of the weather report.

"It might storm again yet," he said. It had been raining and storming for a week straight now and the yard was a mudhole. No one could stop the rain.

"Maybe it won't." Never in her life had she asked him to do something dangerous, but something about today made her feel reckless and desperate. Like leaving him to rot in that chair one more day could somehow doom them all.

"I hate to go by myself," he said.

"Take your dog, then. Nothing's gonna happen to that monster."

He looked at the dog near his feet. Catfish stood, stretched his back, and then set his tail to swinging. He shook his broad head, ears flapping.

She watched her husband's face and knew he was making a list of what he needed and what might call for repair. He was trying to remember where he'd left everything.

CHAPTER FORTY-EIGHT

Ollie saw the old man walk out of the garage as soon as he turned down their lane in the new subdivision. He was surprised to see him outside. Then he noticed the boat hooked to the pickup. Now that was something he hadn't seen in a while.

He pulled in alongside the boat on the narrow concrete drive. It looked like rain, and that would spot the perfect shine he'd achieved with yesterday's washing. What he needed was a garage like his dad had now. He got out of the truck and glanced over at the house next door. A little boy stood under a lowered basketball goal with a basketball in his hands.

"Let's see you dunk it," Ollie called, but the boy just stared at him with a scared look on his face, as if Ollie were someone or something he'd been warned about.

Ollie stared back for a while, waiting for the kid to at least attempt a shot, but the boy stood there like a mannequin in a sporting goods store. What the hell is wrong with him, Ollie wondered as he walked around the front of his truck. Ah, the suburbs. Finding his parents living in one still felt like going to the zoo and discovering a dolphin in the monkey pen, flapping its tail in the dirt and making those creaking noises. He didn't know how much longer they could live on their own, anyway.

The old man was back in the garage, and Ollie found him filling his left arm with life jackets and cushions and the stuff he used when he went fishing. The dog wasn't around for once.

"Don't tell me you're fixing to take the boat out," Ollie said.

"I'm fixing to take the boat out."

"By yourself?"

"No."

"That part's good. Who's going with ya, then?"

"I reckon Catfish'll go with me. He's one person who can still stand my company."

Ollie watched him haul his gear out, walking all hunched over like a desert wanderer, one arm around a pile of stuff and the other working the cane. If someone were to kick his cane out from under him, he'd go down like a sack of rocks, because anymore he relied on it like a third leg. Ollie leaned against his mom's car and said nothing as Frank loaded the equipment into the boat. He didn't have a lot of time before he was supposed to go out with Summer and was just swinging by here to borrow the old man's weedeater since his own had crapped out on him. He tried to figure out how much time he had to waste, arguing with his dad.

When Frank walked back in the garage he didn't look up.

"I'd go with you myself," Ollie began, "Cept I gotta go out with Summer tonight, since we got a babysitter lined up and all."

Frank looked at him and nodded, but said nothing. He began to sort through the rods that stood in a corner, a jumbled lean-to of monofilament and graphite.

"You ought not be going fishing by yourself," Ollie said.

"I told ya I'm not going by myself."

"I mean without another person in the boat."

The old man took about four rods and started out of the garage with them, carrying them parallel to the ground so the tips wouldn't get jammed in the rafters overhead. Ollie followed him out—the trip took about ten minutes.

"How long's it been since you had this boat out?" he asked.

Frank lowered the rods into the truck bed. "I guess it's been since we moved out here, anyway. Too long, I reckon."

"So, what? Like three years? And now all of a sudden you decide to take it out, when it looks like rain and all?"

"That's about right."

"Will it matter if I say I think that's a bad idea?"

"Not to me it won't."

Ollie stood against the truck while Frank walked back into the garage. His dad was maybe a foot shorter than he had been. It was like he was shrinking away before his eyes. How many more years before he only came up to Ollie's waist? His knees? Is that how it would end—with the old man literally shrinking until no one could see him? Maybe he'd get lost in the weeds like someone's forgotten pet turtle.

Frank came outside with a paddle and dropped it into the boat. "I reckon I better get my dog and get going," he said.

"Yeah, well. Watch your ass out there." Ollie felt awkward saying anything that might seem sentimental so he quickly asked, "Where you going, anyway?"

"Out to the river. To Chesterton's."

"You been out there in a while?"

"Not really. No."

"Well, it ain't the same way you remember it."

"I know how that goes," Frank said. He turned and started toward the house.

"You care if I borrow your weedeater?"

The old man just lifted his arm to acknowledge him.

Ollie figured he'd grab the weedeater and run inside and say hi to his mom real quick. Already he'd been here longer than he'd planned. Any fool with a sober mind could see fishing alone was a stupid thing to do. But he'd already told his father he shouldn't go and it was obvious he was still going. He knew they'd stopped listening to each other a long time back and it seemed a little late in life to start again now.

CHAPTER FORTY-NINE

The clouds to the west looked heavy and dark again, and Frank drove with the windows down, as he always had. The air blowing through the cab felt charged and it seemed likely another round of storms was coming. But there were worse things than getting wet, and if a squall hit before he got to the river they'd wait it out in the truck. His dog didn't mind storms, but he knew plenty of them did. Being on the river in a thunderstorm got a little hairy, but sitting one out in a pickup made you happy to be alive, and he figured that would be the case no matter how old he was. It felt pretty good to pull this boat down the road again. He hadn't driven out this way for a long time and now the gravel road was paved with some conglomerate of asphalt chips and oil.

Chesterton had been dead for almost a year, but Frank thought he could still launch from the gravel bar on what had been his property. An obituary had run in the newspaper but Frank didn't remember what killed him. He recalled that Chesterton died in a nursing home, where he'd lived out the last couple of years of his life. Frank hadn't made it to the funeral because he hadn't gone to any funerals since Chub's and he didn't plan on going to any more. Well, he thought, he guessed he'd make it to his own.

Driving out 600 West took him right by one of the two entrances to the new park. LOGJAM STATE RECREATIONAL AREA the huge wooden sign read. It was painted black with yellow letters wood-burned into it. It stood probably twelve feet high on a stone foundation of river rocks.

They claimed the park was doing well with the tourists. Even now there were two cars lined up at the gatehouse, waiting to pay the entrance fee. Whether those tourists did anything to help this town or the folks who had lived here their entire lives he couldn't say. He'd overheard their son telling Ethel about the beach—how the little girl couldn't go there often enough. He supposed that was fine, but then again you couldn't expect a child to understand the cost of things when all she felt was the sun, sand and water.

In the side mirror the trailer tire looked fine. He'd drug out the air compressor from the garage and refilled it, but he couldn't locate a puncture. Probably just a slow leak around the bead. You couldn't leave a tire sitting like that for so long and not expect problems. It surprised him the other one was all right. As he drove he wondered about what he'd forgotten. He didn't have any frozen bait anymore, but he brought the cast net and hoped to throw it over some shad.

Catfish rode along next to him on the bench seat. Once in a while the dog would notice something passing by that offended him and he'd rise to all fours barking and growling, his tail slapping Frank in the face. The Dog

Prince, ruler of everything he saw or smelled. People in their yards would look up as the old truck and boat bounced by, a dog barking at them from the passenger seat with his entire head hanging out the window. Frank never scolded him. These were all new houses along here, built after the lake, and he didn't give a shit about these people.

When they reached Chesterton's he was surprised to see more houses like the one he lived in now, low-slung and vinyl-sided, standing in the old cornfield. The lane along the edge of the field had become a shared border between the yards of four modular homes. He slowed down and looked back toward the river—the trees marking its edge were still there. He didn't think houses could be built on a floodplain, but somehow the developer had gotten around that. Or maybe, since the lake had been constructed, the river was no longer considered wild enough to flood.

Grass hadn't grown well on the old lane, the soil was so compacted from years of tractor traffic, so the original path was evident. He turned off the road, humped up over the culvert they'd left in the ditch, and drove along the seam between the yards, the trailer bouncing and squeaking. A man walked out of the nearest house and stood staring, hands on his hips, and Catfish barked at him.

Near the river it looked familiar. The same sycamores grew from the mud-packed banks, and the smell of the river came through the windows. Catfish jumped and spun on the seat.

"Hush up now," he said to the dog. "Sit down."

He brought the truck to a stop and shut off the engine. Parked where he was, he could just see the water moving beyond the tree branches. The current seemed slower but the water remained the same brownish-green color of a snapping turtle's shell.

He opened the door and Catfish all but pushed him over as he bolted to the ground. "Slow down, you yellow son of a bitch!" he yelled. The dog ignored him, rushing around in circles with his nose held low, drawing in tremendous inhalations. Frank took his cane from the bed. The ragweed was taller than he was, and he had to push through the thick, rich-smelling plants to reach the river. A few saplings had rooted on this bank, their trunks as thick as fingers. Catfish plowed ahead of him, carving a narrow trail, and Frank heard him splash into the water.

The weeds stopped at the rock of the river. When he stepped free of the ragweed, burrs sticking to his clothes, he saw Catfish cavorting in the shallows, the river splashing and dripping off his belly. As before, the gravel bar stretched from this bank out into the current. The river still dimpled and gurgled over the riffle. It still smelled like the river. He found a gnawed-smooth beaver stick and threw it into the water, and Catfish surged forward, waves breaking in front of his chest, and set off swimming. The current pushed the stick downstream, but he overtook it, bit down, and spun about, his tail trailing him, ruddering back and forth not unlike a yellow snake following.

Frank searched the weeds as he returned to the truck, looking for large pieces of driftwood or rocks that might harm the trailer. He lowered the tailgate and moved his rods to the boat. Then he told the dripping dog to jump in, which he did. As he shut the tailgate, Catfish leaned over and licked his face.

He backed the trailer into the ragweed and the outboard clanked against the stern as the weeds bent and were swept under the boat like corn folding before a combine. When the trailer reached the gravel bar he shoved his door open against the foliage and undid the tow strap and checked the drain plug. Catfish watched all of this from the bed, but when Frank lowered the tailgate he jumped out and splashed into the river again. Overhead the sun lay hidden behind a gauze-like layer of cloud cover.

But the outboard wouldn't start. It had fired on the first pull for decades, but now the old Evinrude couldn't find it within itself to start one more time. He jerked the cord, listened to the motor turn over and quit, jerked the cord again, listened to the motor turn over and quit, rested for a moment while massaging his sore hand, and then jerked the cord again. Catfish ran from bow to stern, jumping over the bench seats and scattering the rods and tackle. He'd climbed into the boat easily enough—somehow understanding that's where he was meant to go—but now being on moving water was too much for him. It wasn't fear.

The slight current slowly spun the drifting boat as they floated downriver. Catfish spotted a pair of mallards paddling away in haste along the bank and threatened to jump in, front paws sliding on the gunnel. Frank swatted his rump and pulled his tail to keep him onboard.

Taking the cover off the motor wouldn't do any good—he'd checked the spark plug earlier. He'd poured the old gas out and pumped fresh into the tank. Squirrels chattered and barked at them from the branches overhead as Frank laid his arm atop the outboard's cowling and tried to catch his wind. Pulling a starter on a dead engine could wear out even a young man, he thought. Here and there sprouted the ripples from fish and turtles.

He braced for a few more tries and the second pull worked—the motor sputtered and white smoke bubbled from the water above the prop. With the outboard still in neutral he twisted the throttle and the engine rose in pitch and vibration. Catfish, head cocked, studied the sound. Frank dropped the transmission in gear and the outboard coughed then steadied as the boat lurched forward. Catfish sat back on his haunches near the front bench and

Frank chuckled. Water dog.

He didn't feel like throwing the cast net yet so he kept the bow pointed downstream. The motor needed to warm up, anyway. Every spring flood changed the river: logjams might break apart and recollect downstream, a cutbank would erode further. And, through the first few bends, it seemed like those seasonal changes were the only things he'd missed.

But then the river grew wide and fat. In narrow stretches where the current used to quicken and sluice around caught logs, now the water lay swollen like a rat-fed snake, nestled against the upper edges of its banks. Dying trees stood flooded, their roots waterlogged and branches bare. He leaned from side to side to peer around Catfish, who posed at the bow like a hood ornament, ears flapping with the breeze. Frank watched as the river he'd known all his life turned into a waterway he'd never met.

He followed the old channel through another bend. Here, he recognized some things, like that old oak tree high on the ridgeline. And the tremendous split beech that lightning cracked but didn't kill. The deep hole on this outside bend where Chub once hooked a thirty pound flathead, and Frank almost freed it with some bad net work at boatside. But as he grew closer to what had been Pearson's land, he could no longer tell if the river had changed so much or if his memory had failed him completely.

And then, the unfathomable: the banks began to spread. The river before them opened up like a field of water, stretching across a cove under a bank of gray clouds. The jon boat moved out of the riverbanks and floated onto the widest span of water it'd ever touched. Like stepping from a shaded forest onto a treeless plain. Catfish looked at him. The boat drifted without power because Frank hadn't realized he was no longer twisting the throttle.

"Jesus H. Christ," he said.

Another boat was visible across the open water, anchored off the far shore. To the left of it lay an expanse of even bigger water. This was merely the upper end of the reservoir, where the river brought its load of water and slowed to a stop.

Catfish left his perch and moved to the stern, shaking the boat as he leapt over the benches. His wet paws slid on the aluminum and the boat rocked. He licked Frank's face before he got pushed away.

"Jesus Christ," Frank said again.

He'd fished rivers his entire life and a reservoir of this size would've been a shock to him even if he'd traveled to see it. To find it here, where he'd left his river a few years ago, was enough to send him into confusion as pure and hot as sunlight.

He needed to see more—to understand how large this lake could be, and how far gone his river was. He opened the throttle and the boat's nose lifted.

Catfish staggered before sitting down. The water darkened from brown-green to blue. The boat moved with the reservoir's rhythm as it lifted and fell over the slight waves. The man in the other boat saluted as they drew closer but Frank didn't acknowledge him as they motored on toward the mouth of the cove.

When the full lake revealed itself he gasped. He could barely see across the expanse of it. Houses dotted the shoreline—some complete, others a skeleton of framed lumber—standing among the trees that grew right to the water's edge. The lake wandered back into coves and cuts everywhere he turned, some appearing as lakes themselves. A few other boats were moving across the way, one of them powering across the surface as fast as a car could cruise down an interstate. Out here the waves kicked up by the faster boats undulated until they collided with other waves. Frank felt the little jon boat buck underneath him and Catfish cowered. His narrow boat was a good vessel for the shallow, snag-filled river but was ill-suited for this kind of water.

Gone were any ideas of fishing, but he wanted to keep looking until he could process what his mind couldn't grasp. Maybe if he saw something he could place, that would in turn place him. He motored out across the lake, the bow thudding as it walloped the bigger waves. Catfish knelt with his belly on the bottom of the boat, eyes below the gunnel. Frank picked a house on the far shoreline and aimed for it. A deep-v pulling a skier crossed in front of them and the waves it kicked up hit them a few seconds later.

The lake was maybe a mile across here, he guessed. Maybe more. And about three times as long. Nearing what might be the center, he realized the body of the reservoir swept to the left around a bend. Like a river would've. Like the old river had.

And then the knowledge came to him, like the sudden, angry jerking of a catfish late at night: somewhere under all this water lay his farm.

He slowed the motor and leaned over the gunnel. Deep, blue water. This wasn't the sediment-rich current of a river. This was reservoir water—water that had lost its movement and settled. He strained his eyes, peering into the depths. He and Ethel had left the house standing. Left the barn standing, and the chicken coop. The tool shed, and the silver grain bin. He didn't want to see them torn down, so they packed up what they could move, burned the rest, and left the structures they and others before them had built. He thought the government had probably bulldozed everything before the water rose, but in his mind he imagined all of it standing, as it had for decades, under the water. He thought about fish swimming through the doors of the barn, where his cows had walked and stopped to scratch their backs on the jambs. Those red cows. Some nights he'd slept in the barn when one of them was having trouble calving. Had that really been another time in this same life? He looked now and thought he could see their farm, wavering and distorted. He saw the angles of the house roof and the steep pitch of the barn. He saw Ethel's garden, laid out in careful rows. His fences were still standing.

A sickness rose in his throat and he righted himself quickly. He grabbed the outboard's tiller and twisted the throttle. Something had turned inside him and he didn't expect it to turn back. By God, he and Catfish were going back to the truck and the short stretch of river that remained. This lake. They could have it, and all it had consumed.

The first wave caught them both by surprise, thudding into the boat's side. Catfish leapt to his feet and jumped toward Frank. Another wave hit them as the big dog's feet struck the seat, and he slid across the bench before hitting the gunnel and splashing overboard. Frank turned in time to see Catfish's brown eyes rimmed with white as he fell. He reached out for him with both hands, and as soon as his hand was off the motor it swung into a turn, the prop still spinning at full throttle. Another wave hit the boat as he was leaning over and he felt his ass rising. The water covered his head then and all he could think about was how cold he was.

When he came to he was aware of someone moving him. Someone lifting him with hands placed in his armpits. He was conscious of the sensation of a solid floor under him again, and how good that felt, even then. Voices of men. "Watch that damn boat!" one yelled, saying something about an outboard under power. Someone shook him. Then another voice, closer to his face.

"Wake up, old man. You all right? Hey! Wake up, grandpa!"

A hand holding his cheek and shaking his head.

The two men in new swimsuits laid the old man on the carpet of their ski boat and sped off on plane, the hull sliding over the surface like it was not touching anything of this earth. At the marina they yelled down the Conservation Officers who were gassing up their patrol skiff. As they pulled alongside, one of the officers jumped aboard the ski boat to care for the victim.

"Anyone else overboard?" the other C.O. called.

"No, just this one, we think, just this old man," one of the men said. "But his boat's out there, going in donuts."

The C.O. took off in his patrol vessel, pursuing the captain-less jon boat plowing endless circles out on the lake, throttle wide open and tiller at full turn.

His partner worked to revive the sodden body. An old man, too damned old to be out here by himself, dressed in overalls and a thin flannel shirt. No life jacket. What had he been thinking? And so decrepit he weighed probably a hundred pounds even wet like this. And yet it looked like he might make it. Damned lucky old man. The officer checked his pulse again and called for an ambulance on his radio while the skiers watched over his shoulder and wondered if they might get a reward or something.

The skiers and the C.O. looked at each other when the old man started mumbling. Something about a log. Had he hit a log out there? Unlikely. It was sixty feet deep in the main channel. Nothing down there except for, well, whatever was there before the water rose.

No, wait, he wasn't saying log. He was trying to say something else.

"Get my dog," Frank whispered through blue lips. "Somebody save Catfish."

The officer looked up from where he knelt over the old man. He raised his eyebrows at the skiers from behind his mirrored sunglasses.

"I don't know. We didn't see a dog out there," one said, looking at the other one, who agreed. "Just this old man in a little green boat." They shrugged.

The C.O. stared across the lake and started to reach for the radio on his belt. He'd call his partner, have him keep searching once the runaway boat was secured. Any dog trying to swim away would most likely be hit and killed by the outboard, but they'd look for it. Before he could radio this new information the sound of a siren floated to them. The County Sheriff. The ambulance wouldn't be far behind.

"Just. Not that too," Frank said. They assumed he was talking about the siren. Then the old man lapsed in unconsciousness again, his mind visiting upon him dark and cold visions of water overhead.

Ethel stood at the kitchen sink and looked out the window. One of the neighbors was outside, pushing her daughter on a swing they'd built just last week. The little girl was smiling and laughing, and her mother was shouting triumphantly with each shove. Ethel watched them for some time.

She intended to let him sleep for another hour. The meatloaf would be ready then and he needed to eat. He'd probably wake up mean, but maybe the meatloaf would help. Every afternoon this week she'd fixed his favorite foods, but he hadn't eaten much of anything since the accident. Every evening after dinner, she'd scraped the food from his plate into the trash.

The police had called her from the hospital. Of course it about scared her to death. When she finally got there, they'd just woken him up. He sat propped up in the bed, so pale and ghostly he looked a hundred years old. But his eyes were red and angry. She didn't like thinking about that now—how he'd yelled and been so ugly to everyone. Cussing at the nurses and doctors, jerking the tubes from his arms and pushing things clattering to the tile floor. Shouting for someone to go find his dog.

The accident happened out on the main lake, they told her. She didn't know what made him go out there and he wouldn't discuss it. The police brought the boat back, but many things were missing. Even his cane had sunk. And worst of all the yellow dog was gone.

She herself had driven around looking for him, even though she didn't like to drive anymore and her eyesight wasn't near what it once was. The roads around the lake were confusing and poorly marked—some of them dead-ending in the lake itself—and she'd gotten lost over and over. She'd stop where she saw water through the trees to get out and call his name as loud as she could. She'd yelled until her voice was but a whisper.

Others had searched, too. Ollie and Summer had gone every night after work, and they'd also put up fliers. They'd come by to sit with Frank most evenings. Summer had baked blueberry muffins for him. Ethel didn't like blueberry, so she'd thrown two away every day so it didn't hurt her feelings.

No one found his dog.

Once, about three days after Frank had come home from the hospital, she'd been driving out by the lake, close to where some men were building a house, and she'd called his name. A dog barked somewhere. With her heart thumping, she walked out into the woods, hollering for him. The barking grew closer, and she moved faster through the trees. She fell once, sliding down an embankment, but she carried on, calling out. Finally a dog came to her, wagging his tail and licking her legs. Some little black and tan dog, not half the right size. The stray followed her back to the car, wanting to come home with her. She'd driven away crying, leaving the little dog standing in the road.

She watched her neighbor's child playing on the swing set. Beyond them cars passed on the highway. People going home after work, coming home to their families for supper. She didn't know if Frank would count cars after this. She didn't know if he'd do anything after this.

Across the highway was a field of soybeans, now knee-high. The field sloped up from the road, and sometimes she watched deer on this hill about this time of evening. Even as she thought this, a doe ran out of the woods and into the field. The animal stopped and looked around. Checking for coyotes, Ethel thought. The doe seemed to look her way and then started running. "Well, that crazy thing," she said quietly. "She aims to run right for the highway."

She watched the doe run and saw the tail swinging. Her hands gripped the edge of the sink. Oh my God, she thought. A deer's tail stood straight up when it ran, and those weren't a doe's ears flopping with every stride.

The dog crossed the field, running in leaping bounds, running as if he meant to burst his heart.

She screamed as the car nosed down, brakes squealing. The dog jumped away from the still-shuddering bumper and crossed the highway, running on.

"What in the hell's wrong?" Frank called from the living room. "Ethel?"

Her throat felt so tight she couldn't answer. The animal was blocked from her sight by the house across the lane. She watched its corner and suddenly the big dog appeared, heading straight for her. He crossed the lane in a bound and swept over their yard. And now he was close enough she could see clearly—his pink tongue lolling, the cut on his shoulder and the dried black blood down his leg. His yellow coat was filthy and streaked with mud. But his eyes were the same. She saw that.

And only after she saw all this did she leave her post at the window. She ran down the short hall to the front door and swung it open. She stepped aside just in time to let Catfish stream inside. She hung on the door and tried to catch her breath. She cried there in the hallway until she thought she could stand on her own.

Then she followed the muddy track across their new carpet. Smeared footprints as big as pie plates, soil and water pushed down into the fiber. She would need to clean it up before the stains set, but now she followed the trail. She already knew where it led.